Night of Seduction

Pulling away the wool scarf around her neck, he slipped his hand beneath her long hair to push it out of the way. She instinctively closed her eyes and slid her hands up his shoulders. There was something lulling about the warmth and strength of his arms, the gentleness of his touch. She relaxed as she never had before in a man's arms. His increasingly ardent lips moved down the sensitive skin of her throat slowly, sumptuously, making his way toward the pulse above her coat collar.

She gave a little gasp as his mouth grew hot. . . .

Obsession

OBSESSION

LORI HERTER

BERKLEY BOOKS, NEW YORK

OBSESSION

A Berkley Book/published by arrangement with
Goddard and Kamin, Inc.

PRINTING HISTORY
Berkley edition/July 1991

ISBN: 0-425-12817-2

A BERKLEY BOOK® TM 757,375
Berkley Books are published by The Berkley Publishing Group,
200 Madison Avenue, New York, New York 10016.
The name "Berkley" and the "B" logo
are trademarks belonging to Berkley Publishing Corporation.

PRINTED IN THE UNITED STATES OF AMERICA

10 9 8 7 6 5 4 3 2 1

To Pat Teal and Mark Howell for giving me
the opportunity

Prologue

Sunday Matinee

THE COFFIN sat on a bier in the center of the dark room. Through the yellowed curtain of a high, small window, the last rays of the sun silently glimmered and then vanished. A moment later the lid of the coffin began to open.

Fingers curled, insectlike, over the edge of the varnished wood. Then a long arm, clothed in black silk, emerged from the red satin interior to push the lid all the way up.

A man's head, then his formidable shoulders, appeared as he rose to a sitting position.

Raven-haired and handsome, he exuded a swarthy masculinity. His classic face was of noble character, its lines gaunt, his eyes stunning in their mix of wisdom and tragedy. He angled his chin as his eyes darted this way and that, their whites glistening while he seemed to test the atmosphere.

In one sudden move he leaped sideways out of the coffin with the precise agility of a gymnast disengaging from a pommel horse. Landing lightly on his booted feet, he walked to a nearby pine table. He picked up a small box and took out a match. As he ignited it, the hiss of the newborn flame broke the silence.

He lit a thick candle on the table. The yellow glow cast large shadows of the bier and coffin on the back wall, though the man himself made no shadow.

Lifting the burning match toward his face, he watched the flame for a long moment, as if enjoying its changing shape and color. The wavering light intensified the long planes of his face, and his lustrous black eyes appeared to dance along with the flame. With reverence he snuffed out the point of fire between his forefinger and thumb. Then, with ceremonial care, he laid the spent match on the table.

His eyes seemed lined with sorrow now, sloping downward at the outer corners. He tilted his head to one side and closed his eyes for a long moment, as if in pain. When he opened them, a single tear slid down his cheek. He uttered one word.

"Claudine."

His black garb blending with the night, he balanced with arms out as he moved swiftly along the edge of a rooftop. With lithe grace he jumped from one roof to another along the narrow, 1890s Parisian street, until he came to a two-story town house. A bedroom window on its second floor had been left conspicuously open. Inside, a young woman brushed her long black hair. She wore a nightgown of light blue, which matched her eyes.

He lowered himself from the roof and climbed in through the window. When she saw him, she did not scream, but ran to him with a radiant smile on her face.

"I was afraid you'd never come to me again." A sob choked her voice as she reached up to touch his chin. She stepped even closer and ran her hands urgently over his powerful chest, as if to reassure herself that he was really there.

He enveloped her in his arms and kissed her on the mouth, bending her head back with a passion that was almost savage. In response the young woman pressed her soft body against his with eager, sensual abandon.

"You've come back, you've come back," she murmured. Her hands trembled as she began to untie her nightgown for him, exposing her round breasts.

He took her hands in his, stopping her. "I'd intended to leave you, Claudine."

"Leave me? No!"

"I'm not good for you."

"You're my life!" she protested. "I'm not ashamed of us, whatever my family thinks!"

"But there are those in Paris who are out to destroy me. I must leave the city."

Her face filled with anguish. "Why?"

"I'm not what I seem."

"I don't care if you're a thief or what you may have done. I love you! If you're going, then you must take me with you." She sank to her knees. "Please don't leave me."

He reached down to stroke her white throat as she gazed up at him with pleading eyes. "There is a way that we could be together," he said. "Together forever. Would you like that?"

Claudine's beautiful face brightened. "You know I would!"

"You would stay with me wherever I go? Live by night as I must live?"

Her eyes were alight with eagerness, if not with understanding. "Whatever you ask, I'd do it to be with you."

"The time is short. They're searching for me at this moment. You must gather some clothing and come with me now."

All at once someone pounded on her door. "Claudine, I hear voices in there. Are you all right?"

"Of course, Father. I'm just reciting a poem I learned at school."

"Open the door so I can see for myself."

Claudine motioned her lover to hide in the large pine wardrobe by her bed. When he'd disappeared into it, she adjusted the top of her nightgown and opened the door. Her father, a large man with a handlebar mustache, walked in, glancing around the bedroom in agitation.

Claudine's breaths came fast and her color was heightened, but she tried to look calm. "You see? Everything's fine."

"You haven't seen or heard anything peculiar?"

"Peculiar? Here?"

"There's a maniac on the loose," her father said, alarm in his tone. "He's been spotted in this neighborhood. The police are after him. Some believe he's a vampire."

"A what!"

"I know it sounds incredible. But they have evidence. Close your window and stay alert!" He turned and left, shutting the door behind him. Claudine quickly locked it.

As her lover came out of the wardrobe, she rushed back into his arms.

"It's me they're searching for," he told her, looking steadfastly into her eyes.

She tried to laugh but grew frightened. "They think you're a vampire."

"I am."

Claudine paled and slowly drew away from him. Her face contorted in horror. "How can you be? How can you tell me such a hideous thing? I've shared my bed with you!" She clasped her hand to her stomach. "Is it true? I've made love to . . . a vampire?"

He stared at her with indescribable sadness. "Yes, the man you've loved is unlovable. A creature condemned to darkness and evil. You are my only light, my only hope. God forgive me, but I need you. And I'm going to take you!"

As he moved toward her, she backed away from him to the window. When he caught up to her, he pulled her into his embrace. "I'm no different now from the man you've loved in the past. Come with me."

Claudine tried to pull out of his grasp, but he kept her close. He turned her chin to make her face him and held her attention with a mesmerizing gaze.

"Come with me," he whispered, "and I'll give you freedom, power, immortality. Your fragile beauty will never die. You will see the future and not grow old. Our love can last for eternity, for I'll be at your side, always. We'll never again be apart." His lips drew close to hers. "Never apart."

As he kissed her, pulling her to his chest, she struggled at first, then grew limp in his arms. He drew his mouth away and looked at her. Claudine's eyes had closed in a swoon, her face still tilted up and her neck arched. Gently he pushed the lace edge of her nightgown away from her throat and touched a fingertip to her pulse point.

An unearthly light gathered in his eyes as his mouth hovered over her neck. Yet something caused him to hesitate. "My sweet mortal," he murmured. "It's wrong to take you. But I can't stop myself. Forgive me!" As he opened his mouth wide, his long incisors gleamed, aiming daggerlike at her white throat.

"There he is!" A man in the street below yelled to another as they looked up at the window. "God help us! He's about to bite her!"

The vampire lifted his head from Claudine's untouched throat, his black eyes glazed with desire. He glanced below as some of the men entered the building and began climbing the steps.

He looked back at his love, still in his arms and just becoming aware of what was happening. "I'll return for you!" he vowed, allowing her to sink limply to the floor. "I'll come back!" As he climbed out of the window and swung up to the roof, Claudine began to scream wildly for help. When he reached the rooftop of the next building, he paused to hear her hysterical cries. His eyes grew tortured and his shoulders slumped.

The men ran back out onto the street then, spurring the vampire to hurry on, to jump from rooftop to rooftop, to escape into the dark.

Later, he sat on the roof of a closed outdoor café, leaning against a chimney. Above, over a tree, a huge moon shone among stars. "Claudine, Claudine," he murmured all alone, his voice breaking. "You fear and loathe me now. How can I take you? To bring a lovely child of God into my vile world is despicable, even in my unholy eyes."

He threw a pebble from the roof onto the empty cobblestone street below. "But what am I that I should concern myself with morality?" he mused. "I'm already condemned. Why should I live in this eternal nightmare alone? Why shouldn't I have Claudine for company and consolation?"

He rose and stood on the ridge of the roof. His eyes took on a radiant brightness. Shouting, as if to the stars, he declared, "I may be selfish and depraved, but I will have her!"

He sat down on the ridge again, elbows on his knees, to think. "I'll go to her and take her while she sleeps," he said softly. "She'll feel nothing, only the tiniest pinprick." He smiled. "And then ecstasy more profound than any mortal man can give her. Afterward, she will understand why I took her. She'll forgive me, worship me for it! She'll beg me then to perform the blood ceremony with her. And after I've commingled her blood with mine, she will ease my loneliness for a thousand years."

He turned quickly at the distant sound of voices in the street. "A few days," he promised himself as he rose to his feet again. "A few days out of sight. And then I'll come back to claim her!"

The vampire ran to the far side of the roof and slid down

the drainpipe. He disappeared from sight just as a vigilante party marched up the street searching for him, carrying fiery torches, silver crosses, and wooden stakes as their weapons.

Veronica Ames felt limp as the curtain came down in front of the stage setting of a street. The time had passed so quickly since the play, *Street Shadows*, started, she could hardly believe it was intermission already. Her forehead felt moist and hot, and her heart pounded. As the houselights brightened, she stayed in her seat, recovering, while those around her got up to stretch or buy refreshments in the theater lobby. The program she held in her tremulous hands was rolled up tightly, the black ink on its cover dotted with her damp fingerprints.

The dangerous, desirable vampire had so awed and enraptured Veronica that she had wanted to run up onstage and offer herself to him in place of Claudine! She was so wrapped up in their story that other parts of the plot had gone by her unnoticed.

Was there something wrong with her, she wondered, that she had become this overwrought watching a play? Of course, it was a David de Morrissey play, and she'd been caught up watching his theatrical productions since she was a young teenager. His plays seemed to speak to her in a profound way that no movies, television shows or other plays ever had. And Veronica was an entertainment junkie.

She opened her crushed program and fanned herself, trying to calm her senses. It's only fantasy, she told herself. Imagination, not real life. But what a wonder David de Morrissey's imagination must be, to create such a vampire. If only such creatures really existed, Veronica thought, dreamily, sinking down into her seat. Going to work tomorrow morning was going to seem so dull after these wildly romantic hours in the theater. Nothing in her life, nor any person she'd met, had ever made her pulse pound this way.

People were coming back to their seats. Soon the lights went down, and Veronica pushed herself forward in her seat as the curtain rose again on the darkened stage. Her heartbeat picked up speed as the spotlight revealed the vampire, alone by his candle and coffin, plotting when he would take Claudine. . . .

1

So Eerie and Romantic

"SOMETHING?" Veronica's boss asked, barely looking up from his computer screen. It was Mr. Malloy's abbreviation of "You have something to say?" From experience, Veronica knew what he really meant was "Why are you bothering me?"

She walked from the door of his office to his vast mahogany desk, willing an air of confidence into her stride, her steps pounding out a march cadence. But her ankles grew wobbly in her new high heels, barely up to the demands of making a forceful impression. Hard as she tried to mask her insecurities, she knew Mr. Malloy could demolish her facade with one withering glance from beneath his bushy eyebrows. She knew because she'd played this scene with him before.

Nevertheless, when she got to his desk, she plunged on boldly. "I have a super idea for a feature article I'd like to do, Mr. Malloy."

"Another idea? You've got a busy mind for such a quiet young woman." Mr. Malloy leaned his bulky body back into his chair and looked up at her. His tie was askew and his white shirt had ink stains on the cuffs. She noticed three rubber bands circling his left wrist as he pushed his fingertips through thinning gray hair. "Well? Let's hear it!"

"I saw *Street Shadows* over the weekend," Veronica began. "How was it?"

She smiled. "I think it's David de Morrissey's best play yet."

"And I suppose you want to interview him for the magazine." Mr. Malloy looked amused.

"Well, actually I—"

"I've been trying to do just that since you were in pigtails,

7

Veronica. The man's a recluse. Compared to de Morrissey, Howard Hughes was a party animal."

"I've heard he's eccentric," Veronica said. "What *I'd* like to do is—"

"No, no. Let me guess. Write an article on vampires? We did that two years ago when his last play came out. Anything else?"

"No. I mean, yes." She wished he'd let her finish a sentence. "I don't want to interview de Morrissey. I'd like to try to get an interview with Sam Taglia. He stars as the vampire and he's a local actor. In fact, I found out he and I went to the same high school. He graduated with my older cousin, Harriet. Since I have that connection with him, I thought I might be able to get a good interview."

"What high school's that?"

"Morton East in Cicero."

"Cicero." He chuckled and glanced over her small frame. "You mean, *you're* from the town Al Capone took over?"

"That's ancient history," she said, smiling a little. She was used to such comments about Cicero. "The last time I saw a man walking down Cermak Road with a violin case, he was actually carrying a violin. Besides, I live on the north side now."

"I figured Cicero would produce a tougher breed," he said, still looking her up and down.

What did he expect, a brassy gangster's moll? Veronica shrugged, unable to come up with a good explanation for her frail structure and introverted personality.

He studied her face curiously. "Are you of Bohemian descent?" The western suburbs of Cicero and Berwyn were well-known as Czech communities.

"Half," she said.

"What's the rest?"

"Italian and English." Keeping her hands folded in front of her tan skirt, she shifted her weight from one foot to the other while he scrutinized her. He often acted this way—as though she were a mystery to him.

"Quite a combination. Well . . ." he said, taking a breath. He put his elbow on the arm of the chair and rested his cheek on his thick fist. "The interview's not a bad idea. I'd never heard of Sam Taglia before *Street Shadows* opened, so I didn't know he's from the Chicago area. He'll probably go to Broadway with that play. We *should* do an article on him, but this is something for Rob Greenfield to handle. It falls into his territory."

Veronica's chin went up. "But Rob's from Waukegan," she pointed out. "He wouldn't know about the neighborhood in Cicero. I do. I can bring out how the actor's background influenced him."

"Rob's had a lot more experience than you."

"He's only been here for five weeks."

"He wrote a column for the Waukegan paper for seven years. *That's* experience."

"So how many years do *I* have to put in before you'll give *me* a chance?"

"Look, eagerness is a good quality, Veronica. But I'll decide when it's time to give you an assignment. Meanwhile, you're doing just fine editing 'Upcoming Events.' "

Veronica squared her shoulders, determined this time not to let him dismiss her with a pat on the head. "Mr. Malloy, I've worked for *Windy City Magazine* for a year and a half. When you hired me, you said I'd be given opportunities."

Her boss nodded. "And you will, when you're ready for them." His bushy eyebrows drew together over his nose with a finality that inhibited her from arguing further. He always made her feel as if she were still in a college journalism class, worrying about her grade.

"All right," she said, sounding more curt than she meant to. She turned to go.

"Veronica," Mr. Malloy added, "don't be discouraged. I'm happy with your work. You're careful, accurate, reliable about deadlines. But you need a little more seasoning."

What was she, stuffing for a turkey? "I'm almost twenty-four," she reminded him.

Mr. Malloy tapped his tooth. "This filling's older than that. Tell you what, I'll take you out to lunch on your birthday, and we'll talk more then. How's that?"

Veronica mustered a polite smile, knowing he'd be the last person in the office to remember her birthday when it came. "Thanks, Mr. Malloy." She began to walk out, feeling defeated.

It was a feeling she'd been experiencing ever since she started working there after graduation.

"Oh, Veronica," he called as she stepped through the door.

"Yes?" She turned and held her breath. Had he changed his mind?

"Tell Rob to stop by my office, will you?"

She nodded, too angry to say anything.

About twenty of her co-workers were busy at their computer keyboards or talking on the telephone as she walked back into the main office. Laughter came from the direction of the water-cooler. Moving past desks separated by low glass partitions, she headed toward her own desk in the corner of the large room. The barrette that held back her shoulder-length, dark brown hair came loose. She plucked it out impatiently and stuck it in her skirt pocket.

How did Mr. Malloy judge experience? she wondered. Before he came there, Rob had worked for a small local newspaper as a theater and film critic, the same position he filled now for *Windy City Magazine.* How did sitting in dark, stuffy theaters and writing reviews give him any more practice than she had at interviewing people?

She walked past Rob's cubicle, adjacent to hers. Remembering the message, she stopped and took a few steps back. "Rob, Mr. Malloy wants to see you."

Rob Greenfield stopped typing and looked up. His carefully barbered blond hair and immaculate shirt, vest, and tie gave him a tidy Sunday school appearance. He smiled self-consciously as he pulled his handkerchief from his pants pocket, wiped his nose, and stuffed it away again. His small straight nose was red from a cold he'd had for three days.

"How are you feeling?" Veronica asked, concerned because he looked a little pale.

"Same as yesterday," he replied glumly.

"I have a bottle of vitamin C in my desk, if you want some."

"Thanks," he said, "but I choke swallowing pills. I'll order chicken soup for lunch. What's Ed want?" Apparently he was already on a first-name basis with their boss.

"I think he may have a suggestion for an interview he wants you to do." She found her voice growing a little tart. "With Sam Taglia."

"Oh." He squinted at her, then picked up a pair of rimless glasses from the desk and put them on. "Is something wrong, Veronica?" he asked. The glasses were crooked, one small lens higher than the other.

"No, nothing," she said, lowering her gaze to his desk top, trying to cover her irritation. It wasn't Rob's fault that Mr. Malloy was handing *her* idea to him on a platter. The trouble was, it wasn't the first time. Two weeks ago she'd suggested an article about movies that had been filmed on location in Chicago. Their boss had turned that idea over to Rob, too. If this was going to be a pattern, she needed to figure out what to do about it.

Rob inhaled through his sniffly nose. "Well, are you going to just stand there? Why not sit down and chat a little?"

His watery green eyes looked puzzled and amused behind the concave lenses. Veronica realized she'd gotten lost in her thoughts. "I guess I can come in for a minute," she said with a smile. "But I should get back to work." She sat down on a metal chair opposite his desk.

"You work too hard. You're right next door and I rarely see you, you're so industrious."

She shrugged. "Trying to impress Mr. Malloy."

"He's a tough guy to impress," Rob agreed as his phone rang. When he picked up the receiver, Veronica rose to leave. But he motioned her to stay, so she sat down again, a little reluctantly.

During the half minute he was distracted with the phone call, Veronica studied him, noting especially his thick, luxuriant hair. She recalled how handsome she'd thought he was the first day he came to work for the magazine—lean, square-jawed, wonderfully blond, with classic features.

Rob turned his head toward her then as he ended the call, his crooked glasses giving him a comical look. He'd gone around the office like that for the past three weeks. Some of his co-workers had begun teasing him about it. Why didn't he go to an optometrist and get the glasses straightened? she wondered.

"The screening for the new Woody Allen movie's been changed," he mumbled half to himself as he scribbled a note on his desk calendar.

He tossed his pen down, leaned back comfortably, and smiled at her. Veronica smiled back, unsure what to say, not even sure now why she'd stayed.

"That's a nice outfit," he said.

"Thanks." She tugged at the sleeve of her multicolored sweater.

"So, what's new?"

"Nothing much," she replied at first. Then she added, "I saw *Street Shadows*."

"You did?" Rob's eyes brightened. He leaned toward her as if pleased that they'd found something to talk about. "I saw it on Saturday, opening night."

Veronica perked up at the mention of opening night. "Was David de Morrissey there?"

"If he was, no one knew. He hates publicity."

"I thought for the opening he might have made an exception," she said, disappointed. Veronica wished just once she could meet someone who'd actually seen de Morrissey. His plays were so forceful, she wondered what sort of impression he made in person.

"If I'd known you wanted to see it," Rob said, regret and sincerity softening his voice, "I would have asked you along."

"I went to the Sunday matinee," she told him. "Wasn't it a magnificent production? So eerie and romantic."

Rob took a breath and his expression grew reserved. "I gave it a mixed review."

"Mixed?"

"Well, I think de Morrissey's wrung all he can out of his vampire gimmick, don't you? This is his second play in a row about it. It's time he moved on to something new. He's in a rut."

"How can you say that?" Veronica asked. "He's brilliant! *Street Shadows* has such depth."

"Depth? It's just vampire stuff."

"Dealing with good and evil, immortality, eternity! That has no depth?"

"Well, sure, but he said it all in his last play. In fact, every one of his five plays has been a giant parable on loneliness. An interesting enough theme, but he needs to get off it and move on."

"How did you ever become a theater critic?" Veronica meant to say this in a jesting tone, but she was unable to hide her annoyance.

Rob laughed and lifted his hands in an open gesture. "Sorry my opinion's different from yours. I have a good idea—why don't we have lunch together? Maybe you can change my opinion."

"Today? I can't. I've already got a date."

Rob's jaw dropped a bit. "I didn't know you were seeing anyone."

He must have assumed her lunch date was with a man, she thought. "Thanks anyway," she said, rising. "I'd better get back to work. I doubt I would have changed your mind about the play anyway. You obviously don't understand vampires." She said this in a breezy tone, hoping to end their conversation on a light note.

Rob pushed up his glasses, the humor gone from his face. "Maybe I don't. I'd like to understand *you* better, though."

Veronica decided to ignore the remark. She gave him a polite "See you later" and walked out to her own office.

She remembered she'd once thought she'd like to date Rob. In fact, if he'd asked her to lunch five weeks ago, she would have been ecstatic. His blond hair, broad shoulders, and green eyes had thrown her, and all the other women in the office, for a loop. He'd been wearing contact lenses that first week. She chuckled as she recalled how she and several other women had spent nearly an hour on their hands and knees one day helping him look for the contact lens he'd lost. Unfortunately, it had stayed lost.

After the glasses emerged, Veronica had found other disappointments, little things that shouldn't have been important but somehow diminished him in her eyes. He chewed his fingernails, for example, and ate vanilla yogurt. When he was writing his movie reviews, he frequently asked her how to spell words he could perfectly well have looked up in a dictionary. Unassuming and patient, he could be summed up in one word: *bland.* Still, he was a responsible, capable young man with a pleasant sense of humor. Just the type she ought to go out with. She honestly wished her attraction to him hadn't faded. But it had, and there was nothing she could do about it.

As for her boss, she thought as she took her seat behind her desk, she had to figure out how to acquire some "seasoning" and earn Mr. Malloy's respect. She needed to be more like Katharine Hepburn in *Adam's Rib* or *Holiday,* quick and self-confident and bright, with a ready answer for every occasion. Instead, she apparently didn't know how to advance her career, and she let her boss intimidate her. Somehow all that would have to change.

An hour later Veronica stood on a street corner with a gathering crowd, waiting for the light to change. She squinted to keep grit from blowing into her eyes. Heavy noontime traffic—cars, noisy buses, honking cabs—passed by in a blur. The brisk October wind scattered brown leaves down the pavement from the trees along North Michigan Avenue. Tall office buildings of stone and steel made a stately backdrop to all the lunch-hour hubbub.

Visions of *Street Shadows,* still vivid in Veronica's mind from the weekend, occupied her imagination while she waited. A clear memory of the darkened stage, the glowing moon, and the vampire moving with quick agility from rooftop to rooftop brought the play's rich atmosphere back to her. What a mesmerizing figure the vampire had been! She'd sat on the edge of her seat till the end of the play, longing to live in his night-world with him, half terrified, half envious, totally enthralled. He exuded a heady mixture of power and will and grace that captivated her. How glorious!

People on either side of Veronica began to step off the curb, and she realized that the light had changed. She followed along. On the other side of the street she looked up and found herself standing in front of her destination, the tall marble building called Water Tower Place.

All at once she heard a feminine voice beside her. "In a daze again, I see."

Veronica turned to greet her friend, Caroline Willis, a tall, angular, attractive redhead whom she'd known since their days as roommates at the University of Illinois. "I didn't see you," Veronica said with a smile. "Were you waiting long?"

"A couple minutes." Caroline immediately headed toward the entrance to the huge shopping complex looming over them. "Where should we eat?"

"Our usual place, I guess," Veronica said, hurrying to keep up.

They stepped onto an escalator just inside the building entrance. On the other side of a polished marble partition decorated with green plants, people were descending on another escalator to the lower level. Potted trees and marble columns stood in stately fashion on either side of the moving stairways.

"Something wrong?" Caroline asked, apparently noting her friend's downcast demeanor.

Veronica repeated what her boss had said that morning.

Caroline studied her thoughtfully. "It must be your big brown eyes."

"My eyes?"

"You have an ingenuous sort of look sometimes."

"I do? I'll have to watch more Lauren Bacall movies," Veronica muttered dryly.

"That old actress who said, 'What a dump!'? Why her?" Before Veronica could tell her she was thinking of Bette Davis, Caroline said, "Watch where you're going!"

"Oh!" Veronica exclaimed, tripping. The escalator had reached the top and she hadn't noticed.

"In dreamland again." Caroline chuckled as they moved into the open, central area of the shopping center. "You know, if you walk around your office that way, maybe that's why your boss doesn't have a lot of confidence in you."

Caroline was a certified public accountant, and Veronica valued her opinion. Still, the words miffed her. "It just shows that I have good concentration," she explained. "I get absorbed in my thoughts, or listening to people—like you, just now—and I lose track of my surroundings for a second, that's all."

"Funny, that never happens to me." Caroline glanced at her, thoughtful for a moment. "It must be nice to have your own cloud nine to escape to whenever you want. I'd sure like to escape sometimes. But I seem to be stuck here in the real world," she said, amused.

Veronica shrugged. "Be glad you're normal."

They entered the glass elevator. Their favorite soup and salad place was located a few floors up.

"You know what you should do next time?" Caroline asked

as they stepped to the back of the elevator to allow others to enter.

"What?"

"Don't ask your boss for permission. Just go get your interview, write it up, and turn it in. *Show* him what you can do."

The simplicity of the idea impressed Veronica. She felt like kicking herself. "Why didn't *I* think of that?"

"You've got to be streetwise."

"Yes, but how do you *get* streetwise?"

Caroline laughed as the elevator reached their floor. "I don't know. By living."

Several people glanced at them, smiling at their overheard conversation. Veronica felt self-conscious as they stepped off the elevator.

"So how's it going with Rob Greenfield?" Caroline asked when Veronica fell silent as they walked toward the restaurant. "Has he asked you out yet?"

"He asked me out to lunch today."

"Why didn't you go? You could have called me. I would have understood."

"I preferred having lunch with you."

"Oh," Caroline said, thinking. "Because he got the interview you wanted to do."

"No. He just doesn't interest me anymore."

"The guy you said looks like a young Robert Redford?" Caroline stared at her with some alarm.

"That was only my first impression. He's just your average, everyday sort of guy."

"How can anyone who looks like Robert Redford be average?"

"Rob manages," Veronica said with disappointment in her voice.

"You aren't getting picky again, are you?"

They entered the restaurant, and a young woman came up to seat them. Veronica was pleased to be able to let that question pass.

From their college days onward, Caroline had always maintained that Veronica's criteria for choosing a man were way too high. Veronica didn't really have any criteria, though. She just went by gut reaction. She recalled the half dozen or so men

Caroline had fixed her up with over the years. All very nice, a few even handsome. But somehow, none of them had ever captured her imagination.

The hostess seated them at a small table beneath a hanging basket of pothos. By the time they'd looked at the menu and ordered, Caroline seemed to have forgotten where they'd left off.

"Did you get compliments on the red satin dress?" Veronica asked, referring to a dress for a black-tie banquet she'd helped Caroline shop for.

"I meant to tell you. Tom said I looked fantastic! And I got envious looks from his old girlfriend, too. To think I wouldn't even have tried on that dress if you hadn't picked it off the rack!"

"I'm glad it turned out well. How are the fittings going for your wedding gown?"

"Okay, I guess. Would you come with me to the next one and make sure they're doing it right?"

"I'd love to."

They talked for a while about the bridesmaids' dresses that Veronica and some other friends would be wearing. Caroline's wedding was a month away.

After a pause when the waitress brought them glasses of water, Caroline asked, "Who was the actor you wanted to interview?"

"The star of *Street Shadows*. It's the latest David de Morrissey play," Veronica explained, knowing Caroline had little interest in theater.

At the mention of de Morrissey, however, Caroline's eyes widened, and she seemed about to erupt with some news or gossip.

"What's the matter?" Veronica asked.

Caroline gave a quirky smile. "Tell you in a minute. First, did you like it?"

"Oh, God, yes! That's what I was thinking about when you came up to me outside—how romantic and melancholy the play was."

Caroline drew her eyebrows together. "I've seen the ads. How can vampires be romantic?" She chuckled. "I mean, what do they do? Send their loved one a pint of blood instead of a pound of chocolates?"

While Caroline laughed at her own joke, Veronica smiled patiently. Caroline was a good friend and a bright young woman, but she lacked imagination sometimes. "There's a mystique about vampires," Veronica tried to explain. "The one in *Street Shadows,* for example, is dangerous but also sad and caring. In the second half he breaks into a woman's bedroom and . . . and . . ." She decided it was too erotic to describe in a restaurant. "You just have to go see it."

Caroline looked unconvinced as she took silverware out of a rolled red napkin. "Why don't you find yourself a man and experience all those *and-ands* in real life, instead of watching movies and plays all the time?"

"If I could find the right man," Veronica said, putting her elbows on the table, "I might."

"How about Rob? Sounds like he's interested in you."

Veronica pressed her fingers to her temples. "He's a nice guy, but . . ."

"But what?"

"Oh . . ." What could she say? "He wears crooked glasses," Veronica replied lamely.

The comment apparently struck Caroline's funny bone. Her angular shoulders shook with laughter, and Veronica found herself laughing, too. But Caroline still seemed bewildered, and Veronica wanted her to understand.

"He doesn't have . . . oh, I don't know . . . flash. He's not . . ." Veronica paused, trying to find a logical way to explain what she meant, to appeal to Caroline's cut-and-dried mentality. "I need somebody who can really capture my attention. Like the vampire did, or Robert Redford in any of his movies. If I can't get even one-quarter that excited about Rob to start with, what's the use?"

"But you have to be realistic, Veronica. Number one, vampires don't exist." Caroline counted on her fingers to demonstrate. "Two, in real life Robert Redford may wear crooked glasses, too. Three, you can't get fixated on being 'taken' by some daring and dangerous stranger, because it just doesn't happen that way in real life."

"Yes, but people can't control their feelings," Veronica reminded her, a trace of helplessness in her voice. "I need magic. Nothing else impresses me." As she often did, Veronica felt singled out, different from everyone else.

Concern hovered in Caroline's eyes. "You were like this in college, but I thought you'd outgrow it by now."

Veronica shook her head. "Why would I outgrow it? I've been addicted to old movies since I was five. Both my parents worked, and I didn't have brothers or sisters to play with when I got home from school. Children with no siblings watch a lot of TV."

"Still, you have to accept that every man can't look and act like some movie star you dream about. I didn't meet my fiancé in a daydream. I met Tom at a tax seminar. Not real romantic, but it did the trick."

Veronica nodded and said nothing. She unfolded her napkin and put it in her lap. Caroline meant well, but she didn't understand that what worked for her didn't apply to everyone.

Caroline seemed to sense Veronica was withdrawing from her. She smiled and said in a more jovial tone, "So you need magic, huh? Well, I may be able to play fairy godmother for you."

Veronica looked up. "Not another blind date."

"Nope, this is business."

"Business?" Veronica said, smiling a bit.

"I started to tell you before, I just got a new client—David de Morrissey."

Veronica sat perfectly still. "This is a joke, right?"

"He came to my office early last week to meet with me."

Veronica couldn't believe it. "Really?" she said with doubt, but her heart rate began to accelerate. "How did he pick you?"

"Last year my firm bought a retiring CPA's practice. He specialized in the entertainment industry. One of his clients was the producer of *Street Shadows*. The producer recently recommended our firm to David de Morrissey. When he called, I was assigned to take care of his taxes."

An idea flashed into Veronica's head, a magnificent way to catch Mr. Malloy's attention. She leaned over the table. "Do you think you could introduce me to him, so I could ask him for an interview?"

"That's what I meant about playing fairy godmother!"

The waitress brought their soup and sandwiches. Veronica was too excited to even think about eating now. "How would we arrange it, though?" she asked. "He shuns reporters."

"We'll have to do it carefully," Caroline agreed. She bit into her sandwich and chewed pensively. "I know. Loan me something."

"Huh?"

"Loan me a book or something. Maybe . . . how about your topaz? Let's say I'm borrowing it to wear at my wedding. You know, 'something borrowed, something blue.' Can I, by the way?"

"Sure."

"Thanks. Well, then, bring it to my office next Friday about ten after seven. His appointment's at seven. That way you can seem to meet him by chance."

"Okay," Veronica said, beginning to feel short of breath at the prospect. "His appointment's so late?"

"Our firm had to agree to after-hours appointments if we were to get his account. I suppose it's a way for him to avoid the public. The rich and famous always have special requests."

Veronica picked up her spoon, then put it down again. "What's he like? How old?"

"Early or mid-thirties, I'd guess."

"He must have started young. His first play was produced a decade ago. What else?"

Caroline finished her cup of soup and pushed it aside. "Oh, he's average height and has a trim, muscular build. Actually, he looks very athletic, but he's such a cultured intellectual, I can't imagine him working out at a gym. He's got dark brown hair. About the same shade as yours, in fact."

Veronica felt goose bumps rise on her arms, she was so taken with the idea that she had something personal in common with the lauded playwright.

"He's got blue eyes," Caroline continued. "Sort of an unusual, pale blue. He's a mercurial type of man. You never know what he's going to say next. But he's very polite and dresses handsomely. Sometimes his manner is a little odd, though."

"In what way?" Veronica asked, sitting on the edge of her chair.

Caroline wiped her mouth with her napkin. "Well, you know

how most people will move their eyes and change their position now and then while they talk to you? He sits absolutely still—not rigid, but still—and looks at you without ever blinking."

Veronica tilted her head. "Artistic types are often eccentric."

"Talk about eccentric!" Caroline laughed, rubbing her hands in her napkin. "You know how I hate it when clients bring in all their receipts and papers in a shoe box? Well, he came in carrying this ornate box with polished inlaid wood. He said it was seventeenth-century Italian or something. It looked like it belonged in a museum! He brought out this old key from his pocket to open it. Inside was a mess of papers he's been stuffing into it for years. I hate to even think about sorting through it."

"Really," Veronica said, mesmerized, her brain dancing with all the new information about David de Morrissey and the fact that she was going to meet him. She panicked suddenly. "What'll I say to him?"

"I'll do my part," Caroline said wryly. "What you say to him is *your* problem."

At three o'clock in the morning a pale, eerie flickering light shone from the uppermost rear windows of a large old Oak Street mansion. Constructed in the Romanesque style from rough-hewn, taffy-colored sandstone, the building stood out as a remnant of Chicago's rich past among the art galleries, chic hair salons, and expensive boutiques housed in the brownstones that were its neighbors. It had been built in the late 1800s by a Chicago hotel magnate, and its third-floor ballroom had once been the scene of many elaborate Gold Coast parties.

In the ballroom now the house's current owner, David de Morrissey, was moving a number of low benches closer to the windows, ignoring the creaking, scraping noises he was making. Since he'd bought the mansion more than ten years ago, he was the only person ever to behold the room's spacious wood floor, its large gold-draped windows, its three crystal chandeliers. The only illumination besides the greenish flicker from a corner of the room was the ghostly, tranquil light of the full moon through the bay windows.

David returned to the equipment he had set up in the corner of the ballroom, from which the flickering light emanated. He pressed a button to rewind his videocassette tape to the number he wanted, then pressed the Play button. Immediately the giant screen was filled with the image of Gene Kelly, strolling down a rainy street twirling a big umbrella.

Quickly David picked up his own big black umbrella and sprinted to the middle of the floor. He watched Kelly spin the umbrella in large circles while doing a jaunty side shuffle in front of a colorful store window. David imitated the step, proud of himself. He was finally getting it down.

He'd spent hours playing the dance in slow motion in order to figure out exactly the moves and steps Kelly had used, then more hours trying to reproduce the rhythm and attitude. It deflated him to know that artists like Gene Kelly and Fred Astaire had managed to achieve such creative perfection within their relatively brief careers.

Imitating his screen mentor, David kicked up the tip of his umbrella and caught it. He followed along with the intricate steps Kelly performed under the rain gutter, David pretending that water was pouring down on his face. Then he pivoted around the room in a large circle, the open umbrella in front of him. This was his favorite part.

He moved to the row of low benches set end to end. He'd brought up these step stools from his vast library on the second floor because he'd needed a makeshift street curb to jump to and from. The benches were too high, but they served the purpose. He jumped up and down, over and over, in a light-footed crossover step, while moving forward at a quick pace.

Next he splashed around in a huge imaginary puddle until an imaginary policeman appeared. Finally, smiling, but not the least bit out of breath though he'd been practicing the dance for two hours, David went back to the TV screen and turned off his equipment.

Some rainy night he'd find himself an empty street with a puddle and a curb and a lamppost and do the dance, the music playing in his head. Ever since he first saw *Singin' in the Rain* in Paris in 1952, he'd been enthralled by the sheer joy Kelly exuded while performing. He'd always thought if he could just master the dance, perhaps he could capture the joy. And it worked! The feeling even lasted for an hour or so afterward. It was like really being alive.

It wasn't until the invention of the home videocassette machine—and David's conquering his unwillingness to learn to use such newfangled equipment—that he had been able to achieve his dream. None too soon, either, for his spirits had begun to sink to fearful lows lately.

' He walked across the room to a velvet-cushioned window seat and sat down. Outside in the distance loomed the black Chicago skyscrapers, their windows lit like diamonds, standing staunch and majestic against the moonlit sky.

David liked Chicago. Even at night the city had an energy to it. And yet it wasn't frenzied like New York. Of course, it wasn't Paris or London, but it was fine for now, and perhaps for the next decade or two. After all, his career here was going great guns, his plays even moving on to Broadway. Old Will would have been proud.

The thought of Shakespeare, his great, beloved teacher, disturbed him. He put all that out of his mind.

Where was Darienne? he wondered, looking at the street below as if he'd see her blond head and sleek form down there somewhere. Stupid of him. He didn't know if she was on this continent or even in this hemisphere. She had such a gypsy foot. Always had. But she usually showed up just about the time he needed someone to talk to. Really talk to. Of course, he spoke with his producer and director and others connected with his plays. But that was just shoptalk.

David needed a soul mate, and Darienne was the closest thing he had to that on the whole, lonely planet. Though she was his opposite in disposition, she understood him. It was only natural that she should. Like David, she was a vampire, too.

2

Such Longing for the Fantasy

CAROLINE'S OFFICE was part of a tenth-floor suite her accounting firm occupied in a building near the corner of Randolph and Michigan. Veronica walked toward her friend's door with a mixture of anticipation and anxiety. Fingers trembling, she brushed away a loose strand of hair that had fallen onto the lapel of her navy-blue wool coat.

The thought of being one of the few in the city to actually meet David de Morrissey was almost more than her presence of mind could handle. She pulled off her leather gloves, but her hands were so cold she might as well not have worn them. Her mouth felt cotton-dry. She had to get hold of herself. If only there were a mirror around so she could comb her windblown hair and practice an air of composure. But it was seven-fifteen. She was already a little late, and she didn't want to chance missing de Morrissey because she had taken time to find the ladies' room.

The office suite was almost empty, with only one or two accountants working overtime. Cleaners were emptying wastebaskets and vacuuming floors. The door to Caroline's office stood partly open. Veronica could see the corner of her friend's desk inside. She paused in front of the door for a moment, rehearsing what she would say.

Caroline's voice coming from inside the room distracted her. "Now, about the notices from the Internal Revenue Service I found in your wooden box—"

"Yes, I thought you might have some comment about those."

Was that David de Morrissey? Veronica wondered when she

heard the wry, accented voice. The accent surprised her because she'd always assumed he was American.

"Caroline, I'll be truthful. I've ignored the government just as Daniel ignored the lions."

"So you haven't been filing tax returns. Why not?" Caroline asked.

There was a pause, then he replied in a slow, philosophical manner. "I never think about money. Money bores me. I find no rhythm or poetry in it." His tone changed. "But now that the IRS is threatening to put a lien on my house, and my producer is warning me that I could face jail for tax evasion, I'm beginning to see that money is important. Or that the government thinks so, anyway."

"That's good," Caroline said. "You know you may be audited?"

"I know nothing about any of this. Can you take care of all the rigmarole, including a government audit if it comes to that?"

"Yes, I can." Caroline sounded quite serious now. "But you'll have to give me power of attorney."

"It's yours." De Morrissey's tone was one of whimsical generosity. "Well, then. I assume we're finished?"

Veronica stood by the door, amazed at what she was hearing. Her conscience told her she shouldn't eavesdrop any longer. Go ahead, walk in, she ordered herself.

The door creaked a bit as she opened it farther. She knocked as she stepped into the room. "Excuse me. Can I see you a second, Caroline?"

Caroline glanced up from her desk. "Hi, Veronica!" Then she addressed the dark-haired man seated in front of her in an upholstered chair. "Do you mind a brief interruption, Mr. de Morrissey?"

"Not at all," he said as Veronica walked to the middle of the small, windowless office.

She held her breath as she cautiously glanced at him. His dark brown hair was slightly wavy and curled a bit over his ears and at the back of his neck. From her position she could see only a portion of his cheek, where his high cheekbone angled and formed a smooth plane toward his chin. But she could see enough of his complexion to guess he possessed vibrant good health. In fact, an artist would have had a challenge doing justice to his coloring. His skin had perfect clarity and his cheeks were highlighted with rosy color, as if he'd just come in from skiing a mountain slope. In contrast, the lower part of his face was shadowed by his closely shaved beard. A herringbone jacket of thick, soft wool added even more richness to his appearance.

He turned in his chair. The sweeping gaze of his pale blue eyes stopped at Veronica's face. His eyes focused, questioning. A trace of melancholy in them grew strangely acute as they held hers for a long moment. All at once the sadness vanished. His strong facial features—the flared nostrils of his aristocratic nose, the firm angular jaw, the dark intelligent brows—all worked together to form a stern expression of inward resolve. With a slow, calculated movement he stood.

The impact of the playwright's stare left Veronica feeling like a lump of clay. Sheer willpower made her find her voice. "Please don't leave," she said politely. She assumed he had risen to walk out so she and Caroline could talk.

His face grew almost masklike now. "I'm standing because a lady has entered the room," he explained in an arch, sardonic tone.

"Th-thank you." Nervousness at his superior manner made Veronica stutter. "Please, sit."

"Only if you will first."

"First?" Veronica repeated as she struggled to regain her composure.

"There's a seat." Caroline pointed to a chair against the wall.

"Allow me." De Morrissey said the words coolly as he stepped across the room to place the chair a few feet from his. While he did this, Veronica looked at Caroline in astonishment. Caroline gave a little shrug, indicating she was equally surprised by her client's suddenly formal, courtly behavior.

He held the chair for Veronica while she sat down and then took his own seat. Though Caroline remained behind the desk in the position of authority, Veronica had the distinct feeling that her celebrated, tax-evading client had taken over.

"Shall I introduce you?" Caroline asked, still looking a trifle disconcerted herself.

"Please," he replied.

"Veronica, this is David de Morrissey. Mr. de Morrissey, my friend Veronica Ames."

Veronica tried to summon some poise. "You're *the* David de Morrissey?" she asked, pretending surprise. "I loved *Street Shadows.*"

"Did you?" He raised one inquisitive eyebrow. "I should think my vampire would have frightened a little thing like you out of the theater."

"No, he mesmerized me," Veronica said. "He was magnificent! I'm eager to see the play again."

De Morrissey studied her in the still, unnerving way Caroline had described over lunch the week before. An incandescent light began to flicker in the depths of his eyes. Like a wolf looking into a flame, Veronica thought. She sensed power and desire and hunger all focused on her. Her pulse jumped.

All at once, so smoothly she wondered if she'd imagined it all, his primeval gaze was transformed into a civilized, rather careful smile. "I'm happy you like my work."

Though the words might have been an ideal opportunity to compliment him further and even to ask for an interview, confusion held Veronica back. "I'm sorry to interrupt your conference."

"You're not interrupting," he said in a reserved tone. "We'd just finished."

"No, we hadn't," Caroline interjected.

"I only came by to bring Caroline my pendant for her wedding," Veronica continued as she opened her handbag. She pulled out a small, velvet-covered case and handed it to Caroline.

De Morrissey turned his attention to Caroline. His manner grew a bit more relaxed. "Your wedding?"

"Next month," Caroline told him, stretching across her desk to take the box. "I asked Veronica if I could wear this." She opened the case and showed him the large topaz glimmering on its fragile gold chain. "I wanted to have it for my next fitting to see how it looks with my gown."

"Exquisite." He leaned forward to study it. "A London blue topaz. Emerald cut. Excellent color and clarity." He turned back to Veronica. "Who gave you such a jewel?" he asked as if he had every right to know.

"My parents," Veronica replied. "A college graduation present."

"I would have guessed you received it from a heartsick lover."

Veronica looked into his steady eyes and couldn't tell if he was joking or serious. She wished she could stop feeling like a high-strung, inept actress in his presence, waiting for his cue as to where to move and what to say next.

Meanwhile, Caroline quipped, "She never lets a man stay around long enough to get heartsick."

"Indeed?" De Morrissey watched the changing expressions on Veronica's face, probably amused at her consternation.

He was worse than Mr. Malloy, the way he studied her, Veronica thought. She wished she could think of a comeback to Caroline's remark, but her tongue failed her.

De Morrissey looked back at Caroline. "I wish you happiness in your marriage. Who is your fiancé?"

"His name's Tom Winters. He's a CPA. I vowed I wouldn't marry another accountant, but he loves me and he keeps me laughing."

"The best of reasons to marry him." De Morrissey now spoke in a tone that could only be described as reassuring. He smiled and his low voice lilted with unexpected warmth. "Shakespeare wrote, 'Down on your knees, and thank heaven, fasting, for a good man's love.' "

Caroline laughed. "Sounds old-fashioned, but I'll go along with that."

Veronica enjoyed the quotation, too, and the humorous way he'd recited it. She began to relax a bit. He'd seemed so stern at first, but now he behaved in a cultured, amusing way that she liked. He seemed to take pleasure from the company of women.

When they fell silent for a moment, Veronica wondered what she should do next. Her pendant, the pretext on which she'd come, had been delivered. If she was going to ask for an interview, now was the time. Her hands grew cold again at the thought, but she decided to blunder on anyway. What did she have to lose?

"Mr. de Morrissey, I work for *Windy City Magazine.* I wonder if you would consider—"

"You're a reporter." Suspicion hung on each syllable as the word *reporter* rolled off his tongue. Yet wonder also hovered in his voice and eyes, as if he were surprised that he could *be* surprised.

"I'm not exactly a reporter," Veronica quickly told him. "At least, my boss doesn't think so." She realized as she spoke that she was throwing away any air of professionalism she might have tried to assume. "I mean, I'm the editor of the 'Upcoming Events' section. I'm hoping to move up, and if I could get an interview with you, I know it would impress my boss."

Maybe her stumbling honesty had done the trick. She noticed a hint of softening in the playwright's eyes.

"I never give interviews, Miss Ames. Never! But for you I might consider an alternative. Just this once."

"Please call me Veronica," she said, sitting up straight as she looked at him expectantly. "What alternative?"

"I'll agree to converse with you."

"Sure," she eagerly replied, though she wasn't certain what he meant.

"And I have one condition, Veronica."

Her name spoken in his softly accented tones gave her a pleasant shiver along her spine. "Condition?"

"You must allow me to take you to dinner."

Her sense of confusion about him came back. But she thought of a way she could keep control of things. "I ought to take *you* to dinner, since I'm asking for the interview."

He drew back in an arch manner. "You modern women! I won't have it."

"I insist," Veronica said, bravely holding her ground.

He contemplated her for a long moment, a vertical laugh line creasing his cheek as he gradually smiled. "It's against my principles to argue with a beautiful woman," he said at last. "I accept under protest."

Veronica felt light-headed. An interview with Chicago's famous recluse! "When can we meet?"

"Right now."

"But . . . your consultation with Caroline." Veronica looked doubtfully at her friend, who'd been watching them with lively interest.

"Everything's arranged," de Morrissey said.

"No," Caroline replied. "Actually, we have a lot more to discuss than I originally thought. But since it's getting late, we might as well set up another meeting."

"Excellent." De Morrissey rose from his seat. "Procrastination is one of the things I do best."

"Before you go, I'd like you to sign this." Caroline picked up a paper from her desk and handed it to him. "It's a letter of engagement. It states that you agree to provide the information our company needs, and it lists the services we will perform for you." She offered him a ballpoint pen.

He waved away her pen and pulled his own from his breast pocket. "I prefer a fountain pen. The scratching sounds lend so much more consequence to one's signature." As he wrote his name in a large, flamboyant hand, Veronica couldn't help but notice how extraordinarily long his fingers were.

He gave the paper back to Caroline and thanked her for her time. With a graceful, spiderlike motion of his fingers, he twisted the cap back onto his pen and returned it to his pocket.

He turned to Veronica. "Where are you escorting me?" he asked, extending his hand for her to take.

A vague chill ran down Veronica's spine. She ignored the feeling and put her hand in his while she rose to her feet. The strength in his fingers astonished her, as if his bones were of steel. She let go and swallowed before answering his question. "I've heard you don't like to go out in public places. Where would you feel most comfortable?"

He smiled slightly, the tips of his teeth showing. "With you I believe I would feel comfortable anywhere."

With some trepidation, David stepped into the elevator after Veronica. She'd taken him by cab to the John Hancock Center, a tapering black skyscraper on North Michigan Avenue he'd often passed but never entered. "Where is the restaurant?" he asked.

"On the ninety-fifth floor," she said, pressing the button.

The doors closed and David stiffened. Ninety-five floors. A thousand feet into the sky. He wondered how fast this modern elevator would cover such a distance. Extremely fast, he feared. David didn't know if he could tolerate being separated from the earth at a speed beyond his control. If he could climb the building at his own pace, his body would have time to adjust. But the prospect of being whooshed upward by a powerful space-age mechanism alarmed him. His fingers clutched a small cloth packet in his pants pocket. He remembered then that Darienne had often traveled by plane. If she could do that, then certainly he ought to survive this.

The express elevator began to move so smoothly, the speed was almost imperceptible at first. But soon he could feel its full momentum and it made him dizzy. He leaned against the wall.

Veronica looked at him with concern. "Are you claustrophobic?"

If he hadn't been so addled, he might have laughed. One who had spent each long day of the past four hundred years in a coffin was unlikely to suffer from claustrophobia. "I'll be all right as soon as we stop," he told her.

As he said the words, the elevator reached their floor. The doors opened and they walked out. David felt much steadier, but there was a residual light-headedness from the great height. He'd grown so earthbound.

When the maître d' showed them to a table, David had a new worry. Huge windows walled the restaurant, providing a panoramic view of the city below. Their table was next to a window. David's first concern was reflections. But the lighting had been set up so as not to spoil the view, and Veronica's reflection on the glass was very faint. David felt sure she would never notice there was no reflection from his side of the table.

Once they were seated, Veronica opened her handbag and took out a compact and then a handkerchief, her fingers moving like butterfly wings as she sorted through her belongings. At last she pulled out a pencil and a small notepad.

"What are those for?" he asked, keeping his tone cool. He knew the answer.

"So I can take notes."

Her golden brown eyes glistened as she looked at him. God, she was a lovely creature! he thought. "No, Veronica," he told her in a brusque voice. "I said I would converse with you. I won't let you interview me."

"But—"

"Veronica . . ." He found it so hard to be stern with her. She was such a fragile, innocent little mortal. He wanted to give and protect. And take—though he fought that urge with all the strength his conscience could provide.

"All right," she said, putting away the pencil and paper.

David could tell he'd shaken her again with his high-handed manner. He didn't want to, but could find no other way to deal with her at the moment. She'd come upon him as such a surprise.

"If I say anything significant in our conversation, you'll remember it," he told her in a more friendly tone.

"And you'll make sure not to say anything significant." She looked at him with knowing eyes, as if she understood exactly what tactic he was using with her.

Her gentle teasing made him smile. She reminded him of Cecilia just now. That was why he'd been so immediately taken with her—she was much like Cecilia in her shy but determined manner. In appearance, she was even more beautiful than his great, lost love. Veronica had delicate features, thick, shining hair—almost too much hair—and small, slender hands that moved with such airy grace they vied with her eyes as the focal point of her intensely feminine personality.

She put her handbag away and looked out the broad window now, her head tilted prettily on her slim, elegant neck. Such a lovely, unblemished throat. Its whiteness contrasted with the darkness of her blue dress, tantalizing him. He quelled his desire again, hating himself for his incurable need. He'd fed; he didn't require blood. But the drive never left him completely.

"The cars on the streets look like ants from up here," she said as she leaned toward the window and looked down.

He glanced out the window, but the view brought back his dizziness. City lights spread out far below in radiating patterns, and the lights of the traffic moved along the dark streets as if in slow motion. The sight seemed to delight Veronica.

"Have you ever been here before?" she asked.

"No. This is a first for me. Have you?"

"Once, on a date."

"Are you still seeing the gentleman?" David tried to imagine what type of man would attract her.

"It was a blind date," she said, as if that explained everything. "I liked the restaurant, though. I thought it might be the incognito sort of place you'd like—dimly lit and off the beaten track. I'm sorry about the elevator ride."

"I do like it," David assured her.

"You aren't from Chicago, are you?" she asked.

"No."

"Where are you from?"

"Many places."

"Where were you born?"

Her eyes and her sweet, fragile voice were breaking him down. "Paris." It wouldn't hurt to reveal that, he rationalized. "Where are you from?"

"Chicago's western suburbs. How did you happen to come to Chicago?"

"This conversation is beginning to sound like an interview, Veronica." He tapped his teaspoon on the table to emphasize that she was testing his limits.

She looked chastened. "I'm sorry, Mr. de Morrissey. I'm not sure how you want this to go."

"First of all," he said, pushing his water glass out of the way, "I want you to call me David." She smiled but looked out the window again. "Let me hear you say it," he coaxed in a tutorial manner.

When she brought her eyes back to him, they looked a little frightened. "David," she said. She was very skittish. He wished he could read women's minds the way he could men's.

The waiter came just then, as if on cue to prove David's point. The young fellow was eyeing David's expensive jacket and estimating what tip he'd get. He handed them menus and recited the special dishes the chef had prepared for tonight. David listened with pretended interest, all the while keeping a mild nausea under control. When he was a mortal, he'd loved food. But since his death in 1616, the thought of eating other dead things made him ill.

"I'll have the Saltimbocca alla Romana," Veronica said. "And a small salad."

Her apparent familiarity with an obscure Italian dish made him curious. She didn't seem well traveled. "Why did you select that?"

She grinned. "It's what Louis Jourdan ordered in *Three*

Coins in the Fountain. I'm part Italian and I've always wanted to try it."

David was charmed. She had an affinity for fantasy. If he wasn't careful, he'd soon adore her.

The waiter turned to him.

"I would like a small glass of tawny port," David said.

"And for dinner?"

"No dinner," David said amiably. "Just the port."

The waiter nodded politely, but the astonishment and disappointment his thoughts revealed amused David.

"You aren't eating anything?" Veronica asked.

"I ate at home before I left for my appointment with Caroline." What he told her was true, in a way.

Veronica seemed perplexed. "Then why did you suggest we have dinner?"

"I assumed *you* hadn't eaten. When we agreed to have a conversation, I didn't want you to starve."

She still looked troubled.

"Why don't you have some wine with your meal?" David suggested. He wanted her to relax. She was on guard with him again, and he wanted to glimpse more of what was hidden behind the armor.

The waiter, who had remained in case David changed his mind about eating, suggested a Chardonnay. Veronica agreed and the waiter left.

"There now," David said. "What shall we talk about?"

She lowered her eyes for a moment. Her long lashes made soft shadows on her smooth cheeks as she seemed to hesitate over her thoughts. Looking up, she said all at once, "Could we talk about vampires?"

The word startled David. But in an instant he realized that, of course, she was referring to his play. "What about vampires?"

"Why do you write plays about them?"

It's what I know best, he thought with irony. "Being a vampire would be an unusual existence, don't you think?"

"In your play you showed all the power and danger and romance of the vampire's existence. I found myself really empathizing with him."

"Did you?" David said, sincerely touched. "He intrigued you?"

"More than intrigued me." Veronica put her elbows on the table and leaned toward him. David found himself instinctively leaning toward her in the same pose. "I felt like he pulled me onto the stage with him," she went on. "I wanted to live there with him."

"Forever?" David wondered if she understood the enormity of what she was saying. He saw her expression change from dreamy to distressed. What had he said? "Does eternity frighten you?" he asked.

"I . . ." Her delicate brow furrowed. "It was only a play."

David realized how he'd slipped. Of course, it was all just fantasy to her. But she showed such longing for the fantasy. The potential of her began to excite David.

"Of course, it was only a play," he said in a reassuring tone. "But one reason I wrote it was to explore the idea of living forever. 'Eternity! thou pleasing, dreadful thought!' "

She attempted to smile. "Is that another quote from Shakespeare?"

"No, Joseph Addison's *Cato.* Does all my quoting make me seem old-fashioned? I notice people don't do it much these days."

Her eyes shone again with interest—interest in him. "You have a sort of Old World manner," she said. "I suppose it's because you're from Europe. Though you speak English so well, you don't really seem like a foreigner."

The fact that she was taking notice of personal things pleased David. He loved women who were sensitive to him in small ways. "I was born with a gift for language," he told her. "I know several and speak them all quite fluently."

Of course, he'd had centuries to study, but Veronica needn't know that. He relished making an impression. Her eyes were full of admiration now. God, he was enjoying this! Veronica's sweetness poured over him like a blessing.

The waiter brought their drinks and her salad. Veronica ate only a few bites of the salad and pushed it aside. She took a sip of wine. "Transylvania isn't mentioned in your play. And garlic and the Christian cross don't protect people from the vampire. Does that mean you don't like traditional vampire lore?"

David sipped his port. "You sound as though you've watched a lot of old movies."

She laughed, her eyes crinkling with delight. "Everyone tells me that. It's true, I have."

"I have, too. Actually, musicals are my favorite, especially ones with Kelly or Astaire."

At that, Veronica grew even more animated, her eyebrows rising with exuberance. "*Top Hat* is my favorite Fred Astaire picture. The plot is inane, but the dancing is—"

"Divine," David said, enjoying her spontaneity. "What about Gene Kelly? Which film?"

She put her thumbnail between her teeth while she thought. "*The Pirate.*"

Her choice puzzled David. "Why?"

"He's most sexy in that one."

David smiled. "A woman's point of view."

"But my favorite dance," she continued, "is the long dream sequence with Leslie Caron in *An American in Paris.*"

"Absolutely!" David said. He loved Gershwin, and the dance was the one he wanted most to master, but he didn't have a partner.

"That sequence is just about the most romantic thing I've ever seen," Veronica went on. "Ever. Except for *Street Shadows.* The scene in the second half where the vampire breaks into Claudine's bedroom to claim her equals it."

David was more than flattered. To have her compare his play to a work he valued so highly! "You really think so?"

"Yours wasn't a dance, but still there seemed to be a choreography to the scene. A rhythm in their . . . I mean, in the way the vampire seduced her and then bit her. It was like a dance."

David grew more intrigued with Veronica by the moment. *Lovemaking.* That was the word she couldn't say, he was sure of it. *A rhythm in their lovemaking.* He longed to explore this. He knew it was intrusive of him, and she was already embarrassed by the subject. But he couldn't seem to stop himself.

"You're right, it was choreographed. I spent several nights rehearsing Sam Taglia and the actress who plays Claudine, until they performed it to my satisfaction."

"Did you, really?" Her eyes met his, fascinated.

"You see, I was hoping to show how life, death, fear, and love are all intertwined." He watched her face as he spoke. She seemed to absorb every word. "Eternity itself is a romantic idea. It's like that moment of forgetting during the sex act. For an instant you feel as if you exist forever, floating free, with no beginning and no end. Lovemaking gives mortals a fleeting glimpse of eternity."

Veronica's cheeks colored. Her hand jerked against her water glass.

David's unusual agility enabled him to catch the glass before it spilled. Carefully he set it upright on the white tablecloth. He reached across the table and lightly ran his thumb down her cheek. "But you wouldn't know about lovemaking, would you?"

Veronica looked as though she would have preferred to be in another city at that moment. "I think," she said, drawing her brows together, "we ought to change the subject."

David regretted distressing her, but he wanted so much to know her innermost self. Despite the warnings of his conscience, she was becoming important to him. He closed his hand over hers. She tried to pull away, but he kept hold.

"It wasn't my intention to embarrass you. You're so beautiful, looking at you makes my thoughts rush ahead into territory you may not be ready for. You're inexperienced with men, aren't you?"

Veronica swallowed, then nodded reluctantly, as if she'd decided it was no use to pretend otherwise.

"You're wise," David said, stroking his thumb over her fingers. "You're too lovely to let yourself be taken lightly. And innocence has an aura all its own."

"I wish it wasn't so obvious," Veronica said softly, managing a weak smile.

David squeezed her hand. "It isn't obvious," he said, lying a little for her sake. "I'm discerning about people. A playwright has to be."

The waiter arrived with Veronica's dinner. "I'm not hungry now," she said, staring at the veal dish.

"Veronica, please don't let this conversation upset you." He spoke in a soothing tone. "I've learned some of your secrets. Perhaps you'll learn mine."

She chuckled. "I'd intended to find out all about you, and instead, you learned everything about me."

"Oh, no. I have myriad questions about you. *Why* are you so untouched? How do you stay that way in the modern world? How do you feel about it?"

Veronica's expression grew forlorn. Her voice was barely audible. "Those are all things I wonder myself."

"You must feel a little lost, a little out of step."

"I do." Her eyes welled with tears. "You've described it exactly."

Another romantic soul, adrift in a humdrum world, looking for beauty and finding only elusive glimpses of it. She was a dreamer, as was he. David wanted to take this young woman under his wing and teach her all he'd learned. There was so much he could tell her. In return she might give him sweetness, softness, and warmth. And companionship such as he hadn't known in almost four centuries. It would be like communing with an angel.

Pushing his warning conscience aside, he allowed his mind to suggest all the pleasant possibilities Veronica presented. She was unlike any woman he'd met before. Except, of course, Cecilia. Somehow, being near her, he felt full of hope. This old planet might not be so bleak, after all.

"Try to eat a little, Veronica," he coaxed, patting her hand, "or you'll be hungry later. I'll tell you what—to make up for all my probing, I'll do something for you."

"What?"

"Tomorrow night you may come to my home and interview me. Bring your notepad and pencil. Bring a tape recorder, if you like! You have shared your feelings with me, and I trust you."

Her expression changed to one of cautious happiness. "You'll answer my questions?"

"I reserve the right to hedge," he said. "But I'll do my best."

Late that night David walked alone in the Rush Street district, as he often did, to think and observe. It was a neighborhood of narrow streets, unimpressive really, with two- or three-story buildings, some with modernized facades. On Friday and Saturday nights it hummed with young people, drinking, eating, and pairing off like insects in the heat of summer.

He passed a singles bar called Mother's and heard rock music and laughter, but wasn't tempted to go inside. He was distracted, thinking of Veronica.

She was so unlike the rest of her generation, he thought. He remembered the days when women had to keep themselves chaste in order to be considered worthy of a respectable husband. But Veronica had remained untouched for her own reasons, which intrigued him. He'd always found purity a mystery.

David reminded himself that perhaps purity attracted him because he was himself so far from pure. He represented all that was impure. He had stolen purity from death itself!

He passed groups of young couples, laughing, hanging on to each other, all the joys of life before them. The evenings they spent in these noisy bars, these dingy streets, were only a passing period of their lives. Five years from now most of them would be married, settled down somewhere, raising children. But in five years David would be exactly the same, still walking these streets alone, an outside observer with nothing to look forward to but more empty nights.

What right did he have to yearn for Veronica? It was immoral of him even to think of pursuing her. He should leave her be.

But—like the lines he'd written for the vampire in his play— why should he concern himself with morality, being what he was? God no longer watched over him, he was convinced of that.

Unlike the vampire he'd created for the stage, however, David was still ruled by his conscience. He couldn't justify tainting an innocent. And yet he needed someone like Veronica. He was desperately lonely. And he sensed she needed someone, too. What if he could keep their relationship limited? If they fulfilled each other only on a spiritual level, would that be so immoral?

The soothing smell of liquor came to his nostrils as he passed another singles bar. It gave him a yen for a glass of port, but he knew better. One small glass a week was all he dared take. Alcohol evaporated from his system so slowly, any more might be toxic. In addition, too much alcohol made him far too emotional. He had to be content with the mellow glow the one glass had given him.

Or was it the lovely Veronica who had done that?

It was one o'clock in the morning, but Veronica lay wide awake in bed. Her white cat, Felix, dozed on top of the covers against her hip, purring.

David de Morrissey had both frightened and fascinated her. He was as handsome and imposing and manly as any of the leading men in the old movies she loved—Errol Flynn, Tyrone Power, Cary Grant. Maybe that was why he had sometimes unnerved her. It had been like living out a scene with a man who was larger than life. And yet, at other moments, she'd felt almost at home with him.

Felix nudged his head under her hand, wanting to be petted. As she stroked his soft fur, she decided that, movie fantasies aside, she'd felt a distinct rapport with David de Morrissey in spite of his probing questions and sometimes imperious manner. She wondered how she'd allowed the conversation to reach such an intimate level.

But he hadn't made fun of her inexperience. He seemed to understand without her having to explain or justify herself. She liked that.

In fact, by the end of the evening she'd been enthralled with his looks, bearing, and manner. He'd seemed so protective when he offered to escort her home by cab. Still, something had told her she was in over her head. It was why she'd refused his offer and taken the cab home alone.

Maybe it was the strength of *her* attraction to *him* that scared her. She'd never felt this strongly before about a real-life man. She hoped this time she wouldn't wind up disappointed and retreating to her dreams. Maybe with David the feeling would last.

3

A Fortress with Great, Solid Walls

AS VERONICA walked down Dearborn Street toward the building where she worked, she caught sight of Rob Greenfield a few yards ahead of her. She hurried around others in the morning rush hour crowd to catch up to him.

"Hi, Rob," she said.

He turned and grinned. "You sure look bright-eyed and bushy-tailed!"

"So do you." She tried to figure out what was different about him, then realized what it was. "Where are your glasses?"

"I finally got my lost contact lens replaced."

His wheat-colored hair and green eyes sparkled in the morning sun. Veronica couldn't help but admire his crisp, blond perfection. But compared to David de Morrissey, he seemed boyish and lacking in substance.

"Well," she said with a puckish grin, too excited to keep her news to herself, "I have a little bombshell to drop on Mr. Malloy this morning."

"You do? Going to let me in on it?"

Veronica hesitated, reconsidering now whether she should tell either of them yet. But why not? David wouldn't agree to let anyone but her interview him. Mr. Malloy couldn't replace her with Rob on *this* assignment. Rob might as well know, too. "I've got an interview lined up with David de Morrissey."

"You have what?" His question was tactful, as if he thought she were confused.

"I met him last night through a friend, and he agreed to let me interview him tonight."

"Met him! What's he like?"

41

"Handsome and cultured. Exciting. Debonair." Veronica could have gone on and on.

They reached the entrance to their building, and Rob opened the door for her with an astonished expression. Both headed toward the stairs to the second floor, rather than take the elevator. As they climbed the steps, Rob's expression changed by degrees from stunned to grim.

"What's wrong?" she asked as she unbuttoned her coat. "I thought you'd be happy for me."

Rob raised his eyebrows, but his expression remained far from happy. "Sure, I have to congratulate you. Getting an interview with de Morrissey is quite a coup. How did you do it?"

"I had a long conversation with him. After he got to know me a little, he trusted me."

"Trusted you, huh? He's not expecting anything in return, I hope."

His parental tone surprised her. "What do you mean?" she asked.

"You're not that naive. You know what I mean."

"Rob! What a thing to insinuate."

"Well," Rob went on as they reached the second floor, "of all the newspaper, magazine, and TV reporters who must have asked him for interviews over the years, it's odd that the only one he agrees to see is you. I think he 'trusts' you because you're young and inexperienced. Not to mention pretty. And you admire him so much, you probably swooned at his feet! He happened across the only chocolate-covered cherry in the box and decided to snatch it."

"It's not like that," Veronica said, appalled. "He's a gentleman through and through."

"God, he's got you under a spell already! You won't even be a challenge for him."

Rob's reaction amazed her. Until now he'd been so even-tempered she wouldn't have been able to imagine him angry. "You've never met him. How do you know what he's like?"

"There have been stories floating around about de Morrissey for years," he replied darkly.

"What stories?"

Rob maintained his grim expression but said nothing.

"Well, if you believe irresponsible gossip, I have nothing

more to say to you." She left him at the doorway and headed toward Mr. Malloy's office. As she walked, she took off her coat and threw it over her arm. She adjusted the bow of her red blouse and smoothed her hair with a brisk motion. For once she didn't care whether every strand was in place or not. She had news that would stand Mr. Malloy on his ear!

"Something?" Mr. Malloy said when she appeared in his doorway.

"Yes, something," she said, striding up to his desk with a confidence she'd never felt before in his office.

He looked up from the advertising layouts in front of him and lifted one bushy eyebrow. "Well?"

"I've got an interview tonight with David de Morrissey."

He stared at her, his hazel eyes widening.

"It's true," she said. "I wondered if you had any input—questions you'd like me to ask, a certain slant you'd like me to take for an article about him."

Her boss leaned back and tossed his pencil onto his desk. "How did all this happen?"

Veronica told her story again. "At first he was adamant about not giving interviews, but I talked him into it," she finished with a bit of embellishment. "I'm meeting him at his home this evening."

Mr. Malloy grinned and shook his head. "Damn it, Veronica, you're a mouse, but you can sure pack a wallop when you want to! Congratulations, young lady!"

"Thank you!"

"Ed, may I say something about this?" Rob's voice came from the doorway. Veronica turned, wondering how long he'd been standing there.

"What have you got to say?" Mr. Malloy asked. "How come *you* didn't pull this off?"

"I don't have a high voice and long eyelashes," Rob muttered, walking in.

"Because you didn't even try," Mr. Malloy said.

Rob looked chastised. "No, sir, I didn't. I agree, Veronica's pulled the proverbial rabbit out of a hat. I only hope de Morrissey doesn't view *her* as his prize bunny."

"I'm sure I can handle this interview professionally," Veronica said.

"I think I should go along when she visits his mansion," Rob told their boss. "We can both interview him."

"What!"

"Why?" Mr. Malloy asked, ignoring Veronica for the moment.

"I'm a theater critic. I have the expertise to question him intelligently."

"I can come up with questions just as intelligent as yours!"

"I also think," Rob said, raising his voice to drown out Veronica's, "that she shouldn't go alone to his home, especially at night."

Mr. Malloy leaned forward, putting his elbows on his desk. He rubbed his nose. "All right. Let's discuss this. First, Veronica got this interview all by herself. She deserves the chance to handle it on her own, without you horning in."

"Thank you," Veronica said.

"On the other hand," he went on, "I see what you mean about her going there alone."

"Mr. Malloy," Veronica objected. "I'm capable of taking care of myself. I expect to be treated the same as the men in this office."

Ed Malloy stroked his chin. "Look, Veronica, I'm just an old relic with antiquated ideas. That feminist stuff is all very well when it comes to fair laws and equal pay. Personally, I'm relieved not to have to hold doors and watch my language for you women anymore. But when it comes to a young gal like you going all alone, after dark, to the lonely mansion of a playwright who's certified weird, well . . ."

"I'll be perfectly safe! As I told Rob before, David is an absolute gentleman."

"*David?*" Rob mimicked.

"He asked me to call him by his first name."

"That was gentlemanly of him." Mr. Malloy traded glances with Rob.

Veronica was getting fed up. They didn't value her judgment enough even to believe her eyewitness account of David! "Why do you assume the worst about a man you've never met?" she asked. "He's famous and he hates publicity. Wouldn't it be foolish of him to try to take advantage of me? The moment he did, he'd make headlines."

Both men shifted their positions uneasily, as if neither had a good answer to her argument.

"There have been rumors concerning de Morrissey and women, though," Mr. Malloy said.

"What rumors?" Maybe her boss would tell her what Rob had not.

"Something in the papers a few years ago about strange screams and a scantily clad blonde seen escaping out of his window in the middle of the night."

"That's ridiculous," Veronica said, unable to imagine David involved in such goings-on.

"I heard something similar on the radio once," Rob said. "I was listening to WLS on my way to work. A guy who runs a rare-book shop next to de Morrissey's mansion called in and said he heard . . ."

Rob paused and glanced at Veronica, then, looking back at Mr. Malloy with a faint blush, he continued. "He heard, shall we say, passionate cries coming from de Morrissey's mansion. It was summer and the windows were open. At first the store owner almost called the police. The screams were so wild, he was afraid someone was being murdered. He complained the noises went on all night while he was trying to do inventory."

"De Morrissey must have stamina!" Mr. Malloy said with an earthy chuckle.

Veronica felt uneasy. Did David have a lover? "So he's a healthy male. What's odd about that?" she said, trying to turn their stories around to favor David.

"There are other rumors, too. In fact, I *know* people who say they've seen eerie lights in his upper windows at all hours of the night," Rob said. "A while back I met an investigative reporter from the *Tribune*. He was putting together an article, but couldn't get anyone who knows de Morrissey to talk. He found out by scouting around that de Morrissey lives all alone in his huge house, has no hired help, is never seen coming or going, never even has garbage to be collected. The reporter couldn't find any women who claim to have had a relationship with him—or men, either. There are no photos of him. An understudy in his play said de Morrissey insisted on night rehearsals, at which he would sit far back in the empty theater and speak only to the director. An actor who happened to catch a glimpse of him described him as pale and sickly looking."

"Sounds like he might be strung out on drugs," Mr. Malloy suggested.

"He looked perfectly healthy last night," Veronica told them. "Besides, those rumors don't even jibe. If he's totally alone and doesn't go out with women, where did the blonde come from? If he's sickly, how could he keep a woman screaming all night? Because he writes about vampires and doesn't like to be in the public eye, everyone makes him out to be weird. It's tabloid-style trash!"

Rob shrugged.

"Still, he's not exactly Billy Graham," Mr. Malloy said, scratching an eyebrow. "I think Rob should go along."

Veronica squared her shoulders. "Mr. de Morrissey agreed to meet with me and only me. He won't talk if I show up with Sir Galahad here. If I don't do this alone, we'll lose the interview."

Mr. Malloy looked up at Rob. "Guess she's got us over a barrel," he said, a trace of admiration in his tone. "All right, Veronica. You're on a roll! Ask him what you want. Any quote will be news. Just be careful. Got a canister of Mace in your purse?"

Promptly at eight that evening Veronica parked her car in an empty space in front of David's mansion on Oak Street. Street lamps dimly lit the massive, medieval-looking stone building with its projecting dormers and steep gables. It looked like a fortress with great, solid walls for protection against the outside world.

When she opened her car door and got out, a gust of cold wind off Lake Michigan whipped her hair across her face, stinging her skin. She hurried up the sidewalk and turned onto the cement walk that led to the heavy, wooden front door beneath a high arch. Awed by the imposing entrance, she looked for the doorbell. She found only a small metal cover where it appeared a doorbell button had once been. An ornate bronze knocker was nailed to the door. She was about to use it when she heard a window opening above.

"Veronica?"

She stepped back a few paces and looked up. It was David, leaning out a window on the top floor. "Yes, it's me," she said.

He smiled down at her. "I'll press a button. Open the door when the buzzer sounds and then climb the steps all the way up."

"Okay." She waved to him and then walked back to the entrance. In a moment the buzzer sounded and she opened the door.

Inside was a large oval hall painted creamy white with an Oriental carpet on the floor. The spiral staircase, she noticed when she looked up, rose to a high domed ceiling and was bordered with elaborate molding. The decorative inner door to the ground floor rooms was shut and dead-bolted. When she reached the second-floor landing the door there was also bolted shut. She was out of breath by the time she'd climbed to the third floor. David was waiting for her at the top.

"They built this house without an elevator," he said. "My apologies."

"The exercise is good for me," Veronica told him as she caught her breath.

He looked the same as he had the night before—an intelligent, sophisticated, commanding man with pale eyes and high coloring. He seemed relaxed and amiable. Looking at him made all the stories she'd heard earlier from Rob and Mr. Malloy sound preposterous.

He held open the door for her. She walked into a large, bay-windowed living room with pilasters lining the walls and more decorative molding around the ceiling and doorways. The room was decorated in a comfortable, traditional style, with oak furnishings. The upholstery and the floor-to-ceiling draperies were of a rich fabric in shades of green, coral, and yellow, patterned with large flowers, their stems and leaves entwined, and highlighted with butterflies, dragonflies, and bees. A sparkling chandelier hung from the ceiling, and brass lamps with silk shades were lit on the sofa end tables. A large fireplace with a marble mantel graced one wall, its log fire adding warmth and coziness. Veronica's shoes sank into the luxurious pile of a vast, colorful Oriental rug that covered the entire room.

Conscious of her windblown state, she looked around for a

mirror but found none. "Is there a mirror somewhere? My hair—"

"Anyone as lovely as you has no need of a mirror," he said. "There's a bathroom just over there, but the mirror broke years ago and I never replaced it."

"That's okay," she said, combing her hair with her fingers. She looked around her in wonder. "Your home is beautiful. Did you decorate it yourself?"

"I hired a professional decorator," David replied, taking her coat from her. He hung it in a small closet, then stood near the door, arms casually folded, and watched her move around the room as she admired each piece of furniture. "The decorator came here one evening, and I told her what I wanted, selected the fabric from swatches she'd brought, and gave her a check. She took care of it all while I was . . . away. When I returned, everything was finished and waiting for me. I was very pleased."

"I can see why." Veronica looked at the objects in a lighted curio cabinet. "Are these vases antiques?"

"Yes, they're from many places," he said, walking up to her. "That one there is Victorian." He pointed as he spoke. "And that, eighteenth-century French. I've collected them in my travels."

"Do you collect antique furniture, too?"

"I did, but I tired of it. In fact, the first floor is full of old furniture that I don't want to live with, but can't part with for sentimental reasons."

As he smiled down at her, Veronica noted how striking he looked in his tawny cashmere jacket. The collar of his white silk shirt was unbuttoned and he wore no tie. His bared neck looked as strong as a marble column. Though his shoulders were broad, they were not so developed that they spoiled his elegant line. She could see from the way his shirt tapered smoothly over pectoral muscles toward his belt that he was trim and fit. Dark brown pants, perfectly pressed and creased, and polished brown shoes completed his expensively casual attire. Immaculate though he looked, she couldn't help but sense that the rich clothing camouflaged a raw, imposing, thoroughly masculine body.

Veronica swallowed, trying to collect herself. His strong

presence and manly bearing were making her pulse grow rapid. "I brought a tape recorder. Is that all right?"

"I said you could, didn't I? Would you like to sit with me on the love seat?"

The warnings Rob and Mr. Malloy had given her surfaced again in her mind, giving her a twinge of trepidation. But she didn't want to look as if she didn't trust him. "Sure, the . . . the couch would be fine."

They sat down, a decorous space between them. Veronica noted again the striking pattern of the upholstery. "I like this," she said, running her hand over the seat cushion. "The flowers look so real. And the butterflies and dragonflies give it so much life."

"Exactly," he said with warmth, looking at her with eyes that seemed to grow more blue. "You see it as I do. I chose this material precisely because it shows the exuberance of nature. The brightness of flowers and busy-ness of insects—all the products of sunshine, the joy of a summer afternoon in a meadow. When I look at it, I can almost feel the sun warming me, even at night like this."

Veronica marveled at how finely tuned he was to everything around him. She felt inadequate to interview him at the intellectual and artistic level he deserved. But fate had given her this opportunity, and she had to do her best.

Taking the small tape recorder out of her handbag, she placed it on the graceful, carved oak coffee table in front of them. "I ran out and bought this on my lunch hour," she confessed. "I'm not sure I know how to work it."

"I'm afraid I can be of no help. Gadgets confound me."

Veronica pressed the Play and Record buttons together as the instructions had said. The tape began to roll. "Looks like it's working right. I'm going to take notes, too, just in case."

"Good idea." He seemed amused as he watched her take a small notepad and pen from her purse. He sat facing her, leaning his side into the love seat, his arm over its low back.

"Okay," she said, putting her pen to the paper as she turned a bit to face him. "First of all, why did you agree to an interview after all these years?" She couldn't help but be curious.

"There are so many strange things written about me, I felt it was time to show that I'm fairly normal, after all."

"Great," she said with a smile, reassured that Rob and Mr. Malloy were wrong. "You said you were born in Paris. Would you tell me what year?"

David looked at the table for a moment. "I'm thirty-four. Does that answer your question?"

"Sure. What did your parents do for a living?"

"My parents?" He seemed startled. "I . . . they didn't really have a line of work. They were aristocrats."

"Really," Veronica said as she scribbled. "So the de Morrisseys are a wealthy family?"

"Indeed."

"Do you have brothers and sisters?"

"I did. They're deceased."

"I see. And your parents?"

"Also deceased."

Veronica felt sad for him and uncomfortable at having touched on tragedies in his past. She decided not to ask any more about his family for a while. "When did you come to the United States?"

"I came to Chicago ten or twelve years ago. I've lost track."

"So you must have written your first play when you were about twenty-four?"

He raised an eyebrow, as if puzzled.

"Well, you're thirty-four and your first play was performed ten years ago. I know because I'd just turned thirteen when I saw it."

"Yes, of course," he said, smiling. "I was twenty-four."

"How were you able to write such a profound and polished play when you were so young? You even won a Tony. You must have been only a few years out of college."

"I studied Shakespeare a great deal, and other classic writers."

She chuckled at his modesty. "Well, lots of people read Shakespeare, but they don't turn out magnificent plays. It seems to me your ideas, your insight and wisdom, would have taken years of experience to develop."

He lifted his shoulders in a nonchalant shrug. "Thank you for your compliment. But obviously, my work is curdled cream next to Shakespeare's. A better question is how did Shakespeare achieve his level of genius in his modest life span?"

"Would you like to be a modern-day Shakespeare?"

His eyes instantly took on such a hostile look, Veronica felt as if her heart stopped for a moment. She'd thought it was an innocuous question. "I'm sorry, did I say something wrong?"

He put a long finger to his temple and massaged it lightly. His expression softened as he seemed to grow more comfortable. "Yes, of course I'd like to be a modern Shakespeare," he said with a smile that didn't reach his eyes. "Who wouldn't? But I'm afraid God supplied the earth with only one Shakespeare, and there will never be another. William Shakespeare was God's gift to us. And His punishment."

"Punishment?" Veronica asked. "I don't understand."

The angry glare seeped back into his eyes. "Surely you must have other questions to pursue."

"Yes, of course," she said quickly, feeling her forehead break out with perspiration. "I'm sorry if—"

"No, don't be sorry," he said with more patience. "You have no way of knowing what topics are not to my liking. Please continue."

He seemed almost contrite now, yet still wary and something else, some other emotion she couldn't quite identify. Veronica felt her momentary fear of him subsiding. For some reason she found herself reaching out to touch his jacket sleeve.

"I want this interview to be pleasant for you," she said. "If a subject I bring up is difficult to talk about, then we'll drop it."

His grim mouth eased, and his eyes grew almost luminous. She wondered if there was something unusual about the lighting in the room or if she were having a minor hallucination, for she felt certain his eyes were deepening in color. They weren't the light powder blue of only a few minutes ago, but a vivid, robin's-egg hue. How odd. Before she could steal an additional moment to think about it, he startled her by taking hold of her hand as she withdrew it from his sleeve. His strong fingers folded snugly around hers and he brought her hand to his lips in a feathery kiss.

"Your sensitivity touches me, Veronica."

She managed what must have been a silly smile. "No, I just—"

"Don't argue." His voice lilted with warmth now. "You're

very special. I would willingly answer your questions all night
long, just to sit in your presence and feel your sweetness wash
over me."

His sudden change bewildered her. "David, you shouldn't
say things like that."

"You should hear compliments like that every hour." He
reached over her shoulder to nestle his fingers into her hair.
"You're so dear. But, you know, if you want to be a reporter,
you'll have to be a little less lenient with the people you interview."

She laughed shyly, his touch disconcerting her. "Why are
you telling me that? You should be glad I let you off easy."

"I am. But you're too giving for your own good. The world
out there is tough, and if you want to get on in it, you have
to be tough, too."

"You sound like my boss."

"No, do I?"

"A lot nicer, though."

"An old ogre, is he?"

"He's around sixty," she said. "Impatient and grumpy most
of the time. He says I need seasoning. Though he was impressed
when I told him I'd gotten an appointment to interview you."

"Good!"

Veronica looked beyond David's shoulder at a curtained
window, feeling depressed now. It troubled her that she was
getting the same advice from so many different people.

"What are you thinking?" David asked.

"Just that . . ." She looked at him, sensing he had the wisdom
to help her. "I don't know *how* to get tough, or seasoned, or
streetwise, like Caroline says I should be. It's as if I understand
old movies better than real life. Sounds funny, but—"

"No, it's not. I know exactly what you mean."

"You do?" She smiled. "Then you're unique, because no one
else seems to. I feel that everyone understands how the world
works but me. And they can't figure *me* out."

"I know how painful it is to feel that way. I was like that,
too. Still am, in many ways. When your instinct is for fantasy
and your imagination is bright and clear, then the real world
seems dull by comparison. And like a dull subject at school,

you don't want to spend any time studying it, though everyone around you takes to it like a duck to water."

"And they think I'm slow on the uptake or in a daze," she said, her throat closing with unshed tears.

"You aren't slow or dazed, Veronica. Never think that. Imagination is a rare gift, and you must value it. Don't let anyone tell you otherwise. Unfortunately, our imagination is hidden to others, and only we can feel the joy of it. You have to learn to transmit it in a form others can see. I do it by writing plays. You need to find some way to express all the wonderful things that are hidden within you."

Veronica listened spellbound. No one, including her parents, had ever understood her or believed in her the way David seemed to. He made her feel proud of herself. Tears began to form in her eyes.

She laughed a little, blinking back the wetness. "You've done a turnabout on me again. Instead of me interviewing you, you're tutoring me."

"I would love to be your tutor."

She studied his face, wondering if he was serious. "Would you? I mean, I'd take you up on that if you meant it. But it's okay if you don't."

"I mean it. It would give me joy. I need something to make me feel I'm worth being here on earth. Writing doesn't always fulfill me that way." His eyes grew distant for a moment. "But to know that I could be of use, of help, to you would give me a satisfaction all its own."

Veronica felt her lips trembling as she smiled. His deep interest in her was so unexpected, it overwhelmed her. She wiped away a tear and then felt embarrassed by her overt emotion.

"Thank you," she said. She straightened her shoulders and tried to compose herself. "Well, I guess we'd better finish the interview, and then we can talk more about this later."

"Of course. I think I heard a click from your tape recorder. Has the tape run out?"

She leaned over and picked it up. "It has. Just a second." She fumbled with the recorder, trying to get the tape out so she could turn it over.

While she was working at it, she heard a noise at the window behind him, like a tapping, then scratching sounds. Peering over David's shoulder she saw something glitter behind the sheer curtain that covered the glass. Focusing her gaze even more closely, she saw a white face with two large eyes that blinked. Slowly the window began to open.

Veronica dropped the tape recorder and screamed. "David! Someone's breaking in!"

4

The Peculiar Way the Moonlight Fell on His Face

A GUST of cold air rushed over Veronica's face as the curtains blew inward and parted. David turned toward the window. As Veronica looked on in shock, a woman peered in, put her arms through to clutch the sill and then ducked her head into the opening.

"Diable!" With this stifled exclamation, David rushed from the couch to the window. Taking the woman's arm, he helped her climb in. Lithely, she extended one long, shapely leg and then the other over the windowsill and onto the floor. When she stood, the hem of her floor-length, ruby-red satin dress swished back into place around her bare feet. The high heel of a red shoe stuck out of each pocket of her white mink coat. A tall, obviously energetic woman, she looked perfectly capable of having climbed in without David's assistance. For all her lively acrobatics, however, she was beautiful, with eyes that held a smile. Her long blond hair was piled on top of her head, fastened with a diamond clip, from which plump, shining ringlets bobbed.

Veronica got up from the love seat and instinctively backed away to the opposite side of the room, until the cold hardness of the marble mantel stopped her. She stood perfectly still, questions racing through her head. Who was this woman? How could she have gotten up to the third floor? Was she some kind of cat burglar? Veronica glimpsed the bright necklace of diamonds and rubies at the blonde's throat, beneath the white mink, and the idea of a burglar seemed even more plausible.

While the woman put her shoes on, David shut the window and pulled the draperies, his movements agitated. He stepped close to the blonde and spoke into her ear. *"Vite!"* Veronica thought she heard him whisper. *"Forge une histoire!"*

Veronica had already forgotten much of her college French, but she thought what he said was either, "Quick! Make up a story!" or "Quick! You'd better have a good excuse!" But he'd spoken so softly, she might have misheard him.

The blonde's pale green eyes fell on Veronica then. "Oh! *Une invitée?*" She spoke in a feminine, throaty voice that reminded Veronica of Catherine Deneuve and other French movie actresses. *"Qu'elle est belle!"* Veronica understood that well enough: "How beautiful she is!"

"*Anglais,* Darienne," David chided her. "Speak English."

Darienne's wide-set, sparkling eyes turned whimsical. "How silly of me! I've just come from Paris," she explained with a thick accent, looking across the room at Veronica. "David, introduce me to this pretty creature."

David motioned to Veronica to come closer. Deciding she had nothing to fear from this dazzling woman who thought *she* was pretty, Veronica stepped away from the fireplace and walked over to them.

"Veronica, this is Darienne Victoire," David said. "Darienne, Veronica Ames."

"How charming to meet you!" Darienne extended her hand. Her fingers were long and slender, sparkling with jeweled rings.

Veronica took the woman's hand, almost as delicate as her own, and was surprised at the ironlike strength her fingers seemed to possess. Like David's.

"It's a pleasure to meet you," Veronica said. Smiling with curiosity, she added, "Why did you come in through the window? And how did you get up to the third floor?"

Darienne blithely glanced up at the chandelier for a moment, its shimmer reflected in her eyes. "Friends," she said, looking back at Veronica. "I asked some good friends to drive me over here, and we brought a ladder because I wanted to give David a surprise. In fact, I ought to wave goodbye to them."

As Darienne went back to the window and pushed aside the drapery, David told Veronica, "She's always pulling things like this on me. Darienne's a tireless practical joker."

While Veronica watched in bewilderment, Darienne opened

the window again, wrapped her mink close around her, and leaned out.

"Au revoir! Merci!" she called, waving to someone outside. She closed the window and came back to them. "They've tied the ladder back on top of the car and they're driving off," she said, taking David's arm and pressing her cheek into his shoulder. "They know how I love to tease David."

She pronounced his name in the French way: Dah-veed. His name on her lips sounded intimate and sensual. Veronica experienced a sinking feeling in her chest. Darienne seemed to possess first claim to him, and there was no way she could compete with such a worldly, glittering femme fatale.

Veronica realized all at once that Darienne was staring at her, her eyes a vivid, emerald green. There was something unsettling about her now, something acquisitive and quick and amoral. Then that aspect vanished as if it had never been there, and Darienne's eyes were full of fun.

"Oh, she's lovely, David," Darienne purred. "Where did you find her?"

"She found me," David said, smiling warmly at Veronica while Darienne still clung to him.

The blonde looked up at him. "Found you?"

"Yes, and now she's interviewing me for her magazine."

Darienne seemed concerned. "Is that wise?"

David's eyes held Veronica's in a steady gaze. "She will bring me no harm," he said in a doting voice.

Veronica would have thought such overt attention to her might make Darienne suspicious or jealous. But the blonde looked back at her now with a renewed delight that puzzled Veronica. She knew Darienne couldn't be his sister. Was she his cousin or some other relation? Were they simply old friends? Or was Darienne his lover, the sort who was willing to share him? The French expression, *ménage à trois,* crept into Veronica's mind. She pushed the thought away, not liking it.

"You interrupted our interview," David told Darienne with amiable bluntness.

"Am I *de trop?*" Darienne asked. "Yes, of course, I'm in the way. Shall I leave?"

"No, stay," he said, taking hold of her hand briefly, urgency in his tone. He turned to Veronica then. "We've been sitting for a while. Would you like to go out?"

"All right," she said, uncertain what he had in mind.

"Darienne, there are refreshments in the refrigerator. Help yourself."

"Thank you," Darienne said with a smile as she took off her luxurious mink and threw it on the love seat in a careless manner. Veronica drew in her breath at the dress revealed underneath. It was an evening gown, intricately low-cut with scoops here and scallops there, cradling a voluptuous bosom which was all the more accentuated by a slim waist. Her necklace dripped diamonds and rubies all the way to her deep cleavage.

Veronica suddenly felt like a string bean. "That's a gorgeous dress."

Darienne grew radiant. "Do you like it? I just bought it in Paris. It's the latest Dior."

"It's beautiful. Your necklace and earrings, too."

"Oh, I've had these for years." Darienne patted the necklace with a pleased smile.

"Did you attend some big event? An opening night, or something?"

"No, *chérie*," Darienne said with a flutelike laugh. "Oh, I do attend opera and ballet, and David's plays, of course. But I never require an excuse to dress up. I *exist* to wear beautiful garments and jewels. They're my passion."

Veronica was astonished, yet she rather liked Darienne's approach. "I'd like to see your closet," she joked.

"I'd love to show you the things I have. You may try them on!"

"Enough of this female chatter!" David said with mock firmness. "Darienne, make yourself at home. Veronica and I have an interview to finish."

After getting their coats out of the closet, they said goodbye to Darienne and left.

As they walked down the staircase, Veronica asked, "Is she an old friend?"

"We've known each other since we were children. She's remained more attached to our homeland than I."

"She goes to Paris every year?"

"Two or three times a year. She loves to shop, as you might guess."

"She's beautiful," Veronica said, looking up at him to see his reaction.

"Yes, she is," he agreed. Veronica could read nothing in his expression or manner that might give a clue as to what status Darienne had in his life.

They reached the ground floor. Instead of going out the front door, David unlocked a door behind the staircase, painted to match the walls, that Veronica hadn't noticed before. It opened to another hallway. "I hope you don't mind," he said, leading her into it. "I prefer not to use the front door. I'm a private person and don't like people observing my comings and goings. We'll use a side door and then go around the back."

"I don't mind," she said, adjusting her long wool scarf around her neck.

They walked down the hall, passing a stairwell to the basement. They came to another hallway and several doors, all bolted. He stopped at a door heavier than the others, unlocked it, and they stepped outside.

The night air was frigid, though the wind seemed to have died down a little. As he turned the key to lock the door again, she remarked, "If you're concerned about security, have you ever thought of having a system installed?"

"A system?"

"You know, with sensors and alarms that go off if someone breaks in."

"Good heavens, no! Locks and keys I can understand. Modern technology upsets me."

She chuckled. Sometimes he seemed so much older than thirty-four. "I guess you don't write your plays on a computer, then."

"Pencil and yellow, lined paper," he said, putting his keys into his pocket as they began to walk along the side of the house. "I mail it to a typist to transcribe."

"A computer is a lot more efficient," she said. "We use them at work. They're wonderful."

"Until they break down. I wouldn't like dealing with repairmen, even if I could get the hang of the technology. Besides, the process seems so detached. I like to touch the paper, cradle the pencil between my thumb and forefinger, empty myself onto the page with each stroke. You can't do that with a keyboard and chartreuse letters that hurt one's eyes while they disappear up a gray screen. It's inhuman."

"I guess that settles that."

He laughed. "I must sound like an old curmudgeon to you."

"Brilliant people have a right to be eccentric."

The sidewalk around the house was not lit, and the building blocked the moonlight, so that they walked in a night shadow. The thick, still darkness began to unsettle Veronica as they moved farther away from the streetlights, and she could barely see where they were going. There was shrubbery along the path—she could feel it brush against her coat from time to time, its sudden roughness making her jump. She began to hesitate.

David took her arm. "Can't you see?"

"No, can you?"

"I know my way. Hang on to me. It's not much farther."

All at once she stumbled on some uneven pavement and twisted her ankle. He caught her to him and kept her from falling. "Are you all right?"

"Yes," she said. But her foot gave way as she stepped on it again, and she stumbled once more.

"Perhaps I'd better carry you."

Before she could reply, she was swept off her feet by one strong arm at the back of her knees and another just below her shoulders. She put her arm around David's neck to keep her balance, though she felt secure. Lifting her seemed no effort for him at all. He carried her as he might have a small child.

The path began to grow lighter as they approached the back of the building. Across the yard she could make out the alley and a distant light from someone else's property.

They moved past the house and into the fenced yard. The full moon came into view now and shed its light. Leafless trees stood along the edge of the property like sinister and lonely sentinels. An iron fence with a gate bordered David's lot. He carried her down a narrow path and paused when he came to the heavy gate.

"I can see now," she said, "if you'd like to put me down."

"I do have to unlock the gate," he said, sounding a little reluctant. He squeezed her to his chest, taking her breath away. "You're a sweet burden, Veronica."

Moonlight on his partly shadowed face picked up the smooth plane of his cheek and the edge of his firm jaw. His eyes were luminous, as though reflecting the light, but he was not looking in the moon's direction. He was looking at her.

Veronica was not used to moments like this. She wanted to respond, but didn't know how. "You're very strong," she whispered.

"Am I? Do you like strong men?"

"Yes," she said with a trembling smile. "Especially if they're going to be my tutor."

"I'm glad I please you." He set her down on her feet, keeping her within the circle of his arms to steady her, but her ankle was no longer weak. She could feel the warmth of his breath on her cheek in the cold air. Her heart began to pound.

He bent toward her. She felt a moment of panic as he brought his mouth to her cheek in an affectionate nuzzle. He trailed his lips to her jaw with feather-light kisses.

Pulling away the wool scarf around her neck, he slipped his hand beneath her long hair to push it out of the way. She instinctively closed her eyes and slid her hands up his shoulders. There was something lulling about the warmth and strength of his arms, the gentleness of his touch. She relaxed as she never had before in a man's arms. His increasingly ardent lips moved down the sensitive skin of her throat slowly, sumptuously, making his way toward the pulse above her coat collar. She gave a little gasp as his mouth grew hot.

His breathing became ragged. He drew his mouth away from her skin, but he kept her near, hovering at the side of her neck. She could feel his heated, moist breath at her pulse point, giving her shivers of desire. Veronica had never wanted a man to touch her so much as she craved David's mouth and hands. She wanted him to kiss her again and demonstrate all the urgent need she felt in him.

But, as though paralyzed by an intense internal argument, he made no further move, except that his fingers clutched her upper arms more tightly, almost hurting her. Veronica feared his profound hesitation was due to guilt—to a feeling that he was being untrue to Darienne.

She took her arms from around his neck. "Don't you like me, David?" She dared to look up at him then.

What she saw in his face made her want to run. Only she was too frightened, too disbelieving of her own perception to move.

His eyes were cobalt-blue, more than luminous now, almost burning in their strength. His mouth was partly open, moist, and she noticed for the first time in the peculiar way the moonlight fell on his face that his teeth were sharp and gleaming.

"David!" she screamed, pushing away from him.

He let her go immediately. As she backed away in horror, a look of terrible self-loathing contorted his face, which was now pale. The unearthly light she'd thought she saw in his eyes vanished, replaced by stark shock.

He turned away and wrapped his hands around the gatepost, leaning his forehead against the iron. "I'm sorry. Forgive me! I didn't want to hurt you."

Veronica continued to back away, watching him, her heart pounding painfully in her chest. She didn't know what to think. It was as though everything had turned upside down for an instant, as though she'd seen the moon turn black and the sky glow white in a lightning flash. But it must all have been a hallucination.

As she studied David's tortured silhouette, her adrenaline level began to subside. Now she felt ashamed for wounding him with her ridiculous reaction. She'd let the soundless night, the full moon, and eerie memories of *Street Shadows* get hold of her imagination. Or perhaps she'd let herself half believe Rob's and Mr. Malloy's ridiculous warnings about David. To imagine glowing eyes and carnivorous teeth! As if David could be a vampire! She would lose him if she let her wild imaginings get the better of her again, if she didn't learn to keep his theatrical vampire separated from the gentle, cultured, flesh-and-blood human being that was the true David.

She hurried to him. "David, don't be upset," she begged, tugging at his arm. "I'm sorry I reacted that way. I don't know what came over me."

He turned his face in the opposite direction. "I didn't intend to—to frighten you that way. You must believe me. I would never harm you, not intentionally."

"I know," she said, running her hand up his broad back. "It was the moon and my imagination. I saw things that weren't there. Please don't feel badly." When he still didn't respond, tears filled her eyes and her voice grew choked. She was afraid the tenuous relationship they shared was already ruined. "I admire you so much, David. I want to be your friend and your student. And I want to make you happy, if I can. You seem so troubled sometimes." Was she revealing her feelings too boldly now? If only she'd had more experience with men, she would know when to say what to him.

He turned to her. His face remained in shadows, but she could feel warmth and affection when he put his hands on her shoulders in a strong, sure grasp. "You do make me happy," he told her. "I feel a unique affinity with you. I sensed it from the first moment I saw you. We've known each other only a short time, but already you're very special to me."

She put her arms around his waist and buried her face in his shoulder. "Oh, David. You understand me in a way no one else does. I need you."

They embraced for several long moments. The world seemed to right itself again. Even the night didn't seem so dark anymore. She drew away then. David got out his keys and unlocked the gate. "Let's walk over to Rush Street," he said, stroking her hair. "Maybe we can find an empty table somewhere. We'll relax, have some port, and finish your interview."

She smiled at him. "That sounds lovely."

As they walked the short distance through the alley to the street, Veronica thought again of Darienne. She took his arm and leaned on him in much the same way she'd seen the blond woman do earlier. "David? Is Darienne in love with you?"

The streetlights were bright enough that she could read his expression easily now. The question seemed to make him thoughtful. He looked down at the sidewalk for a few steps as they walked. "I'm not sure if Darienne has ever been in love with anyone. On the other hand, you might say that she's in love with everyone. Darienne has always been very much her own person."

"Are . . . you in love with her?"

He gazed at Veronica and smiled as if with nostalgia. "I've

known her longer than any other person in the world. I do love her. But I'm not *in* love with her."

His answer satisfied Veronica. It meant she had a chance with him. David could never tutor a woman as independent as Darienne. This fact ensured Veronica a unique place in his life, one that Darienne couldn't share with him. And from that special relationship, perhaps a deep love would blossom. Veronica hoped so with all her heart. She was already falling in love with David.

They walked into Butch McGuire's, a popular singles bar jumping with young people and rock music. Taking Veronica's hand, David led her past the bar, where a group of four or five particularly rowdy young men, mugs of beer in their hands, turned and looked Veronica over. She assumed they'd probably given every woman who entered the once-over. A redheaded man, who couldn't have been more than twenty-one years old, tried to say something to her as she walked by, but she ignored him. David put his arm around her protectively as they moved through the crowd to a small, wooden table just vacated by another couple. Once they sat down, they had to almost shout at each other to be heard above the noise.

"Perhaps this wasn't a good idea, after all," David apologized.

"It's all right," she said. "It's interesting to see you in this kind of environment. Everybody says you're such a recluse."

"I am, in a way. I do like to be in crowds where I can be anonymous, however. I come here to study people, overhear conversations, get ideas for my plays. You'd be surprised the things you hear in a singles bar."

A waitress came hurrying over, a pretty young blonde in a short skirt. When she looked at David, speculation immediately enlivened her eyes.

"Two glasses of tawny port, please," he told her.

"Finally, a customer with some class!" The waitress put paper coasters on the table. "It's a relief to wait on someone who isn't scarfing down beer," she said in a confidential tone, using the opportunity to lean close to him rather than shout. With a wink she added, "I'll be right back with your drinks," and strutted off toward the bar.

"Well," Veronica teased when she was gone. "I see why you come here. The waitresses flirt with you."

"It's a singles bar. Maybe they consider it part of their job."

"Sure."

He shrugged off his coat and helped Veronica with hers. "How about asking me the rest of your questions?" he suggested, his eyes warm with humor.

Veronica could see why women would automatically flirt with him. There was something in his eyes when he looked at one that said, I adore women and I'd like to know all about you. She remembered now that he'd even given Caroline that look when he asked her about her wedding. And, of course, he'd looked at Veronica that way from the time they'd "conversed" at the John Hancock. Veronica couldn't help but wonder now if she was only his latest find.

"What are you thinking?" he asked, studying her with interest, as if she were the only woman in the room.

"I'm wondering what I should ask you," she said as she took out her notepad and pen. It was too noisy to bother with the tape recorder. "What do you think about women?"

"Women. That's your question?" He raised one eyebrow. "Again, I'll refer to Shakespeare: 'To be wise, and love, exceeds man's might.' "

"So women make you think of love?"

"What else should they make me think of?" He gazed at her with the same emotion, it seemed, that he was speaking of. "And while thinking of women, or one woman in particular, any wisdom God may have granted me flies to the stratosphere. It's one of my favorite quotations. In a few words it tells a man everything he needs to know about women and renders him hopeless at the same time."

Veronica chuckled as she wrote down the quotation. "But what do you think of women as people?"

"Absolutely fascinating."

"So how come you aren't married? Or have you been?"

He shook his head. Veronica could see she'd happened upon another tragic event in his life as she watched his eyes grow grave, their color pale. "I was almost married once, long ago," he said. "But she died."

"So many people you've loved have died," Veronica murmured, feeling sad for him.

"It's my fate, I believe."

"Why would you believe that?"

"Because I've created my own fate."

"How? What do you mean by fate?"

He looked at her and smiled in a weary, worldly way. "I don't mean anything. I know nothing about fate or providence. Ask me something else."

The waitress came with their drinks, smiling subtly at David as she set them on the table.

When she left, he lifted his glass to Veronica. "To wisdom and love," he said. She touched her glass to his.

After taking a sip, she decided to ask him some practical things. "When and where do you write your plays?"

"I write them at home, sitting or lying back on my couch."

"When?"

He swished the port in his glass. "During the day," he said, studying the swirling liquid. "When you hear or read stories in the papers that I'm never seen out during the day, that's why—it's because I'm working and I allow no interruptions. I hope you will explain that in your article. I go so far as to make my director schedule some play rehearsals in the evening, so I can attend them without upsetting my daily writing routine."

"It sounds like you're very disciplined."

He put down his drink and stroked his eyelid. "I have to be." He turned his head then, wariness in his eyes as he looked up at someone approaching the table.

Veronica turned to see a young man with red hair, his face full of freckles, walking unsteadily toward their table. She'd noticed him at the bar when they came in. Behind him stood his friends, watching. A couple of them were trying to call him back.

"Hi, there!" he said to Veronica, wavering on his feet as he leaned toward her. "How about a dance? They're playing our song."

Veronica nearly choked at the smell of beer on his breath. "We don't have a song," she said, amazed to have someone bother her like this when she was sitting with a man.

"Sure we do," he said, taking hold of her hand and trying to pull her up.

Immediately David rose from his seat and grabbed the fellow by his collar with one hand. "Look at me," he ordered in a low, deceptively gentle voice. The young drunk could hardly do anything else, David held him with such strength. "You're feeling sleepy, aren't you? Yes, you are. Very tired." And with that the man closed his eyes and fell forward onto David. He'd passed out.

The young man's buddies rushed up. Two of them picked him up, one taking his legs, the other his shoulders, and they carried him out. A third lingered to say to Veronica, "Sorry. He's been staring at you ever since you came in. He thought you were pretty. We tried to talk him out of hitting on you, but what can I say? He's pickled."

"That's okay," Veronica said.

The man walked out of the bar. David sat down again.

"Thank you, David, for rescuing me. How did you do that?"

"Do what?"

"Did you hypnotize him or something? He fell asleep as soon as you spoke to him."

"He was ready to pass out. I had nothing to do with it, except to keep him from hitting the floor."

Veronica pondered this, wanting to believe David's explanation, but not quite sure. Some of her fear from the events an hour ago in back of David's house crept back. The light in his eyes, his strength, and now—did he have mental control over people? Oh, she was being overimaginative again.

"Has this upset you?" he asked, taking her hand.

She looked up to see all the concern and tenderness in his eyes and her fears subsided. "No. I should be flattered he wanted to 'hit on me,' I guess."

David laughed, throwing his head back a bit. Despite her reassurance, she couldn't help but notice his teeth. Yes, his incisors were slightly sharp. And they extended a bit beyond his other teeth. But really, they weren't so unusual, or as frightening as they'd seemed an hour ago in the light of the moon. He certainly didn't look like Dracula in all those old movies. She began to laugh at herself. Dracula! David didn't have a thick

Transylvanian accent, either. Or a heavy cape. And she hadn't
heard any dogs howling lately.

That reminded her, she'd wanted to ask him about the Romanian legends. But she glanced at her watch and noticed it
was well past midnight.

"Is it getting late for you?" David asked.

"I guess I'd better go. I have to work tomorrow. A deadline
got pushed up."

"That's too bad," he said with regret. "Shall I walk you to
your car?"

As they walked back to Oak Street, the prospect of separating from him weighed heavily on Veronica's mind. She wondered if she would ever see David again. He'd said things that
indicated he wanted their relationship to continue, but now she
began to wonder if she'd been naive to believe everything he'd
said, or if she was reading too much into his words. Still, there
was their embrace in the yard, and all the unexpected emotion
they'd shared in the moments after her fright. What an unusual, caring man he was. Veronica felt she had to see him
again. She'd be brokenhearted if he didn't want to continue seeing her.

They were on Oak Street now, and she observed the outline
of David's mansion a half block away. Soon they'd reach her
car. He'd been silent since they left Butch McGuire's. Was
something wrong?

"David?"

He turned his head with a start, as if she'd broken into deep
thoughts. "Yes? I'm sorry," he said, putting his arm over her
shoulders. "I've been neglecting you."

"It's all right. We're almost to your house. I'll be saying
goodbye."

"Never goodbye. The French say *au revoir*—till we meet
again."

"Will we?"

"Of course."

"When?"

He gave her a wry grin. " 'Being your slave, what should I
do but tend upon the hours and times of your desire?' "

"David, will you stop quoting Shakespeare!" she said, laughing.

"I can't help it," he said, massaging her shoulder affectionately through her coat. "I feel poetic when I'm with you."

"Thank you." Her tone grew serious. "But I would like to see you again. Will you call me?"

"Yes. I can't say just now when would be a good time. But I'll call you soon. I promise."

They reached his house and he walked with her to the driver's side of her car. She unlocked the door. Keys in her hand, ready to go, she looked up at him for the last time until they met again. If they ever met again. "If you say 'parting is such sweet sorrow,' I'll—"

"I won't say it. I've Shakespeare'd you enough for one night." He stroked her cheek. "I never thought an interview would be so enjoyable. Have you got everything you want for your article?"

She gazed up at him, feeling such longing. "There are a hundred things I'd like to ask you. But I have enough. Do you mind if I describe your home and your furnishings?"

"No, but I would rather you didn't mention Darienne."

"Of course I won't. I'll respect your privacy. Would you like to approve what I write before I turn it in?" She hoped he'd say yes, because then she'd have an excuse to see him again.

"I trust you."

Her heart sank a bit. Then, remembering something vital, she opened her purse and took out her notepad and pencil. "I'll give you my address and phone number, so you can reach me," she said, writing them down. She tore off the sheet of paper and handed it to David carefully, as if she were entrusting him with her future happiness. He took the paper and folded it, then put it in his inner coat pocket.

They stood in silence for a long moment. His eyes moved back and forth over her face. Apparently he, too, didn't know how to say goodbye. She put out her hand. "Well, thank you. Good night."

His eyes grew luminous and soulful. "Veronica," he said, passion in his voice. "Don't be businesslike with me now. It hurts. It's hard to say goodbye, but let's not be timid and end this evening with a polite handshake." He gently pushed her hand aside and took her in his arms. "We have laughed together and waxed philosophical tonight. I feel such a rapport with you. Don't you feel it?"

"Oh, David, yes! I was afraid to assume how you felt. I told you before that I need you. I meant that with all my heart. I want to spend lots of time with you. And I like it when you hold me in your arms like this. I feel like I belong to you."

There, she'd poured out her soul. She stretched up to kiss him, and he met her halfway. His mouth was warm and urgent on hers. She put her arms around his neck and reveled in the feel of his strong arms around her. She felt giddy and yet secure, not the least bit sorry about showing her feelings for him so flagrantly. Her pride was wrapped up in him, and she didn't mind losing it one iota. "David," she whispered when he released her from the kiss.

He studied her eyes and face lovingly for a long moment. Bending, he locked his arms around her waist and lifted her a few feet off the ground, turning around, looking up at her with incredible joy.

She began to cry and laugh at the same time. "David, what are you doing?"

"You're my prize. I want to carry you off."

"I'd like that," she said as he slowly let her slide against him till her feet touched the ground.

"Would you like that?" he whispered. "Then maybe someday I will." He kissed her again, as ardently as before, then stoically took her by her upper arms and pushed her away from him. "You'd better go now, before I'm tempted to—to have my way with you!" he said, ending with humor in his voice. She wondered what he would have said if he hadn't stopped himself. Did he want her to be his lover? Oh, God, she thought. What happiness if that were true!

"Good night, David. I'll wait for your call. Don't lose my number."

"I won't," he said as she got into her car. "I'll call you within a week."

As she drove away, leaving him behind, his promise rang in her ears. A week seemed so long.

5

I Could Worship You

DAVID RAN up the spiral steps to the third floor, buoyant and brimming with energy. He walked into his living room to find Darienne behind the counter of the wet bar in the far corner of the room. She was at the small, stainless-steel sink, wiping blood off her mouth.

Hanging his topcoat in the closet, he said to her, "I wish you'd let me know ahead of time when you're coming." He tried to show some annoyance, but merely sounded factual. He was in too good a mood. "That was a close call with Veronica."

Darienne put down the towel she'd used to dry her hands and mouth. "I'm sorry. You so seldom allow mortals in your home. How was I to know?"

"Why don't you let me give you a key, so you don't have to climb the wall? Your acrobatics already made the newspapers once when someone spotted you. I can't afford notoriety like that."

"David, I'd lose your silly key in an hour. Besides, I like surprising you." She walked around the counter and put her arms around his waist, pressing her downy cheek into his shirt. "I made up a good story, no? Your little Veronica believed me."

"Waving out the window was a nice touch," David said dryly, hugging her with affection in spite of the way she tried his patience.

He looked at her beautiful face, her cheeks unusually pink from the blood she'd just consumed. Her eyes were lustrous and richly green. He could see already that she needed sex, that she'd come to him for a night of frenzied coupling. But David had Veronica on his mind.

71

He stepped out of her embrace and walked behind the bar to open the small refrigerator underneath. "How many are left?" he asked.

"You have two left," she said with the look of a naughty little girl who expects to be forgiven.

"Two? There were four." He pulled out the two transparent, plastic bags filled with blood that remained in the refrigerator. They were both labeled: Type O, Rh Positive. Whole Blood. Of course, the type didn't matter, only that it was whole blood. Another label named the blood bank from which he'd stolen the bags, and the blood's expiry date. As usual, he had sent the blood bank an anonymous monetary donation afterward to ease his conscience about the theft.

"I put the extra one in my coat pocket to save for later," Darienne said. "I just got into town and I don't have a supply. But if you want it back . . ."

"No, keep it," David said, in a generous frame of mind. He put back the two bags and closed the refrigerator door. "I have to make another visit to the blood bank soon anyway."

"Thank you, *chéri*," she said, coming up to him again as he moved out from behind the bar. She folded both her graceful, white arms around his, attaching herself to him in her possessive, feline way. David admired the way she exuded femininity like rich perfume.

"How was Paris?" he asked.

"Oh, *magnifique!* You should go with me next time. You haven't been there in decades."

David ignored the suggestion. He hated to travel. "You've been away six months. Where else did you go?"

"Lucerne, to visit Herman." She referred to a Swiss scientist, also a vampire, whom she'd met half a century ago and visited regularly. "He's working on a sunblock cream for our kind. Just think, David, we may be able to go out in the sun again, if he can perfect his formula."

"The sun? Lord! What I wouldn't give to see the sun. The shadows of clouds passing over a meadow. A rainbow." Memories of David's youth, his natural life, flooded his mind. "But how can he be sure such a concoction will work?" he asked Darienne.

"He tests it on himself in the first faint rays at dawn."

"He's smearing it on and actually going out in the sun? Well, you may not see much more of him!"

"David, don't be so pessimistic." She tugged on his arm, urging him toward the love seat. "Now, tell me how you met Veronica. I want to know all about her."

"I met her at my accountant's office," he said as they stepped away from the bar.

Darienne laughed at that. "What do you need an accountant for?"

"Yes, it's easy for you to be amused," he said with irritation. Darienne had little concept of daily responsibilities. And she knew even less about the legalities of money than he. "You don't live in any one place, so you never have problems with a government tracing you. I've been a resident here for more than ten years. The Internal Revenue Service has records of the royalties from my plays, and they think I should have been paying taxes all that time."

"How greedy of them," she said with sympathy as they sat down on the love seat. Unlike Veronica, who had stayed carefully at her end of the couch, Darienne sat close to David and draped her arm lightly around his shoulders. "Poor David. But tell me about Veronica."

He smiled, feeling elation at the very thought of Veronica. "The moment I saw her, I knew she was special. Her sincerity touched me first of all. And such beauty—eyes that are innocent and yet can be so playful when she teases me. But she's troubled, and she doesn't know how to get on in life. You see, she's a dreamer, more comfortable in her own mind than she is in the world about her."

Darienne nodded, her eyes bright with interest and understanding. "She's much like you."

"Exactly," David said, feeling a light electric energy dancing through his nervous system. "I think I can help her. I know I can. In fact, she wants me to tutor her. We shared such an immediate affinity, I can't tell you how happy I am for simply having spent the evening with her."

"David," Darienne said kindly, stroking his hair, "you realize you're head over heels in love, and you've only just met her. This has happened before."

"No. With Veronica it's entirely different. I know sometimes I've become enamored with women easily—"

"And always they disappoint you. Or hurt you."

"Veronica won't do that," David said, moving away a bit so that she couldn't toy with his hair. "You saw how sweet she is."

Darienne put her hands in her lap, her demeanor serious now. "Yes, she is sweet. I liked her. I truly did. I would enjoy getting to know her myself, she seemed so interested in fashion. But think hard about this, David. What will you do with this little mortal? Make her one of us?"

David felt a shudder in his chest. "No, of course I can't. I wouldn't take her young life." He remembered now with humiliation how he'd been tempted to take her only a few hours ago in the dark at the back of the house. "I must never even think of it."

"Then how will you carry on with her?"

He leaned back, feeling sure of himself because of his resolve. "I will be her friend, her tutor. Perhaps her lover as well," David said, excitement at the possibility energizing his body. "She doesn't ever have to know that I'm not like her."

"Oh, David," Darienne said, looking down and shaking her head.

Her reaction annoyed him. She was spoiling his happiness. "What's wrong?"

She reached to take his hand. "How can you sustain the deception? And the frustration? Don't you see it's bound to end sadly?"

"If I'm determined enough to have her—and I am!—I'll find the willpower. To gain Veronica's love, I can do anything!" But even as he made this vow, he felt like a hypocrite. He grew angry with himself, remembering, indeed still able to feel, the need for her blood when he saw the pulsing artery in her slim neck. Somehow, some way, he'd have to discover a method to quell his lust. His hands began to tremble.

"David, why do you do this to yourself?" Darienne grasped his hand more tightly between both of hers. "Look, you're growing upset already. Stop this before it begins."

"I'm not upset! I've drunk too much port this week, that's

all. I foolishly had another glass tonight. You know how it affects me."

"And why did you drink it? Because you want to forget reality and pretend everything will be beautiful with this woman. Please, for your own good, put her aside."

"I will not," he said, challenging Darienne with his eyes. Anger and the port began to make his head pound. "I need her! She reminds me of Cecilia."

Darienne got down on her knees and gazed up at him with such intensity he had to look away. "David, you know how I care about you."

"Yes," he said, impatient, not wanting to hear what he knew was coming.

"You've got to stop getting into relationships that will hurt you. Every decade—every year!—you grow worse. Cecilia is gone, and you can never have a relationship like that again because you're not mortal anymore. When will you accept what you are?"

David felt his head reeling. Damn, why did he drink that port! "How can I accept it?" he said, rubbing his forehead. "I wish I'd never gone to Transylvania. Such a foolish, damnable decision—all grandiose pride, thinking *I* would be the one to preserve Shakespeare's work and take on his mantle. His plays have lived on without any help from me. And after four centuries of writing and studying, I can see clearly I shall never become his equal."

He gazed across the room, feeling cold now and filled with disgust. "My noble purpose for becoming a vampire is demolished and seems ridiculous to me now as it lies in ruins in my head. And I'm left to be the evil thing that I am. To think I chose this for my fate!"

He looked to Darienne, on her knees in front of him, for understanding. "Unless I have someone who can give me joy and human affection, what reason is there to go on?"

"David, we have so much that mortals don't," Darienne said, stretching forward to place her hands on his shoulders. "Superior strength, agility, knowledge of the past, and all the possibilities of the future. There's all the time in the world to see everything and do everything."

"Alone?"

"You're not alone. You have me."

"No, I don't," he told her in a rough, ironic tone. He pushed her aside, rose from the couch, and stepped past her. Pacing around the room in restless desolation, he glanced up at the chandelier, which had belonged to his family. Its familiar shimmer brought back the distant past. "I thought, when you asked me so long ago to make you an immortal, that if I transformed you, you would stay with me." His tone grew less harsh as his philosophical side tethered his anger and replaced it with resignation. "But I see you only every few years. And then it's because you've come to me for sex."

Darienne gazed up at him from her position on the floor, looking crushed. "Don't say that, David. It's not true."

"It is," he insisted. "And I accept it. I let you use me because I'm afraid if I don't, I'll lose even you."

"David," she said, standing and hurrying to him. "You won't ever lose me. If I could only make you see the advantages, all the positive, lovely things about being a vampire."

"The constant lust for blood?" he asked, turning away. "Having to spend every day in a coffin, in a barricaded house, in unending fear of being discovered?"

"But, David," she said, taking him by the upper arms and making him face her, "we are superior creatures! I have no fear, because I'm three times as strong as any mortal. I move often so no one ever finds me in the day when I'm vulnerable. And each night I meet so many people and see so many places. I'll be young forever. And—"

"I know, Darienne," he said, shutting his eyes at her barrage of arguments. He opened them and looked at her earnestly. "I wish I could be like you. This existence suits you. You shine in it. But I? I would give all my superhuman powers, my priceless ancient books, my whole amassed fortune, and my career for a quiet, mortal life span with a woman who loves only me."

Darienne was subdued for a moment. "Then perhaps the answer," she said quietly, "is for you to make Veronica one of us—"

"No!"

"Then you must give her up and appreciate what you have—

your writing, wealth, and immortality! And me. You do have me, David, in spite of what you think."

"Why must I give her up?" he demanded.

"Because of what has always happened in the past," she said. "Beginning with Cecilia, who drove a knife into her own heart after you told her what you'd become. And when you pretend to be a mortal with a woman, your blood lust becomes too strong. You don't want to harm her, so you disappear from her life. Or, if you initiate a woman, then she oppresses you with her overwhelming need to be with you. And if you make her a vampiress, she does the same as I did and goes her own way. You never get what you want from a mortal woman, David. And you're left with such a broken heart, it takes all my patience and ingenuity to help you pull through. The past fifty years, your fits of despair have frightened me more and more. I've even worried that you may stay up one morning and meet the sun. It's why I've been visiting you more often."

David nodded. So that was the reason. She'd been visiting him more, not because she wanted to spend time with him, but to keep him from immortal suicide. "Your sense of duty touches me," he said sardonically, stepping away from her.

"It's not duty. I love you."

He turned. "Then live here with me."

Darienne shook her head. "I'm not the domestic sort. I'd feel stifled. But Veronica is a good choice for you. I have a feeling she'd be the kind who, even as a vampiress, would stay by your side."

"If I loathe what I am," David asked, "how can I do that to her?"

"You did it for me."

"I had just become a vampire myself. I didn't understand all the consequences." He pointed at her. "And you begged me."

"And I beg you now, David—for your own good—give Veronica immortality, or give her up!"

He walked to the fireplace and gazed down into the dying embers. His head felt heavy and muddled. "I don't have the reserves to make such a choice," he told Darienne in a strained voice. "I need her so much, and yet my conscience won't let me injure her body or damn her soul. Oh, if God would only allow me to be mortal again!"

Darienne went up to him and ran her fingers lightly up his chest. Her voice was caring and coaxing. "David, I can help you forget your problems for a while. Give your mind a rest. You need some . . . recreation. Let's enjoy ourselves, and maybe tomorrow things will be clearer to you."

He glared at her. "Is sex all you think about?"

"You ought to think about it, too," she said, her voice remaining light, almost frivolous, "to remind you of one of the bonuses of being a vampire."

David knew what she was up to, trying to seduce him with the excuse that it was for his benefit. He knew better. Even as a mortal, she'd had an insatiable desire for men. After she'd become immortal, her desire had changed to demand.

He ought to turn away from her. He had Veronica to think of now. But somehow he couldn't. Darienne was unbuttoning his shirt.

She pulled open the shirt and ran her hands up his bared chest. "Pretend I'm Veronica, if you like," she said.

He might have laughed. To compare Veronica's innocent purity to the wantonness of Darienne! Darienne, who'd lost count centuries ago of the number of men she'd seduced.

She pushed his jacket off his shoulders, walking around him to pull it down his arms. She tossed it aside and did the same with his shirt. Standing in front of him again, she watched his face as she reached behind her and unzipped her dress. Slowly the material released its hold on her breasts. The contours of her cleavage became less plump and more natural. All at once the dress fell away and slid down her hips to the floor, revealing her completely nude body. She'd often come to him wearing flimsy French undergarments of satins and lace, but tonight she'd worn absolutely nothing under her gown. She must be especially eager.

His gaze fell to her full breasts. So lush was their curvature, they were like swollen grapes, firm and provocative with their graceful upward tilt. Her large pink nipples jutted toward him, tempting his masculine resolve to give in to just one touch.

Just one touch. That was what he'd told himself when he was a boy of fifteen, at the moment when those very breasts had become his downfall. If precocious, experienced, sixteen-year-old Darienne hadn't eagerly undraped her exquisite body in front of him, he might have become a priest. Yes, he might have lived a quiet, mortal life in the monastery near his home in Paris, in the devoted service and worship of his Creator. He might have died a peaceful death and passed through Saint Peter's gate to a different kind of immortality.

Instead, he'd given in to his curiosity about what her body had to offer. An hour later he realized he could never live a celibate life. Darienne had never let him forget her historic place in his life, either.

She stepped up to him so that her breasts pressed into his chest, their firm, smooth softness causing a stirring in his groin. "Please, David," she said, her eyes all needy and pleading, like those of a waif without shelter. Darienne had turned seduction into an art form, making a male feel as though it were a great humanitarian act to give her what she wanted. She bent her head and put her lips to his nipple, teasing it with her tongue. Opening her mouth wider, she pierced his skin with her sharp teeth, moaning softly with pleasure as she drew blood. David immediately felt the lustful drive to do the same to her. He tried to fight it. He ought to be true to Veronica.

When Darienne looked up at him again, she smiled and put her arms lightly around his neck. Sometimes, when she was on the other side of the planet and he was all alone, he could still feel her arms around his neck like this, as if she'd never quite let go. "You know how it is with me," she said, uncharacteristically meek. "You're the only one who can satisfy me completely."

Yes, David knew that well. Lust was the only thing that kept Darienne coming back. With her superhuman strength she'd long ago found that mortal men did not have the sexual staying power to give her all she wanted. Naturally, she'd turned to male vampires, who would have the stamina she required. But most male vampires—even those, she would complain, whom she'd created from carefully selected mortal lovers—had lost interest in the sex act once they became vampires. Desire for blood became their foremost craving. In fact, she'd often said that other vampires seemed to think her preoccupation with the mundane sex act rather odd.

But David was different. David had always sought to quell his blood lust. And with his longing for female company, he'd kept his interest in sex. Because of these circumstances, David was literally the only male Darienne knew who could satiate her incredible need.

This fact ought to have given David a feeling of uniqueness, power, and masculine pride. Darienne had often pointed out that if he could satisfy her, he must be the best lover in the world. But he wanted to be needed for something more than sex.

"Oh, David, why won't you respond to me?" Darienne asked in a pleading voice. "Because of Veronica? I don't mind if you love Veronica. I've never minded other women. But you can't forget me. I was your first. I showed you what physical love could be." Her eyes were wide, luminous, their vivid color indicating the depth of her need. "Don't deny me, David, please, oh, please."

David looked down into her beautiful face. She'd been his mistress, his friend and confidante, almost a sister, in some ways his wayward wife, for almost four centuries. He couldn't deny her.

Damn his need to please women! Even Darienne.

"All right, Darienne," he said with a sardonic smile. "But let's try not to break any furniture this time."

He saw tears rise in her eyes as she laughed. She stepped over the folds of her dress, still on the floor, and rushed back to the couch, where she'd left her fur coat. She threw the coat fur side up in front of the fire on top of the Oriental rug. "That will be our bed." She turned to him. "David! You aren't even undressed yet. Hurry."

"We have all night," he said, unbuckling his belt.

"But the night goes so fast when I'm with you."

When he'd undressed, she pulled him down onto the fur with her. Bending over her breasts, he caressed their rounded firmness and took one pert nipple to his mouth. She moaned with pleasure at his touch, all the while fondling him with feathery, quick strokes, until, almost before he'd realized it himself, he was ready. Never having been a woman who needed much preparation, Darienne wasted no time. Sliding her hands around his buttocks and arching toward him, she imprisoned his masculinity within her and held it like a delicious captive, winding her long, slim legs around his.

"Oh, David, you have a magnificent body," she whispered while she ran her hands over his back and buttock muscles. "Use all your strength. Don't be gentle. You can't hurt me."

Rising over her on his elbows in a dominating pose, David began violent, bucking thrusts that would have injured a mortal woman. Darienne made whimpering sounds of delight, which turned to screams as he continued. Her piercing cries, the iridescent, vampiric light of passion radiating from her eyes, and her smiles of superhuman, sensual joy shook away David's initial ambivalence about engaging in sex with her. His own pulse began to race. The real, tangible world around him grew dim as he lost himself to her demanding, erotic embrace.

All at once she gave a loud cry, arching her spine, her head thrown back, while her whole body stiffened with convulsive contractions. He allowed his own release then—he'd learned long ago how to control himself so as to give women the most pleasure—and then relaxed onto her body.

"Oh, David." She sighed, smiling up at him with eyes that looked near delirium with her happiness. She stroked his back but would not allow him to leave her. "Again, David," she begged. "Harder." Pulling his head down, she kissed him on the mouth for the first time, pressing so hard that her sharp teeth made his lip bleed. He responded in kind, thrusting his tongue into her, his own teeth drawing her blood. The taste of it heightened his desire.

"Oh, yes, yes!" she cried when she felt him swell within her once again. She moved her pelvis rhythmically against him, and again he began his hard thrusts. She cried out with each one, her screams growing wild and strange. Panting over her, David pressed his lips in hard kisses along her neck and down her shoulder. All at once he bit into her soft, unblemished skin, his incisors puncturing her and drawing blood. He did this not to drink from her—a taboo among vampires—but solely for the pleasure of the bite, of feeling his teeth sink in and possess her flesh. At his bite she screamed and dug her fingernails into his back until he felt warm blood trickling down his sides and onto her white fur coat.

Soon she reached her climax. Afterward, blood at her mouth

and oozing from her shoulder, she stared up at him, holding his head between her hands as he lay on top of her. "No one can do it like you, my beloved David. Again. Again!"

And so they carried on throughout the night. They changed positions, she sitting on top of him for a while, so that he could fondle and bite her breasts. Next side by side, then chest to back. Each climax built on the last until, near dawn, they coupled in an arduous frenzy, rolling around the room, knocking over the coffee table and a chair, breaking an antique figurine.

By that time Darienne had no more voice to scream. Her climax was marked by her high, wondrous gasp, like the harmonic of a violin string. Then she fell back from him limply. David supported her head as he lowered her onto the carpet. Her eyes half-closed, she lay with a stillness like natural death.

"Darienne," David said, touching her cheek, wiping away a thin trickle of blood from her mouth. "Darienne!" He shook her.

She opened her eyes. They were green, glassy, and dazed. But when she looked at him, they filled with adoration.

"You frighten me when you do that," he said.

She clung to his arms to pull herself to a sitting position. Drying rivulets of blood ran from puncture wounds on her neck, shoulders, and breasts. But the wounds were already closed and healing. She buried her face in his chest, biting and then kissing his skin softly, with reverence.

"Oh, David," she said, her voice little, like a child's. "I love you. I could worship you! Don't ever turn me away."

"You know I couldn't," he said, holding her in his arms.

They remained like this for several minutes, until the slapping sounds of the paper boy throwing newspapers onto the sidewalk outside reminded David that dawn was coming. "Darienne, we've no more time now."

"I know." She reluctantly pulled away. She looked down at her breasts and then got up and walked over to the sink.

"Do you want to stay?" David asked. "You can share my resting place."

"No, David," she answered as she washed blood off herself with a towel. "I have a place."

Again, David realized in a flash of pain that of all the many things in the world Darienne loved, including him, she loved her independence best.

When she finished washing, she tidied her hair and then put on her dress, asking David to zip it for her. "Where are you staying?" he asked. "Is it safe?"

She turned and smiled up at him, fatigue in her eyes, her movements limp, but radiating contentment. "Yes, it's safe. Don't worry about me."

He didn't press her further, knowing she wouldn't tell him the location. "I'll walk down with you and let you out the door. The paper boy might notice if you go out the window."

"Yes, all right," she said, complying with convention this time.

In silence they walked down to the first floor where he unbolted the door. Before she went out she gave one last, long, admiring look at his bloodied, naked body. She leaned up to give him a hard kiss on the mouth. "Goodbye."

"When will I see you again?"

"I don't know."

"Will you be in Chicago for long?"

"I haven't decided."

He took a long breath and nodded. "Goodbye, then."

She smiled at him, touched his chin with her fingertip, and then disappeared out the door.

David climbed the stairs slowly, fatigue overtaking him with each step. When he got to his living room, he straightened the furniture, washed himself, and then used a special solution to get spots of blood out of the rug. He threw away the porcelain figurine.

Without bothering to dress, he turned off the lights and walked back down the three flights of steps. Taking the corridor he'd earlier walked down with Veronica, he descended a creaky staircase into the damp, cold basement. Winding his way along a path through boxes and decaying furniture, he eventually came to a bolted door. With a special key he unlocked it. Inside the dark room, on an ornate bier imported from France, lay his coffin, made of thickly varnished oak and encrusted with gold. He opened the lid and climbed in, stretching out on the white satin, then pulled the lid over him.

As he lay in the stillness, waiting for the heavy, paralyzing sleep of day to overtake him, he thought about all that had happened this night. Veronica and her charming "interview." His promise to be her tutor. Darienne's reappearance. Their urgent, prolonged copulating, physically satisfying far beyond the human realm, and yet so empty. Now he was left drained and alone.

Outside, David could sense the rays of the sun breaking the darkness, bombarding the massive stone walls of his home with an energy that could destroy him. But his narrow chamber with its comforting layer of French soil beneath the lining protected him.

Soon the city outside these walls would be humming with busy citizens going about their lives, pursuing their dreams, dreams he could have no part of. In moments like this the clear memory of his own normal life came back to him. How casually he'd been a part of it all so long ago, never thinking to be happy simply because he belonged to the human race. He'd been in love with Cecilia, planning to marry her in London and raise a family. And then Will had died and everything changed. David had traveled to Transylvania and returned as a vampire. And then, most tragic of all, Cecilia had killed herself, preferring to suffer a mortal death in his arms from a self-inflicted wound rather than let David make her his immortal bride. And now he was an outsider, burdened with guilt, alienated from God, from sunlight, from humanity.

Veronica belonged to that world he could never know again. During the hours he'd spent with her, he'd almost felt like an ordinary mortal once more, falling in love with a pretty young woman. He pictured her face, the innocence of her eyes, the sincerity of her smile. Such purity of mind and intent. Such virginal sweetness. Such fresh, unblemished loveliness.

How could he taint Veronica with himself? He could only compare her purity with his own physical and moral degradation. He was a vile creature of the night, feared by man and shunned by God. Barely human anymore, he was not even capable of faithfulness to his new love. He'd allowed Darienne to seduce him into an orgy of self-indulgence, a frenzied, desperate grasp at momentary sexual oblivion that would have horrified Veronica. In the end, if she found out his awful secret,

Veronica might react exactly as Cecilia had and choose death rather than become the consort of a vampire.

Darienne was right. He mustn't pick such a rosebud; he must leave Veronica alone and allow her to bloom and live out her natural life. She would learn about the world soon enough on her own; she didn't need him to tutor her.

And if he needed her? Well, he was used to pain. Pain was his closest companion.

A tear slid from his eye and onto the satin pillow. He would put aside the fleeting sense of hope she'd given him. There was no hope. Only hope for her, if he let her be.

With irony he recalled the last line of *A Tale of Two Cities:* "It is a far, far better thing that I do, than I have ever done; it is a far, far better rest that I go to, than I have ever known."

But unlike Dickens's Sydney Carton, there was no permanent rest for David, no noble death. Just night after night of wretched loneliness.

Unless, of course, he decided to have a look at the sun. Just one little step, one brief glance, one ray on his skin. And then it would all be over.

6

It's the Vampire Mystique

BY THE end of the following week, Veronica had written a rough draft of her article about David. She hadn't shown it to anyone yet, wanting it to be complete and perfect. As she perused it now, sitting at her desk in her office, she shook her head, put out with herself about all the things she should have asked David but hadn't. Was he currently working on another new play? Had he ever considered writing novels or screenplays? How did he like being famous? What did he think of his audiences? David had lavished so much attention on her, she'd lost track of her interview at least half of the time she'd been with him.

When would he call her? she wondered anxiously. He'd said within a week, and the week was almost up. No doubt he was busy. But she was sure he wouldn't forget her.

Her phone rang and she picked it up quickly. "Veronica Ames."

"The de Morrissey article finished?" Instead of David's reassuring, low voice, it was Mr. Malloy's.

"It's almost done," she said. "I want to ask him a few more questions."

"You're going to see him again?"

"Yes."

"Good. Get a photo. We need a picture of him to go with the article. Take our photographer along."

"I don't know if David would allow that," she said.

"Take a sneak shot of him yourself, if you have to. I want the article and a photo by Monday."

"Sure," she promised, hoping David would call today. It was Thursday already.

She hung up and went back to her work. An idea she'd been toying with came to mind. She wanted to talk to Sam Taglia and ask him what it was like to have David coach him in his part, as David had told her he'd done. But she wasn't sure if she'd be intruding on Rob's interview with the actor. It was time to take action, she decided. She adjusted the waistband of her blue wool skirt and tucked in her striped blue blouse as she walked out of her office.

"Rob?" she said, pausing at his door.

"Yeah? Oh, hi!" He smiled as he looked up and saw her, and he slid his chair back from his desk a bit. "Come in. Sit down."

Veronica reluctantly sat on the metal chair opposite his desk. It wasn't her intention to stay and talk. "I wanted to ask you about your interview with Sam Taglia. Have you got it lined up yet?"

"I haven't been able to get hold of him. The theater referred me to his agent. The agent said he'd call me back, but he hasn't. No one will give me his personal number."

Veronica smiled to herself. She might know of a way to get the actor's number. "I'm asking because I want to talk to him myself."

Rob's blond eyebrows drew together. "Why?"

"I'm not trying to take anything away from your interview. I just want to ask him a few questions about David, for my article."

"Haven't you finished it yet?"

"I keep thinking of things I should add."

"Wasn't de Morrissey supposed to call you?"

Veronica hesitated. "He hasn't yet."

Rob studied her with mock patience. "Now, I hope you aren't going to be heartbroken if he doesn't."

"He will."

"Veronica, the guy may have made a fuss over you, but you have to remember he's wealthy and famous and probably has lots of women at his disposal."

"So why would he bother with me, is that what you're saying?"

She wished she hadn't told Rob about her meeting with

David when Rob had asked her about it the first thing Monday morning. But she'd wanted to show him how wrong he was. Naturally, she hadn't mentioned that David had offered to tutor her, or that he had kissed her. But she had described how cordial David had been, and how he'd rescued her from a drunk. Still, Rob remained suspicious and she didn't understand why. She disliked Rob's older-brother manner with her, too. For once she was glad she was an only child.

"I'm saying," Rob told her, "that you shouldn't take him seriously. He wants you to write a flattering article about him, so he flattered you."

"Why are you bent on making him out to be unscrupulous? First you paint him as some Halloween character living in a lonely mansion complete with shrieks and screams. Now that I've proved that scenario's not true, you're trying to make him out to be manipulative and womanizing. I've met him and I *know* what he's like. *I* should be telling *you* about him, not vice versa!"

Rob pushed his paperweight aside. "I just don't want to see you get hurt, that's all."

Veronica ignored that. "About Sam Taglia—"

"You've already gotten to interview de Morrissey. Why do you need to talk to Taglia?"

"But I won't be asking him about himself. I'll just ask him for his thoughts about David."

Rob got up suddenly and walked a few paces to the window. "Do you have to keep calling him *David?*" he asked, looking at the bank building across the street.

"Why shouldn't I? I consider him a friend."

"It's the way you say it." Rob exhaled, then said wearily, "All right, go talk to Taglia. I guess your article won't overlap mine very much." He stepped back to his desk and perched on the edge. "It may all be academic anyway, if we can't get to him."

"I may be able to find out his private number."

Rob's eyes sharpened. "Really? How, from de Morrissey?"

"No, from my cousin, Harriet, in Berwyn. She went to high school with him."

Rob smiled. "Sounds like it's worth a try!"

"If I find out his number, I'll give it to you. Will that make up for my talking to him, too?"

"It's a deal." Rob stood and extended his hand. "Can we shake on it and be friends?"

"Sure," she said, rising, taking his hand.

"Why don't we have lunch sometime?" he asked, moving along with her as she headed toward the entrance of his office. "Are you free today?"

She was but didn't feel like saying so. On the other hand, she hated to refuse him again, especially now that they'd made peace. "How about next week sometime?" she suggested.

"Monday?"

"Well . . ."

"Okay, I'll check with you next week when you know your schedule better."

"Fine," she said with a smile.

She walked back to her office, took her purse from a drawer, and looked up her cousin's phone number in her personal address book. She dialed the number and waited.

"Hello?" Harriet's out-of-breath voice came on after the fifth ring. Veronica could picture her plump figure, clad in sweats, maybe with a scarf covering her light brown hair.

"It's Veronica. I'm calling from work. Did I catch you at a bad time?"

"I was in the basement doing the kids' laundry. How's everything?"

"Great. Listen, you remember I mentioned Sam Taglia when I was at your house a couple of weeks ago? You said you graduated from Morton the same year he did?"

"Sure. By the way, I saw his mother at Vesecky's Bakery the other day. She said he's getting married, if that's what you wanted to know."

Veronica chuckled at her cousin's logic. "Why would I want to know that?"

"Well, you seemed impressed with him in the play. Besides, it's what *I* wanted to know. I had a crush on him in high school."

"Did you go out with him?"

"We went steady for three months," Harriet said. "Just think, if I'd played my cards smarter, I might have been the wife of a future Broadway star. Instead, I met Ralph and here I am, sorting laundry."

"Even famous actors have laundry," Veronica said.

"Yeah, but what laundry! Silk jockey shorts and cashmere socks."

Veronica laughed, enjoying Harriet's nitty-gritty outlook. "Do you think Sam's mother would give you his personal phone number?"

"She'd think I was still chasing him."

"Well, tell her it's for your cousin, who wants to interview him for her magazine."

"She might buy that."

Veronica laughed again. *Windy City Magazine* is eager to talk to him. Do you think you could get hold of her?"

"Her number's in the phone book. I can give it to you."

"It'd be better if you called, since she knows you. Can you get back to me today?"

Harriet agreed and they hung up.

Within ten minutes her cousin called back with Sam Taglia's number. Since it was morning, Veronica reasoned he might be home now, so she dialed it. A man's voice answered.

"Yeah?" He sounded sleepy.

"My name is Veronica Ames from *Windy City Magazine.* I got your number through Harriet Benda—from high school?"

"Harriet Benda. Harriet Benda!" He laughed. "Whatever happened to her?"

"She got married and moved to Berwyn. She's my cousin."

"Oh. What's this all about?"

"I'm writing an article about David de Morrissey, and I'd like to ask you—"

"Sorry, I can't talk to the press about him." The humor in his voice was gone.

"But, you see, I've already met and interviewed him."

"Come on," he said in a sharp tone. "Who'd you say you are?"

"Veronica Ames from *Windy City Magazine,*" she repeated. "I grew up in Cicero and went to Morton East, too—a few years after you and Harriet graduated."

"And you're really her cousin?"

"On my mother's side. My mother's maiden name was Benda. We lived near Laramie and West Twenty-third Street."

"So why did David talk to you? And when?"

"His accountant introduced me to him, and he agreed to an interview last week. Last Friday, in fact. He was very kind. You can ask him if you want to verify it."

"And what do you want from me?"

"David said he worked with you to perfect some scenes in *Street Shadows.* I just wanted to know your reaction to him. What he was like to work with and so on."

"This is pretty strange. David never speaks to the media. You've got me curious. Have you seen the play?"

"Yes! I'm dying to see it again. You were wonderful as the vampire."

"Okay, Harriet's cousin. Want to come tonight? I'll arrange for a ticket to be held for you at the door. Ask for directions to go backstage afterward. I'll be in my dressing room. We'll see about an interview then."

"I appreciate it!" she said as he hung up.

As Veronica sat in the darkened, packed theater, she found herself mesmerized again by Sam Taglia as the vampire, climbing straight up stone walls, balancing along rooftops, finding his way to Claudine's bedroom. Veronica could sense David's influence somehow, now that she'd met him. Sam Taglia moved with a certain poise and ease that reminded her of David. Even his way of speaking had a poignant elegance that seemed similar to David's.

Veronica could hardly breathe during the scene after intermission, when Taglia, dressed all in black, moved soundlessly to Claudine's bed. Lifting her in his arms while she remained asleep, he carried her to the window. There, as the stage moon darkened and colored lights flashed eerily, he kissed her and pulled her nightgown off her shoulders. As she gradually awoke, he made her wind her limbs around him in an erotic pose, then slowly bent her back over the windowsill in a graceful, rhythmic dance, gradually bringing his mouth closer and closer to the side of her neck. With a quick, savage strike he bit her. Immediately her head fell back in a faint of ecstasy, her long hair flowing out the opened window.

When he'd finished, there was blood trickling down Claudine's neck and chest. She clung to him as he supported her, bringing her back from the window's edge. Weakened by loss of blood, she slid down his body until she was grasping his thighs. She looked up at him as if he were a god.

"Take me with you," she begged.

Veronica, her heart pounding, almost said the words along with her.

"Not yet," the vampire told Claudine. "But soon we'll never be parted again." With that he swung himself onto the window ledge, climbed back down the outside of the building, and swiftly exited the stage through a mock alleyway.

In the final half hour of the play the vampire made Claudine his immortal bride in a sensual, horrific blood ceremony. As they knelt, facing each other on her bed, he opened the wounds in her neck again and drank from her as she clung to him with adoration. Gradually her arms around his back grew weak and dropped, useless, to her sides. She began to die from loss of blood. When she was all but unconscious, he drew his mouth away from her neck and, with his fingernail, cut a slit in his chest. As she took her last breaths as a human, he forced her mouth to his wound and made her drink from him, taking back into her body her own blood now commingled with his. After the final swallow she died in his arms. He carefully allowed her to fall back onto the bed and kept a loving vigil with her as she lay there in death for a full minute.

Then, like a miracle, her eyes fluttered and opened. He held out his hand to her in triumph. She took it and sat up, gazing at him with a new, serene smile from which all innocence had disappeared. As her smile slowly widened, her teeth were fully revealed. She had long incisors now, like the vampire himself.

But instead of remaining with him as his immortal bride, Claudine soon left him to explore all her new vampiric powers on her own. Lonely and isolated, the vampire chose not to return to his coffin that sunrise, describing his desolation in a heart-wrenching soliloquy. In a remarkable stage effect he disappeared before the audience's eyes in a cloud of shimmering white dust at the first light of dawn.

Veronica felt exhausted when the final curtain fell. Her second viewing of the play seemed to have had an even greater

impact on her than her first. She followed the crowd out of the
theater to the lobby. There she used directions she'd gotten at
the box office earlier and made her way past security guards
to the backstage area.

She'd never been backstage in a theater before. The first thing
she noticed was that the sets that had looked so real during
the play looked like just what they were close up—painted facades made of wood, steel, and hardboard. She found it deflat-
ing to see how artificial they really were.

A woman dressed in white passed by, and Veronica realized
it was the actress who'd portrayed Claudine. She still had her
stage makeup on, along with the artificial fangs attached to her
teeth for the final act. Someone shouted some quip to her, and
she was laughing at the remark as she hurried by.

Veronica walked up to a stagehand moving scenery and
asked where the dressing rooms were. She walked in the direction he pointed and came to a row of doors with names on
them. One was marked Sam Taglia. Beneath the name, attached with a thumbtack, dangled a small doll on a string. The
doll had a white face, yellow eyes and fangs, and wore a black
felt cape. There was no body beneath the cape. It was a child's
toy for Halloween; she'd seen them in the card stores.

She knocked on the door. In a moment Sam Taglia opened
it and invited her in. He was still in costume. His black shirt
was made of a silklike material with long, flowing sleeves and
an open collar.

"Are you from the magazine?" he asked. As he spoke, she
noticed how his thick makeup gave him the gaunt cheeks and
stark eyes that were so startling on stage. There were plastic
fangs over his incisors. Close up, all the romance about him,
like the scenery, was just a facade.

"Yes, I'm Veronica Ames."

"Right, Veronica. I spoke with David before the show. He
said it was okay to talk to you."

Her heart jumped. "You saw him? Is he here tonight?" she
asked as she followed him into his dressing room.

"No. I asked the producer to have him phone me. The producer and director are the only ones who know how to reach
him. Sit down," he said, motioning to a wooden chair at the

side of his dressing table. He moved a box of tissues off the chair for her.

She sat down and quickly glanced around. It was a small room that looked old but freshly painted. His street clothes hung on hangers in a plywood wardrobe. The dressing table was covered with tubes and makeup pencils. She noted that his eyelids were darkened, which she realized was why his eyes seemed so vivid that they almost flashed when he was onstage.

"Do you mind if I get my makeup off?" he asked.

"No, go ahead."

He took a large jar of cold cream out of a drawer. "So, how's Harriet? You say she got married?"

"Yes, she has two children."

"She was a nice kid. My mother liked her," he added with a chuckle. "When did you graduate?"

Veronica told him the year.

"I thought you looked young," he said, rolling up his shirt-sleeves to the elbow. "Do they still have the homecoming parade down Cermak Road? 'Maroon and white, fight, fight!' "

She grinned. "Sure. Harriet said you were in the high school plays. Did you know the school auditorium's been declared a historical monument as an example of immigrant accomplishment?"

"I heard. Restored it and everything. All those painted murals I never paid any attention to. What was the school motto?" He put his finger to his nose, thinking. "It was something to do with King Arthur, I remember."

"Oh, uh . . . 'What I will, I can.' "

"Yeah, that's it." He chuckled. "It's funny. Such an elevated thought for that huge, overpopulated old barn." Sam pulled out the chair in front of the dressing table mirror and sat down. "Well, what do you want to know about me and the show?"

"I just want to ask you a few questions to complete my article on David de Morrissey. The magazine's movie critic wants to interview you in depth about your career, how you got the part, and so on. Is it okay if I give him your phone number?"

He shrugged. "I'll have to check with David again before I talk to him. *I* don't mind being interviewed. In fact, I'd like it. But David is so adamant about avoiding the media, I have to be careful."

Veronica took out her pencil and paper from her purse. Unfortunately, she'd left her tape recorder at home. "I'm surprised, too," she agreed. "Usually everyone is eager to get publicity for a play."

Sam unscrewed the cap of the cold cream jar and set it down. "When you sign a contract to do a de Morrissey play, you agree in writing not to give interviews without his permission. It was all so strict, I was surprised they didn't ask me to sign it in blood!"

Looking into the mirror, he reached in back of his upper teeth with his thumb and pulled out a bridge holding the two long incisors, which fit over his natural teeth. He put the bridge in a small box and placed the box in a drawer. "God, I'm always glad to get rid of those. You know how hard it is to project on stage with fake fangs in your mouth?"

Veronica smiled. She noticed that he sounded now like many of the kids she'd known in high school. He spoke in a flat, staccato tone, running words together with a tough carelessness that might have been hard to understand if it hadn't been so familiar to her. It was a Midwestern, blue-collar, city-street accent, with a pattern typical of those of Italian descent. While Cicero and Berwyn were mainly Czech communities, they also had a good representation of Italian, Dutch, Polish, and other ethnic groups.

"You spoke differently on stage," she remarked.

"Yeah, that's my actor's training. You have to learn to enunciate. David made me polish my diction even more." He began smearing cold cream on his face, almost to his hairline. He had black wavy hair, thick eyebrows, and brown eyes.

"Where did you work with him? At his home?"

Sam laughed. "No way. I don't think even the director's been to his home. We worked here at the theater late at night after rehearsals. Sometimes we'd be here till three in the morning. I'd be falling asleep on my feet, and he'd be wide-awake and full of energy."

"Was he difficult?" she asked, writing.

"He's exacting. He knew the effect he wanted. And he could explain it to me brilliantly." He wiped a tissue over his forehead, rubbing off the thick cream and makeup. "He's very—

what's that word—erudite? But doing what he wanted was a whole other story."

"How do you mean?"

He tossed the tissue into a small wastebasket and grabbed another. "They had the sets built according to his design, you know?"

"Did they?"

"You saw how tall they were? The carpenters had constructed a few footholds in the artificial stone walls. The first time David demonstrated what he wanted me to do, he climbed up those sets like nothing, like he was a fly climbing up a windowpane or something." He stopped wiping his face for a moment to demonstrate with gestures how David had climbed. "So I looked at him and I said, 'Hey, I can't do that! How'd you do that?' "

Veronica laughed, thinking he must be exaggerating. "So what did you do?"

"He insisted I try, so I did. And I fell off." He tossed away another tissue. His true olive skin tone was beginning to show through the greasepaint now. "The carpenters had to build extra footholds for me. I don't know how David did it. He seemed surprised that I couldn't imitate him. When I auditioned, I told them how I'd been a gymnast and all. I should have learned mountain climbing instead. Anyway, with the extra toeholds and copying the moves David showed me, I got it down."

"What about the . . . well, the seduction scene, where you climb into Claudine's window? David said—"

"Yeah, he coached me on that, all right." Sam took a breath and threw away the last tissue. His face was clean now. He had handsome, Italian features. As he looked at her to answer her question, his eyes seemed to grow uneasy. "I don't know, I don't like to talk about it. That scene and the blood ceremony scene—they both give me the creeps, you know?"

"But you play them so well."

He spread his hands. "That's because I'm an actor. I can do it, but I don't have to like it."

"How does it bother you?" she asked, curious.

"I sense something I don't like in myself. It brings out my

dark side, and I'd rather not know I have one. Know what I mean?"

"No," she said.

"I told you David could explain things brilliantly. Well, when he explained how I should feel when I act out those scenes, I got caught up in it. He looked me straight in the eyes and suddenly, in my inner self, I knew and I understood. And every time I play those scenes, that dark inner self in me reappears. I mean, I *feel* the lust for power and blood." Sam exhaled slowly. "And afterward, I feel like I ought to start seeing a psychiatrist."

Veronica put her pencil down, a bit unnerved by what the actor had just told her.

Sam looked wary then and self-conscious. "Look, I shouldn't have told you all that. Don't print that, okay? I have a feeling David wouldn't like it if he read I'd said that."

"All right, I won't," she promised. "It doesn't fit in with my article anyway. It's all about David, his home, his work, and so on."

"His home? You mean you've been there?"

"Yes, he invited me."

"God Almighty! What's it like?"

"I only saw his living room on the third floor, but it was very nice."

His brown eyes grew inquisitive as he looked over her facial features. "You're a good-looking girl. How did he behave with you?"

Veronica blushed a bit. "Fine. He was a gentleman."

"Nothing odd happened? Everything was cool while you were there?"

Veronica decided not to mention Darienne, or what had happened in the backyard. "Everything was fine. Although . . ." Something Sam had said made her want to share with him. "I was a little surprised at something that happened when he took me to a bar on Rush Street. A drunk started bothering me. David grabbed him by the front of his shirt, looked him in the eye, said a few words, and the guy passed out. I had the feeling David used some hypnosis technique on him, though he denied it when I asked him."

Sam's dark brown eyes widened slightly, as if in recognition, or perhaps apprehension. "Just between you and me, I'd trust your gut feeling more than anything David tells you." He raised his forefinger. "But you didn't hear me say that, understand?"

"Okay," Veronica said, feeling very uneasy. "Why is David so secretive about his personal life? Do you know?"

"I'm afraid to even speculate," he said, a dark intensity in his gaze. "You interviewed him. What'd he tell you?"

"Just that he likes his privacy."

"Yeah, right."

Both were silent for a moment. Veronica began to put away her pad and pencil. This interview hadn't gone at all as she'd anticipated, and she decided to use only a line or two from it in her article. "When you spoke with David on the phone," she said as she opened her purse, "did he say anything when you mentioned my name?"

Sam studied her. "No. He just confirmed that he'd met you and said it was all right if I talked with you."

"He didn't give you a message for me or anything?"

"Nope."

Veronica lowered her gaze to her lap. She'd hoped David would have asked Sam to say hello for him, or to tell her he'd be calling her soon.

"What message were you expecting?" Sam asked.

She looked up at him. "He promised he'd call me this week, and he hasn't. He said he'd phone in case I had more questions to ask him," she added, fibbing a bit.

"You don't have some kind of crush on him, do you?"

"No, I—"

"Look, Veronica, you're from my hometown and I dated your cousin, so I feel like I should warn you. I'd stay away from David de Morrissey. There's something—not right about him."

"But he was very nice to me."

Sam got up and went to the wardrobe cabinet. He reached into his coat pocket, took out a pack of cigarettes, and lit one. Leaning one shoulder against the wall, he exhaled smoke and then looked at her. "You know, as an actor, I've traveled and met lots of people. A few years ago I met an actor who was originally from Romania. Transylvania, to be exact. You know there really is such a place."

She nodded. "I know."

"He'd moved to the States with his parents when he was a little kid, right after World War Two. He told me that his parents—they'd been farm people in the Old Country—they actually believed in vampires. Vampires were reality to them."

Veronica couldn't help but smile. "Really?"

"His folks told him that in the countryside in Romania, if the cows stopped giving milk, or the crops were failing, or there was a drought, the people would suspect a vampire was haunting the vicinity. They'd go dig up the graves of people who'd recently died. If any of the corpses still looked fresh, and if the body was turned slightly or the head leaned to one side, they'd assume the person was a vampire. And then they'd hammer a stake into the corpse's heart and close the coffin up again."

Veronica felt a chill pass through her. She put her hand to her mouth. "Why are you telling me this?"

He took another puff. "Just so you're aware that there are people in the world who believe vampires exist. I asked this actor if *he* believed in them. Now, this is a guy who was educated in the U.S. He told me he wasn't sure, said he liked to keep an open mind."

"Maybe he was just overly influenced by his parents."

"Maybe."

"Why are you taking him so seriously?"

He chewed on his lip for a moment, then took another puff. He walked back to the dressing table and reached into the top drawer for the small box in which he'd put the dental bridge he wore onstage. "You saw these?" he said, showing the fangs to her.

"Yes."

"When I had them on, did I look like a vampire to you?"

She grinned a little. "Onstage, you did."

"You know, before the play opened, David didn't want me to wear fangs. He thought they looked too melodramatic. But he was argued down by the producer and director, who thought the audience would be disappointed if the vampire didn't have long teeth."

As Sam put the bridge back into the box, Veronica wondered what his point was.

"It struck me as odd at the time," Sam went on after a moment. "I asked myself, why would David worry about me looking too melodramatic in the role? I mean, vampire stories, including this play, have always been pure melodrama. Either that or comedy. The fact that he was thinking about vampires in terms of reality seemed a little strange, you know? Like he was on another wavelength."

She shrugged. "David is very imaginative."

"Yeah, imaginative doesn't begin to describe him." He opened another drawer beneath his dressing table and pulled out a folded newspaper section. He put it on the table and sat down again. Reaching for an ashtray, he tapped the ash off his cigarette. "When we were rehearsing late one night, I was tired and getting a little slaphappy. Just to bat the breeze while they were fixing some props, I asked David how he thought a modern Dracula could elude police. Wouldn't he be leaving bodies all over with telltale fang marks on their necks? I asked. With the scientific technology nowadays, wouldn't the police catch up with him? David told me, without thinking twice, that nowadays a vampire would get his supply from blood banks, not by attacking humans."

Sam picked up the newspaper and opened it, turning a few pages till he found what he was looking for. He folded the page, then showed it to Veronica. "You see this in yesterday's paper?"

He pointed to a headline: Blood Bank Reports Mysterious Disappearance of Blood.

Veronica skimmed the article quickly. It said at least fifty bags of blood had apparently been stolen, though authorities had no idea how they'd been removed from the premises. Employees and the cleaning service were being questioned. There was no sign of a break-in.

She handed the paper back to him. "Are you saying you think David—"

He took hold of her wrist tightly and pointed at her with his other hand. "I'm not saying anything, Veronica. I'm just telling you a few things I know—off the record—and you can put them together how you want. As for this little interview, all I talked about was how I prepared for the role and how I hate my fake fangs. Anything else I said, I didn't say. You understand me?"

The manner in which he spoke reminded her of movies about the Mafia. "I understand. I won't mention anything inappropriate in my article."

"Good." He let go of her wrist. "Sorry, I didn't mean to scare you. This is for your protection as well as mine."

"You mean—are you actually afraid?"

He inhaled on his cigarette a last time and stubbed it out in the ashtray. "Let's just say I'll be glad if this play moves on to New York. I'm a little edgy here in Chicago, living and working right under his nose."

"You mean David?" she asked.

"I don't mean Santa Claus."

"But I met him, and he was incredibly kind to me."

Sam shrugged. "Then maybe it's me. Maybe I'm too wrapped up in this role and it's warping my mind. I told you, sometimes I feel like I need a shrink." He started to get up. "Well, I'll have to ask you to leave so I can change. Hey, you want to see something you *can* put in your article?"

"Sure," she said, rising from her chair.

"Wait outside the door while I change. Then you can walk out of the theater with me."

She waited in the corridor for about five minutes. When the door opened again, Sam came out wearing jeans, a green wool sweater, and a leather jacket. He looked like any ordinary guy now, all traces of the romantic vampire figure erased.

"It's this way," he said. She followed him to a door with an exit sign above it. They walked out onto concrete steps leading down into an alley. Immediately screams and shouts and applause rose from a group of thirty or forty women who'd waited for him, waving *Street Shadows* programs.

As he walked down among them, they clamored around him, like fish in a feeding frenzy. He began signing autographs while some women pulled at his jacket and tried to touch him. One yanked on his hair.

"Ouch! I'm going to have to get bodyguards pretty soon," he said to Veronica. She was trying to stick close to him amid all the pushing and shoving. "This is getting more and more out of hand. You should have seen the crowd Saturday night."

"Looks like you're a star!" Veronica told him as he quickly handed back one program and took another to sign. She felt proud of him, someone from Cicero, like her, getting all this adulation.

"It's not me," Sam told her with a dry chuckle. "It's the vampire mystique."

7

Sometimes with Two People, It Happens That Way

AS DARIENNE sat on David's love seat, languid and comfortable, her sequined sweater shimmering in the lamplight, David couldn't help but envy her. Nothing fazed her, nothing tormented her, nothing ever burst her perpetual bubble.

"What are you looking at?" she asked, eyes sparkling. She'd climbed into his window not ten minutes ago.

"Your clothes," David said. "I don't often see you wearing pants." They were made of some shiny, silky fabric in a pink that matched her sweater. She looked all soft, demure, and cuddly tonight.

"No, I don't usually wear pants when I come to you," she replied. "You're such a traditionalist. But I thought you might approve of this ensemble."

"I do."

"How have you been the past week?" she asked seriously, looking up at him as he stood by the fireplace. "Have you seen Veronica?"

"No," he said, feeling a tightness in his throat. "You were right. It's best if we stay apart. But I know I've wounded her terribly."

"She'll forget, in time."

"She asked Sam Taglia for an interview. He asked me for permission."

"You didn't give it, did you?"

"I couldn't refuse Veronica that. I couldn't hurt her any more than I have. I allowed one of her co-workers to interview Sam, as well."

"Does this actor suspect anything about you?"

"I don't think so," David said, though he felt a twinge of uneasiness. At the last rehearsals before the show opened, he'd read some questions in Sam's mind, questions that, if answered, could put David under suspicion. The actor had marveled at David's agility. David had forgotten just how weak and clumsy mortal men were. If he'd thought ahead, he'd have pretended to slip or to have difficulty while he was demonstrating to Sam how to climb the sets.

"Sometimes I wish you'd give up writing plays and live on your family fortune, as I live on mine," Darienne said. "You wouldn't put yourself at risk then."

David draped his arm over the corner of the mantel. "Carrying on my work was part of my purpose in becoming a vampire. If I give that up, what reason is there to go on? Even that's barely reason enough."

"I wish you wouldn't talk that way," she said, rising from the couch and walking over to him. She ran her hands up the front of his shirt. "You frighten me. You sound like you're thinking of . . ." She didn't finish.

"Don't worry," David said. "I've discovered I'm too much of a coward to follow through."

"What are you talking about?" She ran her finger down his cheek. "Tell me."

"The night you were here last, I went back to my coffin. In the darkness and silence I thought about Veronica and decided not to see her again. And then I toyed with the idea of . . . of seeing the sun once again, one last time. I thought it would be easy, a simple solution to all my agony. Then I considered what might happen. Not the sun turning my body into a small pile of dust, that didn't bother me. But I wasn't sure what would become of my soul. I assume we still have our souls, don't you?"

Darienne chuckled uncomfortably. "I never thought about it."

"I came to the conclusion that we must. A soul abides in heaven, hell, purgatory, or on earth. Ours must still be inhabiting our bodies, no? So if my body is destroyed, does my soul go to meet the Maker, just as it would have if I'd died a natural death?"

Darienne looked uneasy, as though she'd rather have been elsewhere. "David, why do you think about these things?"

"How can one not?" he asked. Every now and then David couldn't help but be appalled at the vacuous nature of Darienne's mind. "At any rate," he said, walking away from her toward a small table by the window, "I realized I was too much of a coward to face the possibility of meeting God. How could He ever pardon me? I committed the same sin as Lucifer himself when I chose to be a vampire."

"What sin is that?"

David exhaled with fatigue. "Don't you remember your religious upbringing at all? I used to see you at Mass."

"But that was four centuries ago. And I only attended because my mother made me. What was Lucifer's sin?"

"Pride. Wanting to be like God," David told her, exasperated. "Remember the story of the fallen angels who were cast into hell?"

"Vaguely."

David rubbed his temples. She was giving him a headache. "Anyway, I was afraid to think how God would deal with me. I don't have the courage to face my punishment. And so, I'm forced to remain here."

She walked over and took hold of his arm, leaning her cheek on his shoulder. "David, David, you waste so much energy pondering such dreary thoughts, when you could be out there enjoying the world."

He leaned his head to the side until it touched hers. "It's all so simple for you, isn't it?" he said, thinking of her almost as a child now. "I wish I could be like you." He turned and kissed her blond hair.

As he drew his head away, he felt a vague distraction, as if something were pulling him away mentally. He could almost hear someone calling to him, yet there was no sound except for Darienne's breathing. Something—he didn't know if it was logic or instinct—made him push the drapery aside and look out the window.

He glanced first at the brownstone across from him and then down at the street. The movement of a car pulling away from the curb opposite his house caught his eye. And then a poignant weight fell on his shoulders as he recognized the car.

"Veronica," he whispered.

Darienne leaned around him to look out the window, too. "Veronica? She's here?"

"The car that just drove away looked like hers."

"Maybe it was another one just like it."

"No. I felt her presence. She must have been sitting in her car, wanting to be near me, wondering why I haven't contacted her." The pain David felt picturing the fragile, innocent mortal he loved, all alone in the dark, longing to see him but afraid to come to his door, was more than he could stand. He turned away from the window and sat on an easy chair, pressing his forehead into the palms of his hands.

Darienne knelt in front of him. "David, just tell yourself that it's for the best. She'll recover soon."

"I wonder how many times she's come here?" he said, shutting his eyes tightly.

"Maybe this was the only time. Maybe she decided she'd been foolish and won't come again. She's young and lovely, David. She'll find another man to comfort her." Darienne stroked his hair. "Just as you have me to comfort you."

David lifted his head. Darienne was looking at him patiently, sad for him but not entering into the emotion herself. If only he could bring himself into that detached, uncomplicated world where Darienne lived, never feeling pain or sorrow, only happiness and joie de vivre. He reached to take hold of her upper arms and pulled her toward him. "Comfort me, then," he told her, his tone harsh and desperate. "Make me forget!"

Darienne smiled her delight. She stretched up to bite his lip, licking the drop of blood that she drew. The scent of the blood aroused David, and he told himself this was what he needed. With rough hands he pushed up the front of her sweater and leaned forward to bite her large, warm breasts. An urgent moan escaped Darienne's throat, while her strong, eager fingers began unbuckling his belt.

Veronica handed in her article to Ed Malloy on Monday. David hadn't called, so she'd polished the piece as best she could with the information she had, which actually was more than adequate. She'd added a sentence or two about how David had personally worked with Sam Taglia to perfect his performance.

She'd ended the article with a paragraph about how the vampire mystique continued on, resurfacing in each new generation, much as legend said the vampire lived on, never growing old. The power of the mystique, she wrote, was demonstrated in the way women mobbed Sam Taglia, who'd merely portrayed a vampire in a play.

These were her own thoughts. She wished she could have discussed the mystique with David, because his ideas would have had far more depth. But David, it seemed, had forgotten her. As the days had gone by and he didn't phone and didn't phone, Veronica couldn't help but wonder if perhaps Rob was right. David must have many women more attractive and sophisticated than Veronica to choose from—like Darienne. Had he only toyed with her and made promises he didn't intend to keep? The disillusionment hurt badly, but if it was true, she had to face it. Doing things like parking in front of his house didn't help, either.

Mr. Malloy read her article immediately after she handed it to him in his office. He surprised her several minutes later when he appeared in the entrance to her cubicle.

"I didn't know you could write so well, Veronica. You've painted a vivid portrait of de Morrissey. Besides that, the article is well constructed and has insight. It's great!"

"Thank you," she said. So, she'd finally made an impression! She'd lost David but gained her boss's respect. The trade, if you could call it that, hardly seemed worthwhile now. She valued David's attention far more than Mr. Malloy's.

"Did you get a photo?"

The photo. She'd forgotten it entirely. "No. David never called me as he promised."

"Can't you phone him?"

"He didn't give me his number. Even Sam Taglia can't reach him. Only the play's producer and director have his home number."

"Can't you reach him through them?"

She shook her head. "If David wanted to talk to me, he would have called by now. It won't help to push the issue. Frankly, I don't think he'd ever agree to a photo anyway. He *is* eccentric."

Ed Malloy grinned. "Yeah, but I got the impression *you*

could twist his arm to get him to do things. You're the only one in the city who ever got an interview out of him."

Veronica straightened in her seat, annoyed. "I have no influence with him, Mr. Malloy."

"Okay, don't bite my head off," her boss said, throwing up his hands. "I'm just saying don't give up yet. Use your feminine wiles."

Veronica pressed her lips together in consternation. When I get some, I will, she thought.

Later that morning Rob asked her to lunch. She'd put him off too long with excuses and decided she couldn't avoid him any longer. It seemed to be obvious that he was interested in her. Perhaps having lunch with a man who admired her would help her get over David, she reasoned.

They left early to beat the lunch-hour crowd. Rob took her by cab to Berghoff's, a nineteenth-century-style German restaurant on Adams Street in the heart of the Loop. The restaurant's decor used lots of varnished wood, giving its several rooms a comfortable, masculine atmosphere.

After they'd been seated and had looked over the menu, they both ordered sauerbraten and imported German dark beer.

"Did you interview Sam Taglia?" she asked Rob. She'd given Rob the actor's phone number.

"Saturday after the evening performance," Rob said. "He gave a good interview."

"Did he say he'd gotten permission from David?" she asked as their waiter brought them water.

"De Morrissey was reluctant. Sam said he'd mentioned I was your co-worker, so de Morrissey agreed to it, but told him this was the last interview he'd allow."

"I wonder if David's angry." She ran her finger down the side of her water glass, making a clear streak in the condensation.

"I wouldn't worry about it," Rob said, studying her expression. "Why should you care?"

"I'm just curious."

"Veronica, you met this guy twice, and you act like you're getting over some long-term affair with him."

"No, I'm not. I've never had a long-term affair. How does anyone know how I'd behave?"

"You seem depressed," Rob added. He looked at her with concern. "How could de Morrissey get you so attached to him in such a short time?"

"He's a unique person."

"Who doesn't keep his promises. I told you he wouldn't call."

"Okay, you told me." She was beginning to lose her patience. "You were right. What more do you want?"

"I want you to forget him and look around you," Rob said in a soft, coaxing way. "There are other men in the world."

Veronica guessed he was referring to himself. And he was right. She ought to get her mind off David. She made an effort to stifle her impatience with Rob and to view him with an open mind—with new eyes, so to speak. Maybe if she tried, she could make herself become attracted to him.

"Okay." She forced a smile. "Shall we change the subject?"

"Gladly."

Both were silent for a while. Veronica straightened her silverware. "Seen any good movies lately?" she asked.

"The new Woody Allen movie's good. I just turned in my review of it."

"How did you rate it?"

"Four stars."

"I guess I should see it," Veronica said. "You usually like his movies, don't you?"

Rob nodded. "His films have layers of depth and a big dose of philosophy, but you don't mind it because of the humor. They seem effortless, but the structure underneath is very intricate. Everything is thought out and placed in the script for a specific reason, from the names of the characters to the background music."

As he went on comparing *Manhattan* and *Hannah and Her Sisters* to the current film, Veronica was impressed with Rob's knowledge and analytical ability. She watched him as he spoke, noting his clear, placid eyes, his classic cheekbones and jawline, the soft fall of blond hair over his forehead. If she could just *feel* something for him—longing, desire, adulation. All those things she'd felt so vibrantly for David. The image of Claudine in *Street Shadows* clinging to her lover, imploring him to take her with him, came strongly to her mind, bringing the sting of tears to her eyes. Oh, David, how could you forget me?

"Veronica, are you listening?"

"I . . . um . . ."

"What did I just say?"

She felt embarrassed. "Sorry, my mind wandered."

"You do a hell of a lot for a guy's ego," Rob said with edgy humor. "You were thinking about de Morrissey again, weren't you?"

She swallowed. "I can't seem to help it."

"What is it about him that's so transfixing?" Rob's eyes searched her face as though he genuinely wanted to know.

Veronica took a long breath. She felt odd confiding in Rob. But he seemed sincere, and she thought getting a man's point of view might be helpful somehow. How could she begin to explain her feelings to him? she wondered. "David understood me. He knew what I felt, my wants and my fears. I think he could have helped me."

"Helped you with what?"

"My life."

"What's wrong with your life?" Rob asked, raising his shoulders. "You're giving one man an awful lot of credit. He's not a psychologist, is he?"

She smiled sadly. "No, I'm sure he's better than any psychologist. They don't get personally involved. David did."

"Then why didn't he call you?" Rob asked gently, as though he were a therapist himself.

"I don't know," she told him. "I don't understand. He was so sincere. He said he needed *me* and that we had a special affinity. It's so hard to believe he didn't mean any of it."

Rob looked grim. "He told you all that? Don't you see now that it was just a seductive buildup? He was trying to get you to sleep with him."

Veronica sat dumbfounded for half a moment. After all she'd told him, Rob still persisted in viewing David as a scheming womanizer. "He never asked me to sleep with him!" she said, her jaw muscles tightening. "And even if he did and I had, it's not your business to speculate about."

"Maybe not, but I care about you," Rob insisted.

"How could you care about me? We don't even know each other that well."

Rob pointed at her. "*You* care about de Morrissey and you barely know *him!*"

"Yes, I know him better than I've known anyone," Veronica replied in a husky voice. "Sometimes with two people, it happens that way."

Rob raked his fingers through his blond hair, mussing it. "You know what that sounds like? Something from those old musicals where two people look at each other, dance once together, and bingo, they're in love for the rest of their lives."

"I don't want to discuss this with you anymore," she said in a cool tone. "My feelings aren't your concern. And I don't want you to make them your concern."

"What about my feelings?"

"Your feelings?"

"I could really be attracted to you, you know?" Rob's voice was growing unsteady. "If you weren't living out some illusion all the time. When I first met you, I thought you were the most feminine, ethereal-looking woman I'd ever seen. I even thought that dreamy look in your eyes was endearing. Until I realized you were only half here and half somewhere else." He snapped his napkin open and put it in his lap. "De Morrissey was exactly the kind of man a girl like you *shouldn't* meet. He figured out how to weave himself into your daydreams. I wish I knew his secret. Now he's taken you off his hook, callously thrown you back into the ocean, and you won't even believe it!"

The waiter brought their plates of food at that moment.

Veronica grabbed her purse and pushed back her chair. "You can take mine back to the kitchen," she told the waiter. "I'm not hungry anymore." She rose, picked up her coat, which she'd been sitting on, and said to Rob, "I'm leaving. I've heard enough."

Rob stood, throwing down his napkin. "Veronica, wait!"

She walked past him. "And don't you dare follow me out."

"So you just left him standing there in the restaurant?" Caroline asked. She was posed on a wooden box while a woman inserted pins at the hem of her white satin wedding gown.

"Just walked out on him," Veronica said, standing to one side in the small fitting room. "I can't believe I did it myself."

"I think you were right," Caroline said. "I don't let men, even Tom—heck, *especially* Tom—pontificate and tell me what I ought to do. I'm proud of you."

Veronica shrugged, somehow not feeling so proud. She adjusted the bouffant sleeve of her turquoise attendant's dress, which she'd also put on for a last check by the bridal shop personnel. "The thing is, I think Rob meant well," she went on. "I just feel so emotionally raw when it comes to David."

"He never called, huh?"

"No."

"That's odd," Caroline said, pivoting a quarter turn at the behest of the fitter. "I don't really know him, but somehow he doesn't seem the type to forget a promise."

"Have you seen him again?"

"He came in briefly last Friday. Of course, we only talked business. He seemed a little quiet, now that I think of it."

"My name didn't come up at all?" Veronica asked, grabbing at a last hope.

"No. I thought about mentioning you, but then decided against it. I have to keep my business demeanor with clients, you know. It wouldn't look good if I seemed to be playing matchmaker."

"I know," Veronica said. "Do you have his phone number?"

"He wrote a number on one of the papers I asked him to fill out. But when I looked at it afterward, I noticed the number ended with two zeros. Just on a guess, I looked up the theater's number in the phone book, and it was the same."

"It's strange how secretive he is," Veronica said, reminded for a moment of Sam Taglia's hints and suspicions.

"In any case, even if I did have his number, it wouldn't be professional of me to give it to you."

"Yes, you're right." Veronica sighed. "I guess I just have to accept that he doesn't want to see me and it's over." She felt tears starting in her eyes and blinked them back.

"Well, that's a fighting attitude!" Caroline mocked. "Veronica, these are modern times. You don't have to play the shy, old-fashioned girl and wait for the man to make all the moves."

"But I don't have his number. And I don't want to send a

message through Sam Taglia or you to ask David to call me. I'd look like I was begging, and I'd just wind up waiting for him like I am now."

"Go to his house and knock on the door."

Veronica's stomach contracted. "I've gone to his house."

"You have?"

"I couldn't get up enough nerve to knock on the door. I saw the lights in his living room windows, though. You think I should have knocked? It seemed so bold. And if he didn't want to see me, it would only make him angry to find me there at the door."

"At least you'd know for sure," Caroline said. "Maybe he'd explain why he never called. Even if he said it was because he lost interest, it would end all your wondering and speculating."

Veronica thought it over for a moment, looking down at the carpet. Its diamond pattern began to make her dizzy. She leaned against the wall mirror to keep her balance. "I don't think I can do it."

"If you had the gumption to walk out on Rob in a restaurant, you can knock on David's door. We women shouldn't let men get away with broken promises. Right?"

"Right," Veronica agreed weakly, following the word with a long, uneven breath. "But maybe not knowing is easier than knowing."

A few nights later Veronica drove her car slowly up Oak Street in the rain. Over her tape player came David's voice from the interview, sounding so reassuring and sincere as he told her, "I would love to be your tutor."

His house came into view. Veronica swallowed hard, feeling as though she must be the greatest fool on the face of the earth. Driving closer, she noticed that the front lights of his mansion were not lit, but a soft, flickering light was coming from windows along the side wall, toward the rear. It looked eerie at first, but then she realized what it must be. From having stayed up late many a night, watching old movies with the lamps turned off, she decided the bluish-gray light must be from a television. She found it odd thinking of David watching TV, but then she remembered he liked old movies, too.

It was almost ten o'clock, and the rain was growing heavier.

She'd hemmed and hawed the whole evening, deciding to go to his house, then changing her mind, even turning her car around twice to drive back to her apartment. But she'd finally decided that Caroline was right. If she could see him once and if he would give her an explanation, at least she would know why he was ignoring her. And then maybe she could somehow put it all behind her and go on. As it stood now, she would be wondering about David forever.

She'd thought of a good excuse for coming, too. Mr. Malloy wanted a photo of David. She could always save face by saying her boss sent her to ask him for a picture. David would probably see through the excuse, but at least she'd have something to say to him when he opened the door. If he opened it. She recalled he didn't have a doorbell. If he was at the other end of the house, would he even hear the knocker?

Carefully, for her movements were erratic from nerves, she parked in front of his house. She got out and hurriedly locked the car door as rain pelted down. Her hands felt as cold as her car keys. She put the keys in her purse and ran toward the door. Somehow she felt as she used to when she was about to enter Mr. Malloy's office. She made an effort to drum up the self-confident look of composure she'd invented to impress her boss.

But when she stepped up to David's big oak door, she felt queasy in the stomach, weak, and dizzy. She leaned against it for a moment. Forgetting everything—her pride, the potential embarrassment—she willed herself to take hold of the knocker. She banged it hard against the metal base. The sharp sound knifed through her, echoed in her ears, seemed to deafen her. She knocked three times and waited.

What felt like a full minute went by, though it might only have been twenty seconds. She found partial shelter from the rain under the arch that projected out high above the door. Not a sound came from inside the house. She knocked again, this time with more force.

Again, no response, no sound. She wrapped her fingers around the knocker, clinging to it, feeling as though she would weep. "David, please answer," she whispered. She rapped on the door again with all her strength. The sharp sound echoed out over the street from the mansion's thick, stone walls.

The answering silence was painful. It wasn't fair of David

to ignore her like this. She must make him hear! She'd see him or die trying—drown on his doorstep waiting, if she had to.

"David!" she cried out on a sob and banged the knocker again. She leaned against the carved wooden door and wept, continuing to knock, but with weakening force. Wind blew the rain in toward the house, chilling and soaking her.

All her dignity was gone now. And if David didn't answer, so was all hope.

8

Damn Morality!

GENE KELLY lifted Leslie Caron in his arms, silhouetted in yellow by a flame-colored fountain in the background, all to the rhythms of Gershwin. Kelly looked muscular, possessive, triumphant; and the actress, sensual, pliant, fulfilled. The dance contrasted masculine strength with feminine softness; it was vividly realized, stunning in its sexual impact.

As he watched the sequence, David remembered Veronica talking about this very scene. All at once he felt such longing and such acute loneliness that he could no longer bear to watch. The memory of Veronica that the film brought back pained him too much.

When David stopped the tape of *An American in Paris,* he thought he heard a faint knock. In the silence while the tape rewound, he heard it again. Three taps in a row.

If someone was at his door, they'd better give up. He never answered to unexpected callers. And then he heard a woman's voice crying out his name, not with his ears so much as in his mind.

Veronica.

Had she come again? Was she at his door now? David turned off the video equipment and once more heard the distant knocking. Quickly he ran from the ballroom down the hall to his living room. He went to the front window and pushed aside the draperies to look out. A heavy rain made everything opaque. But below, illuminated by the street lamp, he saw Veronica's car parked at the curb. He couldn't see his doorway from the window, but when he heard the knock again, he knew for sure she was there. His sharp ears picked up the sound of a woman weeping.

Oh, Lord, what should he do? He'd made the decision not to disturb her life, to stay away from her. But if she was suffering this much pain, what was the moral thing to do? Would she still be better off without him? Or had he already destroyed her future happiness?

If he had, then they might as well be together.

David felt the weight of guilt heavy on his shoulders. Was he being logical and putting her welfare first? Or was he twisting logic to suit his own need?

He walked to the door and paused there, trying to think, to put aside emotion. Veronica's future lay in his hands. His decision whether to answer her knock might set her fate forever.

It was no use. Logic became clouded when he thought of Veronica. He could picture what she must look like, standing at his door in the rain, calling to him and weeping, wondering why he didn't answer.

Then it occurred to him that she must have seen the light from his large TV screen in the ballroom. She knew he was home. How could he hurt her by obviously ignoring her when she was crying out for him? She might lose faith in humanity if he didn't respond, might be scarred emotionally for the rest of her life.

Now it was clear to David that he had no choice.

He opened the door to the landing and bounded down the spiral steps to the ground floor. As he ran he promised himself that he would see her only to explain, to provide her with some plausible reason why they must not see each other anymore. He would open the door, reassure her that he cared for her, yet tell her why it would not be good to continue their relationship. And then he would never see her again.

The plan seemed simple when David reached the ground floor entryway. The knocker sounded again, and he could hear her crying on the other side of the door. Poor Veronica, he thought, her sobs bringing tears to his eyes. What have I done to you?

He began to unbolt the door. Her audible weeping stopped at the metallic sound of the lock. Heart thudding, David opened the door.

Veronica stood there looking up at him, her dark eyes wide and wet, drops of sleet sliding down her hair and coat, looking so forlorn David thought his heart would break.

"David?"

He took her wrist and pulled her into the shelter of his home, then closed the door on the cold outside.

"Veronica, I'm so sorry," he whispered and took her in his arms.

She clung to the lapels of his jacket and her tears dampened his shirtfront. His hand grew cold with the icy wetness of her hair and cheek as he stroked her, trying to soothe her.

"You'll catch cold. Come in and dry off," he told her. He led her to the steps. Blinded by tears, she tripped on the first one. David lifted her into his arms and carried her. As he moved slowly up the steps, Veronica slid her arms around his shoulders and buried her face into the side of his neck, kissing him and crying and whispering his name. David closed his eyes at the pure joy her simple affection gave him. He needed her. She wanted him. How could he tell her they must part? It would break her heart and his, too.

Damn morality! he told himself as he carried her up the stairs like his most prized, most rare, most lovely possession. His arms seemed to grow even stronger, and he felt sure of his decision now. Damn what was good or right or honest! Veronica was his, and even God couldn't make him let her go now!

When they reached the living room, he put her on her feet and helped her out of her coat. He led her to the love seat, and while she wiped away her tears, he went to the bar to get a towel.

David sat next to her, gently blotted her face, then began drying her wet hair. She sat like a good child and let him minister to her. Though she'd stopped crying, her breathing came in uneven little gasps. She was wearing a knit dress in a color that reminded him of parchment. The material clung to her slim body. As she sat with her torso twisted toward him, the fabric draped over her small breasts, defining them softly. Like any normal male, he wanted to comfort and caress her.

Running the towel over her hair one last time, he looked at her and said, "Are you all right now? Are you still cold?"

"A little."

"Shall I build a fire?"

"No," she said, reaching out to him. "Just hold me."

He put the towel aside and drew her into his embrace, pressing her to his chest to warm her, laying his cheek on her hair. "Better?"

"Yes, David."

"What made you come tonight, so late, in the rain?"

She bowed her head against his chest. Her fragile voice was muffled. "I had an excuse—to ask you for a photo for the magazine. But I just needed to see you again. You didn't call me. I wanted to know why."

He stroked the hair at the side of her face. "I didn't call because . . ." David paused, considering what to tell her. "I was afraid I wouldn't be good for you. I didn't want to hurt you by breaking my promise, but I was afraid a relationship between us wouldn't be in your best interests."

She looked up at him, her brown eyes wounded. "Why?"

"I'm considerably older than you."

"Ten or eleven years," she said. "That's not so much."

"But I'm set in my ways," he told her. "I follow a rather restricted lifestyle of my own choosing. I'm not a social creature. If you adapted yourself to my life—and you would have to—you would cut yourself off from people your own age."

"I don't care, David."

"Wouldn't you like to meet other young men of your generation?"

"No," she insisted. "I prefer your company to anyone's."

David found her reply gratifying, but he had to press the issue to justify his decision, once and for all. "You wouldn't prefer a young lover to an old mentor?" he asked, his tone lightly teasing.

She drew away from him a bit and sat up straight, looking at him in a more direct way than she ever had before. Reaching up to touch his chin, she said, "Couldn't you be both my lover and my mentor?"

He didn't breathe for a moment. "Is that what you want?"

"With all my heart."

"Why?"

"Because . . ." Tears filled her eyes as she spoke. "You've

meant so much to me already. I don't think I can go on without you."

So David had his answer. He drew her against him tightly and kissed her mouth as a tear ran down her cheek. As she slid her arms around his neck and kissed him back, he had to be careful not to injure her delicate mouth. He couldn't be as free with her as he was with Darienne.

But David didn't mind the restrictions he would have to put on himself for Veronica's sake. Veronica could give him what Darienne never had, the two things he wanted most in his life: love and constancy.

For these David would give anything. To lie and to pretend he was mortal, to keep himself within the constraints of mortal lovemaking, to be patient with Veronica's innocence—all these restrictions were nothing in David's mind. He would do them all with thanksgiving for her devotion.

A few weeks before, Darienne had convinced him that such a relationship would be impossible. But now, holding Veronica in his arms after knowing the sheer misery of their separation, David felt sure a mortal-style love affair with her not only was possible, but was the best decision he could ever make.

When they drew apart, ending the kiss, David pressed his hand to her cheek. "All right then. I'll be your mentor. And in time, when you wish it, your lover."

She stared at him with huge eyes, her dark pupils growing almost as large as her irises. Her complexion paled.

"What's wrong?" he asked. "Isn't that what you said you wanted?"

"Yes," she said in a near-whisper. "I just can't believe it. You, with me. You scare me a little sometimes."

David was mortified. "In what way?"

"Your eyes. They seemed to shine with an odd light just now when you said 'lover.' "

He'd forgotten the involuntary glow that emanated from vampires' eyes with any high emotion. Smiling a bit while his mind raced for an answer, he told her, "Pale blue eyes dominate in the de Morrissey family tree. Unfortunately, our eyes have the embarrassing characteristic of occasionally catching the light in a certain way, so that they seem to reflect, like a cat's eyes. It's a peculiarity of the genes, I'm afraid. My uncle had the trait so profoundly that a renowned ophthalmologist went so far as to do a thorough study of him, giving him one test after another, shining many types of light into his eyes."

"What did he find out?" Veronica asked, hanging on every word.

David felt complimented that she believed his improvisation. "The doctor speculated that there was an unusual amount of some substance—whatever it is that lightning bugs possess— that caused the phenomenon. Now this was all very informative. But he had no cure to offer my poor uncle, who had to go on the rest of his life frightening people, as I did you."

Veronica leaned against him, relaxed now, looking up at him face-to-face, amusement in her eyes. "I like to listen to you talk."

"I like the way you listen," he murmured, leaning in to kiss her again. As he ran his hands over her back and down to her waist, he began to yearn for more than simple, chaste kisses. But there was time enough for more in the weeks and months to come. She was innocent and he needed to take things slowly, so they could savor every moment together. But what sweetness when he finally possessed her!

"David?" she asked when they drew apart. "You won't ever leave me alone again, will you?" Her brown eyes searched his, looking for reassurance.

"No, Veronica. I'm convinced now that it's better for us to be together than apart. But if you ever regret your choice to be with me, then you must tell me."

"I won't regret it," she told him, her eyes wide and earnest. "How often will we see each other?"

"Is several nights a week too often?"

"Not for me. I'd come every night, if you asked."

He kissed her forehead. "Let's take things carefully at first, and see what works best. I'm afraid you can't come every night, Veronica. You work and you need your sleep."

"I know," she said. "So do you."

The profound difference between her life and his, shown by her innocuous remark, gave David a moment of pain. "We'll see what works best," he repeated, collecting himself. "I'll give you my private phone number, so you can always reach me. That is, only in the evening. I don't like to be disturbed—"

"While you're working during the day. I know," she said with a smile. "I wouldn't want to interrupt progress on your next play. Are you writing one?"

"Toying with some ideas," David replied. "I haven't actually begun writing it." And he realized for the first time that if he spent most evenings with Veronica, his "progress," as she'd put it, would be very slow indeed. He wished he *could* write during the day instead of lying helplessly in his coffin. But it didn't matter anyway. If he had Veronica, he wouldn't need to bury himself in his work. In fact, at this moment, David didn't care if he ever wrote again.

Veronica seemed to be mulling over something. "There were so many questions I wished I'd asked you when I wrote my article about you. One of them was what your next play was about."

"I still can't answer that, but you may ask me the other questions."

She laughed a little and shrugged. "Too late. I handed in the article on Monday. My boss liked it as it was. Except . . ." She hesitated. "He did want a photo of you. I told you before, it was the reason I used to get up the nerve to come here."

David smiled. "Then I'm grateful to your boss for being the means to bring us back together. But I have no photograph to give you."

"Can I bring a camera and take your picture?"

David's heart sank. He wanted so to please her. "No, Veronica," he told her gently. "I don't want any photographs of myself published. It would spoil my anonymity. Now I can go where I want, and no one knows who I am. I refuse to have my privacy invaded by people wanting my autograph and so on." There was another reason, too, but he couldn't go into that.

To his surprise, she nodded with equanimity. "I told my boss you wouldn't allow it. He wanted me to sneak a camera in and take a picture of you." She grinned. "But of course, I won't."

Her loyalty touched David. "Perhaps I could give you something else that might please your boss almost as much as a photograph."

"What?" she asked as he got up from the couch.

He went into a small room adjacent to the living room. It

was set up like an office with a desk and file cabinets, but he seldom used it. He picked up a script lying on the desk, brought it back into the living room and handed it to Veronica.

He watched her lift the unmarked manila cover to read aloud the title page: " '*Street Shadows* by David de Morrissey.' " The words were written in his own hand, as well as the date and the city. Quickly she leafed through a few more of the handwritten pages, then looked up at him in wonder. "Your original manuscript?"

"Scribbled in fountain pen. My typist mailed it back along with her transcribed copy. It might be considered valuable. Perhaps your boss would be satisfied taking photographs of the title page or the first page of the text."

She smiled with delight. "I'm sure that'll be fine. Wait till I show this to the people at the office! I'll return it as soon as I can."

"You may keep it if you like," David said, sitting next to her again.

"I may?" She folded her arms around the script and held it against her as if she were holding a child. Her eyes were bright with unshed tears. "I'll cherish it, David. Thank you."

A unique feeling of peace settled over David as he absorbed the gratitude in her eyes and listened to her heartfelt words. It amazed him that such a trifle could please her so much. He'd never met another woman like her. Even his memories of Cecilia faded in Veronica's soft, warm radiance.

This evening would mark the beginning of a new era for him, David realized. Veronica was his. The world would never seem lonely again.

9

I Cried to Dream Again

THE NEXT morning Veronica walked into her office cubicle and carefully set the parcel she was carrying on her desk. Because it was still raining, she'd wrapped her treasure in tissue paper and then in plastic. She set down her umbrella and took off her raincoat. After shaking off drops of water, she hung it on the wooden clothes tree in the corner.

As she walked back to her parcel, Rob came in. He hadn't attempted to speak to her since she walked out on him in the restaurant a few days before.

"Veronica?"

"Yes," she said, wiping the plastic dry with a facial tissue.

"Are we going to ignore each other forever?"

"I'm not ignoring you," she told him.

"Look, I'm sorry if I got carried away giving advice that day at lunch."

"Unasked-for advice," she said calmly, her tone almost light. "You were also judgmental and a busybody."

Rob seemed taken aback. "Anything else?"

"That covers it." She was surprised at herself. She couldn't remember ever having had the nerve to talk to anyone so plainly before.

Rob took a deep breath. "Will you accept an apology?"

"Sure." She turned to him and mechanically offered her hand.

He shook hands with her, looking a bit amazed at her manner. "What's that?" he asked as she started to unwrap the package.

"I'll show you." Her heart began to beat faster with pride

124

as she took off the plastic and then carefully pulled away the tissue paper. Inside was the script. As Rob looked over her shoulder, she opened the cover to the title page so he could see.

" 'Street Shadows,' " Rob read aloud. " 'By David de Morrissey.' Well, well. Handwritten, too." He looked at her. "Where did you get it? You haven't seen him again—"

"Yes, I have. He gave it to me," she said, smiling as she lovingly ran her fingers over David's name.

"I don't understand you, Veronica," Rob said, shaking his head. "Can't you see the guy's an insensitive egoist? He forgets you, ignores you, then gives you a lousy script from his own play to make up for it."

"Do you know how valuable this is?"

"It didn't cost *him* a cent," Rob pointed out.

"He gave me this to have it photographed instead of a picture of himself. He said I could keep it. It wasn't meant to 'make up' for anything."

Rob exhaled. "Okay, let's have a look at it." He took the script from her and began leafing through it. "Doesn't he know how to type?"

"David feels closer to his work writing it by hand." As Rob quickly and cavalierly turned one page after another, she added, "Careful, don't tear it."

Annoyed, Rob closed the manuscript and dropped it back on the desk. "There," he said, wiggling his fingers menacingly over the book. "You probably don't want it tainted with my fingerprints, either."

She picked up the script and hugged it protectively. "I have to show it to Mr. Malloy and then the photographer. So, if you'll excuse me," she said, waiting for Rob to step out of her way.

"Sure, I'll excuse you." He stepped aside. "But, if I may ask, how did you excuse de Morrissey for ignoring you?"

Veronica's jaw tightened. "He had his reasons for not calling me, and I had my reasons for forgiving him. And none of those reasons are any of your business."

When she started to walk out, Rob stopped her by taking hold of her elbow. "Are you going to go on seeing him?" he asked, a raw huskiness in his voice.

"I'm not ten years old and you're not my father, Rob. I don't have to report to you who I see or what I do."

Rob let go of her arm abruptly. "All right. Fine!" He seemed to relent a bit. "But if you ever need someone to talk to, I hope you'll come to me. You may have to look hard to find me," he added with sarcasm. "Apparently I blend in well with the paint on the walls."

Darienne clung to David's arm as they strolled down Oak Street toward Lake Michigan and the beach. It was shortly after midnight. When she'd shown up at his home a little while ago, David had asked her to take a walk with him. The wet streets indicated it had continued to rain during the day, but now the night air was clear and crisp. Somehow, to David, the change in the weather seemed appropriate.

"Something has happened, David?" Darienne asked. She wore a flowing, gold lamé dress, high-heeled shoes, and her mink, cleaned now of bloodstains. Diamonds sparkled at her throat.

"Yes, something's happened. How did you know?"

"By the way you asked me so quickly to go *out* for a walk, even before I could take my coat off. Afraid my new gown may be too seductive?" she said with amusement, looking up at him.

"You know me too well."

"Yes, I do. So. Is it Veronica?"

"Yes."

"She came to your house again?"

"Last night. She pounded on my door, weeping."

"And you couldn't keep yourself from comforting her," Darienne surmised, her tone wise. "And so?"

"And so I made a new decision. She is as miserable without me as I am without her. Therefore, I concluded, we must be together. What's done is done. I believe our destiny was sealed the day we met, and I have no will left to try to change it, either for her sake or mine." He looked at Darienne, waiting for an argument.

She was silent as they walked several steps. Finally she smiled up at him, her beautiful eyes full of warmth. "Then I wish you both well, David."

"Thank you. I hoped you would understand. I love her."

"Then you'll make her one of us?"

David felt a pain of tension between his shoulder blades. "No. I'll pretend to be mortal." He said this with a finality that he hoped would dissuade Darienne from arguing the matter.

She gave a slight nod, her blond hair gleaming under the street lamp they were passing. "Veronica is different," she said, as if trying to be positive. "Maybe it will work."

They walked on in silence for a long while. David was relieved that Darienne seemed to be accepting his decision. But there was one more matter he had to broach with her. "Darienne?"

"I know, David." She sighed and glanced up at him, a resigned smile on her face. "You want to be true to Veronica. So there will be no more of our delightful couplings."

"Yes, that's it," he said with some regret, knowing what Darienne's disappointment must be. "I know our special relationship means a great deal to you. But Veronica wouldn't understand. I won't risk losing her, not even for you."

"I don't want you to risk anything on my behalf, David," she said, taking his arm more closely. "But one day, in time, Veronica might understand and be willing to share you with me."

David felt unsettled at the thought. And humiliated. Did she look upon him as she might a piece of clothing, to be loaned by one woman to another? "I wouldn't count on that!"

Darienne merely smiled, looking like a glamorous Mona Lisa.

"Will you stay in Chicago now?" he asked.

"Perhaps for a little longer. I've noticed some intriguing young men on Rush Street this year. I may stay and sample a few, you know?"

"What do you mean, 'sample'? Not—"

"No, no. Calm yourself," she said, laughing. "These days I use blood banks only, like you. I mean sample them sexually. Try them on for size, so to speak. Mortal men never have enough stamina, but they're better than nothing. Actually, I find American men can really be quite charming in bed. Do you think it's all those hot dogs they consume?"

"Darienne, really!" He smiled in spite of himself. "Tell me, how do you manage it? You ask them to take you home with them?"

"Sometimes. But I have a place I can take them, too."

"Where?" he asked, curious only because she never wanted to tell him.

"Now, David, I don't want you keeping track of me."

"You keep track of *me*. Sporadically," he added, under his breath. "And unexpectedly."

She clicked her tongue. "Am I such a nuisance?"

David couldn't help but feel thankful for Veronica and that she was Darienne's opposite.

"Don't worry," Darienne assured him. "I won't walk in on you and Veronica unannounced. I'll knock first, or something."

"That makes me feel much better," David said in an arch tone as they entered the tunnellike underpass beneath Lake Shore Drive. In a few moments they came out the other end at the sandy edge of Oak Street Beach. The stars and moon seemed more brilliant now over the quiet, dark expanse of Lake Michigan.

Darienne ran her gloved hand up his arm. "Tell me, have you coupled with Veronica?"

"Americans say 'make love.' No, I haven't."

"She's a virgin, isn't she?"

"Yes."

"You'll have to be so very gentle, David," Darienne said with concern.

"I know."

"How long will you wait to make love with her?"

"I'll leave that up to Veronica."

"Poor thing. She'll probably be frightened, especially when she sees your manly *équipement.*"

"Darienne!" David chided as they stepped onto the sand.

"Do I embarrass you?" she teased.

"Yes, and don't you relish it! But since we're on the subject, maybe you can advise me. I've never actually taken a woman's virginity."

"What?" Darienne seemed absolutely amazed.

"No, I haven't."

"What about Cecilia?"

"Of course not. She was a proper girl and wanted to wait till we married."

"Not even that little *italienne* you were so taken with in Milan around 1900?"

"I disappeared from her life before anything took place. I've always done that with chaste women. My conscience has never allowed me to destroy what's pure." Guilt threatened to overtake him, and he reminded himself of his decision. "But with Veronica, our emotions are too overpowering for me to vanish from her life."

Darienne took off her shoes to walk barefoot on the cold, wet sand. "What precisely did you want to ask me?" she said, looking at him with curiosity.

"I think Veronica is willing, but sometimes she's afraid of me. I don't know how she'll react. Were you frightened—I mean, did the act upset you the first time?"

"Mon Dieu, I can barely remember," she said, pausing to look at her footprints in the sand. "No, I'm sure it didn't frighten me. I was ready and eager."

There was something David had occasionally wondered over the centuries. This seemed an appropriate time to ask. "Who did deflower you, by the way?"

" 'Deflower' me? You sound so ridiculously old-fashioned! It was the young priest, Father Armand. Don't you remember? Well, of course, it was all hushed up, so maybe you never heard."

"Father Armand!" David repeated in disbelief. He was the very priest from whom David had sought advice about entering the priesthood.

"I'm sorry to shock you, David," she said, laughing, "but you wanted to know. Why haven't you asked me this before?"

"I did, the first time I slept with you. You refused to tell me. You're such a secretive woman, I haven't asked since. After the first quarter century, it didn't seem important anymore. Did he seduce you?"

Darienne seemed to have to think about it. "No, I suppose you could say I seduced him. It's so long ago, who can remember? I do remember it was a pleasant experience. Poor Father Armand was chastised and sent away, though."

"So that's what happened to him."

"And I was locked in my room for six months to pray for forgiveness." She laughed. "My mother allowed you to visit because you were so very pious. She felt you'd be a good influence. It's all so amusing to think back on it now."

David didn't share her amusement. He remembered Darienne's mother arranging with his mother to take him along on visits to Darienne's palatial home. While the two women talked, David was sent to visit Darienne. When he asked why she was confined to her room, his mother told him only that she was doing penance, but he must not ask for what sin.

Being a dutiful young man, he did what he was told and followed his instructions about praying and saying the rosary with Darienne. The mothers had thought the rebellious sixteen-year-old girl might respond better to the good influence of someone her own age than she did to that of her elders and clerics. Only they hadn't counted on Darienne's lack of conscience and her perfect willingness to sin again. Nor had they—or David—realized how vulnerable the repressed adolescent was to temptation, and how easily his studious cloak of sanctity could be torn to shreds.

David put aside his impatience with Darienne's blithe attitude about it all and directed her attention back to his original question. "What about Veronica? As a woman, can you give me any insights as to how she'll react?"

"I think you're right. She may be willing but frightened. She seems quite sensitive. Unless you initiate her first," Darienne suggested. "Then she'll come to you eagerly."

"No! I won't take a drop of her blood."

"Then you'll have to calm her the way all mortal men reassure a virgin."

"How?"

She laughed. "David, if you don't know, *I* certainly don't. No man has ever had to soothe *me* into bed."

"I see your point," David said with a sigh.

Having reached the shoreline, they walked along the water's edge and listened to the waves lap onto the sand. Beyond them the vast lake expanded to the dim horizon.

"I'm sure you'll know instinctively what to do for Veronica, David. You're very sensitive to women." Darienne's eyes sparkled with admiration as she looked at him. She rose up on her toes to kiss him softly on the mouth. "And I'm sure," she continued, with certainty in her voice and smile, "that Veronica won't be disappointed. Oh, I envy her! To have you for her first experience. Only—poor thing—you'll spoil her. After you she'll never be satisfied with anyone else."

Over the next few weeks David saw Veronica almost every evening. She always drove to his mansion, but not until after she'd eaten dinner at home. David made the excuse that he got hungry in the late afternoon after writing all day, and therefore ate his evening meal early. They spent their time together in a variety of ways. Sometimes they sat and read Shakespeare, sometimes they went for a walk. They spent two evenings at the opera and one at the Chicago Philharmonic. Afterward, they talked about what they'd seen or read or heard. If Veronica had questions, David would answer them. She listened with such rapt attention, he knew his ego could become puffed up in no time if he wasn't careful. Already he'd noticed a definite tendency to pontificate.

Their meetings, so far, were innocent, as if they were close friends or a tutor and his favorite student. They parted around one or two in the morning with nothing more than an affectionate kiss. But David couldn't remember ever having been so content, so happy to be on earth.

One evening they went to a production of *The Tempest* at a small theater in Evanston, a suburb to the north. As usual when they went any distance, Veronica drove. David refused to own a car.

Afterward, they left the theater and walked to where she'd parked the car on a side street. The theater's small lot had been full when they arrived.

"Can you remember that passage about dreaming?" she asked, taking his arm when they came to a patch of slippery sidewalk. A freezing rain earlier had left an icy glaze on the streets.

" 'We are such stuff as dreams are made on'?" he quoted.

"No. Something Caliban said."

David thought a moment and then remembered what she must be speaking of. " 'In dreaming, the clouds methought would open and show riches ready to drop upon me; that, when I waked, I cried to dream again.' "

"Yes, that." She looked thoughtful, her long lashes cast downward, her mouth parted and wistful.

"That passage appeals to you?"

She chuckled and tilted her head. "It doesn't 'appeal' exactly. But it sort of describes how I feel sometimes."

"Go on," he coaxed as they walked past a closed dress shop.

"I tend to daydream a lot, especially at the office. When I 'wake' from the daydream, I always want to go back and dream again, because my surroundings seem so dull."

"What do you daydream about?"

She smiled self-consciously. "You, lately."

David's chest swelled. "I know what you mean. I can think of nothing but you when we're apart."

They exchanged affectionate glances and then a little kiss. Afterward she looked around her and stopped walking. "You know what?"

"What?"

"We're walking in the wrong direction. We parked the car back there." She pointed behind them.

David smiled. "What can you expect from two dreamers?"

They did an about-face, and she took his other arm as they retraced their steps. "But how can I make myself stop daydreaming?" she asked.

"I don't think you should. How can you stop what's natural?"

"But people notice it. Especially my boss. The other day he asked if I was in Wonderland or Never Never Land."

"What goes on in your mind is no one else's business," David said. "I told you once before, you should value your imagination."

"But it gets in the way of doing my job."

"If your job doesn't hold your interest, maybe you should consider working at something else."

Veronica looked as though he'd pulled a rug out from under her feet. "But I don't know anything else. I majored in journalism in college. Working for a magazine was what I aimed for as a career."

"Why?"

"Because I thought I'd like to write. And a magazine seemed more exciting than a newspaper."

"Maybe you should be writing fiction instead. How about a novel?"

She looked downcast. "Selling novels is pretty chancy. I have to support myself. Besides, I wouldn't know what to write about. I don't really have much to say to the world."

"I'm sure you do," David said, putting his arm around her. "You just haven't learned enough about yourself yet. You're so young."

"Mr. Malloy keeps reminding me of that, too."

"Does he? I thought he liked your article about me."

"He did. But he hasn't given me any new assignments."

"Life takes patience, Veronica."

As they approached her car, she said, "That's why daydreams are better. You don't need patience. You don't have to figure out what other people want. You don't have to fit in. In a daydream you can be where you want to be. When I'm alone, I'm never bored."

David thought about her words while she unlocked her car door. He could remember feeling exactly how she'd described when he was still a mortal. But now he hated his own company.

He made no reply to her observation, not really knowing how to advise her. Some tutor I make! he thought.

When she'd gotten into the driver's seat, he closed the door and walked around to the passenger side. "Don't you live somewhere up this way?" David asked, changing the subject.

She nodded as she started the engine. "My place is between here and your house."

He had a curiosity about where she lived and what her home looked like. "Can we stop there?"

She seemed surprised. "You want to see it?"

"Yes, if you don't mind."

"It's nothing like your mansion, but I'll take you there. You'll have to watch out for my cat, though."

David stiffened. He didn't know she kept an animal. "Why? Does it bite?" he asked, keeping his voice light.

"No, Felix likes people and loves to be petted. That's the trouble. He'll get white fur all over your suit!"

In about fifteen minutes she pulled into a parking space in

front of a three-story brick apartment building on a quiet street. After she unlocked the door of her second-floor flat she opened it slowly, looking down at the floor. David understood her caution when he saw a white, furry head peek around the door.

"Hi, Felix," she said in a high voice. She bent down and picked up the cat. "I was afraid he'd run out," she told David as she walked in. "I don't like him out at night. He gets into fights with other cats."

David closed the door behind him and followed her into her living room. She put the cat on the floor, and he twisted himself around her legs, purring. Many years had passed since David had seen a cat up close. He'd forgotten what graceful creatures they were. He watched, fascinated, while Felix stretched up on his hind legs, forepaws on Veronica's blue coat, begging for her to scratch behind his ears.

"He's a beautiful animal," David murmured.

"Thank you. I've had him since I was fifteen. My parents kept him for me while I was away at college. Want to pet him?"

David hesitated. "Cats don't usually like me."

"Some cats are standoffish, but this one's friendly." She picked up the cat again and, holding him in her arms, turned to David. "Go ahead, pet him. Put out your hand first, so he can smell."

The expression in the cat's gold-green eyes instantly turned wary as he stared at David for the first time. As David slowly moved his hand toward Felix's nose, the animal's ears began to flatten. When his fingers came within two inches, the cat spit, then began to growl low in his throat.

"Shh!" Veronica said, putting her cheek against the cat's head. "I've never seen him act this way."

All at once Felix twisted in her arms and leaped over her shoulder. He hit the ground running and disappeared into the next room.

Veronica took a few steps following her pet. "I'm sorry," she said, looking back at David with shock. "I don't understand."

But David understood that animals always instinctively recognized a predator. "Don't apologize. Cats just don't take to me. I don't know why," he lied, his voice revealing more sadness than he wished.

Veronica walked back to him. "Let me take your coat."

David stood motionless, unable to respond, his eyes fixed on a red mark on the side of her chin.

Veronica was bleeding.

"What's wrong?" she asked.

David swallowed, choking down his lust as the scent of her blood reached his nostrils. "You have a small cut," he said, longing to put his tongue to it and taste. But if he did, he would only crave more.

As if becoming aware of the injury herself, she put her fingers to the cut and then looked at the blood on her fingertips. "One of his claws must have scratched me when he jumped," she said.

She looked up at David and her expression changed again, this time to fear. Had she glimpsed bloodlust in his eyes? Or perhaps she'd seen their vampire glow again. He couldn't feel the change in his eyes, only the intensity of his need.

She tried to smile. "Take off your coat. The closet's over there. I'll go wash this off." She backed away from him uneasily, then turned to go into the kitchen.

David took off his coat and hung it up. He sat down on the couch and tried to pull himself together. He had to have his intense drive under control when Veronica returned. He closed his eyes and took several long breaths. Opening his eyes, feeling somewhat quieted, he made an effort to notice his surroundings and get his mind off what had happened.

Her small living room was modestly but tastefully decorated in soft tones of off-white, aqua, and terra cotta. He felt comfortable in the casual atmosphere and began to relax. He noticed that Veronica had chosen solid colors in simple forms—no busy flower-and-insect pattern here. The couch and two easy chairs opposite were upholstered in a nubby, eggshell-colored fabric. The carpet was aqua and the curtains, like the walls, were eggshell. The terra cotta highlights came in the ceramic lamp bases, the large pots with live plants scattered around the room, and throw pillows on the furniture. On one wall was a bookcase filled with books, small plants, and decorative objects: a large beribboned porcelain cat, a ceramic vase, a miniature carousel horse.

David reached for a magazine lying on the glass-topped coffee table in front of him. It was an old issue of *Life*, May 1988, with a photograph of Clark Gable and Vivian Leigh from *Gone with the Wind* on the cover. As he leafed through, he found a number of pages inside with row after row of small reproductions of every *Life* cover dating back to 1936. This must have been a commemorative issue. As he glanced over historic covers featuring Garbo, Sandburg, Roosevelt, and Churchill, he could remember that era so clearly. He'd left England and moved to New York in the ominous, late 1930s and had remained there until the war ended. Darienne had spent those years underground, retiring to her coffin for almost a decade to completely avoid all the unpleasantness. That was Darienne for you.

But David remembered the period as one of the more interesting ones in his life, as he monitored the ravages of the two countries he loved most, England and France, from the relative safety of New York City. In the process he'd gotten used to Americans. When he'd visited America in the nineteenth century, he'd found it to be an uncouth place with sprawling, haphazard cities and its western regions not yet tamed. He had barely been able to understand the American accent—so flat and devoid of elegance, he'd thought at the time.

But while living in New York in the late 1930s and early 1940s, he'd slowly revised his earlier impressions. The nation had evolved since he'd last seen it. He began to be impressed with the pace and promise of America, which at that time was playing the role of rescuer of his homeland and powerful ally of England. How could he not admire America?

And now he was in love with an American—who knew nothing of any of this, except what she'd seen in movies or read in history books.

Veronica walked back in, carrying her coat over her arm. She smiled at him and walked to the closet to hang up the coat. David thought she looked calm, but wondered if it was just a facade to cover a lingering fear.

"Would you like something? Coffee or tea? I have some cake, too."

"No, nothing, thank you," he said, watching her walk around the sofa toward him in her shy, graceful way. "Sit down with me."

She did, but at more of a distance than usual. She was wearing a green wool dress with a wide belt. It buttoned down the front, and the collar was open, displaying a pearl necklace. He looked at the side of her chin. The scratch had stopped bleeding, and there was only a small pink mark.

He reached to touch her chin and turn her head a bit. "Is it all right?"

"Sure. It wasn't deep. I found Felix hiding under the bed," she said, shaking her head. "He never behaves that way. When I came home from work earlier and fed him, he was fine."

"Don't worry about it. Perhaps in time he'll get used to me," David told her, though he knew this would never happen. "I've been enjoying your magazine." He picked it up from his lap.

Her beautiful dark eyes seemed to light up a bit. "I saved it because Rhett and Scarlett are on the front. It has pictures of all the old covers inside."

"I've been looking at them."

"Maybe someday you'll be on the cover," she said with a smile. "No, maybe not, since you don't like publicity."

David chuckled. "It would be a difficult choice for me if the opportunity arose."

"You'd be immortalized if you made the cover of *Life*," she said.

The irony of her statement made him pause to collect his thoughts. "I like your apartment," he said finally, putting the magazine back on the table. "It reflects your personality. Beautiful and uncomplicated."

"Thank you—I think. Uncomplicated? Is that a good trait?"

She seemed to be relaxed now, like her usual self. David relaxed, too, and thought about her question. "I feel it's a good trait. Complicated people can drive others crazy. There's a peacefulness about you."

"Oh." She sounded disappointed. "I'd rather you thought I was exciting. More like Darienne."

She always came back to Darienne. Her worries about the blonde's place in his life did a lot for his ego, but he hated to see her troubled for no reason.

"No one is more uncomplicated than Darienne," he said, reaching across the space between them to take her hand. "Darienne has only one goal—to enjoy herself. She's like a queen bee. When she shows up, the hive starts humming. With you

I feel as though I'm at a mountain lake on a summer day, all serene and restful."

"I don't sound very stimulating," she said, looking down and running her fingertips over his knuckles.

"On the contrary, I find you very stimulating."

"In what way?" She looked up.

"The way you're touching my hand right now. No, don't stop."

She grinned and slid closer to him. Ah, that was better, he thought. His pulse began to pick up as he put his arm around her and drew her close.

"David?" she said, toying with his hand again. "You know the love scene in the play, where the vampire bites Claudine? What was your inspiration when you wrote that scene?"

Oh, Lord! he thought. What a question! What made her ask that? "I just imagined it. Like you, I daydream."

She looked up, her face close to his. "It's very erotic. You showed Sam Taglia exactly how to play it, too. You must have a vivid imagination."

"I do." He kissed her softly on the mouth.

"No one inspired you for that scene?" she asked, her eyes such a rich brown as she gazed at him, he lost track of her question for a moment.

"You did," he said.

Her mouth quirked prettily. "You wrote it before you ever met me."

"Then it was the anticipation of meeting you."

"Did you kiss the Blarney Stone? You have such a way with words."

"I'd rather kiss you."

She sighed, consternation passing through her eyes. "Oh, David," she whispered and stretched up to kiss him.

David gathered her in his arms, eager to experience all her warmth and femininity. He tangled his fingers into her thick, soft hair and deepened the kiss, always careful not to injure her. She slid her arms around his neck and pressed herself against him.

They'd ended each evening together this way. Her open affection was reassuring, but it challenged his resolution to let *her* choose when they would finally make love.

David's pulses were soon racing as her kisses grew more heated than usual. He moved his hand along the side of her waist and then up over the soft rise of her breast. He'd caressed her breasts through her clothing before, but whenever he tried to unbutton her dress, it always became just the moment when she decided she ought to go home. If he could step out of himself, the situation would have amused him. Four hundred years old, experienced with women of many nationalities and epochs—even rated as the best in the world by one female—and here he was, confounded by a virgin!

It occurred to him that they were at her house this time, and she couldn't leave. Should he use the opportunity to press the issue? he wondered. God, he wanted to have her! But he didn't want to frighten her, either.

As he caressed her while they continued to kiss, he could feel the nub of her hardening nipple through the material of her dress. Knowing she was aroused made his own need more intense. "Veronica, let me touch you."

She put her hand over his, cupping her breast, and looked down, as if in embarrassment.

"Are you frightened of men?" he asked when she said nothing.

Her eyes were glassy with tears when she looked at him. "A little."

"Why? Did someone hurt you once?"

She shook her head.

"Why, then?"

"I've just never let a man touch me. I'm not used to it. I'm afraid where it might lead."

"But you're twenty-three. Surely you must have let a man at least unbutton your dress."

She shook her head again.

"You haven't?" He could barely believe it, but she looked so painfully embarrassed he had to. "Why not?"

"I never met a man I wanted to touch me that way."

"No one?"

"Ordinary men—I mean men I meet in my everyday life— never seem to interest me. Like Rob Greenfield at work. He likes me, but . . ." She lifted her shoulders in a helpless gesture. "I just can't get interested in him. It's always been like that."

"But you are attracted to men?" David asked, a little confused.

"Oh, yes," she said, her eyes widening. "You know, movie stars, men in my imagination, the Vampire in your play. Though, when I met Sam Taglia in person, he seemed ordinary, too. I've always been more attracted to men who don't really exist. They just exist in my mind, perfect and larger than life. When I meet real men, they never measure up to my daydreams, so I'm disappointed and I don't want them." Two tears streamed down her cheeks. "It's awful to be this way. You know how embarrassing it is to be almost twenty-four and still a virgin? And to know it's all my own fault, even though I can't seem to do anything about it?"

David wiped away her tears with his fingertips, thinking about what she'd revealed. He could understand now why she was so different and so untouched. Her active fantasy life had kept her from experiencing what she fantasized about. It boggled his mind to think what a vivid imagination she must have, that it was strong enough to damage her this way. If only he could delve into her mind. He could have a mental union with her if he initiated her. But he reminded himself firmly that that was out of the question. But, oh, to feel what she could feel! To understand a woman's secret desires through the mind of a woman who excelled in creating such desires was an almost overwhelming temptation.

Perhaps she could tell him. "If I could see what you envision as the perfect man, what would I see?" David asked her.

She stared at him, her eyes welling again with tears. Suddenly her face crumpled and she turned away from him, weeping.

"My God, I didn't mean to upset you," he said, hugging her. "What is it?"

"It's you," she said through her tears.

"What about me?"

She took a deep breath to steady herself. "You're the perfect man. You're beyond my imagination."

The news stunned him for an instant, and then he smiled. "Then doesn't that solve everything? I want you. You want me. The problem seems very simple. In fact, there is no problem."

She shook her head, tears threatening again. "Yes, there is.

You're an experienced, worldly man. You'll be disappointed with me. And then I'll lose you."

"You won't lose me," he said, stroking her hair. "On the contrary, I'm finding your innocence, and the reasons for it, fascinating. It would be impossible for you to disappoint me."

"You think so?" she asked, the pupils of her eyes growing large as she looked at him.

"I'm sure of it."

"I do want to make love with you," she confessed, making his heart jump. "But I'm still afraid."

"Of what?"

"I don't know. Will it change me? Will it change us? What about the future?"

David was thoughtful for a few moments, considering her questions. "I imagine it will change you and us. You'll become a woman, fully. And we'll grow even closer. As for the future, I want to be with you always. I can say that with certainty."

"David." Her mouth formed the word, but her voice seemed to fail her. Her eyes became dewy again and she looked down. He could see she was too full of emotion, too overwhelmed by their conversation to make any decision tonight.

He kissed her forehead. "I think you're tired, Veronica. I'll go and let you get some rest. Shall we meet again tomorrow night?"

She looked a little dazed, but smiled. "Yes," she said, hugging him. "I'll get my car keys and drive you."

"No, don't. You need your sleep. It's late and you have to work tomorrow. I feel like walking, anyway."

"But it's too far to walk."

"I'll catch a bus or a taxi. Don't worry."

She looked unsure but got up from the couch with him as he walked to the closet to get his coat.

"One more thing," he said as they stood by the door together to say goodbye. "I love you."

Her eyebrows drew together as if in pain, and she closed her eyes. "I love you, David. You're all my dreams come true." She leaned against him and put her arms around him. In a few moments she looked up, a new awareness in her eyes that made her seem even more a woman. "I'll come to your bed soon. I want to consummate our love, too. But I need a little time yet."

"I understand," he said, his heart full of joy. "Till tomorrow night?"

"Till tomorrow."

They kissed and then he left. As he walked down the steps and headed toward the street, he replayed the things they'd said to each other, to cherish and remember them.

But one thing repeated itself and weaved through his mind ominously. "I want to be with you always," he'd told her. Unless he transformed her, made her like him, "always" was impossible. The thought tormented him.

He shut it out of his mind and refused to think about it anymore. Veronica loved him and would be his. For now that was all that mattered.

10

Through It All, His Eyes, His Eyes, His Eyes

ABOUT SEVEN o'clock in the evening Veronica drove down Division Street on her way to David's house, taking a different route than usual because an auto accident had caused a detour. The Rush Street area, to some minds, was actually centered at Division and State, a couple of blocks from the point where Rush Street ran diagonally to join State Street. There Houlihan's, Mother's, and Butch McGuire's—Butch McGuire himself claimed to be the "father of the singles bar"—stood in a row along a narrow sidewalk, all sharing the same compact, old, white-and-green, three-story building.

The traffic moved slowly, and Veronica absently gazed at the pedestrians on the sidewalk, mostly young men and women in casual dress. Above their heads hung a sign showing a red heart against a blue background with Mother's painted across the heart in large, yellow letters. Next door, beneath the white-and-green awning of Butch McGuire's, Veronica noticed a blond woman who looked familiar. Glancing at her more closely, Veronica was almost sure she was Darienne. But she was wearing a short, white leather skirt and a zippered, white leather jacket, clothing Veronica wouldn't have thought Darienne would have in her closet.

When the blonde happened to look toward her, Veronica waved and stopped the car. Darienne stepped into the street and walked up to the passenger window, which Veronica lowered with the press of a button.

"Veronica?" Darienne asked in her sensual, throaty voice. "It's a nice surprise to see you!"

"You're on your way to David?" She pronounced it Dah-veed, of course, reminding Veronica of her long-term "friend-ship" with him.

"Yes, I'm going to his home," Veronica replied. She hesi-tated, feeling a compulsion to speak to Darienne, yet not sure if she should. As she studied the blonde, who was bending to look into the car window, she sensed a similar hesitation on Darienne's part.

Darienne broke the awkward silence. "I'd like to talk to you."

"I would, too. Want to get in?"

Darienne opened the door and sat in the passenger's seat.

Veronica drove to the corner and turned, looking for a park-ing space. She continued turning corners until she found herself on Division again, where she pulled into a newly vacated spot. They were a few doors down from Butch McGuire's, where they'd started.

"It's good to see you," Darienne said. "David mentions you all the time."

"You've seen him?"

"*Mais oui,* I often visit David." Veronica felt self-conscious as Darienne looked her over, her lively, light-hued eyes noting Veronica's hair, her face, her gold earrings, her coat. "You look so pretty," Darienne said. "David is good for you, *n'est-ce pas?*"

"He's wonderful," Veronica replied. There was so much she wanted to ask Darienne, but her questions embarrassed her.

"I can see you're in love with him." Darienne smiled, reach-ing out to brush Veronica's long hair back over her shoulder with a sisterly gesture.

Veronica decided to take the bull by the horns. She looked directly at Darienne. "Are *you* in love with him?"

Darienne's smile grew more serious but didn't disappear. "I love him, but not the way you do. I have no hold on him." She checked herself. "No, that's not quite right. I do have a claim on him, but it needn't concern you. He's devoted to you, *ché-rie.*"

Veronica nodded, still troubled. She traced her gloved hand over the curve of the steering wheel.

"What is it?" Darienne asked in a nurturing tone. "You can

speak with me about anything. I think we need to have this conversation."

Veronica turned to her. "Have you ever slept with him?"

"Yes."

"Oh." Veronica faced the front window again. She'd half expected that answer, but it still came as a shock.

"Veronica, I know you're not experienced in the world, but it's best not to be naive."

"I know," Veronica whispered.

"David and I have been lovers on and off for many years. In fact"—there was a definite tinge of pride growing in Darienne's voice as she spoke—"he lost his virginity to me when he was a boy of fifteen."

Veronica couldn't help but look at Darienne with wide eyes. She couldn't even imagine David as a boy. And to picture him at that age with Darienne! "Are you older than he is?" she asked.

Darienne smiled and twisted the diamond in her earlobe. "I'm one year older. But, psychologically speaking, I'm much older than David. There's a small part of him that always stays a little naive. And he cherishes that part of himself. It's why he loves you, I think. With you he can be innocent again. I, on the contrary, was never naive. Even as a child, I could view the world clearly, and I liked what I saw. David . . ." Darienne shook her head. "David would like to change the world, you see."

"Change the world?"

"That's why he writes such profound plays, all full of angst. Did you know that when he was a boy, he wanted to be a priest?"

Veronica looked at her, astonished.

"It's true. But I changed all that." Darienne was gazing out the front window and seemed to become distracted as she watched a couple of young men walking down the street.

"You mean, because he slept with you?" Veronica asked, prodding her to continue.

Darienne replied matter-of-factly. "I trained him well. You'll enjoy him." She looked at Veronica. "You haven't yet, have you?"

"Haven't . . ." Veronica felt her face grow warm.

Darienne laughed. *"Chérie,* you can talk of these things with me. I'm a woman, like you. Well, almost like you. Do you have things you want to ask me about sex? Don't be embarrassed. I want to help."

"Why?"

Darienne's expression grew pensive. "Because I care a great deal about David's well-being. He needs you to be happy. If there's anything I can do to enhance your relationship with him, then I want to do it. It's not just for him and for you, but for me, too."

"For you?" Veronica couldn't help but be confused as to where Darienne thought she stood in all this.

"David and I have a long history. Whenever he and I are both unattached, we become lovers, as we were in the beginning. You must understand this, Veronica. My relationship with him has never ended and never will. But he and I have different outlooks. If we're together too much, we get on each other's nerves. Still, when I'm away for long periods of time, I worry about him. If I knew that he had you to look after him and keep him happy, then my life would be perfect."

Veronica couldn't quite grasp all that Darienne was telling her. There seemed to be something about it all that didn't add up.

Darienne's gaze was focused out the window again at the same two men, who now stood talking under the lamppost in front of Butch McGuire's. "It's getting a little stuffy in here," Darienne said. "Why don't we go outside?"

They got out. Veronica walked to the sidewalk and leaned against the front fender, where Darienne had already taken a seat. The blonde sat with her beautiful legs crossed at the knee, allowing her short skirt to hike up despite the evening's thirty-degree temperature, dangling her high-heeled shoe from her toe.

To Veronica, she looked like the fifties' Brigitte Bardot and the sixties' Catherine Deneuve rolled into one. Darienne unzipped her leather jacket partway, allowing a glimpse of her voluptuous cleavage. The total package of sexual knowledge and delight she presented completely undermined Veronica's confidence. If David had experienced all Darienne's sensual skills, how could he ever be happy with a self-conscious virgin?

Veronica leaned against the fender in her navy-blue coat, buttoned to the neck, and thrust her hands in her pockets, while Darienne continued to look speculatively at the two men about thirty feet away. One was tall, broad-shouldered and blond, wearing jeans, boots, and a cowhide jacket. The other was dark-haired, slimmer, dressed all in khaki with an army jacket. They both appeared to be about twenty-five. Veronica thought they were a little young for Darienne, who, she calculated, must be about thirty-five—though Darienne could have passed for almost any age.

"Think they'll come over?" Veronica asked her.

"Maybe. If not, I'll go over there—drop my handkerchief or something," Darienne said with a wry chuckle. She looked at Veronica, green eyes alight. "But I'm forgetting why we're here. Now there must be something you want to know. Ask."

There was something, something Veronica ought to have discussed with her doctor, or at least with Caroline, but was too embarrassed to do so. "Well," Veronica said with hesitation, leaning toward Darienne and lowering her voice. "I don't know much about contraceptives."

Darienne looked puzzled. "I'm not familiar with the word. Do you know it in French?"

Veronica swallowed. "Things to keep you from getting pregnant," she whispered.

Darienne's eyes widened in surprise, and then she laughed. "You're so prudent! Let me put your mind at ease. You needn't worry about that with David."

"Why not?"

"He can't have children." Darienne lifted her hands. "So you see? There's no problem. It makes the relationship so much more pleasant when there are no worries, *n'est-ce pas?*"

"Yes, but why can't he have children? Do you know that for sure?"

Darienne's usual, open expression grew a bit circumscribed. "I know it for certain. I'll let David explain to you why, if he chooses."

Veronica nodded slowly, wishing Darienne would say more, but at the same time almost relieved to find there was something Darienne *wouldn't* talk about.

"And there's something else you needn't worry about when

you and David are together," Darienne added. "Diseases. Even blood diseases. He's immune."

This was too much. "How can he be immune?" Veronica asked. "No one is immune! Did a doctor tell him that?"

Darienne pulled at the diamond in her ear again. "Perhaps I shouldn't tell you so many private things about David," she said. "I should let him explain all that in his own way. I wanted to put your mind at ease, that's all. Is there anything else you want to know? I mean, about sex."

Veronica felt as if she were lost in a mental maze and shook her head.

Darienne smiled at her, the sisterly look back again. "You seem apprehensive. David will be very gentle with you."

"What kind of lover is he?" Veronica asked, wanting to know as much for herself as to find out about his relationship with Darienne.

"David is simply the best lover in the world," Darienne said with reverence in her voice.

Veronica couldn't help but smile at what must be an exaggeration. "How can I make him happy after he's known you?" she asked, losing her smile as she spoke the words. Tears stung at the back of her eyes.

"What a question!" Darienne said. "Of course you can make him happy. I have nothing to do with what's between you and David."

"How can you not? You're so attractive and experienced. How can I compete?"

"Don't worry about competing! He loves you because you're not like me. He'll enjoy teaching you all that you don't know. He'll be gentle and worship you with his body, and you'll both be so happy." Darienne blinked. "How silly, this makes me cry! It's like a Valentine, picturing you with him. He'll be so thrilled with you."

Tears of anxiety welled in Veronica's eyes. "I hope. What will you do, now that David and I are together?"

"Me? Have fun!"

"You won't miss him?"

Darienne's gaze grew luminous—almost iridescent. "I won't come between you and David. But," she said with a tiny, knowing smile, "I told you that a part of him will always belong to me."

Veronica wanted to ask what she meant by that, but some inner voice told her to leave well enough alone for now. Besides, Darienne was distracted again. Veronica turned to find that the two men she'd been staring at were ambling down the sidewalk in their direction.

"I guess I ought to be leaving," Veronica said, not wanting to get involved in Darienne's escapade.

"You shouldn't keep David waiting," Darienne agreed. She leaned closer and whispered in Veronica's ear as the two men approached. "Go make love with David tonight. He wants you so. He'll make you deliriously happy!"

"You ladies like to have a drink?" the man in the cowhide jacket asked.

"Perhaps," Darienne said, pushing herself off the fender of Veronica's car. She stepped up to the men and smiled. "I'm Darienne Victoire."

The two men introduced themselves. Veronica was too bent on getting away to take note of their names.

"And who's this?" the other, dark-haired fellow said, smiling at Veronica.

Darienne turned back to her. For a moment Veronica was afraid she wanted to pull her in and make a foursome. But Darienne said to the men in a doting, liquid voice, "She is my good friend, but, *alors,* she has to go. She's in love, you see, and she's on her way to a rendezvous. So we mustn't keep her." Darienne took her by the shoulders and pressed her cheek lightly against Veronica's. "Good night, Veronica. I'm so glad we had this talk. Go make David happy."

Veronica felt both embarrassed and amused. And touched somehow. "Good night. Thanks for the advice."

"It's nothing. *Au revoir.*" Darienne let her go and stepped back to the men.

As Veronica walked around the front of the car to the driver's seat, she looked back and overheard their conversation.

"Are you French?" the blond man asked as he looked over Darienne's attributes.

"*Oui,*" Darienne replied. She promptly took both men's arms, walking between them, and the three began heading to-

ward the doorway of Butch McGuire's. "Do you speak
French?" she asked.

"Nope," one of them said. "But I'm willin' to learn."

Veronica chuckled as she got back into her car, wondering
how Darienne managed two men at a time. Maybe it was better
not to even speculate, she thought as she started the engine.
Besides, she had her own evening to think about.

She turned the car down State Street to Oak and pulled up
in front of David's house. David was watching through the
window for her. She got out of the car and waved as she walked
up the sidewalk. He buzzed the door open and she climbed the
spiral staircase to the top floor.

They hugged and kissed as they always did when she arrived
at his home. He was dressed more casually tonight than she'd
ever seen him before, in a thick, dark blue cotton sweater and
gray slacks. While he took her coat to the closet, she said, "I
just talked to Darienne."

"You saw her?" David said, hanging up her coat. "Where?"

"In front of Butch McGuire's. I parked and we talked for
a little while."

As David walked back to her, his eyes seemed to arm themselves. "About what?"

"You, mostly."

He took her hand and led her to the love seat. "Can I make
you some tea?"

His change of subject threw her a bit. "All right," she said.
"Thanks."

She watched David walk behind the small bar. He pulled out
a single electric burner and plugged it in, then filled a small
metal, spouted pot with water and put it on to heat. He'd done
this before, but only after she'd begun to visit him on a regular
basis. The first time he used the hot plate, he'd had trouble finding the switch to turn it on, as if he'd never used it before. She
often wondered if he'd gone out and bought it just so he could
serve her something.

The other odd thing was that David never had any tea himself. He fixed one cup for her and that was it. Nor did he ever
have any cookies or cake to go with it. Not that she wanted
any. But she'd thought even a single man would know it was
customary to serve something with tea or coffee. She'd thought

about it the other day, and in recalling each of their meetings since the beginning, she realized she'd never seen David eat. A small glass of port was the only thing she'd ever watched him consume. She did remember his once telling Darienne to help herself to refreshments in the refrigerator, and Veronica couldn't help but wonder what he kept in there. Another question was, why a hot plate and a small refrigerator? His huge mansion must have a kitchen in it somewhere. The living room was the only room she'd ever seen.

Veronica walked up to the bar instead of remaining on the love seat. "Don't you want to know what Darienne said?"

He smiled grimly as he brought out a cup and saucer from the cabinet beneath the oak bar. "Of course." His words were curt.

Veronica hesitated but had to continue. "She wished us happiness."

He raised his eyebrows a bit. "Did she? How nice."

"But she said other things that left me a little confused."

"Darienne has that effect on people."

"What's wrong, David? Are you angry with her? Or me?"

"I'm not angry with you," he said. "But if you want to talk about me with someone, I wish you wouldn't choose Darienne. If there's something on your mind, why don't you come to me?"

"It was pure chance that I ran into her tonight. I didn't plan it. And there are some things that are easier for a woman to talk about with another woman." Veronica felt hurt that he was obviously annoyed, if not angry.

"Veronica, I assure you, you have far more in common with me than with Darienne. She's not a good influence on you, not one you should go to for advice."

"You told me once you loved her. How can you criticize her so much?"

"I can love her and still recognize her faults," David said. "You haven't had enough experience with her to know her as I do."

"Yes, I know about your experience with her." Veronica's voice was hushed.

David stared at her in that still way of his, while the water on the hot plate began to boil. "So she told you we've been lovers."

Veronica nodded.

"Diable!" he exclaimed under his breath as his eyes took on an incandescent light. "Damn her for interfering!"

Veronica felt weak inside, trembling at the unearthly anger in his eyes. "It's not her fault. I asked her."

"You *asked* her if . . ."

"If she'd slept with you."

"Why? What has my past with her got to do with you?"

"I just needed to know, that's all," Veronica said, backing away from the bar a bit because his eyes frightened her. She hated to see him like this—he seemed almost inhuman. "If Darienne was going to be my rival, then I wanted to know and not have to go on guessing."

His voice softened. "Can't you believe me when I tell you I'm in love with you, that no one else even comes close to you in my estimation?"

"But I didn't know what was in Darienne's mind."

"No one knows what's in Darienne's mind. You might as well ask your cat!"

Veronica felt dumbfounded. "If you think so little of her, why have you had such a long-term relationship?"

David lowered his eyes and turned to take the hot water off the burner. He poured water into the cup on the counter between them. "Because I was young and wet behind the ears when I met her."

"She seduced you, didn't she?"

"Lord, what *didn't* Darienne tell you?" Without thinking, he touched the bottom of the metal pot he was holding with the fingertips of his other hand. "Ouch!" he exclaimed, almost dropping the pot. He set it back on the burner and unplugged the hot plate.

"Did you burn yourself?" she asked, leaning over the counter. "Let me see."

He examined the tips of his long fingers. "It's all right."

"But you put your hand right on the bottom of the pot. Do you have some ointment for it?"

"It's all right, Veronica. See?" He held out his hand for her to look at.

She took his hand, cradling it in hers, and looked at his fingertips. There was no mark at all. "It might show up later," she said with concern. "It doesn't hurt?"

"Not at all," he said, reaching up to stroke her face with his burned hand. He leaned over the bar and kissed her, his kiss like a benediction.

In the spell of the moment she said, "I love you, David. I'm sorry if I've upset you."

"It's just that my past with Darienne has nothing to do with you, and I don't want you to worry about her."

"Darienne told me the same thing."

David smiled thoughtfully. "Did she? Well, then, perhaps I'm not giving her enough credit."

"In fact," Veronica said with some embarrassment, "she urged me to make love with you. Which is what I thought was odd, since she told me that she thinks you're a wonderful lover. I would have thought she'd want to keep you for herself."

David carefully reached into a box of tea bags he'd pulled out and dropped one into the cup. "Darienne is basically an amoral person. She has her good qualities, her random moments of nobility, but she has no scruples. 'Live for the moment' is her philosophy. She knows I don't approve of her. And she can't keep me for herself, because she never stays around long enough to do that, even if I'd let her. There *is* a certain sexual attraction between us that I won't deny. But, beyond that, we have little in common, intellectually, spiritually, or philosophically."

Those last three heavy-duty words troubled Veronica. "What do you think you and I have in common?" she asked, afraid of the answer. "I'm certainly not your intellectual equal. And I don't know much about philosophy or spiritual matters."

He smiled and picked up her cup of tea. She followed as he walked to the love seat and sat down, setting her tea on the table in front of them. He pulled her down to sit close to him. "First of all," he said, touching his finger to the tip of her nose, "your intellect and philosophy will develop. Unlike Darienne, you have a questioning mind and are eager to learn. It's on the spiritual level that I feel you and I have a great affinity. You seem to experience the world the way I do, with the same sensi-

tivity and imagination that so many others don't possess.
You're my soul mate. I've searched for you forever."

"You make me feel so special," she acknowledged with awe.

"You are special. It's why you don't fit into the workaday
world you live in. I never did, either. So I live here, alone, away
from the world, and write. But now that there's you, I won't
have to be alone."

"I only feel alive when I'm with you." She was trying to express her own feelings, wishing she could be as eloquent as he.
"My dreamworld becomes real, and there's nothing but us."

"Exactly," he said, taking her into his arms. He kissed her
gently, running his hands over her body, feeling the curve of
her hip, the indentation of her small waist, the rise of her
breasts through her knit dress.

As he caressed her more and more ardently, she recalled Darienne's urgings to go ahead and make love with David. But
then her fear that she could never compete with the voluptuous
blonde returned. All the high-flown language about spirituality
and their special affinity seemed to fade when it came to the
basics of mating, basics that Veronica still knew little about
other than what had been explained once in a brief lesson on
sex in school. Her mother had always been too embarrassed
to speak on the subject at home.

And Veronica's knowledge of the passion of sex came only
from movies, scenes of people writhing together beneath satin
sheets, voicing incoherent whispers and groans. David seemed
so cerebral, it was difficult to imagine him naked and overtaken
by such nonintellectual passion. More than that, it was hard
for Veronica to imagine herself that way.

As David started to unbutton the front of her dress, Veronica
took hold of his hands and stopped him. Breathless from his
kisses, she said, "David, I thought about us making love all day
today. I couldn't get any work done. But now I'm not sure I
can go through with it yet."

"Why?" he asked, his voice and eyes so sad it made her heart
break.

"I . . ." She hated to mention Darienne again, but what could
she do? She might as well be honest; David would want her
to be. "Knowing you've been with Darienne makes it hard. I

understand that you had a life before you met me. But I'm not like her."

"Thank God."

"But, David, I know I'll disappoint you. I'll be silly and clumsy. Darienne understands sex and I don't."

"You only have to experience it once to understand. Don't you want to know what it's like? If you thought about it all day, you must."

She hesitated, then slowly let go of his hands. Her mind raced with old-fashioned proprieties, with the awareness of being different from her peers, with thoughts of the consequences if she did or didn't let David make love to her.

But her body ached for his touch, and she found herself making the decision even before she was aware she had. She began unbuttoning her dress herself. But the knit material was hard to work over the small buttons, especially when her hands were trembling.

"Help me," she whispered, looking up at him. "Teach me this, too."

Gently he took over and unfastened the buttons one by one to her waist. The manipulations of his fingers against her skin gave her goose bumps. He pulled the dress material apart, exposing her small breasts.

He ran his fingertips lightly over her pink nipples, which contracted at his touch into pointed little nubs. As he bent and took one nipple in his warm mouth, she gasped.

"God, you're lovely!" he whispered as he moved to her other nipple. She almost wept at his words and at the acute, beautiful sensations his lips created on her sensitive skin.

He raised his head and kissed her mouth while his hands pushed the dress off her shoulders and down her arms. He drew away a bit so he could help her pull her hands out of the sleeves. She looked down at her body, nude to the waist. An urge to cover herself with her hands threatened to overcome her, but she quelled it, knowing it was foolish now that he'd already seen, kissed, and caressed her. Gazing up at him, she found him looking at her with eyes that positively adored her. Their blue was deep and rich and shone with the light of love.

"I could weep at your beauty, Veronica. You're so precious to me. I want to feel your skin on mine."

In an instant he'd pulled off his own sweater and tossed it aside. Veronica was stunned at his revealed chest. His body was breathtaking in its virility. His shoulders and pectoral muscles were surprisingly developed, while his waist and deep rib cage rippled tightly with each breath he took. In his elegant, tailored clothes, he'd always seemed so refined. The sheer male power those clothes had hidden thrilled and frightened her.

"No wonder you're so strong," she whispered, reaching out to touch his biceps.

He reached around her and clasped her against him, her soft breasts flattening against his chest. The quick movement startled her, the force of him pushing the breath from her lungs. He kissed her then, harder than he ever had before, holding her so tightly, she couldn't breathe. And yet the power of him swept her away, and she didn't want him to stop. She felt herself sinking, losing contact, growing limp. A sharp pain at her lip brought her back. She tried to twist away.

Instantly he withdrew his mouth and loosened his hold. "Have I hurt you? I'm sorry," he said, stroking her cheek as she regained her breath and put her fingers to her lip.

"I thought I felt something." She looked up at him uneasily, remembering that night at the back of the house when his teeth had looked so strange. She drew her hand away, but there was no blood. Still her lip felt tender.

David looked aghast. "I'm sorry. I want you so much, I forget how frail you are. Tell me if I'm hurting you. You must tell me, my angel. I don't want to injure you."

"No," she said, trying to smile. "Don't be sorry. I'm overreacting, I'm sure. I'm not used to men. I didn't realize how strong a man can be."

Gently he pulled her against him, stroking her breast, then running his hand down her dress to her thigh. "I won't harm you, believe me." He kissed her hair, her forehead. "I love you. I need you." His voice lowered to a husky whisper. "I want to be one with you."

Veronica felt herself grow pale. She wasn't sure if she could withstand the experience. She wished now she'd already been with other men, ordinary men. Rob Greenfield, maybe. She probably would have been able to cope, to muddle her way through the sex act with him. And it wouldn't have mattered what happened, because she didn't care about him.

But David was too much for her—too strong, too profound, too overwhelming. And she loved him.

"I . . ." She paused to catch her breath and her wits. "How? Wh-where? Here on the love seat?" She felt foolish asking about logistics. David must think her horribly unromantic. But she honestly didn't know what to do next. And she was scared to death.

Instead of laughing or being annoyed, his eyes sparkled, as if an idea had come to him. "You're absolutely right. This isn't suitable at all. I have a better place to take you."

"Your bed?" she asked, the thought making her feel faint.

He looked at her oddly for a moment, then smiled. "No. Someplace you can't even imagine." He nuzzled his chin to her cheek. "Let's undress and then I'll take you there."

He said the words so blithely, he obviously didn't realize how traumatic it was to her to remove all her clothes in front of him. She saw him unbuckling his belt and turned away, not wanting to watch. Mechanically, trying not to think about what she was doing, she took off her own clothes.

When she'd finished, she shyly turned to him. "Come with me," he said, lifting her into his arms so swiftly, she felt she was floating. Carrying her tenderly, he walked past the bar, through a door, and down a long, dark hall. They passed several rooms, most with closed doors. She managed a glimpse through one door that was open. The room inside seemed completely empty, except for a ceiling light fixture of cut glass that sparkled in the moonlight that shone through a window.

He passed through a large double door of carved wood and entered a huge, empty room bathed in pale silver moonlight. Three magnificent chandeliers glittered from the high ceiling, and long, heavy, gold draperies hung over the windows along one wall. The windows were high, in three groups, with a deep, cushioned, built-in seat below each group.

The polished wood floor creaked slightly as he carried her in. Over his shoulder she could see a wide-screen television set, which seemed totally incongruous, both for the room and for David.

"How do you like it?" David asked as he set her on her feet.

The moonlight made her own skin and David's appear pale and luminous. The moon and the vast, empty beauty of the room made her feel as if she'd entered another world.

"I've never seen anything like this. It looks like a ballroom."

"It is," he said, putting his arm around her and drawing her across the expansive floor toward the nearest window.

"You use this as your TV room?" she asked, smiling as she pointed to the wide-screen in one corner.

"I play old Kelly or Astaire movies sometimes. I try to dance to them."

"Really? You'll have to show me!"

"Someday. Not now." He picked her up in his arms again.

Veronica realized with a stab of panic that there was no way out now, no detour. David had brought her here especially to make love, to give her her first sexual experience.

He laid her on the velvet cushions of the window seat. The windows were built out from the wall of the mansion, like bay windows. Looking around her from where she lay, she found glass on three sides and overhead. She could see the stars and the moon as she gazed up.

"It's like being outside," she murmured. In the distance were the black outlines of skyscrapers, their lights like little diamonds, set against the midnight blue of the clear sky. The sheer quiet and beauty of it made her relax a bit. "This is a wonderful place."

David carefully swung himself over her, and gradually allowed the weight of his body to sink onto hers. She was afraid he would crush her, but instead, his body felt warm and comfortable on top of hers.

"Am I hurting you at all?" he asked with a little kiss.

"No."

Raising himself on his elbows, he looked out the window and then down at her, smiling. "You don't know how many times I've sat alone at this very window, waiting and wishing for you."

"But we've been together almost every—"

"I meant before I ever met you. When I had no one and my world seemed so empty. You fill every void. There's no other woman for me but you, Veronica. My adorable little innocent. You're completely mine now."

Veronica's heart began to thud and her chest began to rise and fall beneath his with her anxious breaths. "David, I'm scared."

"Of me?"

"Yes."

"I won't harm you. I promise. I promise."

"Will I change? Will it change us?"

"It is a type of transformation, I suppose," David said, his eyes melancholy, yet luminous with reflected moonlight. "You won't be quite the childlike creature you are now, I'm sure. I'll miss the old Veronica but welcome the new. This can only bring us closer, unite us in body as well as spirit."

Veronica swallowed and whispered, "Then make love to me, David."

Cradling her head between his hands, he brought his mouth to hers and kissed her, long and gently. His hands traveled down her arms, to her breasts, tantalizing her nipples with deft strokes of his thumbs. His mouth left her lips, moved over her throat without touching her, and went to her breast where he teased her nipple again. The sensation sent little shock waves through her, making her writhe softly against him.

He moved his hand down her smooth stomach to the place between her thighs no man had ever touched. It embarrassed her at first, but instantly his touch sent such a transfixing sensation through her, she cried out softly. She'd grown moist, and he used her secretions as a balm on her body's most sensitive area, his fingers urging and caressing her, slipping inside her now to tantalize her more, until she grew delirious with pleasure and need.

She closed her eyes and put her arms around him. "Oh, David, I've never felt this way before."

"You must tell me what you want, what gives you the most pleasure."

The pleasure he spoke of was becoming so intense, it was beginning to be painful—a type of urgent tension she'd never felt before.

"David!" she cried, putting her thigh over his. "It's too much."

"Shhh. I'll soothe you." He took his hand away.

"Don't stop—"

And then he moved against her, and all at once she felt him enter her, a thick, velvet shaft, too big for her body to allow. Her eyes shot open and she looked at the moon as if for help as she cried out in pain. Tears spilled from her eyes and down her cheeks as she clutched him in panic.

"I'm sorry," he whispered. "I didn't want to hurt you, but it can't be helped." He stayed still over her and wiped the tears from her face with his hand. His own eyes were pale as he hovered over her. "Is it better?"

And all at once she noticed the pain was gone. All she was aware of was that David was inside of her, filling an empty place she hadn't realized existed until this moment. She smiled and said in a breathless voice, "So much better. You make me feel whole."

A tear ran down his cheek. Then his mouth met hers in a joyous kiss while his body began to move with long, languid thrusts, causing a whole new sensation to spring up within her. Sensual whimpers came from her throat with each pull and push. He drew his mouth away, as if to concentrate on the center of their lovemaking, and Veronica lay back and closed her eyes, stroking his back and small, firm buttocks. She'd never felt such pleasure, such closeness with another human being.

But again the pleasure grew into pulsing urgency and then to demand. "Oh, God, David. David. Oh, David . . ."

As his thrusts grew stronger, he gripped her upper arms more tightly and drew his mouth along her chin in a series of heated kisses. His mouth moved down her neck, slowly, almost reluctantly, as if he didn't want to but couldn't stop himself. When he reached the pulse point at the side of her neck, his mouth stopped, resting on her skin. She felt him press his tongue into her artery as if to feel its pulse. His breathing grew erratic.

Instinctively she moved her head away, sensing something was not right. He drew back then and looked down at her, his eyes a radiant cobalt-blue that penetrated to her core. And yet they were full of anguish, anguish mixed with sexual desire and something else. Something that seemed like an unwholesome passion.

Veronica pressed her hands against his shoulders, wanting to get away. She gasped for breath and began to cry.

"Don't be afraid. It's all right," he told her. "There's nothing wrong. Nothing wrong. I won't hurt you."

He looked and sounded so desperately sincere, she stopped fighting him and tried to relax. But the unearthly light in his eyes remained, unnerving her. She looked away, out the window at the moon.

"What's wrong? Tell me."

"Your eyes," she said, her face averted. "They frighten me."

"Then don't look at them. Don't think about it." He moved against her in his slow, sensual way. Quickly, so quickly it seemed to her obscene, her desire for fulfillment returned.

She closed her eyes as the momentum between them increased, until she could barely stand it. "David, it's too much! I feel like I'll die if this goes on." Forgetting, she looked at him. His eyes were still iridescent and strange, but now they mesmerized her while she grew supercharged with building passion. She couldn't take her gaze from his. His eyes shone on her with love and warmth and heat, transfixing her, bringing her to a new realm that was beyond the physical.

With a last, savage thrust of his pelvis that should have hurt her, her body exploded in ecstasy. She cried out, clinging to him, as wave after wave of supreme pleasure surged through her. He stiffened and she felt his fulfillment within her at the same time. For a few moments time ended, disappearing along with gravity and heat and cold, and she felt as if she were floating with him on a cloud of moonlight, through the radiant atmosphere, up amongst the dazzle of the chandeliers as lights burst and flashed about her. And through it all, his eyes, his eyes, his eyes . . .

And then everything softly settled into place. There she was, lying on the window seat beneath David, spent and deliriously fulfilled, while David lovingly stroked her hair back from her face. His eyes were adoring, reflecting the moonlight now, as any other pale blue eyes would.

"Are you happy, Veronica? Have I pleased you?"

"David." She put her arms around him tightly to hug him. They sat up on the seat, and Veronica leaned against him, burying her head between his neck and shoulder. "I'm so happy. So happy with you. I love you so much."

He seemed to hesitate. "I didn't mean to frighten you."

"It was me, David," she said, hugging him closer. "Silly me and my imagination." She reached up and stroked his cheek. "I'll never be frightened of you again. Not after tonight."

As David lay in his narrow chamber at dawn, he thought back on his sweet moments of rapture with Veronica. She'd delighted him as no other woman ever had with her fragile, supple body, her soft sighs of pleasure, the loving, innocent way she'd given herself to him.

She'd stayed with him almost the whole night. They'd talked, they'd watched *An American in Paris,* even tried to imitate the dance sequence with humorous results. He'd never experienced such an enjoyable night. Finally she'd given herself to him again, with eagerness this time and no trace of fear.

The only detail to mar David's complete happiness had been his strong urge to take Veronica's blood. He'd thought he had managed to mentally subdue his bloodlust, but he hadn't foreseen that she would shed a few drops when he took her virginity. The scent of her blood combined with the heated pulsing of the artery in her throat had brought back his need in spite of his self-control.

But when she gave herself to him again a few hours before dawn, he'd regained full command of himself, and their second coupling had been unshadowed by his darker side. He and Veronica would be able to maintain a normal, mortal relationship, he was sure of it now.

Poor Veronica, he thought with concern. He had the day to rest, but she had to go to work after being with him all night. He'd reminded her that she needed her sleep. But she'd wanted him again, and he hadn't been able to deny her or himself that tender ecstasy. He hoped she would be all right during the long day, while he rested and dreamed of her. Veronica, the beautiful new angel of his night world, his godsend just when he was about to lose all hope.

If only God *had* sent her to him. In truth, David felt as if he'd stolen her from God's protective care. And someday, no doubt, David would have to answer for his action. But it didn't matter. Veronica's love was worth any punishment.

11

A Little Mystery She'd Always Wondered About

ROB GREENFIELD didn't have a lot of insight into women, but he'd have had to be blind not to see the change in Veronica. And it wasn't hard to guess who had robbed her of that innocent, untouched quality. She had to be sleeping with David de Morrissey.

Why should he care? Rob asked himself as he watched her pass his office. She was walking slowly, as if too tired to move. Through the glass partition he could see her enter her cubicle, yawning as she took off her heavy coat, almost too exhausted to lift it onto the clothes tree.

She was late again, too, he noticed. She'd been late every day for the past week—since Friday, to be exact. In his angrier moments Rob sometimes toyed with the idea of confronting her and telling her he knew exactly when de Morrissey had seduced her: last Thursday night. He didn't know the hour, but he could guess it must have been late. She'd come in on Friday looking as if she hadn't had any sleep. But in her eyes and around her mouth there had been a knowing, self-satisfied sensuality he'd never seen in her face before.

She'd been such an ingenuous, unworldly young woman, Rob thought with pain. Why did de Morrissey have to take her?

And why had it been de Morrissey? Always, with Veronica, everything centered on David de Morrissey. David says this. David likes that. Rob hated his own jealousy, his feeling of insignificance. His shoulders slumped as he leaned back in his chair. Other women seemed to think him attractive. There were at least two in the office who constantly angled to go to lunch with him, even invited him home for dinner. Why not the one woman he'd wanted?

Should he have come on tougher? Bolder? Or would Veronica have been more attracted if he'd given her the cold shoulder? Sensitivity, patience, sincerity—traits he'd thought a woman like her would appreciate—had gotten him nowhere. He might as well have been a store mannequin for all she'd ever noticed him.

Still, despite her obliviousness of him, he cared about what was happening to her, what she was letting de Morrissey do to her. The notorious playwright might have spoiled her innocence, but he wasn't going to ruin her life, not if Rob could help it.

Rob got up and looked through the glass partition into her cubicle. She was sitting at her desk now, her chin in her hand, ready to fall asleep. Her hair, which she usually kept so neat, was windblown, and she hadn't combed it. Softly disheveled, it tumbled about her shoulders. As she sat there, shadows under her closed eyes, Rob thought she looked like a beautiful doll that had been played with too roughly. If he didn't take some action, she'd soon be broken.

He got up to head for the door, automatically straightening his tie as he went. Noticing the habitual gesture, he suddenly undid the Windsor knot and took off the tie, tossing it on his desk. He unbuttoned his shirt collar, shrugged off his jacket, and rolled up his shirtsleeves to the elbow. Veronica needed to see him differently, some instinct told him. And she needed to see that he meant business.

Rob strode into her office and stopped directly in front of her desk. Veronica was dozing and didn't even notice him.

He spoke softly but sternly, imitating their boss. "Gonna make your deadline?"

She lifted her head with a start and looked up. "I'll have it—" The sight of Rob stopped her. "What about my deadline?"

"What if I'd been Ed Malloy?"

"What do you mean?" she asked. With her fingertips she rubbed her bleary eyes. The lids looked heavy.

"What kind of impression would you have made on the boss, sitting there asleep?"

She took a long breath and exhaled. Rob couldn't help but notice her soft, full lips. He'd always thought she had one of the most kissable mouths he'd ever seen. Her lips were naturally full, but today he noticed they seemed swollen. De Morrissey's work, no doubt. The unwanted vision of Veronica being used by another man swept through Rob's mind and fed his anger. Why did she go on seeing the playwright? He couldn't believe that a young woman as delicate as Veronica would *like* such treatment.

Then again, Rob thought, maybe he was trying to keep her on some pedestal from which she'd gladly fallen.

"I guess Mr. Malloy wouldn't have been impressed," she admitted. "I'll get myself some coffee."

"You need more than coffee. You need to get some sleep at night."

"I've been having trouble sleeping," she said.

"Why don't you ask him to give you a break?"

She stared up at Rob. "Who?"

"Your insatiable playwright."

Rob watched her blush, confirming his suspicions. He swallowed the exploding jealousy within him. His purpose was to help her, not make accusations.

"I don't know what you mean," she said in a testy voice.

Rob walked to the back of her office and picked up a metal chair. He slid it across the low-pile carpet to a position close to her chair and sat facing her.

"What are you doing?" She shoved her own chair back a few inches, as if trying to keep a distance between them.

"I want to talk. Since our offices don't have doors, I'll have to keep my voice low."

"Talk about what?"

"Your affair with de Morrissey."

Her jaw dropped. "Why are you so sure I'm having one?"

"It's pretty obvious. You used to come in on time, looking fresh and neat. And awake. Something must have changed in the past week. I figure it's a man keeping you up all night, and it's not hard to guess who that man is."

"Why assume that? I might be up taking care of a sick relative."

Rob had to laugh. "Are you?"

She wet her swollen lips. "I don't see how this is any of your business."

"Maybe it's not. But I'm really worried about you. If Ed hasn't already noticed your excessive fatigue, he's going to see your work going downhill. By the way, I've covered for you a couple of times."

She brushed her hair away from her face, looking puzzled. "Covered for me?"

"Ed went by your office looking for you before you came in late yesterday. I told him you were in the ladies' room. And earlier in the week, when you'd fallen asleep at your desk, I saw him coming and headed him off with some excuse so he wouldn't find you that way."

Her brown eyes looked guilty and a little scared. "Thank you. I didn't realize."

"You've got to manage your life better," Rob told her, feeling for her now. Obviously she'd gotten caught up in something she didn't know how to handle. "If your personal life interferes this much with your job, pretty soon you won't have a job."

She nodded a little, her eyes moist. "I know, but how can I control such a strong emotion?"

Rob had a sick, sinking feeling in his stomach. "What strong emotion?"

"I love David. He loves me. It's so hard for us to separate after we've been together." Veronica's voice was soft, sensual, full of adoration. Her eyes were dreamy, as though she were lost in her own feelings, as if her lover were before her now in her imagination. "He gives me so much, and he lets me give it back," she went on, her voice dwindling to a whisper. "I want to be with him all the time."

Rob felt envious, not only of David de Morrissey for winning Veronica, but of the profound bond she seemed to have experienced with him. Her desire seemed unhealthy, but so potent Rob wished he could experience such a love himself. He tried to keep hold of his natural common sense. He had to make Veronica realize her relationship was bad for her.

"You sound like you're under a witch's spell," Rob told her, attempting to chuckle but not succeeding. "If he loves you, why is he stressing you beyond your limits? Why does he keep you out so late? Doesn't he sleep at night?"

"He says he doesn't need much sleep. It never seems stressful to me when I'm with him. He's often told me to go home and get some sleep, but I can't leave, knowing I could spend the time with him instead."

A suspicion crossed Rob's mind. "He's not making you do drugs, is he?"

"No, of course not! He would never do anything to hurt me."

"But don't you see, he is? Pretty soon you'll be so run down you'll get sick."

"I've been taking vitamin C," she said, opening up her drawer and pulling out the bottle to show him. "B complex, too."

Rob smiled. "Vitamins aren't enough. You need rest."

"I need David."

Rob leaned toward her, looking her in the eye, his tone gentle but insistent. "Veronica, something's wrong here. You sound like you're obsessed, not in love."

"I *am* in love! How dare you tell me what I feel?"

"All right, all right," he said, leaning back, realizing he'd never convince her otherwise. "Can't you work out some more sensible schedule if you have to go on seeing him? See each other on weekends, like most people do."

"But he works weekends, too."

"He writes every day? So you never see him during the daytime?"·

"No."

"What, does he live like a vampire so he can identify better with his characters?"

"Rob!"

"Well, you have to admit it's pretty strange. And you're letting him alter your whole life to suit his."

"He's brilliant and maybe a little eccentric," Veronica said, opening the vitamin C bottle and taking out two tablets. "I don't mind giving up my convenience for someone as remarkable as he is."

"You're giving up more than convenience. You're giving up your mental and physical health!"

"You're getting melodramatic." Her tone was impatient as she set the two tablets on a piece of paper.

"Veronica, look at you. Your eyes are bloodshot, you're too

tired to work, and you're obsessed with this guy. Is he that good in the sack that he's worth all this?"

She set down the bottle sharply, making the tablets inside rattle. "I won't listen to you talk about David in such a crass way!"

"I'm just trying to make you see what he's doing," Rob said, sitting on the edge of the chair, gesturing sharply. "You think he's showing love for you? He's using you up! When he's had his fill and worn you out, he'll throw you away."

"David loves me!"

Rob jerked back his chair suddenly and got to his feet. He was fed up trying to reason with her. "You're just naive! Looks like you'll have to learn a tough lesson the hard way."

She shook her head at him, her eyes fiery. "You think David's like other men. But he isn't at all. He's far superior in ways you can't even imagine."

Her blind devotion irked Rob. "Pretty soon you'll be deifying him. Already you're sacrificing your body on his altar!"

"Get out!" she whispered harshly, angry tears starting in her eyes.

Rob wished he could retract what he'd just said. Anger was getting the better of him, too. This wasn't at all how he'd wanted his talk with her to go.

"I'm sorry I said that," he told her quickly. "For your sake, I hope you're right about de Morrissey. But if not, remember: I'll still be here for you when he's long gone."

Veronica clung to David, her head resting at his shoulder while his arm around her kept her close. They were out walking near Washington Square, an open park of grass and trees across the street from the Newberry Library. It was after midnight. They walked along the sidewalk in front of the library. The building was made of stone, and its high, arched windows looked dark and a bit ominous at night.

"I need to try to get home earlier tonight," she told David. "I'm not getting enough sleep."

"I know you aren't," he said with concern, giving her an extra squeeze, "and tomorrow's a work day for you. I'm sorry I'm monopolizing your time."

"It's my fault." She gazed into his eyes. They were translucent in the dim light of the street lamps. "I hate going home. I'd rather stay with you." Yearning overtook her as she felt the swaying of his strong body as he walked. "Will we make love when we get back?"

Desire mixed with sadness in David's eyes. "But we just decided you need to go home and sleep. And we already made love tonight."

"Why does it have to be this way?" she said, sighing. "Why do I have to trade you for sleep?"

"This is what I tried to warn you about." David sounded as if he felt guilty. "That you'd have to adjust your life to suit mine. I'm sorry, there's no other way. We'll have to be more strict with ourselves. I don't want you becoming ill."

They were approaching the steps and the arched main entrance of the library. "Maybe there's another way," Veronica said hesitantly. David looked at her, waiting for her to go on. She swallowed. "Maybe we could live together. I'd be at work during the day, so I wouldn't be in your way when you're writing. And that way we'd have more time for everything."

His eyes shone with a quiet light. "You'd really like to live with me? How I wish we could."

"But why not?"

Before David could reply, someone darted out from the shadows of the library entrance and stepped in front of them. He was a tall man, taller than David, with untidy blond hair and wearing a shabby coat. In his hand he held a gun pointed at David.

"Pull out your wallet or you'll get hurt!"

Veronica turned cold, staring at the gun. She looked up at David, afraid for him. David, however, seemed grim but calm. "I'm not carrying much money."

"Gimme what you got, or I swear I'll blow your head off!" He followed the threat with crude language.

David did nothing, as if thinking about the situation. Veronica was astonished. "Give it to him, David."

David took his wallet from his pants pocket, opened it, and took out all the bills he had—three dollars.

"You got more than that!"

"I haven't."

"Open it out! Where's your credit cards?"

"I don't use them," David said, showing him the sections of his almost empty wallet.

The man spit out an expletive, grabbed the wallet, and threw it onto the sidewalk. He leveled his gun at Veronica. "Let's have your purse, lady."

"Don't go near her!" David warned, stepping closer.

The man turned the gun toward David again. "Stay where you are!"

"I've had enough of this." David's voice was cold as death. "Move away, Veronica."

"No, David—"

David pushed her away from him, keeping his eyes on the mugger. She stepped backward, losing her balance for a moment. When she looked up again, David was moving slowly toward the man, despite the gun pointed at his chest. His eyes had taken on their strange cobalt sheen, radiating icy power.

The mugger appeared struck with horror, his mouth half-open, his face stiff with fear. "Get away from me!" he told David, who kept moving closer to him until the gun was only an inch from his coat.

"Look at me," David said.

The man's eyes widened in terror. "No!" He fired the gun.

As Veronica shrieked, David bent forward, clutching his chest. The mugger backed away, then turned and started to run.

Instantly David went after him, in spite of his obvious pain. He grabbed hold of the man from the back and lifted him off the ground, then hurled him onto the concrete sidewalk with such force that Veronica could hear bones break.

She felt sick to her stomach but rushed to David's side. He was bending over the man, checking his carotid artery for a pulse.

"He shot you!" she wailed, tears streaming down her face. She took David's arm. "We've got to call an ambulance."

"I'm all right." David stood up and looked at the crumpled body at his feet. "He needs one, though."

"You must be hurt," she said as she unbuttoned David's overcoat. "I saw the flash. I heard the shot."

"The gun misfired."

She opened his jacket and saw a dark spot on his shirt. In

the dim light she couldn't tell if it was red, but she was sure it must be blood. "David, we've got to get an ambulance for you!"

He took hold of her shoulders. "Calm down, Veronica! I'm all right. We'll call an ambulance for him."

She glanced at the mugger, who still lay motionless on the sidewalk, then at David, who obviously had regained his strength despite his momentary pain and now seemed to feel perfectly well. Maybe the gun *had* misfired. Maybe the mark on his shirt was from the flash she'd seen. How lucky David was! she thought. Thank heaven!

David picked up his wallet from the sidewalk, took Veronica's hand, and hurried her down the street in the direction they'd come from.

"We've got to call the police, too, and report this," she said.

"No."

"But—"

"No police! I don't want publicity. The ambulance driver will contact the police, and they can make what they want of the incident."

"But he's a criminal."

"If he lives, I think he'll have learned his lesson."

"I wonder if anyone saw it happen," she said, glancing at the park across the street as they raced along. She couldn't see anyone among the trees, but it was too dark to be sure.

"We'll have to take that chance."

His attitude upset her. She understood his desire to avoid publicity, but someone had tried to rob him, had even tried to kill him. Surely justice should be done. Also, if David had seriously injured the man or even killed him, and there were witnesses, wouldn't it be better, she asked herself, for David to report the incident himself?

Soon they were back on Oak Street. David stopped at a pay phone in front of a hair salon down the street from his mansion. He fished through his pockets for change.

"Why don't we just phone from your house?" she asked.

"They might trace the call."

Veronica hadn't realized until then just what lengths he would go to to avoid publicity. A man had almost murdered David, and he was worried about being traced!

He found a coin and dialed 911. "There's an injured man lying on the sidewalk in front of the Newberry Library," David said and hung up. He turned to Veronica. "Quickly, let's go home."

In a few minutes they walked into David's third-floor living room. As soon as he turned on the lamps, Veronica went up to him. Before he could take his coat off, she ran her hand down the front of it—and found a hole about the size of a dime.

"David!" she exclaimed. "The gun didn't misfire!"

Quickly she looked underneath at his jacket and found a similar hole. Beneath that his white shirt also had a hole, rimmed with a small amount of blood. "You're shot!" she cried. "We've got to call a doctor!"

"No!" He shrugged off his overcoat and jacket, then unbuttoned his shirt. "Look. I'm all right."

She looked closely at the spot beneath the hole in his shirt, just at the front of his rib cage, below and to the left of his sternum. The skin was discolored there, mottled and pink beneath traces of dried blood. But there was no break in his skin, no bullet hole.

"Are you satisfied?" he asked, his tone gentle as she carefully moved her fingers over the spot.

Of course she was relieved to see he wasn't badly injured. But she didn't understand. "How can you have bullet holes in your clothes and not be shot? You weren't wearing a bullet-proof vest."

"It must be one of those freak things. Perhaps a faulty bullet."

Veronica couldn't help but think of another explanation. According to all the old movies, vampires could be shot and not be affected. The creatures perhaps felt momentary pain, like that David had seemed to experience, and then they recovered. She also couldn't help but think that such an explanation would also account for David's extraordinary strength, demonstrated in the way he'd hurled the mugger to the ground.

But it was impossible. Vampires didn't exist.

"What are you thinking?" David asked, studying her face. "You look so dreadfully somber."

She shook away her thoughts. "I—I just don't understand

how he could have shot you at close range and yet the bullet didn't hurt you."

"Why don't you just be happy that I'm all right?" he said in his softest, most reassuring voice. He took her in his arms and stroked her hair, kissed her forehead. "Isn't that the most important thing? Why worry what quirk of nature or fate spared me?"

Veronica nodded, relaxing in spite of her doubts. His voice and his touch always had that effect on her. She put her arms around him and pressed her cheek to his chest. "I'm so relieved you weren't hurt."

David took off her coat and threw it on top of his on the love seat. He drew her to him again, holding her in his arms, his face close to hers. "I was afraid he would hurt you," he told her. "I used more force on him than I needed to, but only because he'd threatened you."

"Where do you get such strength?" She searched his blue eyes for an answer.

"From you."

She smiled. "David."

"You won't think any more about this incident, will you?" he asked. There was a slight edge in his tone. "It's over and we both survived it unscathed. We must forget it now."

"It'll be hard to forget."

He bent and kissed her warmly while he brought his hands to her breasts and caressed her softness. His sensual touch lulled her, then aroused her.

"How can I erase your memory of tonight?" he asked.

"You know how," she whispered, her fingers trembling with desire as she unbuttoned her blouse.

David's lovemaking made Veronica forget the experience for several hours. But during the next few days she couldn't help but wonder how David had survived the shooting. In addition, there had been reports in the papers and on television about a man with a fractured jaw and four broken ribs who'd been picked up, unconscious, gun in hand, in front of the Newberry Library. Some accounts mentioned the anonymous phone call that had alerted medics and police. But more attention was paid to the man's account of what happened. In fact, it had been picked up as a humorous story for use at the end of the nightly TV newscast.

The man told police from his hospital bed that he'd been attacked by a crazed man with superhuman strength and phosphorescent eyes. This was *after* he claimed to have shot his attacker through the heart in self-defense. Since the hospitalized man had a long arrest record, his truthfulness was doubted, especially since his story was so bizarre. Police were arranging for him to be given a psychological examination.

Veronica was glad David had escaped all the publicity. But the fact that everything the mugger told police was true—she'd witnessed it herself—weighed on her mind. If she told anyone what she'd seen David do, they would think she was crazy, too. Was she? She remembered Sam Taglia saying that after being around David he felt as though he needed a psychiatrist. What kind of man was she in love with?

On Saturday, at Caroline's house, Veronica was still trying to ignore the nagging doubts at the back of her mind. Caroline's wedding was to take place at a nearby church in a couple of hours. In her turquoise gown, a lace and ribbon confection pinned into her upswept hair, Veronica was fastening the topaz pendant around Caroline's neck. She went to work then on the tiny pearl buttons at the back of the bride's stunning ivory gown.

Caroline's parents, the three bridesmaids, and a photographer were in the living room. Caroline had asked Veronica to help her dress because her mother was too nervous.

"Don't miss any," Caroline said, referring to the small buttons.

"I won't. There sure are a lot of them."

"They probably cost five bucks a button, too." Caroline still couldn't get over how much the dress had cost, and often commented on it.

"If I were getting married, I'd be happy to splurge on the wedding dress of my dreams. You only get to wear one once."

"That's exactly my point," Caroline said.

"What is?" Veronica was stuck at a buttonhole that seemed too small for its button.

"All that money for a dress I'll wear once!"

"Oh, Caroline!" Veronica chided as she squeezed the button through the hole.

"So when are you going to get the wedding dress of *your* dreams?"

"Me?" Veronica sighed. "Who knows?"

"How's your romance with David?"

"It's . . . fine," Veronica said, not knowing what else to say.

"He mentioned you the last time he was in. I thought there was something a little fragile about him when he said he'd been seeing you."

"Fragile? David?"

"Like you could break his heart," Caroline said. She twisted to look at Veronica, a grin on her face. "Is he in love with you?"

Veronica hesitated at the buttons. "Yes. I'm in love with him, too."

The button jumped out of Veronica's fingers as Caroline turned around to hug her. "That's great! He's incredibly wealthy, you know. He's even mentioned Swiss bank accounts. You marry him, you'll be a rich bitch for sure!"

"Just what I always wanted to be," Veronica stated dryly. "I've only known him a month and a half. It's too early to be thinking about marriage."

"It's never too early to *think* about it."

"He's pretty set in his ways," Veronica said carefully. "I don't know if he'd want to get married."

"Well, you can work him around that. Have you and he— you know—" Caroline rocked her outstretched, lace-covered hand back and forth.

"I've slept with him," Veronica admitted.

"Wow! So you finally found someone real to replace all those imaginary men in your head!" Caroline hugged her again. "I'm so happy for you!"

Veronica laughed. "David *has* been wonderful."

"Just between you and me," Caroline said, lowering her voice, "what's he like? He seems like such a cultured egghead in my office. Though he's pretty flaky when it comes to accounting. I can't imagine him, you know, between the sheets."

Veronica couldn't help but remember that she'd never been with David between sheets. They always made love in the ballroom, on the window seat, under the moon and stars. "He's an exquisite lover," Veronica said, reverence in her voice. "I'm sure no one else could be like him. He transports me to another world."

"Wow!" Caroline exclaimed in awe. "You're making me envious. You've got to marry him!"

A few weeks ago Veronica would have agreed. David was all she wanted. But her doubts about him were becoming too strong to ignore. Suddenly the conflict between her desires and the fears she had been trying to dismiss was brought to a head by Caroline's reference to a marriage between her and David. If David was supernatural, what did that mean for her?

"Veronica, what's wrong?" Caroline asked, noting the change in Veronica's expression. "You look like you're going to cry."

At that, Veronica burst into tears. Caroline made her sit on her bed and plopped down next to her. "What's wrong? Maybe I can help."

When Veronica thought she could control her voice, she tried to explain. "I'm afraid David may not be normal."

"You mean he's bisexual or something?"

"No." Veronica swallowed, knowing how ridiculous this would sound. "I'm afraid he might actually be a . . . a vam—" She could barely say the word aloud now that it had become reality for her.

"A vam—" Caroline repeated, confused. "A vampire? That's not what you meant, is it?"

Veronica nodded, new tears starting.

Caroline quickly felt her forehead. "Do you have a fever? Do you feel all right?"

"Other than being tired from staying out late every night, I'm fine. David only lets me see him at night. Never in the daytime. Don't you think that's strange?"

"He writes during the day."

"That's what he says."

"Well, you can't conclude he's a vampire on the basis of that!"

"He's unusually strong," Veronica went on. "I've seen him throw a man to the ground like a bale of straw. I've seen his eyes glow in an unearthly way. His teeth are unusually sharp.

Sometimes, accidentally, he's injured my mouth when he was kissing me."

"Some guys just kiss like that," Caroline said, waving her hand nonchalantly. "I've had a swollen lip or two myself the next morning. Maybe he's strong because he lifts weights. As for his eyes, blue eyes always pick up light in a reflective way. Tom's eyes are like that. Your vivid imagination is carrying you away again, Veronica."

"But a few nights ago we were out walking. A man with a gun came up and wanted our money. He shot David. I saw the gun go off against his chest. At first David doubled over in pain, and then within a minute he was fine. That's when he threw the man to the ground."

"That sounds like a news report I—"

"Yes! That was us. The man is hospitalized because David picked him up in the air and threw him down so hard I could hear his ribs crack."

"Well . . ." Caroline shook her head. "There must be some logical explanation."

"And it happened like the mugger said, after he'd shot David point-blank. And when we got back home, I found the bullet holes in David's clothes. I could put my finger through them. But he only had a slight discoloration on his skin."

Caroline rubbed her nose. "Do you think you could have heard that news report and fallen asleep afterward and dreamed that it happened to you and David? You do look tired. If you've been out late all the time, maybe you're beginning to hallucinate a little."

Veronica put her hands to her temples. "No, I don't think I dreamed it."

"I've had things happen where I couldn't be sure if I'd dreamed it or lived it. Little things, anyway."

"I'm sure it was real," Veronica said. Of course it had happened. But David had wanted her to forget it as though it had been a bad dream.

"Let's look at this another way," Caroline said, sounding very logical. "Vampires don't exist. You know that, right?"

"People in Transylvania think they exist. Sam Taglia told me."

"They do?" Caroline was astonished. "Well, those people are

probably rural and uneducated. My grandmother still believes if you break a mirror you'll have seven years of bad luck. She only had an eighth-grade education. You know better than to believe in vampires, Veronica. Bites on the neck, stakes through the heart, can't see them in mirrors—all that's nonsense."

"That's another thing. David has no mirrors in his home. And I've never seen him eat."

Caroline took a long breath. "Look, I've got to get married in a little while. I don't have time to answer all your arguments. But I'm sure there *are* answers, Veronica. Will you just believe me when I tell you David couldn't possibly be a vampire? I've seen him several times now, and other than keeping incredibly messy financial records, he seems like a perfectly normal guy to me. God, Veronica, you've been sleeping with him! If he was a vampire, wouldn't he have bitten you by now? Isn't that what vampires do?"

Veronica nodded. "But what about the bullet holes?"

"Maybe his shirt button got in the way and somehow deflected it."

Veronica hesitated, envisioning David's clothing. "The hole *was* right by a button," she said, suddenly hopeful that Caroline's explanation could be right.

"Speaking of buttons . . ." Caroline turned her back so Veronica could finish her task.

"Oh, right. Sorry." Veronica laughed a little as she continued buttoning the bridal gown.

"So," Caroline said, "have I convinced you? You've got to get a grip on that imagination of yours!"

"I suppose you're right. I got so involved when I watched his play, maybe I transferred some of the vampire fantasy to real life."

"It could be psychological, too. Maybe you're afraid of committing yourself, so your imagination invents reasons why you can't marry David."

"I hadn't even thought of that." Veronica wondered if that was possible.

"Is David coming to the wedding?" Caroline asked, hopeful. "I wondered if you'd ask him, since you're dating him."

"I did mention it. He said he couldn't break his writing routine," Veronica replied, her uneasiness returning a little. "You know how he is. He never goes out in the daytime."

As Veronica left the wedding reception and drove to David's house that night, she felt uplifted from the fears that had plagued her for the past several days. The more she thought over Caroline's practical suggestions about David, the more she believed her friend was right. Of course David wasn't a vampire! How could she even have thought something like that about the man she loved? She wondered how Caroline could be so patient with her ridiculous ideas.

The afternoon wedding had gone smoothly. Veronica hadn't tripped walking down the aisle as she'd worried she might. Assisting Caroline with her flowers and her veil during the ceremony had also gone off without a hitch. Caroline had never looked more radiant, and Veronica had cried as Caroline and Tom repeated their vows. Her friend had entered a new phase of life, and Veronica was happy for her.

The dinner and reception afterward had been fun. Veronica had danced quite a bit and enjoyed herself more than she had in a long while. Or rather, she realized, she'd enjoyed herself more than she usually did in her everyday life. Her other life with David—she'd begun to look at it that way—was, of course, beyond anything she could hope to experience with friends, relatives, or acquaintances.

She parked in front of David's house. Lifting her long skirt, she rushed to the door and knocked. The buzzer sounded and she hurried up the steps to the third floor.

David greeted her at the top landing, wearing the jacket and tie he'd worn the night they first met. After they kissed, he hung her coat in his closet, then turned to look at her.

"How beautiful!" he exclaimed, walking around her to admire her from all angles. "The color suits you."

"Thanks. You should have seen Caroline. Her wedding gown was gorgeous!"

"Did you enjoy yourself?"

"Yes, but not as much as if you had been there." She sidled up to him, draping her arms over his shoulder. "You should have come to the reception, at least."

"Maybe," he said, looking as though he was enjoying her

nearness. "But it wouldn't have worked out well, even if I had. My producer's negotiating with a theater in New York, and I've been on the phone all evening. I'm expecting him to call back. I hope you won't mind the interruption."

"Is *Street Shadows* going to Broadway?"

"If we can get the details worked out, yes."

"That's wonderful!" Moving in front of him, she rose up on her toes to kiss him. She straightened his tie playfully and tugged on the ends of his shirt collar. "You'll be the toast of Broadway."

David laughed and put his hands at her waist. "You should go to weddings more often. I've never seen you in such an imp-ish mood."

She smiled. "I'm happy because of you. Because there's us."

His eyes showed the odd mixture of melancholy and joy she'd grown accustomed to but never quite understood. "I'm happy we're together, too."

"David? You didn't have a chance to answer that evening when I suggested we live together." She felt a bit nervous, afraid he might consider her too forward or too presumptuous. "Have you thought about it?"

"I've thought about it a lot." His eyes met hers, their blue as clear and vivid as a stained-glass window in the sunlight. "I love you more than anyone, more than the world. But I think it may be too soon. There are many adjustments we would both have to make. There's a great deal we have yet to learn about each other. I think we ought to continue as we are for a while. And then we'll see." He smiled. "You aren't too disappointed, are you?"

"No. I've been going overboard about a lot of things lately," she said in a self-deprecating tone. "You're being wise for both of us, I'm sure."

David's face took on a brooding expression. "I hope I'm being wise."

His telephone rang in the small office adjoining the living room. The sound seemed to jar him. "I'm sorry, my angel. I have to get that."

"Go ahead," she told him with a quick kiss.

He walked into the other room, and soon she could hear his voice on the phone. She sat down on the love seat and looked around his living room, enjoying the colors, the lively patterns, the comfortable atmosphere. Would she ever call this place home? This room and the ballroom had grown so familiar to her, they felt like home already.

David seemed to be deep in conversation, and Veronica had the feeling it would be a long phone call. She got up and ambled around the room, then stood by the fireplace for a moment looking at the gentle flames.

All at once a thought came to her. She had the opportunity now to investigate a little mystery she'd always wondered about: What did David keep in his refrigerator? He'd never opened it when she was present, though he'd once offered Darienne refreshments from it. Why shouldn't she peek inside it while he was occupied?

She walked quietly across the room, glancing at the doorway to his office. He was too far inside the room for her to even glimpse him, though she could still hear his voice. A few more steps and she was behind the bar. She squatted, took hold of the metal handle, and pulled open the refrigerator door.

At first Veronica couldn't figure out what she was looking at. Piled neatly in stacks were plastic bags of some dark substance with long plastic tubes sticking out of them. Curious, she reached in and pulled one out. A chill ran up her hand from the cold plastic, then permeated her body as she read the label: Type O, Rh Positive. Whole Blood. A second label bore the name of the Chicago Independent Blood Bank.

She stared in disbelief, then wanted to scream, but she couldn't. "David," she said with a weak gasp. All at once she felt ill. She stood up, stumbling, still holding the bag of blood. A numbness crept into her head, a ringing sounded in her ears, and the lamps began to grow dim. She reached out for the bar counter for support as she felt herself blacking out. No, she couldn't faint. She wouldn't let herself faint . . .

"Veronica!"

She turned her eyes in the direction of David's voice. The realization that he'd discovered her forged its way into her consciousness. Inhaling raggedly, she willed herself not to pass out.

Her vision began to clear. David stood staring at her, his eyes pale and wide with shock. He started to move toward her.

She backed away from the open refrigerator to the wall behind her. Weakly she held up the blood bag in her hand. Trying to find moisture in her mouth to speak, she asked in a whisper, "Why do you keep blood?"

"I—it's for research. My next play." His face was suddenly white and gaunt, as if he knew she would never believe him.

"You're a vampire!"

Slowly he held out his hand toward her over the counter. "Veronica, please calm—"

"Tell me!"

He stared at her a long, anguished moment. "Yes. I am a vampire."

The blood bag slipped out of her hand to the floor. She recoiled from him. All she could think now was that she had to get out of there. Alive.

Her hair and shoulders brushing the painted plaster, she edged along the wall until she was no longer behind the counter. Quickly her eyes took in the room, the couch and chairs in the center, the fireplace, the distance from there to the door. She'd have to run toward the fireplace to avoid going by David and then make a break for the door. All this she ascertained in a split second.

"You needn't be frightened of me, Veronica. I've never harmed you, have I?"

The image of David in the moonlight at the back of his house flashed in her mind—his sharp teeth, the unnatural desire in his eyes.

Ignoring his question, she made for the couch, ran around it, and then to the fireplace. When she turned to head for the door, she found David standing three feet in front of her.

"You can't outrun me," he stated gravely. "You can't outmaneuver me. I'm far more agile than your cat. And just as harmless to you."

"Let me go," she begged, breathing hard as she started to back away again.

"I'll let you go. I promise," he said softly. "I won't even try to touch you now. I only ask you to recall the many times I've touched you and loved you. Never once did I injure you. Though I was tempted to taste from you, I did not."

He looked down for a moment, as if to compose himself. Lifting his eyes to hers again, he continued. "Over the next hours your mind and soul will absorb the truth of your discovery about me. I plead with you—remember all the times I might have taken your sweet blood and did not." He moved away from her and stepped behind the love seat, completely clearing her path to the door. "Go now, if you must."

Veronica didn't think twice. She fled to the door, scrambled down the steps and out of his house in sheer terror.

12

Before Any Ideas Became Set in Her Mind

THE FIRE had died hours ago. David sat on the couch, his grief spent, feeling hollow, numb, and cold. Veronica was gone. He'd lost her for the reason he'd lost Cecilia so many years ago, because of the vile thing he was. He only hoped Veronica would not go so far as to take her own life, as Cecilia had.

What was there to do? Could he possibly find a way to make Veronica trust him again? In addition to their love they had a strong sexual bond, something he'd never shared with Cecilia. Veronica must realize, once she thought about it, how often he'd had the opportunity to take her blood. Wouldn't she see that she could trust him?

Perhaps, but he had to face facts. The shock of finding out the man she loved was a vampire would probably outweigh reason.

And while he was facing facts, how long did he really think they could have gone on as they were? Try as he might, so many times he'd felt his bloodlust threatening to overcome his willpower. It might have taken years, but inevitably the night would have come when he'd have held her in his arms and been unable to resist.

He straightened his back as a new thought came to him. Was there a chance he could overcome her revulsion? She might even want to be initiated, once she got over her shock. Some women did. He'd always compared her with Cecilia, but it might be that she wouldn't react like Cecilia at all.

It was clear he needed to talk to Veronica, and the sooner the better, before any ideas became set in her mind. Maybe all wasn't lost. He couldn't change what he was, but he had a right to some happiness, didn't he?

Veronica twisted and turned, trying to find a comfortable position. Her white cat, Felix, nestled closer to her. She'd been sleeping fitfully since she'd gone to bed at midnight, after checking and rechecking that her doors and all her windows were locked. Opening her eyes, she instinctively looked toward the window in her bedroom. The venetian blinds were closed and the curtains pulled shut over them. Glancing at her digital clock on the small nightstand next to her bed, she saw it was almost 4:00 A.M. Next to the clock her lamp was still lit because tonight the darkness frightened her. Felix looked up at her with round eyes, as if sensing her fear. She petted him until he began to purr and put his chin on his front paws.

Lying back, closing her eyes, she fingered the small silver cross she'd dug out of a drawer. She wore it around her neck over her white flannel nightgown. The pendant had been a confirmation gift from her aunt when she was thirteen. She'd seldom worn it, but tonight she was thankful she'd kept it. The cross was her only protection if David came for her.

Images from *Street Shadows* kept appearing in her mind—the vampire climbing in through Claudine's window, the mesmerizing way he'd bitten her in her sleep. The images were as clear as if she'd seen the play an hour ago, and they chilled Veronica, keeping her from sleep. She was terrified David might come to her that way, now that she knew what he was.

No wonder the scene in the play had seemed so real. No wonder Sam Taglia had felt corrupted acting it according to David's precise demonstration. The scene, the whole play, must be based on David's own experience—as a vampire. But was it possible? She'd suspected the truth, had even confided in Caroline, and yet she had never really believed it. Now she had to. Her beloved David was an unnatural being, something to be feared, something akin to the powers of darkness that no one understood. But why had he spent so much time with her? What had he wanted from her? Her blood? Her life? Her soul?

Veronica's eyes felt heavy, and she told herself that she needed to sleep. She must stop thinking about all of this. It was nearly four o'clock. He wouldn't come anymore tonight.

Maybe he would never come. Tomorrow she would figure out what to do. But now she needed sleep. . . .

The soft lamplight penetrated her closed eyelids, changing, now brighter, now darker, now white, now red. Sparks of light as if from a chandelier spun around her, and she was floating in a cool, silent breeze. Now soft noises, a tinkling like ornaments when the Christmas tree is shaken, a gentle whoosh of fabric on fabric. The wind was cold on her face, bracing and exciting. A thick shadow fell over her, blocking the light, and then all was still and black.

Her eyes flew open. David was standing beside her bed, looking down at her.

"No!" she exclaimed, pulling the covers up for shelter, moving to the opposite side of the bed.

The cat arched his back and spit, then jumped to the floor and raced out of the room.

"I won't harm you," David told her, his voice almost matter-of-fact. He was wearing a sweater and pants beneath his open overcoat. He shrugged off his coat and threw it at the foot of her bed. Behind him the window blinds were pulled up and the curtains fluttered in the cold wind coming from outside. He turned and shut the window. "Sorry about the lock. I think I can fix it." He pressed the metal back into shape with his bare hands and moved the lever to lock the window again. "There now," he said, turning to her.

"Wh-what do you want?" she asked, barely able to speak as panic turned her body to ice.

"To talk."

"No." Beneath the covers she took hold of her cross.

"We must talk," he insisted kindly. "May I sit down?"

As he walked around the bed to where she was huddled, she lowered the blankets from her chin. Holding the small cross in her fingers, she extended it toward him as far as the short necklace chain would allow.

"Oh, my," he said with sad amusement. "I haven't seen you wear that before." He leaned over her to look at the cross more closely. "A gift? Or did you go out and buy that somewhere tonight, thinking it would protect you?"

"God will protect me!" Veronica said, clinging to her last hope.

"I suppose He may, if He chooses," David mused. "Perhaps a lightning bolt down my back? I wouldn't blame Him. I'd deserve it. But short of our Maker's intervention, the only thing that can protect you from me—is me. And I will."

He sat down, though she hadn't said he could. "Why won't you trust me?" he asked in the reassuring voice she'd grown to love. "I won't harm you."

Veronica scrambled across the bed, slid off the mattress, and stood by the window. "You're a vampire!"

"I'm still the man who loves you."

"But you're . . . d-dead."

David winced, as if her blunt statement bruised him. "A technicality," he replied. "I have a different kind of existence. But I do exist! Do I look dead to you?" He stood up and held his hands out at his sides. "Or 'undead,' as they like to say in the movies? Did you think of me that way when we made love?"

Veronica shut her eyes, horrified at the knowledge of what she'd done. She put her hand to her mouth. A combination of a scream and a sob escaped her constricting throat.

"Am I such a monster to you now?" David asked, his own voice breaking.

The ache in his voice compelled her to look at him again. She saw how the blue of his eyes had grown so pale it was barely a color at all. His face looked gaunt, drained, filled with sorrow. She found herself beginning to feel guilty, though she didn't know why she should. He was a vampire. He had tricked her by pretending to be a normal man. If he was in pain now, it was his own fault. He was a monster!

Still, he seemed to be so deeply sensitive, as full of tender emotion as when she'd believed him to be normal. She remembered she'd always thought of the vampire in *Street Shadows* more as a human being than as some ghoulish fiend. Maybe she was wrong to think of David differently now because she'd learned something she hadn't known before. David seemed still to be David.

She looked at him, studying him a trifle more calmly now, and with awakening eyes. "When were you born?"

"In 1582," he replied, looking at her with a curious, slightly perplexed expression.

"In Paris?"

"Yes."

"When did you die?"

"Here we are together, our future in the balance, and all you want is facts?" he said. "We need to talk about us."

"I'd like to know."

"I died in 1616 in Transylvania."

Transylvania. The real Transylvania? "Why were you there?" she asked.

David sighed as if fatigued. He stepped around to the foot of the bed, pushed his coat aside, and sat down. Bending one knee onto the mattress, he turned toward her. "I went to Transylvania to find out if the Eastern European folklore about vampires was true. I wanted to become one myself, so I set out to find a vampire who would transform me."

Veronica was astonished. He'd chosen to become one? "Why?"

"I'd gone to England from France to study with William Shakespeare. He was my beloved mentor for fifteen years. I wanted to become a playwright of the caliber he was." David's face was grave and wistful.

"When Will died in April of 1616, I was overcome with grief and consumed with the fear that he and his work would be forgotten. I quickly safeguarded his manuscripts, which were not yet in print. But I was afraid that wasn't enough. Future generations, I imagined, would lose interest, and his genius would not survive time. I also became burdened with the truth that it would take more than a normal human lifespan to develop my own writing skill to Shakespeare's level."

David paused and shook his head, as if angry with himself.

"Go on," Veronica said.

"I'd heard the legends of vampires and the idea of becoming immortal obsessed me. If I were immortal, I thought, I could remain on earth throughout the future to see to it that Will's plays and sonnets were not forgotten. And I would have all the time I needed to polish my own talent. With that dual purpose in mind, blind to all other logic, I traveled to Transylvania, where vampires were said to exist. I found a vampire—an uneducated, brutish creature. But he served the purpose. I died and awoke as a vampire myself."

Veronica felt a new chill overtake her and shivered in her bare feet and flannel nightgown. But she couldn't take her eyes off David, trying to imagine him doing all he'd just described. "Do you . . . have you ever . . . ?"

"Bitten anyone?"

Veronica nodded, swallowing a knot that seemed to have formed in her throat.

"I have," he replied, lowering his gaze. "Infrequently, at various times and for various reasons. It's always something I consider carefully before I act." He paused and tilted his head. "At least, I try to."

"How often do you need . . . ?" Again, she couldn't say the word.

"Blood?"

She nodded.

"To feel healthy and look normal, I need blood at least every week. Otherwise I grow pale and lose some of my strength. It's happened now and then when I couldn't get into a blood bank in time."

"What about before there were blood banks?"

David smiled a bit and studied her. "You're really thinking this through, aren't you? I've never killed anyone for blood, if that's what you mean. I used to live off animals, mostly."

Veronica put her hand to her stomach and felt her gorge rise.

"It sounds ghastly, I know," he said, looking at her with understanding. "But it was my only choice. Their blood isn't as satisfying, either—probably comparable to some of those low-cal foods you mortals eat nowadays. Sometimes I'd take sustenance for a while from someone I'd initiated, but that circumstance has been rare. The invention of refrigeration was a godsend to us vampires as well as mortals."

Veronica was starting to feel dizzy and light-headed. She sat down on the edge of the double bed, a few feet away from him. "What do you mean by 'initiated'?"

He eyed her for a moment, as if conferring with himself about how to answer. "A mortal is initiated when a vampire has drunk from him or her. But only a relatively small amount of blood is taken, so that the mortal recovers."

Veronica put her hand to her mouth to keep her lips from trembling. She didn't know why she wanted to ask her next

question, but she had to know. Pulling her shaking fingers away
from her mouth, she asked, "Is it pleasurable to you, to drink
from someone?"

"Yes," David responded simply. A trace of cobalt light
began to appear in his eyes. "The experience is as profound as
the sex act. More so. Most vampires vastly prefer it to sex, in
fact. I'm different that way. My sense of morality won't allow
my bloodlust to take over. But the drive is always there."

Veronica's mouth had grown dry, and she tried to wet her
lips. Again she had a question that, she felt, if she had been
in her right mind, she wouldn't ask. Her voice came out as a
whisper. "Have you ever wanted to drink from me?"

"I've longed to taste from you, my angel," he replied, his
eyes softening even as the light in them grew more intense. "But
I made a vow to myself not to. I'd hoped only for a normal
relationship between us."

"Why?" The perverse disappointment she felt shocked her.

"For your sake. I thought I could keep my secret from you,
so that I wouldn't have to involve you in the darker side of my
world. But you've suspected me for some time, haven't you?"

Veronica nodded and looked away. Her mind was reeling.
Racing. She had to quell her desire to know how it would feel
to be "initiated." "What happened when you were shot?" she
asked instead.

"The bullet passed through my body. I felt a momentary
pain, and then the wound instantly began to heal. If you'd
thought to look, you would have found a bullet hole in the back
of my clothes, too." He picked up his coat and turned it. In
a moment he put his finger through the hole in the back of it.
"See?"

Veronica edged forward to look, then leaned back and covered her face with her hands. "David, this is all so hard to accept. I suspected what you were, but I forced myself not to
believe it."

"I know," David said.

She felt the bed shake. When she pulled her hands away from
her face, she found him moving toward her. He sat near her,
but not so close as to touch her. Somehow she wasn't frightened
of him anymore, though common sense told her she ought to
be.

"I wish with all my heart," he told her softly, "that I could change myself into a mortal again, so that you and I could share a normal life together."

Tears filled her eyes. "You did really love me, then?"

"I *do* love you! Don't speak in the past tense about something so dear, so vital to both of us."

The fact that he still wanted her was more comfort than she could have ever hoped for. Suddenly she didn't care what he was, only that he existed and that he still needed her as much as she needed him. A sob broke her voice as she asked, "What will we do?"

"That's up to you," he told her gravely.

"But I don't even know the choices," she said, wiping the tears from her eyes with the wrist ruffle of her nightgown.

David looked at her with so much love, it made her want to weep more. As if disciplining himself, he turned his gaze to the window and spoke quietly. "One path is to end our relationship and never see each other again." His voice was unsteady. "I'll honor your decision, if that's what you choose. In many ways that would be your wisest choice."

How could never seeing David again be wise? Of course she knew the answer to that question, but the answer didn't seem logical to her anymore. "What else?" she asked.

"We can go on as we have been," he said. His eyes rose to the pleated drapery valance. "Though I'm not sure I can guarantee that I'd never give in to my desire for your blood. I promise you that I would try. But you'd be taking a risk."

"I know," she said with new understanding. "Is there another choice?" She held her breath, waiting.

He paused and turned to look at her again. After staring at her in his steady, unblinking way for a long moment, he said, "I could initiate you."

"What would happen then?" she asked in a hush.

"Then you would be under my power."

She took a breath. His words enthralled her.

"You and I would have a bond between us that would extend over time and distance," he continued. "I would be able to summon you whenever I wanted. You would have great difficulty resisting me. And in the same way you would be able to call me. We would always be united in this way, even if we were separated for many years. You would never be able to disconnect from me, for as long as you are mortal."

"Until I die?"

His eyes were still and shining. "Until you die. Or unless, in due time, you become an immortal, too."

"A vampire?" Veronica stared at him as her mouth dropped open. "Me?"

David smiled slightly. "Darienne likes to say 'vampiress.'"

Veronica sat up straight. "You mean, Darienne is a vampire, too!"

"You're surprised?"

"I only thought of you," Veronica said. "It never occurred to me that Darienne— Did you make her one?"

"Within a year after I'd been transformed, she asked me to initiate her. Afterward, she wanted to be like me, so . . ." He didn't finish.

"The blood ceremony," she whispered, remembering the play. "And that's why you and she have such a special relationship," she said slowly, envying Darienne's place in his life.

"Don't misunderstand," he said. "Darienne is no longer under my power. Once she died and became a vampiress, she acquired her own power, equal to mine, and grew extremely independent." He told her this, Veronica detected, with reluctance, as if hoping she would not choose the same path as Darienne.

Veronica sat in silence for several moments, considering all he'd said. "What do you want me to do, David?"

"This is your decision." His expression was resolute, as though he did not want to sway her mind in the smallest way.

"What do you hope I'll decide, then?"

The light in his eyes changed, and he looked away. He seemed to be grappling with some inner torment. She wished he would just say what he wanted and not worry about swaying her judgment. She wanted his guidance. And his love.

"I won't tell you what I want," David answered at last, disappointing her. "I mustn't influence you. You don't have to make a decision tonight, Veronica. This is too enormous a choice to settle in a few moments. You must think it through."

She sighed, feeling troubled and frustrated, wanting it all to be settled so she'd know where they stood with each other. "When will I see you again? Tomorrow?"

Again, he smiled a little, his eyes full of warmth. "You still want to see me, knowing what I am?"

Veronica reached to touch his hand. "I can tell you're the same as before. You're still kind and gentle. I'm not afraid anymore. I love you, David. My feelings haven't changed."

He started to move to her, then hesitated. "Will you let me hold you?"

In spite of what she'd just said, a small tremor of fear edged up her spine. But she smiled and leaned toward him, holding out her arms.

As he clasped her to him, she closed her eyes, marveling at his strength, his indestructibility. He kissed her mouth, her hair, her eyes. She sighed at each caress, feeling inexpressible relief to be in his embrace again. "Will you make love to me?" she asked, winding her arms around his neck.

She noticed him glance at the digital clock beside her. Looking herself, she saw it was almost five o'clock.

"I can't stay," he told her, his eyes filled with regret. "Dawn will come soon and I'm far from home."

Veronica stiffened, recoiling from him just a bit. "You have to go to your coffin," she murmured, visualizing for the first time exactly how he passed the daylight hours.

He released her gently, as if understanding her revulsion. "I must rest in my coffin during the day. Otherwise the sun would destroy me. It's a necessity of my existence—just as blood is."

Veronica wrapped her arms around herself, feeling an icy chill. "Oh, David, I can't imagine you that way."

"Lying still as death in a coffin? We must all face that prospect eventually, one way or another." He reached and took her hand. His long fingers felt warm over hers. "You need time to adjust to all this," he said. "Perhaps it's better if we don't see each other while you make your decision about our future. You need a clear mind. You need sleep. When you're with me, I'm afraid, you have neither."

He rose and picked up his coat. "I'll leave by your back door now. Take as many days as you need. I'll be home each evening. When you're ready, you'll find me there, waiting for you to come to me with your answer."

13

The Thought of Being Under His Power

VERONICA WAS working in the file room, hidden among banana-yellow metal cabinets taller than she. Under the bright fluorescent lights she busied herself looking up everything she could find on ethnic food. Mr. Malloy had assigned her to do research for an article on the big Taste of Chicago event held each summer in the Grant Park area near Buckingham Fountain. "Find some new angle," he'd told her. At least he was giving her a chance to do something besides update the coming events column, Veronica reminded herself as she poked through the dusty files. At the moment she was in the corner looking under the letter *C* for Chinese cooking.

It was hard to concentrate. Foremost on her mind, ever since David had come to her almost a week ago, was her decision about their relationship. Ordinarily she might have talked about such a major life choice with her parents, or better yet with Caroline. But, of course, she couldn't discuss this because she had to protect David.

He'd given her four choices, but Veronica had decided she really only had two. To stop seeing David altogether was unthinkable, and she wasn't ready yet to choose immortality as a vampire, either. That left either going on as they had been, or initiation.

The thought of being under his power allured her, thrilled her. To share a mental bond with David that would tie her to him even when they were apart was more than her heart could have longed for or imagined. And when they were together, how close they would be!

But how would it affect her life? To be bonded to him for

194

the rest of her time on earth! For the present she couldn't envision herself ever wanting to be free of David. But as she grew older, would she change her mind? How would she feel in her thirties, in her forties, and even older?

For now maybe she should tell David she'd like to go on as they had been. She had so many questions.

"Veronica?"

Startled, she turned quickly at the male voice and hit her wrist on the sharp corner of the open file drawer. She looked up to see Rob coming in, then examined the scrape across her inner wrist, which began oozing a little blood.

"I thought you'd gone out to lunch like everyone else," Rob said, walking up to her. "Hurt yourself?"

"It's okay," she answered, going back to the files.

Rob stopped her by taking hold of her wrist. "Let me see." He held her hand in both of his. "It's bleeding a little," he said. He reached into his pocket to pull out a clean, white handkerchief.

Veronica tried to pull away. "It'll stain."

"That's okay." Rob pressed the white cloth against her skin.

Veronica couldn't help but remember David's reaction when her cat had scratched her. By comparison, she found Rob's nurturing ministration touching. Rob was so human.

"You don't have to mother me," she said with a smile.

He looked at her with an exasperated expression. "I was hoping you'd see it more as a knight-in-shining-armor sort of thing."

"Thank you, Sir Lancelot."

He grinned wryly and pulled the handkerchief away. Twisting her wrist a bit so he could see, he said, "I think the bleeding's stopped." He tucked the handkerchief back into his pocket but didn't let go of her hand. His eyes met hers with kindness and affection. "I've been meaning to tell you, you look a lot better the past few days."

"I've been getting more sleep."

"Does that mean you've stopped seeing de Morrissey?"

"Not exactly."

"What, exactly?"

Veronica wanted to remind him it was none of his business, but hated to get into another argument. They had to work together, and their relationship had been on tenterhooks since their last angry exchange. "David's been busy the past week," she lied, "so I haven't been seeing him."

"You seem to improve when not seeing him," Rob said. "Why don't you make it permanent?"

She pulled her wrist out of his grasp. "I told you. I love him."

Rob's green eyes took on a brittle, glasslike quality. "You still refuse to consider that there might be other men in the world?"

"I've chosen David," she said, turning back to the file drawer.

"Are you sure he's chosen you?"

"Yes."

"As his one and only? Do you know for sure he hasn't got other women?"

Veronica hesitated. Darienne immediately came to her mind.

"You're not sure, are you?" Rob took her by the shoulders to make her face him.

"David is unique," Veronica told him, defensive and suddenly feeling a strong sense of conviction. "His life has scope and depth. He adores women and he's sensitive to our feelings. Many women must have loved him. It would be immature of me to expect to be the only woman in his experience. If there are one or two that he still has an attachment to, I can't help that."

Veronica could hardly believe she'd said what she had. The statement was contrary to all the romantic ideals she'd carried in her head since childhood.

"In other words, you're willing to share him?" Rob asked, incredulous.

Veronica swallowed and looked at the floor. "I'm the one he loves most, I'm sure of that."

"Number one concubine, that's what you want to be?"

"To have David," she said with emotion, "I'd do anything."

All at once Rob shook her harshly, startling the sweet visions of David from her mind. "Veronica, this is sick! You're obsessed with him. That's not love!"

"If it's not, then it's even better than love!"

"I'll show you what love is."

Rob drew her to his chest roughly and kissed her hard. Her

breath remained caught in her throat while his mouth was fixed hotly on hers for a few interminable seconds. She felt his aggressive passion, his attempted claim on her, but could not respond.

It wasn't at all like kissing David. She could never lose herself in Rob's embrace. Where was David's tender voice, the unsettling blue of his eyes, his reassuring, enveloping presence, the superhuman intensity of desire she'd come to crave? She was just standing here in this dusty file room being manhandled and put upon. A great nuisance was all it was, and she stoically endured the kiss until Rob let her go.

When he looked at her, disappointment, anger, and embarrassment were all vying for prominence in his eyes. He'd felt her complete lack of response, and they both knew it.

"Guess I don't measure up," Rob muttered.

At least he wasn't going to try pretending otherwise. "It's not your fault," she told him, attempting to be kind as she stepped out of his grasp. "I love David and no one else can even come close. Maybe you should follow your own advice and look for someone else."

Rob's eyes glittered with suppressed emotion as he said, "Yeah, maybe you're right!"

She watched him walk away, feeling sorry for him, but at the same time overjoyed for herself. Rob had unwittingly helped her make up her mind. His kiss seemed to prove that she would miss nothing, would have no future regrets, if she chose to be with David for the rest of her life. And if that was going to be her choice, why not be David's in the way that she could experience his love to the fullest degree?

Why not initiation?

David bent in front of the marble fireplace, arranging logs to build a fire. The early December evening was cold. And lonely. He hadn't seen Veronica in a week, and he was growing anxious to be with her, to know what she'd decided. For her own sake, she ought to stop seeing him. But David knew she needed him as vitally as he needed her.

Or maybe that was only what he hoped. Maybe she had realized she'd be better off staying away from the shadowed vampire world she'd unknowingly slipped into.

David crumpled a piece of newspaper and pushed it between the logs along with some kindling. And where was Darienne? he wondered as he worked. He hadn't seen her for weeks. Maybe that was just as well. He'd told Darienne he couldn't continue their relationship because of Veronica, but he suspected Darienne had other ideas. She always did. If she'd decided to leave Chicago for a while, so much the better, in case Veronica did choose to continue with him.

David lit a match and tossed it onto the newspaper. As the flame took hold and grew, he moved the ornate screen back into place in front of it. While he stood watching the fire for a moment, he thought he heard a car door shut outside. Quickly he moved to the window. Pushing aside the drapery, he looked down and saw Veronica walking up the sidewalk to his door. The sight of her made his chest swell with renewed hope.

She looked up and waved, smiling. David didn't hesitate. He rushed out of his living room and bounded down the spiral staircase, four or five steps at a time. Just as the knocker struck, he opened the door and swept Veronica into his arms.

The feel of her next to him brought immediate solace to his loneliness. He looked down into her face, so fresh and young and sincere. Tears shimmered in her golden brown eyes as she wound her arms around his neck and stretched up to kiss him. The warmth of her lips heated him as no fire ever could. She was showing him her love just as she always had, as if reassuring him that she'd adjusted to her new knowledge of him. He had to restrain himself from weeping over the momentous fact that he hadn't lost her.

"Come upstairs," he said, pulling off her knit cap and taking the woolen scarf from around her neck. "I just made a fire."

"I've missed you," she said, putting an arm around his waist as they began to walk up the steps together. "I'm sorry I took so long, but I wanted to be sure before I told you my decision."

"It's all right," David insisted. "I wanted you to be sure."

When they reached his living room, he took her coat and hung it up. She was wearing the soft, parchment-colored knit dress that showed her graceful, feminine form so sublimely. He smiled to himself. She must have sensed it was his favorite and chosen to wear it tonight. He loved the way she always wanted to please him.

As she stood in front of the fire, warming her hands, David approached her from behind and put his hand on her shoulder. "Don't torture me. What have you decided?"

She turned and looked up at him. The fire backlighted her hair, and her eyes were full of a radiance of their own. She seemed to vibrate with warmth as she said, "I want you to initiate me."

Profound love surged through David's heart. But there was also fear and guilt. She was asking him to change her forever. Would she hate him someday, as he hated himself? In a horrid moment he realized how selfish he was.

"What's wrong, David?" Her eyes moved back and forth over his face. "I hoped you'd be happy."

"I am happy that you want that special bond with me. But do you understand the consequences? You'll never be the same."

"I don't want to be the same! I've only been truly happy in my life since I met you."

"You'd be entering a different world—the world of vampirism." David put all the gravity into his voice he could. "Though you wouldn't be a vampire yourself, you would be a part of our dreary existence all the same."

She smiled and slid her hands up the front of his sweater. Her touch gave him a warm shiver, reminding him of how much he wanted her, her body and her blood.

"Your world seems magical to me," she told him. "It's *my* life that's dreary. I want to be as close to you as can be." She leaned up and kissed him on the mouth with a heated pleasure that made David realize how much he'd changed her already. Because of him, she was no longer the innocent who'd blushed when he'd guessed she was a virgin. He'd made a woman of her, and she obviously was happy about it. Should he take her adoration and yearning for him to another level?

He drew his mouth away from hers, his body already responding to her sensuality. "You must understand completely, Veronica. You would be like . . ." David fought with himself over telling her all of the unvarnished truth. But his conscience won the battle. "You would be like my slave. You would be able to refuse me nothing. Where I was concerned, you would have no free will. Giving me comfort, sex, your very blood would be all you could think about. When away from me during the day, you would probably feel alienated and bereft."

He paused a moment. "I've never experienced the initiated state myself," he continued, "but I've observed it. Even Darienne, independent as she was as a mortal and now as a vampiress, was like a child in my hands after I'd initiated her."

Veronica's eyes welled with tears and she grasped the front of his sweater, making her hands into fists. "Giving you everything is all I think about now. I *want* to be like a child in your hands. Nothing could sound more beautiful to me. Don't you see? I'm your slave already."

David took an unsteady breath and then clasped her to his chest. It was as he'd told himself all along: she was unhappy in her life. She needed him. Maybe he was rationalizing his moral conscience away, but he was going to give her all of himself that she wanted, just as she was so willing to do for him.

"All right," he whispered with finality. He kissed her softly.

She breathed a ragged gasp, almost like a sob, only she wasn't crying. Her eyes were wide and shining as she looked up at him. "How will it happen? I'm a little afraid, like when we made love the first time."

He smiled. "But you like making love now."

"Yes!"

"You'll like this, too, my sweet angel."

"W-will it hurt?"

"Less than losing your virginity did."

She grinned a little. "How will you do it? Is it like in the movies? You bite me on the neck?"

David chuckled deep in his throat. She was so adorable—the way she always had questions, the way she relied on movies for her information about everything. "I'll open your artery with a prick of my teeth." His bloodlust heightened as he talked about it. "After I've drunk, you'll feel weak, maybe lightheaded for a while. But you'll soon recover."

"Will I feel it when you open my . . ." She was growing pale.

"I'm sorry," he said, stroking her cheek. "I shouldn't have described it so graphically. You may feel the bite, but you won't mind it." He held her face in his hands. "I'll do it while we're

making love. All you'll be aware of is the new, even more profound pleasure we'll be giving each other."

She inhaled roughly, her eyes limpid with longing. "Then
do it, David."

The stars and moon dazzled Veronica as she fleetingly opened
her eyes. Their midnight beauty became a part of her, just as
David was a part of her. She lay naked beneath him, enjoying
his weight on her body and the fulfillment of his flesh made
one with hers. As she held on to him more tightly, running her
hands over his heated skin, gasping with the ecstasy of each
forceful thrust, she thought only of the moment, of the joy of
being with him. If she'd begun their lovemaking with a trace
of persisting anxiety, David, like a magician, had quickly made
her apprehension disappear. David was the magic she'd needed
since she was born. He was everything and he gave her everything. She wanted to give back to him. She had no fear.

"Oh, David, David," she whispered, saying his name like an
incantation while he conjured all the hidden corners of sensuality from her body. She felt the tension within her reaching that
wondrous point of no return. In a moment she'd be among the
stars.

As if sensing her need, he lifted himself above her on his elbows and began powerful thrusts that thrilled her while they
knocked the breath from her lungs. His eyes were radiant and
frightening, their cobalt-blue more penetrating than the moonlight, more comparable to the sun in its intensity. But the
frightfulness of his eyes exalted her now, intensifying her pleasure to an overpowering level. She could never look away from
him, not now. His eyes were more beautiful than anything on
earth. His eyes must be like glimpsing heaven.

"Ohhh . . ." she moaned, the pleasure becoming unbearable.

"Are you all right?" David asked, his voice husky with
arousal. "Tell me what you'd like."

"David," she breathed, smiling as she looked at his face
above hers. "Just don't stop. Don't stop." She inhaled sharply
as he thrust again in an urgent, transcending rhythm. "Oh,
David, oh, David . . ."

All at once she felt the familiar tightening beneath her stomach, the momentary stillness, as if the world had stopped. And

then her body burst with sensation. The room seemed to spin, and soon she was in that other realm he always took her to, the realm of crystal lights and ethereal splendors that lay just beyond earth's natural plane.

But now, instead of softly settling back to find herself lying on the window seat, spent and fulfilled with David in her arms, she was still among the lights. And there was a coolness all about her, as if she were floating in a pool or gentle stream of water, clinging to David as if he were a floating buoy. And there was no particular direction in which they moved together, but only an increasingly languid gliding through the coolness as the crystal lights grew dim.

She felt herself falling into a voluptuous swoon, still holding on to David, reveling in the pulsing of his flesh within her body as his pleasure came to culmination. The feeling of oneness with him grew stronger than she had ever experienced it before. She slid her hands over his smooth back, to his head, as if to comfort him further. But she was growing so limp and delirious with the pleasure of their oneness, that her hands slowly fell away from him. And she lay there so languid in his embrace that everything, the lights, the coolness, even the pleasure gradually faded, faded . . . until there was only David . . . until he was the only reality, the only truth in the world. And she had become not just a part of him. She had become . . . David.

"Veronica. Veronica!"

She heard David's voice as if he were shouting from the top of a deep well.

"Oh, God. Veronica, wake up!"

Gradually she realized he was shaking her, but she didn't have the strength to speak or open her eyes.

"What have I done? You weren't supposed to die! Come back to me!"

"David." Her lips formed the syllables of his name.

"That's right. Open your eyes, Veronica. Look at me."

She willed her eyes to open, but they wouldn't respond. Only a flutter. Only a glimpse of David's face. Blood at his mouth.

"Veronica, can you hear me?"

She tried to nod.

"Stay with me—stay with my mind. Don't let yourself pass into the other realm. Do you hear?"

Veronica nodded, more strongly this time. She was aware of a new feeling, or rather a new presence. She could sense David's thoughts. Not articulate words, the way he spoke them. But she could feel his panic, as if it were her own.

Again she willed her eyes to open. All at once her eyelids lifted. She saw David's face, his blue eyes pale, yet rimmed with bright red. His skin was aglow, his cheeks as red as if he'd been in the sun too long. There was blood on his chin and smeared near his mouth.

"Are you all right?" he asked. Again she felt, as well as saw, his anxiety.

"Yes."

"Lie still. You need fluids. I'll get you some water."

She tried to reach for his hand. "Don't leave me."

"Only for a moment," he assured her. "No more than a moment."

"No," she protested weakly, but he walked away.

Slowly, summoning all her remaining strength, she moved her head to the side and watched him rush across the dark ballroom to the doorway. He vanished in the blackness of the hallway beyond. She felt something that was akin to pain. The pain increased with each step he took away from her. She needed to be near him! Why was he going away from her?

And then, as if he were right next to her, she could feel his nurturing emotion, as if he were saying, *Stay calm. I'll hold you in my arms in a moment.* She would have cried with the comfort it gave her, if her eyes hadn't felt so dry. Her mouth was dry, too, and it was difficult to breathe.

In the distance she heard a higher-pitched voice. For a moment she wasn't sure if she'd heard it with her ears, or with her mind. She heard it again, and then David's. The voices came from beyond the ballroom, beyond the hall. Someone was in his living room. It was Darienne.

Veronica began to breathe faster, feeling threatened, feeling alone. Darienne might take David from her, distract him with her beauty and her body. *David, don't leave me. . . .*

"She knows you're here! Why tonight of all nights?"

"I hadn't seen you for a while. It's good I came. You're in such a state."

Veronica could feel David's anger toward Darienne as she heard, with her ears, their voices in the distance. Their voices grew louder as they came down the hallway.

"I lost control. I needed her so," David said, his voice full of wretched guilt. "I know I took too much. She's such a little thing."

"Keep calm, David. If necessary, I can take her to a hospital."

"How would you explain the marks?"

"I'd think of something plausible. You can count on me."

In a moment Veronica could see them across the large ballroom, coming in from the hallway. Darienne was wearing her white mink over a glittering gown, and David was still unclothed. David rushed to Veronica's side, a tall glass of water in his hand.

"You see?" he said, smiling at her through his anguish. "I'm back. You must drink this."

Veronica weakly lifted her hand to his, only wanting to touch him, not caring about the water.

He looked at Darienne. "Can you help her sit up?"

"Of course, but let me check her first," Darienne said, coming close. She held a towel in her hands. Leaning over Veronica as David was, she said, "Veronica, it's me, Darienne. Do you recognize me?" Her voice was sweet, as if she were hovering over a sick child.

"Yes," Veronica whispered.

"Good." Darienne sat down beside her and touched the towel with a blotting motion to the side of her neck. "There now." With her other hand she felt Veronica's forehead, then gently pulled her lower eyelid back from her eye. Last, she felt the pulse at her wrist. "Are you thirsty?"

Veronica nodded.

"Good! Then we must have you sit up so you can drink." Darienne changed her position, sitting behind Veronica now, and lifted her gently, supporting her against her shoulder. The towel slipped from Veronica's neck, stained bright red. Veronica paid it no heed. She was more entranced with the sight of David hovering over her with such devotion.

"What do you think?" David asked Darienne anxiously.

"I think you did take a little too much, but she'll be all right. Now give her the water."

"My hand is shaking. You give it to her."

Darienne took the glass from him and held it to Veronica's mouth. "Now take small sips. Little by little. Soon you'll feel stronger."

Veronica had trouble swallowing and choked on the first sip. Darienne waited patiently, like a lavishly attired nurse, until she could continue drinking. David knelt next to Veronica and took her hand as she slowly drank all the cold water. When she'd emptied the glass, a chill began to creep through her body, making her feel as if she were freezing.

"She's shivering," David said with alarm.

"It's all right," Darienne told him softly. "Don't be so agitated. One would think you'd never done this before!"

"I never wanted anyone as much as her. Look what I've done to her."

"Shhh! Don't upset her," Darienne said, carefully slipping off her mink while Veronica still leaned against her. Veronica could feel the brush of fur against her bare back as Darienne pushed her forward a trifle. "Don't pay any attention to David, Veronica. He worries about everything. And they used to say *women* were hysterical! You're going to be all right."

She had the coat off. David leaned forward to support Veronica as Darienne draped the coat around her naked body.

"There. Is that better?" Darienne asked.

Veronica closed her eyes at the warmth of it. "Better."

"I think you should drink something hot. David? Can you get her—?"

"Tea. I can make her some tea."

"Just the thing."

"No!" Veronica said, reaching for him as he began to rush off.

"I won't leave you for long," David told her. He leaned forward and held her in his arms for a moment. Weak as she was, his strength comforted, then aroused her. "Be patient, my angel. Our bond is new, and I know it's hard for you to be separated from me. But you will adjust. Right now we need to help you get your strength back. I'll be gone for just a little while.

Darienne will sit with you." He kissed her forehead and then gently let her fall back against Darienne's shoulder.

Veronica tried to resist, but she was too weak to cling to him and keep him close. As he walked out of the room, she could feel the pain of their separation increasing again with each step he took. She would have wept and begged for him, but she still had enough feminine pride not to let her rival, Darienne, see her behave so pitifully.

When he'd left the room, Darienne said, "Can you sit up on your own?" She pushed Veronica upright and held her steady. Veronica remained there for a moment and then grew weak. "Here," Darienne said, taking hold of her again. "Lean against the window frame behind me." She got up and helped Veronica edge over to the end of the window seat, where she could rest her back against the wide frame that held the side of the bay window. Darienne sat on her other side, facing her. Veronica felt angry and bereaved at having to trade David's loving presence for Darienne's company.

"I'm glad we have a few minutes alone to talk," Darienne said. "Girl talk, the way we did once before, remember? Things David needn't hear."

Veronica was leaning her head against the frame, but she turned slightly so she could see Darienne. She was all blond and shimmering in her diamonds and a green, sequined gown that clung to her generous curves. By comparison Veronica could only feel pale and skinny wrapped inside the thick, luxurious fur Darienne had loaned her. "What things?"

"I'm still your friend, Veronica. Don't let David come between us. Now that he's initiated you, you will have a relationship with him that's very special and very strong. Stronger than life itself. Nothing I do can weaken it. I'm happy for you. I want you and David to be together."

"You want something from him, too," Veronica said, knowing she was too vulnerable now to be making accusations, but unable to resist.

"Only a little something," Darienne said with an air of innocence. "Nothing that will alter your relationship with him. Now that you have been initiated into our private circle, you will be my *petite soeur*. Do you know?"

"Little sister?"

"*Oui!* I'll teach you things about our existence that David won't, or can't. Because, despite all his vampire powers, he's still only a man. And men, you must have realized by now, never will understand things the way we women can."

Veronica smiled, her sense of rivalry with the other woman fading, as it had the first time they'd talked alone. Darienne's ideas were always so different, so blithely rebellious. Whether her conclusions about men were true or not, it was fun to listen.

"There! It's good to see you laugh," the blonde said, her green eyes lively with humor. "David will be pleased to see you laugh. He's so worried about you. It's a good thing I decided to come by. As usual, my instincts were right."

"How long have you been here?"

"Oh, perhaps an hour."

"You were here while we—"

"Don't be embarrassed. I climbed through the window and saw your clothes where you'd left them on the living room couch. I knew that you and he were somewhere, enjoying each other. I didn't peek through the keyhole, if that's what you're concerned about. I must say, this is a lovely place." Darienne glanced briefly up at the stars through the slanted window above them. "I wish I'd thought of it."

The last remark brought back Veronica's doubts. "You want to go on making love with David, don't you?"

"How sweetly you put it, 'making love.' No, that will be for you to make love with him. I only want to couple with him."

"Couple?"

"You know the French word, *s'accoupler?*"

"To mate."

"*Oui.* That's all I want. If you become a vampiress yourself, you'll understand why only David can satisfy me completely. I do require him. Only now and then, you understand—I travel a great deal. But I've known him much, much longer than you, and I claim a certain right. We're sisters now. And sisters ought to share, *n'est-ce pas?*"

Veronica looked away. Somehow she'd expected this, but it was hard to envision David with Darienne and not feel deeply threatened.

"Don't worry," Darienne said in her most soothing voice. "I'll stay out of your way for the present. I wouldn't want to disturb this most precious time you have with him right now. Enjoy it, Veronica. It won't be the same once you choose to become a vampiress."

"How do you know I will?"

Darienne lifted her shoulders elegantly, making the sequins glisten. "It's inevitable."

"How will it be if I do become . . . what you are?"

"Ah, you see? You're curious already. You will be more free and independent than you can imagine. Believe me, being dead is much freer than being alive ever was. You will stand beside me and David as an equal, with all our powers and strength." Darienne reached out and touched Veronica's hand. "Perhaps you'll want to travel with me. David is such a stick-in-the-mud about going anywhere." She drew her hand away. "But a word of advice first. Don't get too curious too quickly, as I did. My only regret about becoming a vampire is that I cut short my special time with David."

"When he first initiated you?"

"So, he told you?"

Veronica nodded. "What do you regret?"

Darienne tilted her head in a wistful pose. "The mental bond between us. We understood each other much better then than we ever have before or since. It was the only time in my life that I felt innocent. I worshiped David as if the earth turned around him. I felt a physical ache whenever we were separated. Just as you must feel now," she said, squeezing Veronica's fingers.

It comforted Veronica to know someone understood. "David said it would get less acute. Does it?"

"I believe so. I didn't let it go on long enough to find out. I begged David to let me drink from him."

"Drink from him," Veronica repeated, remembering the horrific, erotic blood ceremony in *Street Shadows*. A hot shiver coursed through her.

"Darienne, what are you telling her?" David's sharp voice interrupted them.

Veronica turned to the door. David, dressed now in his sweater and pants, his face clean, walked in holding a cup with steam rising from it.

"I'm telling her the facts of life as I know them," Darienne said, lithely getting up from the window seat. "You sit next to her. She wants you so."

"Don't you listen to her, Veronica," David said as he stepped up to them. "Darienne's version of the facts is as fluffed as that coat of hers." He sat next to Veronica and held out the cup. "You look so much better now," he said, gazing over her face with love. "Can you drink this?"

"Yes." Veronica reached to take the cup and saucer. "Thank you."

"She'll be fine," Darienne said. "She looks fragile, but she's stronger than you think."

"And what have you been telling her? I felt her anxiety. Or was it jealousy? I want to know what you said."

"Moi?" Darienne replied innocently. "What would I say? You know how we women like to talk. You've often commented on it. If you'd listened to us, you would have been bored to death—forgive the expression. Did I say anything to upset you, Veronica?"

Veronica glanced up from the cup of tea she was sipping. The blonde's beautiful, smiling eyes looked down on her with sisterly affection and secret understanding. Veronica had never had a sister. "No, you didn't say anything that upset me."

"There, you see?" Darienne said to David, playfully. "You're always accusing me of things. Aren't you ashamed now?"

David took a long breath. "Ashamed? I'm not that stupid. We'll talk about this another time." He paused as he looked at Darienne. "But I do thank you for helping me care for Veronica. Your cool mind was useful for once, and I'm grateful."

"I was happy to help," Darienne said, reaching out to touch Veronica's long hair. "I've grown fond of her." She addressed Veronica. "Do you feel warmer now?"

"I feel good," Veronica said. She felt much stronger. And now that David was near her again, she was growing aware of his masculine presence in a way she'd never experienced before. It was as if her body and mind could meld with his, as if they were a spiritual unit. She set down the empty cup by the window and leaned against David, who immediately took her into his arms. She could feel the reality of his love in a tangible way now, as if when she touched him, she touched his emotion, too.

And the touch fired her own sense of herself, her own emotion, and made her feel strong and invincible. She realized that what she was able to experience now was his vampiric strength, as if she possessed that very strength herself.

"You two look lovely together," Darienne said, still standing a few feet away. "Just like a Valentine. I must go now. Dawn is coming."

"Dawn. Yes, you're right," David said, glancing at the sky through the window.

Immediately Veronica could feel the impending separation on his mind. It cut like a sliver of ice. "Don't leave me, David."

"No, not yet," he assured her, kissing her forehead. "We have a little while. But I will have to go downstairs soon. You may stay here and rest."

A sob constricted her throat. "But I need to stay with you."

"Shhh. God, I can feel your pain! Remember, angel, you'll be in my home, near me. When the day ends, we'll be together again. It's hard at first, but you'll get used to our separations."

"No," she said, clinging to him. "I'll die if you leave me."

"You won't die," he told her. Instantly she could feel his fear return. "You're all right."

"David," Darienne said. "She means die spiritually and emotionally. I remember the feeling. It was dreadful. Maybe if you held her tightly for a while. She needs to feel you."

David slid his arms beneath the coat, his hand brushing Veronica's nipple as he did so. Her eyes closed in a wince at the sensation of his touch, like pleasurable pain. Her lips parted and met the taut skin of his jaw with a heated, worshipful kiss. He'd unwittingly awakened a profound erotic need more powerful than she'd ever known. Her breaths came faster. If only she could feel him within, experience their union just once more, to quench this terrible longing.

"David? Please . . ." Her voice reflected her agony of desire as she shook the coat off her shoulders and pressed her naked body against him. "Make love with me again. Make love to me."

"You're too weak."

"No, I'm not. Please, David? I need you."

"But you're not strong enough right now," David said with tenderness, running his hands up and down her back as if to comfort her. The action only aroused her more. As if sensing that, he stopped.

"I feel so strong now," Veronica insisted. "I've never felt so strong. Please give me yourself before you go."

"Go ahead, David," Darienne said as she picked up her coat and put it back on. "There's time yet. She needs you now as she never will again. You'll enjoy it, too."

"But she's lost so much blood. She hasn't the strength."

"She may not have the strength to get through the day without you, unless you appease her. You know how to be gentle, David. You won't hurt her. Give her what she wants." Darienne wrapped the white fur around herself. "Oh, I envy her!" she said wistfully. "I wish I could stay and watch."

"Darienne!"

"But I won't," she said, amused. "Goodbye."

Veronica pulled away enough to watch the vampiress glide out of the room, her gown shimmering beneath the hem of the coat. "Goodbye, Darienne," she called out in as firm a voice as she could muster, realizing she wasn't as strong as she felt.

Darienne turned, smiled, and blew them a kiss. When she was gone, Veronica looked up at David. "She's right. I feel like I'll wither away unless you make love with me now. My whole being craves you. It's such an ache, David. I feel so desperate for you. It frightens me."

"Then we'll make love," David said, smoothing back her hair. "But we have less than an hour."

Veronica shifted herself on the seat cushion and lay back, opening her arms to him. "Hurry, then."

David pulled off his clothing. In moments she felt the sheer bliss of his flesh entering her. Already she took comfort, sensing her driving need for him becoming appeased. And as he slowly and gently made love, she felt whole and strong and profoundly serene.

"David," Veronica whispered a short time later as she held on to him tightly. He could feel her writhing body nearing its climax beneath him. "Drink from me again," she pleaded.

These were the words he'd feared she'd say. It was one reason he'd been reluctant to lie with her again so soon. "I can't," he told her. "Not for a while. You must be content with love-making."

Disappointment seeped into the sensual glaze of her eyes. But she accepted his answer, and he felt she understood. He increased the urgency of his thrusts inside her sweet, tight body and kissed her hard, hoping to satiate her new desires as best he could without taking more of her blood.

Soon Veronica cried out with ecstasy. She arched toward him as her head fell back, and he felt the contractions in her belly. He allowed his own release then, enjoying all the delight her lovely, mortal body provided. And with their new blood bond, he felt a more profound intimacy with her than ever before. It sustained him so, emotionally, that whatever physical heights they reached together now seemed almost irrelevant.

After clinging together to savor the sweetness of the moment, David began to draw away. The sun would rise in only a matter of minutes.

Veronica tried to pull him back. He prevented her, and lifted himself away from her body. Kneeling beside her as she lay gazing at him with longing, he said, "I must go. There's no more time."

Tears filled her eyes, but she nodded. "Can I stay here?"

"You'd better. I'm afraid you may still be too weak to drive home. It's Saturday. You don't have to work?"

"No," she said, smiling a bit.

"Thank God. Rest until you feel strong enough, if you decide to go home. Or you may stay until evening, but I'm afraid there's nothing here for you to eat. I'll get you a blanket."

He left and in moments came back with a blue wool blanket. He covered her soft, naked body with it. Checking the wounds on her neck, he was pleased to see there was no further bleeding. He'd feared she might bleed again with the intensity of their lovemaking.

He stroked her hair. "Will you be all right after I leave you?"

A tear streamed from her eye back into her hair. "I'll ache for you. But I'll be all right knowing we'll be together tonight."

"I'll long for you, too, my love. I've tasted your blood, and you're a part of me, now."

He took two keys he'd brought back along with the blanket and put one of them in her hand. "This is a key to my home.

No one else has one. I want you to be able to come here whenever you want."

He took the other, smaller key and held it up. "This key opens the door to my resting place. If you find the pain of separation too great, you may come to me."

"Will you know I'm there?" she asked, her brown eyes wide and soulful. "Will you be asleep?"

"I fall into a heavy sleep, but I believe I would wake for a few moments if you came to me. Don't be frightened by the way you find me. I lose all my strength in the daytime. Only my coffin, and the earth from my homeland that lines it, preserve me from the sun's destruction. I won't be able to speak, and I won't be able to even reach out to touch you." He smiled. "But you may touch me."

Veronica nodded like a serious child being given instructions on how to care for a new pet. David kissed her, amused and touched by her ingenuous sweetness. "You're my favorite person in all the world," he whispered. "I trust you as I've never trusted anyone."

She gazed at him as a new tear streaked back into her hair. "I love you, David. Only you in the whole world."

"And I love only you." He put the small key into her hand, folded her fingers over it, and kissed her delicate knuckles. "I must go now." He looked out at the sky which was no longer quite so black. There was no time left. Now he could smell the dawn. "Until tonight." He kissed her quickly on the mouth and then hurried from the room, leaving his clothes on the floor where he'd left them.

He looked back once as he reached the hall. Veronica was lying on her side now, huddled knees-to-chest beneath the blanket, as if she were back in her mother's womb. She'd reached for his sweater and was using it as a pillow, nestling her cheek into it longingly. When he turned, she looked at him. As their gazes met across the wide, empty ballroom, a silent message of love passed between them, mind touching mind, emotion melding with emotion.

They were one.

14

A Small Price to Pay

VERONICA AWAKENED slowly from a deep sleep. With a languid movement, she turned onto her back. Bright light filtering through her closed eyelids disturbed her. She opened her eyes partway and had to turn her head to the side, the light was so harsh. Putting her hand up to block it, she found herself in the empty ballroom. She chanced another look toward the glare and realized it was the bright sun coming in through the frosted windows above and to the other side of her. She could bear the intense sunlight for only a moment before she had to turn her eyes back to the more muted, interior light.

As she sat up on the window seat, the blanket fell away from her. She was naked. At once everything came back to her, all David had done, all she'd begged him to do. She picked up his blue sweater and held it against her chest, hugging it. Concentrating on him, she began to experience a profound lethargy. Soon her own heartbeat was slowing to match his as he lay in his resting place somewhere below the ground, underneath the mansion.

Veronica shook her head slightly to keep herself just on the edge of their mental union. If she allowed her mind to go any closer, she felt she might be swept into a lethargy herself.

It was Saturday, she remembered. She looked at her watch. Almost noon. Her parents were expecting her to visit them today. Much as she longed to stay until the sun set again, she realized she mustn't do anything that would cause her parents to worry about her. Her union with David had to be kept secret at all costs, and that meant keeping up a normal appearance to everyone else she knew.

Without thinking, she turned to look out the window. The light blinded her again, its intensity so strong it was as if the sun had begun to radiate three times its normal amount of brightness. Her new sensitivity must be due to her connection with David. The thought warmed her. This was how much she belonged to David, that she could even share some of the burdens of his existence!

She stood up, a bit unsteady on her feet at first. But she felt reasonably strong. Her mouth was dry. She folded the blanket and left it on the window seat, then picked up David's clothes and carefully folded them. Carrying them over one arm, she reached for the two keys he'd given her and the empty water glass, then headed across the ballroom floor.

Veronica hadn't seen the room in daylight before, and she admired it as she walked. Shining gold draperies that reached from floor to ceiling framed the three sets of windows. They were hung ornately, with gathers at regular intervals to give the material a scalloped design. The rich wood of the floor was polished to such a gloss that it reflected the sunlight and hurt her eyes. In one corner, incongruous with the room's old-fashioned elegance, stood David's wide-screen television.

She entered the hallway and glanced at the several doors she passed by, wondering what was behind them. She peeked into the one room whose door was open. It was empty but clean. There was a closet and a draped window and a ceiling light. It might have served as a guest room at one time.

When she came to David's living room, she got a drink of water from the bar. Her clothes lay in a haphazard pile on the couch, and she recalled how anxiously she'd undressed for him the night before. She quickly put on underwear, the knit dress, and her shoes.

It was a little past noon now. If she was going to visit her parents for the usual length of time, she'd have to leave soon. But she couldn't leave without seeing David. She took the two keys he'd given her and started down the spiral staircase. When she reached the second floor and saw the locked door, curiosity got hold of her. She tried the larger key in the lock and found it worked.

Slowly opening the door, she peeked in. Books were what she saw, floor-to-ceiling bookcases filled with them! She decided to take a few steps into the room and soon found herself wandering down aisle after aisle, from room to room.

The entire second floor was a vast personal library. Everything from ancient Greek tragedies and the works of Plato and Aristotle, to Malory, Shakespeare, and Shelley, to Hemingway and Capote, to modern plays by Stoppard and Mamet, and even screenplays by Robert Towne and Woody Allen. There was a whole section of French authors: Hugo, Molière, Racine, Baudelaire. There were books on art and music, architecture, geography, and myriad other subjects, old and modern.

By the time Veronica had scanned all the shelves, a half hour had passed. The enormity of David's interest and knowledge overwhelmed her and made her feel inadequate. Why had he chosen her? She might have a university degree, but she had actually learned little of the world. What she had learned in college was how to be a good student, how to write on a test what a professor required for an A grade. She'd forgotten most of what she'd learned a few days after every exam. And she had never traveled. Vacation trips with her family to Wisconsin were the farthest she'd ever been from Chicago. Why hadn't David chosen a woman with an intellect to match his own?

Tears gathered in her eyes, and she fled to the staircase, ashamed to even be in his library. She locked the door and walked down another flight of steps to the first floor. Against her better judgment, unable to deny her curiosity, she unlocked the door and opened it. Furniture met her eyes. Old furniture, haphazardly placed and getting dusty, as if in some forgotten antique store. Carved wood tables and desks with delicate varnishes, and chairs and couches upholstered with velvets and tapestry materials. Remnants of David's past, she guessed. She didn't walk in, because there was no more time to explore.

After locking the door again, she found the hidden corridor and went down the creaky flight of stairs that took her below ground level to the basement. The atmosphere grew cool and moist as she reached the door. She unlocked it. A musty odor greeted her as she walked in. She moved down an aisle between crates and boxes filled with contents she couldn't imagine. Here and there were more pieces of antique furniture.

As she looked around her in the dim light coming from the small, curtained windows at ground level, she grew acutely aware that she was physically very near to David. He hadn't told her exactly where his resting place was. He must have known she'd find it the way a speck of iron will find a magnet.

She moved down a maze of aisles through the length of the house until she came to a door that was locked. Hands beginning to tremble with anticipation, she took the small key and turned it in the lock. The door hinge whined as it swung open into darkness on the other side.

There were candles, a metal candle holder, and matches on an old table next to the door. She put a candle into the holder and lit it, wondering if David had left these for her to find. As she held the candle out in front of her through the open door, the flickering light illuminated the small, windowless room.

She walked down the three steps beyond the door. As she moved into the lower room, her eyes growing accustomed to the dark, she spotted a large object in the candle glow. In the middle of the small chamber stood a magnificent, rectangular casket fashioned of wood and encrusted with gold. Beneath it, supporting it, stood a thick table of about the same dimensions. She walked toward the casket with silent reverence and laid her hand on the gold leaf decorating the lid.

David's coffin. Her sense of his presence grew overwhelming, and she began to breathe more deeply. After setting the candle and holder on the floor, she took hold of the edge of the lid with both hands. It was quite heavy, but it moved smoothly and silently, as if the hinges were kept well oiled.

Beneath the lid she found David, lying on white satin. Tears blurred her vision. She blinked them away. After pushing the lid open as far as it would go, she bent to pick up the candle again. Holding it over the open coffin, she studied her beloved. His eyes were closed. One hand lay at his side and the other rested over his abdomen. The strength of his broad shoulders, muscular arms, and deep chest was dormant now, and he appeared like a finely chiseled statue. Like Michelangelo's *David,* only reclining instead of standing.

His face also looked perfect and at peace. The narrow, aristocratic nose, the high cheekbones, the regal arch of his eyebrows, the brown hair that matched her own—all these Veronica noted with love and adoration. Hesitant at first, but quickly growing sure of herself, she put her hand out to touch the arm that lay across his chest. His skin was cool, as if his body temperature was low, but it wasn't cold. She ran her fingers softly across his bare chest, over the male nipple, to his shoulder. Gently she pressed her fingers into his thick shoulder muscles with a massaging motion, wanting to reassure him that she loved him and would take care of him and everything would be all right while he rested.

David's eyelids trembled for an instant, and then his eyes slowly opened. His blue eyes seemed opaque and unfocused, with an iridescent sheen, like the inside of a seashell. She leaned over his face, holding the candle near, hoping he could see her.

"David, it's Veronica."

His head turned to her a fraction of a degree. The corners of his lips formed a small, calm smile, while his eyes took on a soft glow that radiated love. From the edge of her vision she noticed the long fingers of the hand over his abdomen slowly lift and extend toward her. She took hold of his hand and held it in her own. His fingers closed around hers smoothly, spider-like.

The communion of their touch as she looked into his eyes was silent and serene. She bent and kissed his mouth. A hint of cobalt filtered into the strange iridescence of his eyes. "I love you," she told him, her voice full of emotion. "I love you."

His eyes filled with inexpressible adoration. Then, as if he could no longer forestall the deathlike lethargy, his eyelids slowly shut.

With gentleness she removed her fingers from his weakened grasp and lovingly pressed his hand to his chest. She closed the coffin lid over him, ran her fingers one last time over the gold and wood, and then walked out with the candle.

After locking the door again, she tried it twice to make sure it was sealed, then left the basement. She felt uniquely at peace now, having experienced David's peace. They had communed for a few perfect moments, moments that would sustain her until sunset.

Veronica drove home to shower and change. She put the car's visor down in an attempt to block the sun, which continued to irritate her eyes.

When she unlocked the door of her apartment, she opened

it carefully, knowing her cat, Felix, would be there to greet her. His small head and big eyes peeked up at her from around the opening door. She walked in, closed it and bent to pet him.

Instead of putting his head beneath her hand as always, Felix backed away from her, ears flattening, and spit. It was the same reaction he had given David.

"It's me," she said in the high voice she used to talk to her pet. She put out her hand so he could smell her. Instead, the cat hissed and growled, then ran away into the kitchen. She followed and found him scratching at the back door. Then he jumped to the kitchen window, from which he'd escaped one day the previous summer.

When she leaned across the sink and tried to pick up her pet, he fled from her, to the front door in the living room. He scratched, then banged his body against the door, trying to get out.

"No, no," she said, coming after him. "It's all right." But Felix continued to throw himself against the door over and over, desperately attempting to flee. "Stop it!" Veronica said, beginning to cry. "You'll hurt yourself."

But the cat kept trying to get out until finally she saw a spot of blood in the fur on the side of his face. Tears filling her eyes, she quickly opened the door. Felix ran out in a flash, down the steps and across the front yard, then across the street where he disappeared between two houses.

Veronica knew she'd never see him again.

Around two-thirty she pulled up in front of her parents' brick bungalow in Cicero. She adjusted the rearview mirror so she could look at herself and took off her sunglasses. Squinting in the bright daylight, she checked her face. She'd put on some blusher to conceal her paleness and some makeup to hide her red eyes. She'd finally stopped crying about her cat. He was gone, and she had to accept his loss as a small price to pay for belonging to David. She only hoped some kind person would take in the animal and care for him as well as she had.

Moving the mirror to reflect a bit lower, she checked the large, multicolored scarf she'd tied around her neck, over her rust-colored sweater. After her shower she'd changed into a casual pants outfit. All traces of blood had been washed away, but there remained the two small wounds David had caused.

Veronica cherished the marks, but had to keep them hidden. She adjusted the scarf more securely, grabbed her jacket and got out of the car.

Her mother greeted her at the door. "You're late," she said. "I was getting worried."

Marie Benda Ames was Veronica's height, but about forty pounds heavier. She dyed her gray hair brown, perhaps a shade too dark. Her features were similar to Veronica's, except that she had hazel eyes, a lower forehead, and more flesh around her chin and neck. She wore a red cardigan sweater over a blouse and black skirt. There was a Santa Claus pin on the sweater.

"I was cleaning my kitchen," Veronica explained, following her mother into the house. It was an excuse she knew her mother would approve of and never question. Keeping house was a major preoccupation of Marie's, and she seemed to assume her daughter had the same sense of duty.

"Dad went out to buy the Sunday paper," Marie said. "Would you like me to put the kettle on for instant coffee?"

"No, thanks." Veronica took off her jacket, hung it in the hall closet, and sat down in one of two worn, flowered easy chairs placed by the curtained front windows. Between the chairs was a darkly varnished table with a large lamp on it. The base of the lamp was shaped like an urn patterned with green and pink flowers, and its shade was frilly. Veronica had always hated it.

Her parents' home never changed. Doilies were everywhere, as were inexpensive knickknacks. The upright piano she'd taken lessons on briefly as a child stood in one corner, unused, but sheet music for "Silver Bells" was propped up on it as though someone might want to sit down and play at any moment. Her mother changed the music according to the season: "Easter Parade" at Easter, "Grand Old Flag" at the Fourth of July, "Autumn Leaves" in the fall. Maintaining order was how her mother got through life: keeping house, observing holidays and seasons, keeping track of the quarterly interest on the family savings accounts.

"Look in the sideboard in the dining room," her mother said with a smile as she settled down on the dark brown, nubbytextured couch and picked up her knitting. "I got you something at Olympic."

Veronica chuckled. "What is it this time?"

"A cut-glass candy dish. It's really nice."

Marie exemplified the Bohemian fondness for saving money, and kept an account at nearly every one of the numerous savings and loan companies that lined Cermak Road. When one institution offered a toaster or some such attraction to those who added a few hundred dollars to their accounts, Marie would promptly and personally transfer the required amount from another savings and loan to the one making the offer. The "gifts" she received this way she usually passed on to Veronica, since she had no need for them herself.

Veronica walked into the dining room, with its lace-covered table and sturdy old chairs. The word *Veronica* was carved on one of the seats, a permanent reminder of her mischief-making at age five.

She opened the beveled-glass cabinet built into the wall above the polished wood sideboard. Among the "good" set of dishes and assorted figurines and teapots, which were rarely used, she found a small, corrugated cardboard box. As she brought it back into the living room, she opened it and took out the glass dish, a sticker on it indicating it was made in West Germany.

"Thanks, it's pretty," Veronica said, sitting down again. She wondered what on earth she'd do with it. "Anything new at the bakery?"

"Lonnie quit," Marie said, referring to one of her co-workers. Marie had worked at a Bohemian bakery on Cermak for the past fifteen years, wrapping up *houska,* a braided egg bread, and *kolacky,* fruit-filled pastries, and other baked goods for customers. Because of her seniority, she got Saturdays off.

As Marie chattered about Lonnie, Veronica couldn't help but feel the boredom creeping up on her that she'd experienced most of her life. The things that were of vital interest to her mother seemed mundane to Veronica. As a child, at home alone after school while her mother worked, she'd turned to the late-afternoon movie on TV to stimulate and entertain her. Soon her own mind had become as full of fantasy as the movies she watched. But the world of her imagination had no relevance in the real world. She'd lived a full life in her head and walked through the everyday world around her without ever fully becoming a part of it.

Until David. Now she was a part of something real that she could hold on to, that she could touch. The thought of him, of being with him tonight, would make these duty-laden hours with her parents pass quickly, she promised herself.

"I saw Harriet at the bakery the other day," Marie said, referring to Veronica's cousin. "She was all thrilled that you'd interviewed that Taglia boy. She said she wants to go see the play he's in, but her husband won't take her."

Veronica sighed. "Ralph's such a dolt. If you see her again, tell her I'll go with her."

"She'll like that." Marie studied Veronica as she put the candy dish back into the corrugated box. "Are you okay? You seem tired or something."

"I'm okay," Veronica answered quickly. "I've been working hard lately."

"That's a colorful scarf. How come you're wearing it?"

Veronica hesitated. "Why not?"

"You've never worn scarves much."

"Well, I do now."

Marie looked at her daughter with the judgmental eye that made Veronica's jaw muscles tense. "It's too much around your face, especially with your hair so long. Aren't you ever going to cut it?"

Her mother always seemed to want her to look as she had when she was eight years old, with short straight hair and bangs so carefully clipped you could line up a ruler underneath them. She had always discouraged any trace of sensuality. Veronica had the urge to tell her that not only did she have no intention of cutting her hair, but she wasn't a virgin anymore, either.

Fortunately, her father chose that moment to come through the front door, a thick copy of the Chicago Sunday *Tribune* under his arm. "Hi, kid!" he said when he saw her. He reached over and tugged on a lock of her hair. Veronica grinned and said hello.

Fred Ames was a tall man, his features showing a mixture of Italian and English ancestry. His hair was graying and he'd been putting on weight for the past several years. "Boy, it's getting cold out." He set the newspaper on the coffee table in front of the couch and went to hang up his coat.

"The weatherman said a cold front was coming in," Marie told him. "It's supposed to go down to twenty tonight."

Veronica closed her eyes. The weather. Every morning of her childhood, her mother had given her the weather report when she woke her up for school. Every evening perfect silence had to be maintained when the weatherman was on the TV newscast. Veronica wasn't sure if her mother was preoccupied with meteorology because it was the only part of the news report she understood, or because it was the only part that had any bearing on her life. Presidents and distant wars might come and go, but the weather would determine what to wear to work the next day.

"A cold front, eh?" Fred repeated.

"Right," Marie said. "And the windchill factor will make it feel like zero. Not to mention the lake effect."

Veronica started to laugh, the conversation struck her as so funny.

Her parents looked at her. "What's the matter?" her father asked, smiling but not understanding.

"Nothing." Veronica tried to compose herself. "How are things at work?"

"Not bad." Fred sat on the couch beside Marie. He worked at a nearby mail order company. He and Veronica's mother bought most of their clothes at a discount through the catalog. "We'll be getting the Christmas bonus next week. Hey, we need to get a tree!"

"We sure do," Marie agreed.

"There's a place up by Roosevelt Road. We could go for it now. Want to, Veronica?"

They spent the next hour picking out a Christmas tree, just as they had when she was little. While they did so, a light flurry of snow began to fall—the lake effect, her mother pointed out. For some reason, as they walked from tree to tree comparing one to another, Veronica found herself blinking back tears.

All the things she'd taken for granted in her life because they'd always been there, unnoticed like a frame around a painting, suddenly began to seem rich in their own quiet way: Christmas trees and *kolacky* and the Sunday paper; the ugly lamp in the living room; her parents, hardworking even though they lacked inspiration, content with the limited parameters they'd set for themselves.

Why was Veronica different? Why hadn't she accepted her life? Her college education could have broadened her interests while still leaving her happy with a routine day-to-day life. What had she missed by escaping into her fantasies?

They finally took home a Scotch pine, tied to the top of her parents' old Chevy, and carried it up the front steps. By five o'clock, as daylight was beginning to wane, they had it set up in the living room.

"We'll decorate it after supper," Marie said, turning on the lamp.

"I can't," Veronica told them, a keen sense of anxiety coming over her. "I have a date."

"You do?" Marie was always hinting that Veronica should be on the lookout for a husband. "Someone you met at work?"

"No." She touched her scarf, making sure it covered the marks on her neck. "Caroline introduced me to him."

"You'll have to bring him home for dinner some night."

Veronica hesitated. "Sure, Mom. Speaking of dinner, I can't stay."

"You have to get ready," Marie said, understanding. "Where's he taking you?"

Veronica rubbed her forehead. "I don't know. He likes to surprise me."

"What's he do for a living?"

"He's a writer. I'd better go now." Veronica walked toward the closet for her jacket.

"Well, have fun." Marie helped her on with the jacket. "Leave off the scarf, though," she said, stuffing the long ends of it inside Veronica's collar. "It doesn't do a thing for you. And why don't you pin up your hair?"

"Mom—"

"It'd be so much neater," Marie went on as Veronica opened the door and stepped out onto the cement porch. "I like your hair *off* your face."

"I know."

"And not too much makeup. You might think men like that, but they really don't."

Just as Veronica was losing her patience with all the parting instructions, she heard the echo of her own name, as if on the wind.

She stood transfixed. *David!* The sun was just setting behind the brick homes across the street, and the sky was almost dark. And David was calling to her to come to him. She was so far away. Oh, why hadn't she left sooner?

"Goodbye, Mom, Dad," she said as she hurried down the steps. "Have to go."

Her parents watched her from the doorway, looking puzzled. "When'll you be back?" her father asked.

"I don't know," Veronica answered distractedly as she reached her car. "I'll call sometime."

"David!" Veronica cried as she rushed up the winding staircase to the third floor.

David came down half a flight to meet her. He picked her up in his arms, kissing her, and brought her into the living room.

"I'm sorry I was so far away," she said, clinging to him as he set her down and held her near. "All the time it took to drive back from my parents', I could have spent with you."

"It's all right." He ran his hands over her body, beneath her jacket. "We have lots of time and many nights together."

Veronica shed the jacket and tossed it on the floor. She was in a frenzy to be near David. Pulling her sweater over her head, she tossed it aside, too. She undid the knot in her scarf and let it slide off her shoulders. David reached out to touch the marks on her neck. She closed her eyes at his caress. As his hands moved down to her breasts, she unbuttoned his shirt.

The ethereal glow was beginning to show in his eyes. "You came to me during the day, didn't you? Or was it a dream?"

"I came to you." She smiled up at him. "I held your hand and I kissed you."

"And you told me you loved me." A small tear formed at the corner of his eye.

"Yes, I told you," she murmured, pressing her breasts against his bared chest. She moaned softly at the feel of him. The tremendous need to be one with him overwhelmed her. "David—"

"I know," he said, lifting her in his arms again. He began taking her down the hall toward the ballroom.

"Will you take my blood?" she asked, her arms around his neck.

"It's too soon, my love. Not for a while. You would grow too weak."

"All right," she said, disappointed. She wanted to give him sustenance. She wanted him to need her for his very existence.

"You give me so much just by being here," he told her as he crossed the ballroom in the darkness. "By giving me your sweet body to love, by giving me all your devotion and affection. No one else gives me what you do."

He set her on the window seat, where she drew him to her, eager for him to appease her ache.

They made love for hours.

After midnight David suggested they go out for a walk. They dressed, put on their coats, and left. David grabbed his black umbrella just before they walked out the door.

"It's only snowing a little," she told him, putting the hood of her jacket up over her head.

"It might turn to rain," he said. She saw a gleam of delight in his eye.

They walked at a leisurely pace, enjoying the night. The air was clear. The wind had died down, and there were gentle snow flurries that did not accumulate on the ground, but only made it wet, so that the streets reflected the street lamps, car headlights, and signs. The lights of the night were easy on Veronica's eyes after the harshness of the sun. The night appeared more beautiful to her than it ever had before, a fantasy world with snowflakes like confetti slowly falling all around her. She felt like celebrating.

By 3:00 A.M. they found themselves on North Michigan Avenue, approaching the dark, gothic Tribune Tower and the Chicago River just south of it.

"Well," David said, stopping and looking about him, the mischievous gleam back in his eyes. "This will have to do."

"For what?" She grinned up at him.

"For singin' in the rain."

She realized why he'd brought the umbrella. "No, you aren't! Are you?"

"The street's empty," he said. Only an occasional car had passed by as they walked. "It's not rain, but snow flurries will have to suffice. Watch."

As she took a few steps back to give him room, David grabbed hold of the black umbrella by the middle and jumped to a nearby lamppost, hanging by one arm and holding out the umbrella with the other. He began to sing.

And Veronica began to laugh. Not that his voice was bad. On the contrary, he sang very nicely. It was just the daring impulsiveness of it all! In a way, it was unlike David. And in a way, it was like him exactly.

He walked jauntily down the street, then did tap steps in front of a store window, twirling the umbrella in front of him. He kicked the tip of the umbrella up and caught it in his hand, never missing a beat. Opening it over his head, he continued in such a fun-loving way, with such light and elegant steps, that he looked like a marionette bouncing from strings. All at once he jumped out into the street and went round and round in a large circle, holding the umbrella out in front of him. Veronica thought he looked like a child having fun in street puddles. Putting the umbrella overhead again, he jumped back to the curb, and combined a balancing and crossover step.

Veronica laughed and cried at the same time, enraptured by the giddy exuberance of it all. She was enormously pleased to see David so happy, so uninhibited, so full of life. She had given him this happiness, she knew. And she felt only love and thankfulness that they had found each other, that she was here for him.

When he finished, he tossed the umbrella aside and swept her up into his arms, turning her around until she began to grow dizzy. He stopped then and kissed her as her head still reeled a bit from his force and strength.

When he set her down, they saw ahead of them the Wrigley Building, its white surface lit by floodlights against the night sky. Its central tower rose above the rest of the building and displayed a large built-in clock near the top. The twenty-five-story edifice gleamed so, it shone like the sun in their eyes, only not so bright that they had to turn away from it.

"Look, David, isn't it beautiful?"

"Let's climb it!"

"Climb it?"

"It's easy. I'll carry you." He took her hand and began to cross Michigan Avenue toward the building.

"But, David, I don't think—"

"Don't think. Just leave it to me."

When they reached the white building, he hoisted her onto his back, her legs wound around his waist and her arms tightly around his neck. He kicked off his shoes. Digging his fingers and toes into cracks in the stone, he began climbing straight up the side. When they were two stories up, Veronica panicked. "David, I'm scared!"

"Don't look down. We'll be up there in no time. Hold on!"

She shut her eyes and didn't look for several seconds. When she opened them again, she could see out across the river from a new perspective as the Michigan Avenue Bridge below grew smaller.

David moved up the side of the building like a grasshopper moving up a stalk of corn. First he climbed the main part of the building, seventeen or eighteen stories, then continued up the narrower tower several more stories. They passed the two-story-high clock set into the stone and stopped at a ledge above it. There they sat down, their legs dangling over the edge, as below them the huge minute hand cranked downward toward 3:15.

Veronica shivered from the cold of the stone she was sitting on and from fear. She'd never been this high without glass or a railing to keep her from falling.

"Hang on to me," David said, putting his arms around her. "I won't let you fall."

She wrapped her arms around his chest and leaned her head against his neck. In a few moments she'd settled down, taking on David's calmness. Now she saw only the beauty of the city all around her—the many skyscrapers with their windows lit in random patterns; a floodlit fountain below, its waters glowing like dancing gold; the silent, wide river off to the right, bordered by buildings and the lights from Wacker Drive; the Michigan Avenue Bridge crossing the river below their feet, just in front of the Wrigley Building.

Veronica pointed off to their left to a tapering black skyscraper looming far above all the others. "There's the John

Hancock Center, where I took you to dinner. Except I was the only one who ate," she joked.

David looked at it, a smile in his eyes. "I treasure that place. It's where I first realized I'd fall in love with you."

They kissed and David adjusted the hood of her jacket more closely over her head, to keep her warm. She glanced down at the river, whose waters moved soundlessly far below them.

"Did you know that the Chicago River flows backward?" she said.

"How can it do that?"

"They altered the gradient somehow and reversed its flow so it wouldn't pollute the lake. It was done long ago. Before I was born."

"That's not so long ago," David murmured in a doting voice.

For some reason Veronica thought of his library and the feeling of inadequacy she'd experienced there. "David, why did you pick me? I don't have much knowledge or culture, and you have so much."

His eyes took on an inner light. "Culture can be learned. But a loving nature, sensitivity, and imagination, such as you possess, are difficult to acquire if one isn't born with them. What's charming—and a little sad—is that you're so unaware of your own qualities—you don't appreciate them. You're unpretentious and sweet, but you undervalue yourself. Yet *I* value you more than you can ever know."

Veronica couldn't help but shed a few tears at his words. "I never felt worthy until I met you. My life will be different now. With you I feel I can do anything in the world."

In fact, Veronica felt not only as if she could do anything, but as if she and David owned the world. And the world was more beautiful than either of them had ever imagined.

But the loveliness of the night faded toward dawn. They reached David's mansion just in time. He returned to his coffin as sunrise was breaking. Veronica stood over him, holding his hand and speaking softly to him until the deathlike lethargy closed his eyes and stillness took over his body. She kissed him and closed the coffin lid. It was so hard to leave him.

She went home to sleep for a while herself—and to wait for the night to fall so she could come to him again.

15

The Consequences of Love

ON A Monday morning early in January, Rob Greenfield looked through the glass partition of his office at Veronica's empty desk. She was late again, and Rob was growing concerned. Though he didn't know why he should be. After the day he kissed her in the file room, he'd kept his distance. Obviously she didn't want him. But he couldn't stop his feelings for her. Wise or unwise, he'd fallen in love with her.

For a while he'd thought she'd gotten her act together again. She'd been looking better and getting to work on time. Then, all at once, she'd gone back to her previous pattern. Rob knew Ed Malloy was growing annoyed with her inconsistent effort. But what should Rob say to her? She resented any advice. And, as she always pointed out, it was none of his business.

Rob ran his fingers through his hair in irritation and sat down at his desk. He had a movie review to crank out. It was no use worrying about a woman who wouldn't even admit something was wrong.

He turned on his computer terminal and called up the appropriate file. Over the weekend he'd gone to see a new Disney film. Reviewing children's movies always made him a little uneasy. He had no idea what youngsters liked nowadays. He only had his own childhood to go by, and back then he hadn't seen many movies or watched a lot of TV. As a kid, he was more into playing baseball with his friends and annoying his older sisters by hiding frogs in their beds. He hadn't really discovered movies until high school.

Rob typed a few opening sentences and got stuck. He leaned back in his seat and tried to think through his judgments about the film. If he had children of his own, he could ask them what they liked and didn't like, maybe even quote some of their opinions. God, he'd enjoy that! But he wasn't even married yet. And now he'd let himself fall in love with the wrong woman.

Great! His mind had drifted to Veronica again. Annoyed with himself, he tore yesterday's date off his calendar pad and threw it in the wastebasket.

He might have been able to forget Veronica if she didn't look so much like someone who needed rescuing. It was obvious she'd latched on to the wrong man, and Rob foolishly kept hoping she'd realize that. Something had to give. She couldn't go on much longer the way she was.

"Seen Veronica?"

He looked up to find Ed Malloy in his doorway. Rob quickly tried to think of some excuse to cover for her. Then he decided, why bother? His excuses were wearing thin. "No, I haven't."

"She's been late a lot the past few weeks, hasn't she?" Ed said, rolling up his shirtsleeves. "I'm going to have to have a talk with her. You know what her problem is?"

"Yeah. David de Morrissey."

"Well, she may have to choose between him and her job," Ed muttered. "I thought you had the hots for her yourself."

Rob felt heat come to his face. "Not anymore."

"Oh. I was going to suggest you try romancing her away."

"I don't think anyone could pry her away from de Morrissey."

"Sure you can! Half the women in the office are after you," Ed said, putting his hands on his wide hips. "Veronica's a nice kid. I hate to see her mess up her life."

"She's not my responsibility. A guy can get burned only so many times."

Ed nodded as if he understood. "De Morrissey must really be something. Of course, she's the dreamy-eyed type. I suppose a wealthy playwright—"

"It's more than that," Rob said, pushing the keyboard away from the edge of his desk. "I think he's got her on drugs. She claims he hasn't, but what else can it be? The change in her appearance and behavior is so marked."

"I hate to think so, but you may be right." An unusual silence came over the office. Ed turned and glanced over the room behind him. "Here she comes now. She looks sick!"

Rob immediately got up from his desk and looked through the glass partition toward the entrance. As everyone in the office paused to notice, Veronica was walking slowly among the desks, her coat open, grabbing on to chairs to support herself. She appeared extremely pale and weak. The sight shocked Rob. He'd never seen her look so ill. "Looks like she might faint!" he said and moved past Ed into the main office.

When he reached Veronica, he took hold of her under her arms to help support her. "Are you all right?"

"Just a little dizzy," she said.

"Are you sick? The flu?"

"No. I . . ." Her knees began to give way.

Ed Malloy rushed up as other co-workers approached, murmuring surprise and concern. He put an arm around her from the other side. "There's a couch in my office. Let's get her in there."

Veronica seemed to regain a bit of strength then. Rob had the feeling, from the frightened look in her eyes, that she had realized what sort of appearance she was making in front of her boss and everyone in the office. Her adrenaline must have kicked in, for she grew more secure on her feet as they walked, and she tried to pull away from the two men's assistance.

"I'm all right now," she said when they walked into Mr. Malloy's private office.

"I want you to lie down for a little while anyway." Ed guided her to the couch, helped her off with her coat, and made her sit down. "Put your feet up," he said. "That's right." She obeyed her boss and stretched out.

Rob looked on, worrying what to do for her. He would have loosened her collar, but she was wearing a turtleneck sweater. "Can I get you some water?" he asked.

"Yes, please," she replied.

Rob rushed out to the watercooler. When he came back, he found Ed Malloy had pulled up a chair and was sitting facing Veronica.

"You're going to have to take better care of yourself," he was telling her.

Rob handed her the water. She sat up and drank it all as if she were thirsty, then handed the paper cup back to him.

"More?"

"I'll get some later," she said, trying to smile. "Thanks."

Rob figured he might be intruding, since they were in Ed's office. "I'll get back to my desk, then."

"No, stay, Rob," Ed said, eyeing him in an urgent way that indicated he thought Rob might be helpful in this situation.

"Sure." Rob walked around Ed and sat on the thick arm of the leather couch by Veronica's feet. She'd leaned back against the armrest again, looking self-conscious about having two men staring at her.

"I hate to pick this moment to get tough with you, Veronica, since you're not well," Ed said. "On the other hand, maybe it's just the right time for a lecture. It looks to me like your personal life's getting out of hand. You can rightly say that your love life is none of my concern. But it is my concern when you come to work late nearly every day, and now you come in ready to pass out."

"I'm sorry," she said, pushing her hair back and sitting up more. "I'll do better."

"What's wrong?" Ed asked. "You used to be the most prompt person in the whole office."

"I . . . stay out later than I should," she admitted, looking down at her hands as she fidgeted nervously.

"I understand you're still involved with David de Morrissey," Ed said.

She looked up at Rob then, her eyes accusing. But Rob felt angry and unapologetic.

"Don't blame Rob," Ed told her. "I pumped him for information. He's just as concerned about you as I am."

Veronica answered with tight lips and a cool voice. "Yes, I'm seeing David de Morrissey."

"Does he hang around with a fast set?" Ed asked.

She looked puzzled. "What?"

"What kind of people does he associate with?"

"No one."

"You and he don't go out with other people or to parties?" Rob asked, trying to put the question more clearly. He knew

what Ed wanted to find out—if de Morrissey took her to gath-
erings where drugs were passed around.

Veronica's expression grew odd, as if she wanted to laugh.
"No, we never see other people."

"So you're always alone with him?" Rob asked, anger almost
making him choke on the question.

"Yes, if you have to know!"

"Now, Veronica," Ed said sternly, "Rob's just trying to help
me get to the root of this. And we're both trying to help *you*.
I've got to be frank with you. Another few weeks of tardiness
and preventable ill health and I'll have to fire you. If you'd been
in an accident or caught pneumonia, it'd be different. But
you're letting yourself go down the tubes because of a man. It
shows a lack of good judgment and it's made you highly unde-
pendable. I can't let that go on. I've got a magazine to run."

Veronica grew pale and looked chastened. Rob felt sorry for
her, but he was relieved Ed was saying all this. Rob had warned
her this might happen.

"Now," Ed continued, "if he's got you on drugs, then I can
help you get into one of those drug programs."

"I'm not on drugs!" she said, visibly upset.

"Alcohol?"

"No."

"Something must be draining you!" Ed said.

She looked frightened again, Rob noticed. As if she had
something to hide. But what could she be hiding? "Is de Morrissey into sadomasochism?" Rob asked. Ed glanced at Rob in
astonishment, but he turned to Veronica to watch her reaction.

She looked at Rob, then Ed. "I've heard of that, but I don't
know—"

"Bondage," Rob said. "Whips and chains."

"No!" She seemed appalled. "How could you think I'd go
along with that?"

But Rob noticed a doubtful expression pass through her eyes,
as if she'd caught herself saying something that wouldn't bear
scrutiny. "What *does* he do to you?" Rob asked.

"N-nothing," she replied.

"We're only trying to help you," Ed said, his voice uncusto-
marily gentle now. "You can tell us. It won't go any further
than this office."

Veronica backed as far as she could into her corner of the leather couch, her eyes growing not only angry, but something more. Protective, Rob decided. She was protecting de Morrissey.

"All he does is love me!" she said in a vehement, hushed voice, making it clear she would be pushed no further.

Rob and Ed exchanged exasperated glances. "All right," Ed said, getting up and pushing his chair back to its original position. He looked at Veronica, who was shifting her legs off the couch. "It's up to you whether you want to keep your job or not. I can't straighten out your life for you."

"I want to keep my job," she said in a more contrite tone. "I'll do better, I promise."

"Okay," Ed told her. "I'll give you another month. If you're not back in the groove by then, you're out! Understand?"

"Yes."

She stood up. Rob noticed she was still unsteady on her feet. He walked over to her, to help her out if necessary.

"And just a piece of advice, Veronica, from an old geezer who's been around and seen a lot," Ed said. "Get out of that relationship. I don't know what de Morrissey's into, but he's no good for you. You'd better wise up. Fast!"

Veronica paled again while her brown eyes took on a hard defiance that dismayed Rob. Before she could say anything that might get her further into trouble with their boss, Rob grabbed her coat, took her arm, and urged her out of the room. "Come on," he said. "Let's get back to work."

She complied and they walked through the maze of desks toward their cubicles. On the way several people stopped her to ask if she was all right. "Fine, thank you," Veronica said to each one. By the time they reached her desk, Rob noticed a sheen of tears in her eyes.

"I'm sorry Ed was so hard on you, but you had to know it was coming," Rob said.

"I know." She grabbed a tissue from the box on her desk and dabbed at her eyes. "I'm just realizing that so many people care about me," she said, smiling self-consciously. "I didn't know."

"Of course people care."

"I've never felt like I was one of the team, you know?" She crumpled the tissue into a tight ball in her hand.

"Why not?"

"I've always felt a little different."

"I don't see why you should."

"Because I don't know what seems to be common knowledge to other people. I don't think like everyone else. It puts a distance between me and others."

"But you have friends," Rob said. He realized she had a poor self-image, something he previously hadn't been aware of. She was so beautiful, he'd always assumed she must be popular and sociable in her own circle.

"I have a few friends. Not many."

"And de Morrissey? How does he fit in?"

"He makes me feel strong and whole," she replied, her eyes brightening, but only for a moment. "At least when I'm with him, I feel that way."

"I'm your friend." Rob felt full of emotion despite his previous vow to forget her. "I could make you feel appreciated, if you'd let me."

Her eyes glazed with new tears. She seemed genuinely touched, as if for the first time he'd reached through her outer shell and made contact with the fragile personality beneath.

"Thank you," she said, quickly turning away.

The barrier was up again. She was afraid of the real, human contact she needed, he realized. And somehow de Morrissey had tapped into that need and had overcome her fear. So much so that he'd taken her over completely.

"Can I get you anything?" Rob asked.

"I'm okay."

"Did you eat breakfast this morning?"

"No."

"Well, maybe that's why you're feeling faint. I'll get you something out of the sandwich machine downstairs. How about some tea with it?"

She smiled a little. "All right. Thanks."

She looked grateful and shy now. Rob would have taken her in his arms if they hadn't been at the office with people glancing with curiosity through the glass. But if he had tried to embrace her, she would probably have pushed him away. Rob wondered if what he was seeing now might be a crack in de Morrissey's grip on her. Then again, maybe it wasn't. But the possibility gave him new hope.

Before going out to meet Caroline at lunch time, Veronica went to the ladies' room. When she looked in the mirror at her reflection, a tremor of fear ran through her. For the first time she saw herself as everyone else must have seen her. She looked extremely pale, her face a sickly white. There were dark circles under her eyes and her cheeks were becoming gaunt. She was losing weight because she'd been skipping meals, forgetting to eat in her urgency to be with David after work, and in her rush to get to work each morning because she'd overslept. And, of course, she wasn't sleeping enough.

This morning she'd almost fainted because David had taken her blood again last night. Finally. She'd been waiting all these weeks since the first time, and he'd kept refusing. But at last he'd given in to her pleas. The deep ecstasy of those moments was worth anything. Anything. Her eyes closed at the memory of it as her hand went to the side of her throat. *Oh, David* . . .

The door to the ladies' room opened, startling her. One of her co-workers said hello and walked into one of the stalls. Veronica glanced into the mirror again. She looked awful. What could she do? She didn't want to give up one moment of the time she spent with David, but she had to keep her job. It was as if she was leading a double life. Her nights were a fantasy with David. She never felt tired when she was with him. Her days were long and dull, working at a job that no longer excited her or seemed to hold any potential.

Why couldn't she quit and spend all her time with David? She could live with him there at the mansion, protect him during the day while he rested. She could give him her blood for sustenance and her body for love. In return she was sure he'd take care of her.

Still, logic told her it would be an odd life with only David in it. And when Mr. Malloy had threatened to fire her, the possibility of losing her job had stung her. Her job had once given her life some definition and goals. Working there had made her feel as if she had a place in the world.

It was all too much to think about now. Caroline was waiting. Veronica dabbed on some makeup and left.

She met Caroline at Marshall Field's in Water Tower Place. Caroline had called that morning and asked her to come and help her pick out some suits that were on sale. They met by the front entrance. It was rainy and low clouds hung over the city, enveloping the tops of the skyscrapers in thick mist. Despite the obscured sun, it was still too bright for Veronica, and she wore her sunglasses.

"Are you sick?" Caroline asked with great concern as soon as she saw Veronica take her glasses off.

"A touch of the flu," Veronica lied as they entered the building.

"Maybe you should go home."

"No, no. Come on, let's look at suits. What did you have in mind?"

Caroline hesitated, eyeing Veronica as they walked. She swallowed, as if recovering a bit, and said in a brighter tone, "I don't know. Something to wear to work that looks business-like."

Veronica knew Caroline hated to shop. She didn't really like being an accountant, either, though she was good at it. Caroline had said back in college that she wanted a secure profession that would put bread on the table. Her true interest was archaeology, but after taking a few college courses in the subject, she had put it aside.

"Do you ever wish you'd become an archaeologist?" Veronica asked as they walked into the section that displayed women's suits. "You wouldn't have had to worry about clothes."

Caroline sighed. "Sometimes. But I'm doing well in accounting, and it's how I met Tom. It's working out."

"How was Hawaii?" Veronica was referring to her friend's honeymoon.

"Gorgeous. Crowded with tourists, of course, but what can you do?"

"And how is marriage treating you?"

"Now that the honeymoon's over?" Caroline made a comical expression. "Just between you and me, dating was more fun."

"Really?"

"Sure. There's the anticipation of seeing each other. There's the preparation for each date. He escorts you to nice places. There're all the questions: Does he love me? Do I love him? Is he the one I should marry? It's exciting and even a little scary. But after you're married, the suspense is all over. And you have to adjust to a guy who keeps producing dirty underwear he wants you to wash. But that's life. Single people worry that they're not married, and married people reminisce about when they were single. Nobody's ever one hundred percent happy."

I am, Veronica thought with a hidden smile. Her relationship with David would never be a disappointment.

Yet there was something Veronica admired about people who settled for less than they dreamed of. Anyone who could cope with daily life without escaping into fantasy was really rather brave. Braver than Veronica. Facing the real world took guts.

On the other hand it was fantasy that had led Veronica to David. And now she was living a dream others couldn't even imagine. Still, her life was getting so divided that she could hardly deal with the real world anymore. Even holding down a simple job was too much.

"What are you thinking about?" Caroline asked as she sorted through suits on a rack. "You're so far away."

"Just about what you were saying."

"You're still seeing David?"

"Yes."

Caroline grinned. "Well? Do you think you'll marry him?"

Veronica felt edgy at the question. How could she ever *marry* David? "According to you, it's better not to."

"Nah. That was just talk," Caroline said with a wave of her hand. "Marriage is security. Security is worth more than romance. Everyone gets old, and it's nice to have someone alongside you that you can depend on."

Everyone gets old. The words unsettled Veronica. Of course, *she* would age—and David wouldn't. She would have to become what he was in order to keep their relationship the same. She began to breathe unsteadily and felt a little dizzy again.

"Veronica, are you okay?" Caroline asked, touching her arm.

Veronica took a deep breath and got hold of herself. "I'm fine. I'm fine."

Was that the answer—to become like David? She would have all the physical strength she needed. She could live with David, rest when he did, and be awake when he was. No more dual life. She could be with him as she was now, forever. And she wouldn't have to deal with the real world anymore. It would be only David and his beautiful night world.

But what about her family? Her friends? She supposed she would never see them again. But surely David was worth giving them up for, wasn't he?

David sat next to Veronica on the cold sand looking out at the blackness of the lake. It was close to one o'clock in the morning. The moon was partly hidden behind clouds. She'd been telling him how she'd almost fainted at work, how her boss had threatened to fire her. As David listened, a frozen feeling clutched at his heart.

"It's my fault," he said, angry with himself. "I should have foreseen this. I've been selfish, wanting you so much. We have to be strict about getting you home sooner."

"I don't care about my job."

"Of course you do." Her words startled him. "When I first met you, you wanted so much to get ahead in your career."

"That was before I knew you the way I do now. Everything's changed. You're the most important thing."

It was the initiation that had made her think this way. He had to try to reason her out of this state of mind quickly. "Veronica, I explained to you before I took your blood that you would become like my slave. But you must try to fight that. I haven't been exercising my mental control over you, so you can resist your pull to me if you try. It's not that I don't enjoy your devotion, but you must hold on to your own life and the things that are important to you. Otherwise you'll lose yourself in me."

She looked impatient with him and troubled. It grieved David to know that he was the cause of her problems instead of the solution, as he'd once thought he could be.

"It's hard for me to see what's important anymore," she told him. "When Mr. Malloy threatened to fire me, I thought, 'No,

I can't let that happen.' But then, when they kept questioning me about you, it became clear to me that you were more vital to my life than anything else."

"Listen to me," David said, massaging her shoulder through her coat. "You can have both. It's just a matter of discipline. We've been indulging ourselves, and that has to stop. I want you to have a life of your own. You need to develop yourself as a person. You're too young to be cutting yourself off from everything to be with me."

"But—"

"No *buts*. We must be strict with ourselves, starting tonight. In a little while I'll send you home, so you can go to work tomorrow rested. You've got to get back that old goal of yours— to impress your boss and do well."

Veronica nodded slowly, as if he were making some sense to her. "I was thinking just today, when I was with Caroline, that I've missed a lot by clinging to my daydreams. Lately I think I've begun to see things a little differently."

David was curious and pleased. "How?"

"Well, take Rob Greenfield, for instance."

"The one who interviewed Sam Taglia?"

"Right. He was attracted to me, but I never could get interested in him. He used to seem ordinary and unexciting." She smiled. "Especially after I met you."

David was glad to hear that, but wondered why she was bringing up this other man. "He seems different to you now?"

Veronica was thoughtful for a moment, as if still trying to sort it out herself. "I see things about him I never appreciated before I shared a bond with you. Rob's only a mortal, and he has none of your experience and abilities. But he does his best despite his flaws and faults. He's persistent and makes the best of things. He's kind and warm and so human. He reaches out to people. I wish I could have been like him. And Caroline, too. Even my parents in some ways. They all go on, accepting their limits, seeing value in what they have. They don't feel a need to escape like I did."

David was growing more and more troubled listening to her. Not because of her talk about another man, but because of her perception of things. "Veronica, it was always my hope that you could draw value from your fantasy and from me and apply it to your *life*, to make your life more vivid and your goals more rewarding. I didn't want you to choose between two worlds. I wanted you to combine them."

"But I don't think I can." Veronica shook her head. "It's all confusion." She glanced at him, as if to reassure him. "Not now. I never feel confused when I'm with you. But during the day, I'm sad that I've always been different from other people. And I want to join in and be a part of them. I want to keep my job. And then I think of you, and the yearning for you makes all the rest seem unimportant."

Her words upset David so much that he had to get up and walk away a few paces. God, what had he done to her? He was so enamored with her, he had failed to fully realize how young and inexperienced she was, how unready to deal with the consequences of love with a vampire. How could he have been so thoughtless?

She ran up to him and took hold of his arm. "What's the matter? I can feel how upset you are."

"This has all gone wrong. And it's my fault."

He could sense her taking on his distress moment by moment. How could she be independent if she was connected to him? How incredibly blind and stupid he'd been to let himself think he could do her good! It was all rationalization to justify possession of what he'd been so desperate for: her love.

"But, David, don't worry. I've thought of a way to make things right. Couldn't I just stay with you?"

He looked at her in agitation. "What do you mean? Give up your job?"

"Yes." Her eyes were wide and hopeful.

"But then you would be giving up your own life, don't you see? I want you to be a complete person, not an extension of me."

She paused and grasped his arm more tightly. He could sense what she was about to say, and it pained him to the core.

"Make me like you, and I can be independent," she said, her voice full of eagerness. "I'd be as strong as you and Darienne. I'd be your equal. Let me drink from you."

So Darienne *had* brought that up when he'd left them alone for a few minutes. Leave it to Darienne to put ideas in her head, to try to manipulate things to go the way she wanted. "You shouldn't listen to Darienne."

"Don't be angry with her," Veronica said. "I'd already seen the blood ceremony in your play. I'm glad she explained it all to me. If I were what you and she are, I could live with you—and live *the way* you do. I'd be in your world totally. And I'd be yours forever."

David felt her sincerity. He knew she wouldn't leave him, the way Darienne had, if he transformed her. And he desperately wanted to have Veronica at his side forever. He didn't think he could go on without her sweetness to sustain him.

But his moral sense dictated that he do what was best for her. He'd already made one mistake. He must not make another.

"Do you want an existence where you'd have to constantly hide what you are?" he asked. "Do you want the torture of constant bloodlust? Sweet as you are, you would change overnight into a creature who thrives on the blood of others. You'd be cut off from the rest of the world. You'd be alienating yourself from God. Do you know what it's like to feel that you've made a choice that can never be forgiven?"

She looked frightened, but her voice was bold. "You manage to survive all those burdens! And Darienne seems happy. I don't see that there's any other choice, if you want our relationship to go on. Either you make me like you, or you'll have to give me up someday. If I stay mortal, eventually I'll die."

"You think you have the perfect solution, but you don't understand what you're saying," David told her with anguish.

"All I know is I want to be with you!"

He took her in his arms. "I understand what you're going through." He ran his hand over her hair, trying to calm her. "But we can't make this decision yet. It's best if we continue as we are for now."

"Why?" she said, tears in her voice.

"Because we haven't given it enough time. The situation as it is may work out for you yet."

"But even if it did," she said, "I'll still grow old someday. What will we do then?"

How could he argue with her? He'd known the consequences all along but had refused to face them. "That's many years away," he told her, taking a parental tone. She usually obeyed when he spoke to her as a father rather than as her lover. "You're barely out of childhood."

Her eyebrow quirked. "I'll be twenty-four next week. I want you to stop treating me like a little girl."

Even that tactic of his didn't work as well as it used to. She was growing older before his eyes. He was tempted to exert his mental power over her but refused to allow himself. "I understand these things better than you," he said, taking on a sterner voice. "You must let me decide when the time is right."

"How long?" she asked.

"I don't know."

She sighed in frustration and then tears began to fall. "This is so hard, David."

"I know," he said softly, holding her closer in his arms. "I know."

16

A Clean and Simple Idea

ROB HAD just left his cubicle and was walking toward the file room when he remembered he'd left on his desk a list of movie directors to research. He turned suddenly and found himself colliding with Veronica.

"Sorry!" he said, putting his hands on her shoulders to steady her. "I didn't know you were behind me."

"It's okay." She smiled and knelt to pick up the file of papers he'd knocked out of her hands.

"I'll help," he said, squatting beside her. As he gathered the photos and clippings together to put them into the manila folder, he added, "Still doing research on Taste of Chicago?"

"Yes. I keep trying to come up with new angles, and Mr. Malloy keeps rejecting them."

"He's tough to please. He wants me to do an article on directors who got their start in Chicago." Rob looked up at Veronica. He noticed the scarf she wore was askew. Beneath it there was a red mark on her skin.

"What happened to your neck?" he asked, reaching out to push the scarf aside.

Instantly she flinched and adjusted the piece of silk to cover the mark. "It's nothing, just a scratch."

"Did I do that when I bumped into you?" Rob didn't see how he could have, but the small cut on her neck looked fresh.

"No, of course not," she said as they both got to their feet.

He was holding the file in his hands, and she tried to take it from him. Rob held on to it. He took her arm and made her step back into his office. There he quickly pushed the file into her hand to distract her while he pulled the scarf aside with his other hand.

"Don't!" she said, trying to stop him.

She wasn't successful, and Rob managed to get a good look at the injury on her neck. There were actually two marks. Two small puncture wounds, open and moist, but not bleeding. They were at the side of her neck, one about an inch and a half above the other.

Veronica finally managed to pull his hand away. She looked up at him with anger, but there was also fear in her eyes. "I can take care of my own cuts and scrapes, thank you!"

"How did you get those?"

Her eyes did not meet his as she answered, "I fell."

"Fell?"

"With a—a glass in my hand. The glass broke, and when I fell down onto the pieces, they cut me."

"When did that happen?"

"Oh, I don't remember," she said with impatience. "Last week."

"There should be scabs by now if you did it last week."

"Well, maybe it was only a few days ago. I have to go."

As she hurried out, Rob followed her. "You know, now that I think of it, you've been wearing scarves a lot lately."

She walked faster. "So it's a new style I've picked up. So what?"

"Nothing," Rob said, and he let her move ahead of him. She walked on to Ed Malloy's office, and Rob continued to the file room.

His heart was beating unsteadily and a clammy feeling had come over him. What should he think about this? he wondered as he walked down the aisle between the yellow file cabinets. Could she really have fallen on glass and gotten those marks? He supposed it was possible. But she was awfully vague about when it happened, and the wounds looked as if the injury had occurred only a few hours ago. She was unnecessarily defensive about it all, too—just the way she was always so protective of de Morrissey.

"Oh, God!" Rob muttered under his breath. What he was thinking was ridiculous. Impossible! Everyone knew vampires were just superstitious folklore. They only existed in novels and movies.

And plays. Plays that David de Morrissey wrote with such a sense of realism that they totally mesmerized audiences. Was it because he had an unusual dramatic gift? Or were the plays he created so vivid because they were taken from his personal experience?

And Veronica—she showed all the traditional signs of being under a vampire's influence: wounds on her neck; wearing clothing that hid the wounds; paleness and weakness; protectiveness of a man to whom she was so devoted. You might almost say she was under his spell. And de Morrissey himself reportedly lived like such a recluse there in his mansion that he also could fit the vampire image. Veronica had said she and he never saw anyone else.

A sickening chill ran through Rob. If what he was thinking was true, then Veronica was in great danger.

But it was all so preposterous! How could a rational, educated man like himself contemplate even for a minute that Veronica had come under the spell of a *vampire?* He ought to just forget all this nonsense and get back to work.

Rob realized then that he'd still forgotten to bring along the list of directors he wanted to look up. Without a moment's further thought, he decided to do that research later. Instead he headed for the last aisle of cabinets, to find the file drawer marked *V.*

After spending the next few hours reading up on vampires, Rob knew a few things he hadn't known before. For one thing, the idea didn't originate in horror stories of the nineteenth century. Evidence showed that humans had believed in vampires since the beginning of civilization. Such lore was found in ancient Egyptian, Assyrian, and Chinese cultures. Even old Tibetan manuscripts believed to date back as far as 2500 B.C. mention blood-sucking creatures with large teeth. Vampire lore was thought to have originated in the Orient and had found its way to Europe through Turkey and the Balkans.

Rob also found an article about porphyria, a class of genetic diseases, that some scientists felt might be responsible for the lore about vampires and werewolves. The disease created a painful sensitivity to the sun and caused lips and guns to be drawn taut, so that teeth were exposed to look like fangs. The eating of garlic could make this condition even worse. Today the disease was treatable by injection, but in the Middle Ages, drinking large amounts of blood was the only remedy that could have provided similar relief. Did de Morrissey have this disease? At least this theory had some medical plausibility, Rob told himself, trying to keep a rational state of mind about an irrational subject.

There were further files on Vlad Dracula, a Romanian prince born in Transylvania in 1431, who tortured and impaled his enemies on stakes. Bram Stoker was believed to have used this historic figure, combined with traditional Romanian vampire folklore, in creating his gothic novel about Count Dracula in 1897.

From these articles, and from books he borrowed that evening from the public library, Rob drew up a list of the following "facts" about vampires:

1. They cannot be seen in a mirror and cast no shadow.
2. They never eat or drink.
3. They possess enormous strength.
4. They cannot be photographed. A photo of a vampire will turn out bluish or appear to be that of a skeleton. Nor can an artist paint a vampire. The likeness always turns out to be that of someone else.
5. They fear the sun, a crucifix, garlic, religious wafers.
6. They are immortal, unholy, and ruthless. They exist by night and survive by sleeping in coffins by day.
7. They must carry a little of their native earth with them wherever they go. Such earth must line their coffins.
8. They can be destroyed by a wooden stake through the heart, a silver bullet, exposure to the sun.
9. A vampire will draw blood from the living until his victim dies. This can happen all at one time, or little by little. But if he wishes to transform the person into a vampire, he mixes his vampire blood with that of the living person. When the person dies, after drinking the commingled blood, he or she will rise from the grave as a vampire also.

Now, Rob thought as he completed this list a few nights later in his apartment, just what was he going to do with this information? If he had any common sense, he'd light a match to it and forget all the "knowledge" he'd gleaned. Surely it was all the stuff of nightmares, arising from the mysterious, collective unconscious mind of humanity.

And yet, how else could he explain what he had observed about Veronica and her connection to de Morrissey? He'd done some research on the playwright also and learned little more than he already knew. Nowhere was there a photograph of de Morrissey; even Veronica had failed to obtain one. Nowhere was it recorded when and where he was born. Apparently no one had ever seen him in the daytime, and only rarely at night. And there were his vampire plays.

But all this was anything but conclusive. Such meager evidence would never hold up in a court of law. What did Rob expect to do—report de Morrissey to the police? What a great laugh they'd get out of that!

If Veronica was truly in danger, it was up to Rob to do something about it. But what?

First of all, he had to prove *to himself* that de Morrissey was a vampire. If he could get into the playwright's mansion somehow, maybe he could find his coffin. And what if he found it? What would he do, drive a stake through de Morrissey's heart?

Rob felt icy cold and nauseated suddenly. This was unbelievable! he thought. All for a woman who didn't even care for him.

But Rob had no choice other than to try to rescue Veronica. There was no one else who knew of or would believe her situation. And without de Morrissey around to mesmerize her, she might even come to care for Rob one day. Lately, now and then, he'd noticed she showed a warmth toward him that she'd never shown before. There was hope. Only the evilness of David de Morrissey stood in the way.

Rob had to stop him.

David looked behind himself as he and Veronica walked down Oak Street late at night. He put his arm around her protectively.

"Is something wrong?" she asked.

"No," he said, deciding not to worry her. But he felt as if someone were watching them. He'd had this feeling for several nights now. Sometimes he'd thought he'd seen the same car, a white one with what appeared to be a convertible top, parked or driving down his street. He'd seen the car pass as they were out walking. He'd caught a glimpse of the driver, too, a young blond man. Unless it was some nosy reporter, David knew of only one person who might be following them.

"Has Rob Greenfield said any more to you since he saw the marks on your neck?" David asked. Worried sick, she had told him about that the night after it happened.

"Not about that," she said. "Just about work. I guess he's forgotten it, like you thought he would."

David had told her that, trying to ease her apprehension, but he had quietly continued to worry. "Tell me, what does Rob look like?"

Veronica smiled. "Why? You aren't jealous."

David took a playful tone. "Of course not! Just idle curiosity."

"He's blond, and about your height. The women at the office think he looks a little like Robert Redford did when he was younger."

"An Adonis, is he? And I suppose he drives one of those sleek sports cars you women like so much."

"He has one of those Volkswagens with the top that comes down."

David wouldn't have known a Volkswagen from a school bus, but the removable top sounded right. "What color?"

"White."

So, perhaps it was her heartsick swain following her around. But what had Rob made of the marks on her neck? Did he suspect?

"Why are you asking all this?" she said.

"I just want to know what my competition is," David told her. "I may have to buy a car just to impress you."

Veronica's shoulders shook with laughter. "You're going to learn to drive?"

"No. I'd just leave it parked out in front. You could drive it."

"That might be fun. We could go drag racing."

"I don't even want to know what that means," David said with dour humor.

She leaned against him and put her arms around him. "No, it's not your style at all. You don't need to impress me, David. You know I'm yours. Have you thought any more about our future together?"

He knew she meant her transformation. "I've decided it's still too soon to decide. Lately we've been doing well, getting you home early. And then we have the weekends." He bent his head to kiss her, thinking of the night-long ecstasies they shared when she didn't have to work the next day. "I think we can go on as we are."

"But, David, we can't go on forever this way. Only if I'm like you—"

The thought of making her like him still brought David inner torment. "Let's not talk about it tonight. It's a beautiful evening. Let's just enjoy being together. You'll have to go home soon."

"But that's what I mean. It's hard for me. I'm one person at night and another during the day. I still feel confused when I'm at work. Sometimes I even wish I'd never met you. It upsets me."

"You wish you'd never met me?"

"I shouldn't have said that," Veronica told him hastily.

"No, don't apologize. I just want to understand."

She hesitated. "I don't think real life can ever satisfy me now. But I'm beginning to see how young I am to be losing contact with the world. I've missed life altogether. If I hadn't met you, I might have still adjusted and learned to appreciate a normal, ordinary life."

She stopped, as if waiting for David's response. His throat was too constricted with pain and unshed tears to speak. Instead of helping her, he had ruined her chance at a happy life. Why did he destroy everything, everyone he touched?

"But when I'm with you, I forget all that," she continued, her tone positive now, full of hope. "I'm only aware of all the beauty and joy you give me. That's why I know that I'd be happiest if I were like you. I wouldn't have the real world pulling me back anymore."

David swallowed and tried to compose himself, not wanting her to see how distraught he was. "It's getting late. We'll talk

of this another night. Let's walk back to your car now. You
need your rest."

"David—"

"Do as I say."

"Sometimes you treat me like a three-year-old. That's another reason—"

"I know, I know. Just for now, indulge me. Be my little girl
again. Be the unknowing innocent who asked me for an interview." In spite of his efforts at composure, a tear ran down his
cheek. She reached up to brush it away.

"I'm sorry," she said. "I didn't mean to hurt you."

"No, not at all. You're just changing more quickly than I
expected, and I like everything to be the same. We'll work all
this out. Somehow."

She seemed troubled as they turned to head back to her car,
which was parked in front of his house. They walked in silence
until they reached it. There she turned to him and they kissed
with much emotion, as if clinging to something that was myste-
riously fading. Veronica began to cry.

"Shhh. Don't weep," he told her. "Everything will be all
right. Will you come tomorrow night?"

"Of course I will!" She kissed him again with energy and passion, causing such a fusion of will between them in that moment
that it seemed to prove how vibrant their love was. With difficulty they separated. The temptation to spend the remainder
of the night together was overwhelming. But David urged her
into her car.

As she drove off, he stood on the curb watching her car move
away from him down the street. He could feel the increasing
distance of their separation and the sadness within her. Then,
in the next moment, another car drove by, following hers. The
car was white with a removable top, and its driver, a stern-faced
blond man. David caught the flash of the young man's eyes
upon him as he passed by.

De Morrissey didn't look at all as Rob had expected. In her
article for the magazine, Veronica had described him as darkly
handsome with kind, intelligent eyes. Rob had told himself that
this description was probably the product of her blind admiration. But he'd gotten a good look at the playwright when he

drove by him last night, and with reluctance Rob had had to agree. Except for the eyes. Rob hadn't seen any kindness in them, only suspicion and cunning. De Morrissey's clear, light-hued eyes might have been carved from ice. Looking into them from his car window for only a fraction of a second had given Rob the willies.

So what was he doing here in front of de Morrissey's mansion on his lunch hour? What if the playwright wasn't a vampire; and what if he'd noticed Rob following him and Veronica around every night for the past week? If he went up to his house now and de Morrissey answered the door, he'd have a lot of explaining to do.

On the other hand, if de Morrissey was a vampire, then he ought to be sleeping in his coffin now, at noon. But what if he had some depraved assistant who guarded him during the day? In the movies vampires often had such human watchdogs. Then de Morrissey would know for sure that someone was on his trail.

As he buttoned his overcoat and got out of the car, Rob wished he'd had some experience as a private detective. He walked up to the mansion and looked for the doorbell. There wasn't any, only a heavy, brass knocker. He took hold of it and knocked strongly on the door. As he waited, his heart began to pound. All he heard from behind the door was absolute silence. He knocked once more, and then a third time. Again, only silence. Instead of walking back to the safety of his car, he stepped around to the corner of the house. A locked iron gate crossed the walkway that led along the side of the house to the back. He could see the heavy iron fence extending to the back of the building.

Rob looked around. Cars were driving by, and people were walking down the sidewalk across the street. He waited a few minutes. When he thought no one was around to see, he climbed the high fence, almost impaling himself on spearlike iron decorations on top. He dropped to the other side and crouched by some bushes. No alarms went off. No sirens. Apparently de Morrissey didn't have any elaborate security system.

As Rob walked along the side of the house he came to a door that was dead-bolted shut. He reached the back of the house and tried the doors and windows he found there. Everything was closed tight and locked. Every window was heavily draped. There was no way he could find out anything without breaking and entering. Since Rob had no experience in committing such a crime, he decided not to smash any windows. He couldn't help Veronica if he was in jail.

As it was, he might get arrested for trespassing if someone had seen him scale the fence and had called the police. Or someone might be watching from the mansion, for that matter, though the thick-walled stone house seemed coldly devoid of life.

He'd found out all he could for now, he thought, and he'd better get the hell out of there. He walked back to the gate, waited until the street was empty, and climbed over it again. Perspiring as he quietly hurried back to his car, he got in and drove off.

After a few minutes, Rob calmed down. It was over; he'd made it. But all he had found out was that no one answered de Morrissey's door during the day. He needed to get into the house somehow. That was the only way he'd find any proof that the recluse playwright was a vampire.

By the time he parked near the office, he had concluded that the only way he'd ever get into the mansion was with a key. And he knew Veronica had a key. He'd followed her there from work several days in a row and had seen her unlock the front door. If he could just find a way to get into her purse . . .

It turned out to be remarkably easy. That afternoon, when she was on her way to the file room, Rob asked her—claiming he was pressed for time because of a deadline—to do an hour's worth of research for him on some obscure director from Chicago. "I've covered for you several times with Mr. Malloy," he told her, wringing his hands as if he were terribly nervous. "Do you think you could return the favor by helping me out?"

"Sure," she said, looking genuinely concerned. "I'll be glad to."

Rob felt guilty about the ruse. She was so sincere about coming to his aid. But, he reminded himself, it was all for her own good. While she was gone, Rob went into her office, pretending to look for something in case any of his co-workers was watching. He found her purse where he'd often seen her put it, in the bottom left-hand drawer of her desk. Quickly he fished through the compact, wallet, and other objects in the leather bag, until he came upon her key chain. There were several keys, and Rob didn't have a clue which one might unlock de Morrissey's mansion. And then, by accident, his hand came across something hard wrapped in a handkerchief and stuffed into the purse's side pocket. He unwrapped the handkerchief and found two keys, a larger one, such as might undo a dead bolt, and a smaller one that looked curious and old. Something told Rob he'd hit pay dirt.

He took the two keys and put them in his pocket, then placed the purse back as he'd found it. Nonchalantly he sauntered out of the office, then out of the building, and walked down the street to an office supply store that duplicated keys. Within fifteen minutes he was back at Veronica's desk, wrapping the two original keys in the handkerchief and stuffing the bundle into the pocket of her purse. He put the purse back into her drawer and walked to his own desk again, scanning the large office as he did. His co-workers were all busy at their computer terminals or huddled in conversation. No one seemed to have noticed him.

When Veronica returned a half hour later with the research Rob had asked her to do, he thanked her profusely. Veronica smiled and seemed touched.

Rob left work an hour and a half early that afternoon and drove back to de Morrissey's mansion. He parked half a block away and walked up to the house. As a precaution he knocked first, but again no one answered. He took the larger, newly made key out of his pocket and, fingers shaking, tried it in the lock. Like magic, the door opened.

Rob walked into the large, oval hallway with its spiral staircase and Oriental rug. Stopping to listen for any hint of a sound, he heard nothing. He closed the door behind him.

Rob spent the next forty-five minutes exploring the huge house. He found that the key to the front door also unlocked the bolted inside doors on each floor. The maze of old furniture on the first floor astonished him. The library on the second floor amazed him even more. The third floor, however, was the most intriguing, because it seemed to be the playwright's living quarters. The rich, comfortable decor surprised him. Was this how a vampire lived? No cobwebs and foul odors?

But there weren't any mirrors, Rob noticed. Nowhere, not even in the bathroom. The wet bar drew his curiosity. Rob opened some of the cabinets below the bar and found a few cups and glasses and a single bottle of port. There was a hot plate and a teakettle. He opened the small refrigerator.

The sight of more than a dozen full plastic bags of blood made Rob's skin crawl. Even if he never found a coffin, this was proof enough! Why would anyone need to keep a refrigerator full of blood? Unless de Morrissey had the disease he'd read about, porphyria, and used the blood to treat himself.

Rob shut the refrigerator with a shiver. He walked down the hallway and soon found himself in a magnificent ballroom, empty except for the wide-screen TV in one corner. There were no two ways about it: undead or alive, de Morrissey was certainly odd!

As he glanced out the windows, Rob noticed the sun had disappeared behind buildings and the late-afternoon light was beginning to dim. If there was a vampire in the mansion, Rob knew he'd better get out before sunset. But he hadn't found a coffin yet, and he wanted that final proof. He felt in his pocket for the small key and pulled it out. If he were a vampire, where would he keep his coffin? Rob asked himself. In a room with a separate lock and key? But where? He hadn't checked the basement yet.

As he left the ballroom and walked back down the hall, he passed several doors. The coffin might be behind one of them, he supposed. He tried one nearby and found it unlocked. When he opened it, the room was empty. The door next to it was already open, and that room, too, was empty. Across the hall he tried another door. Inside he found stacks of what looked like manuscripts lying on bookshelves along all four walls. Rob stepped in to look at them more closely. There were manuscripts of all de Morrissey's plays on one shelf, all written by hand with de Morrissey's signature, the year, and Chicago scrawled on the cover page. On other shelves were manuscripts for other plays and novels with various dates and places: Paris, London, Vienna, New York, Rome. Their dates went all the way back from the middle and early 1900s to the early 1800s.

On another shelf were deteriorating, handwritten pages dated in the 1700s and a few from the 1600s. Some carried the de Morrissey name as the author. Others had other names. But the handwriting was all the same—except for two manuscripts that appeared to be very old and fragile. These had been penned by a different hand and were signed "William Shakespeare." Their titles were *Hamlet* and *A Midsummer Night's Dream.*

Awed, Rob left the room and closed the door as he had found it. The next door he opened looked like a costume rental. The room was larger than the others and held racks of clothing from various periods. Rob knew little of historical fashions, but many of the clothes looked like costumes he'd seen in movies. They all appeared to be men's clothing. Had de Morrissey actually worn all these in past ages?

The next room was smaller and contained what appeared to be his current wardrobe, with shirts, ties, sweaters, blazers, and suits. It looked similar to Rob's closet, except there were more clothes, and they appeared to be a lot more expensive.

Realizing that time was speeding by, Rob closed the door and walked to the living room. Looking out the window, he saw the light waning even further. The basement, he told himself. Before he left, he had to get a look at the basement.

He closed and locked the door and moved quickly and quietly down the spiral staircase all the way to the bottom. At first he couldn't find any way to get to the basement, and then he noticed a door painted the same color as the wall, and scarcely distinguishable from it. He opened it, walked down a dark corridor until he came to another stairwell, and went down the steps to the bottom. There he unlocked a door and found himself among more old furniture and storage boxes. The place was like a maze.

Starting to sweat under the pressure of time and the danger of hunting a vampire, Rob walked up and down zigzagging aisles until he came to yet another door. He tried the key he'd been using on the other floors, but it was too big. He dug out the smaller key, and with hands that trembled he fit it into the lock. The door opened.

In the dimming light from the basement windows Rob could barely make out the interior of the room. He saw candles and matches on a table next to the door, but there was no time and his hands were shaking too much to use them. Pulling a pen-sized flashlight out of another pocket, he turned it on and shone it into the room. The beam of light found what appeared to be an ornate, oblong, carved wooden box. It was about the size of a coffin, though more elaborate than any he'd ever seen. Rob's hands turned cold, and a moment of panic gripped him. He ought to go and open the box to make sure de Morrissey was in it. But he had a mental image of himself opening the coffin and de Morrissey's hands reaching up out of it to grab him by the throat.

Besides, the sun was fading fast, and if he didn't get out of the house very soon, de Morrissey might find him there. He couldn't rescue Veronica if he was dead!

Deciding to open the coffin some other day when the sun was high, Rob quickly closed the door and locked it. He began to retrace his steps out of the basement, using his penlight to find the way. The light from the windows was gone. Unfortunately he took a wrong turn and became lost. After several minutes, sweating profusely while his hands remained cold with fear, he found the stairs up to the ground floor. He ran up, hurried out the front door, and raced back to his car.

None too soon. In less than a minute he saw Veronica's car pass his and pull up in front of the mansion. Sinking down into his seat, he watched her through the steering wheel as she walked up to the house. She had her key ready, but seemed startled to find that the door was already unlocked. Rob realized that in his panic to get out of there he had forgotten to lock it. Damn! She would tell de Morrissey, and they'd be suspicious that something was wrong.

As soon as she went in, Rob looked up and noticed the lights were already on in the third-floor front windows. A feeling of faintness came over him. He must have missed de Morrissey by no more than a minute.

He leaned his head back on the headrest and tried to calm himself. They might just assume that one of them had forgotten to lock the door. In any case, no one had seen him, so he was safe. He had to plan what to do now.

It was Friday night. From having observed them for the past week, Rob guessed that Veronica would probably stay at de Morrissey's house all night. That thought conjured up images of what they would be doing together in the house. The anger and revulsion he felt made him push the images aside. Now was the time to keep a cool head.

He had to have a plan to destroy de Morrissey. Rob was certain now that the playwright was very much a vampire. The refrigerator filled with blood, the coffin, the manuscripts in his own hand dating back to the seventeenth century had convinced him. The fact that Rob was planning to rid the earth of a creature that had survived for hundreds of years was awesome and terrible. But he had to use his wits and accomplish it for Veronica's sake, not to mention any other victims of the vampire.

What should he do, come back tomorrow at noon with a hammer and a wooden stake? The idea almost made him gag, and he felt the blood draining from his face. But how else to destroy the vampire? Rob had no idea where to get silver bullets, nor did he know how to use a gun. It was either the stake or . . . the sun. Now, there was a clean and simple idea.

Yes, why not let the sun take care of David de Morrissey?

"Are you sure everything's all right?" Veronica asked as David walked down the spiral steps with her before sunrise.

David wasn't sure. She'd told him about finding the front door open, and he'd already had the odd feeling that someone had been in the house while he rested. But he couldn't be sure if the feeling was from some faded dream, or if someone had actually entered his house. He had found no evidence of anyone's being there.

"David?"

"I'm sure," he told her, hiding his suspicions so she wouldn't worry.

"We'll just have to be more careful about locking the door from now on."

"Right," David said. He put his arm around her as they reached the ground floor hall. As he reached to open the front door, Veronica stopped him.

"It's Saturday," she said. "I could stay here all day, just in case. I can sense you're edgy."

David toyed with the idea for a moment. If she stayed, he would be more protected. But if someone was prowling around, she might be in danger. She would be here all alone. "No," he told her finally. "I appreciate your willingness, but I think it's unnecessary. I can barricade the door to my resting place before I retire. That should suffice. I can put so much furniture and crates in front of it, no one would ever know a door was there. But I'll need extra time, so I must see you off quickly."

"All right," she said. She leaned up to kiss him. The fire of her lips brought back all the sensuous joys they'd shared during the night. As she drew away he could feel her reluctance, but she opened the door herself, as if worried about delaying him.

They walked out to her car. The sky was black, but streetlights reflected off the snow on the ground, making the night seem brighter. In no more than a quarter of an hour, the first rays of the sun would rise above the horizon.

"Goodbye, David," she said, putting her arms around him one last time. "I'll see you tonight."

He kissed her again with adoration. In his mind a subtle new feeling that everything would soon change irrevocably made him hate to let her go. He almost feared never seeing her again.

"David, do you want me to leave?"

"You must."

She nodded, looking troubled, undoubtedly sensing his vague foreboding but, like him, not knowing exactly what she feared. "I love you."

"I love you," he told her with feeling. "Go now, quickly."

She got into her car, looked back at him once through the window, and drove away.

David stood on the empty street for a long moment, looking up and down. Everything was quiet. But something somewhere wasn't right. He couldn't put his finger on it. There was a human presence, male he suspected, concentrating, focusing on him.

David turned around suddenly. There, standing on the walk between David and the mansion, was a blond man of about his height.

"Excuse me," the man said. David could sense he was nervous, but hiding it under a jaunty manner.

"Yes?"

"Are you David de Morrissey? The famous playwright?"

"Why do you ask?"

"Well, I'm a fan of his. If you're he, I'd like to get your autograph."

"And why do you think I am?" David slowly walked toward the man, who seemed to grow frightened at his approach but stood his ground.

"I know David de Morrissey lives in this house. It's been mentioned in the papers. And I saw you come out of the house with the young lady."

David came to a stop about three feet away from the man. "Who are you?"

He hesitated. "Just a fan of yours. I've seen all your plays."

"You know my name. I'd like to know yours."

"Rob," the man said. His green eyes sparkled with fear. David could read him like a magazine.

"Rob Greenfield, by any chance?"

Drops of perspiration gathered at Rob's temples. "How did you know?"

"Veronica has mentioned you."

"Oh."

"So what's your real reason for being here, Rob?" David asked, feeling very much like a spider playing with a fly.

"To . . . to . . . I hoped to get an interview."

Lying, lying, David thought. "Do you love Veronica?" David asked.

The aspect of Rob's green eyes changed. "Yes," he said strongly, without hesitation.

"You're here to try to protect her, aren't you?"

Rob's expression grew hateful, all pretense gone now. "You're destroying her life."

"And what do you plan to do about it?"

Instantly Rob reached into his coat pocket and pulled out a silver cross, about five inches high. He boldly held it up in front of David's face, a look of fearful righteousness in his eyes. He reminded David of the judges who used to burn witches a few centuries ago.

David stood rigid, staring at the cross for a moment, humoring him. "Did you buy that at some religious store or borrow it from a church? It's quite elegant, but it won't protect you from me." To prove his point, he pulled the cross out of Rob's clenched grip and handled it, admiring the smooth gleam of light from the street lamp reflected on the polished, precious metal.

A look of sheer terror passed over Rob's face. He started to back away, to make a run for it.

David reached out and took hold of Rob's coat lapels with one hand. He tucked the cross into Rob's side pocket with the other. "Don't go, Rob. We haven't finished our conversation yet. You imagined you could immobilize me with the cross, keep me here until the sun came up, didn't you?"

Rob didn't answer, but stood there glaring back at him.

"Did you go into my house as well?"

He didn't reply.

David shook him fiercely. "Did you?"

"Yes!"

"You have keys. How did you get them?"

"I took Veronica's and made copies," he said. "What are you going to do with me?"

David was becoming impressed with Rob's courage. Not all men reacted with this degree of honesty and bravery when in a vampire's clutches.

"I won't harm you," David said. "Despite what you may think, I'm a civilized vampire. I'm going to unhand you now. But don't try to run. I can move faster than you, and I can break you in half if I choose."

He let go of Rob's lapels. Rob stood there, knowing he was helpless, but staring at him with cold defiance. Again, David was impressed.

"You must love Veronica a great deal to face me for her sake."

"I do."

"Do you think she loves you?"

"No," Rob replied, his gaze wavering for a moment.

David felt a twinge of sympathy for him. " 'If she think not well of me, what care I how fair she be?' Wither's poem carries some wisdom you might take note of."

Rob's eyes sparked with anger. "If *you* love her, then why don't you leave her alone?"

The question tore at David's soul like a jagged razor. Rob was someone to be reckoned with, after all. The young man had a sense of morality, and he knew how to sting with it. "You are worthy of her," David said, his voice softened with emotion. "You may have your chance to win her away from me."

Rob stared at him. "How?"

"I don't have time to explain," David said. "Dawn is almost here. And the hows and whys won't matter anyway, because you won't remember this conversation." David changed his tone of voice, growing stern. "Now give me the keys you made."

Still looking puzzled, Rob obeyed and took two keys out of his breast pocket. As he did so, David noticed a yellow sheet of paper in the same pocket. "What's that? Give it to me."

Rob handed him the keys and the paper. David unfolded it and found a list of supposed facts about vampires. He chuckled as he skimmed it. "You've even done homework! How very thorough. Not all of this is true, as you've found out. But that's neither here nor there. You won't remember this, either."

"What do you mean?"

"I mean the one thing you don't have written down here is the mental power we vampires have." David smiled as he looked into Rob's mystified and wary eyes. "You never had a chance. Next time use a stake and hammer at midday. Much more reliable. Of course, it's unlikely there will be a next time, because— No, relax, Rob, I won't harm you. Just keep looking at me," David said, concentrating. "You won't remember me or this conversation. You won't remember anything about me, only that I wrote *Street Shadows*. And you'll forget all you know about vampires, too." He focused on Rob until Rob blinked and then looked at him oddly.

"S-sorry, did I bump into you?" Rob said, looking confused.

"Don't worry about it. Are you lost?"

Rob looked around him. "I—yeah, I guess so."

"One too many at the Irish pubs?" David said with a grin.

"I can't seem to remember."

"Happens to all of us. You're on Oak Street. Michigan Avenue's that way," David said, pointing.

Rob looked in that direction. "I think I see my car," he said with surprise. "Thanks. Sorry I bothered you."

"No bother. Good night," David said. "Or should I say, good morning?"

"Yeah, right." Rob still looked confused as he began to walk away. He raised his hand in a salute. " 'Morning." He walked on down the sidewalk toward his car.

David rushed into his home. He could smell the dawn by the time he settled himself in his coffin and closed the lid. At least he was safe now. He'd found the intruder and taken care of the matter.

But Veronica weighed on his mind. She and he couldn't go on as they were, that was clear. Other friends or relatives of hers might suspect, as Rob had. And their relationship had proved to be too draining for her to carry on her normal life.

Willing as she was, David could not turn such an innocent soul into a creature like himself.

There was another path to take that he'd been contemplating the past few days, and he could no longer delude himself into believing there was any other choice. Tonight he must take that path.

17

On That Distant Night

THE NIGHT air had a chill to it, but the atmosphere lay so still and quiet over the city that Veronica didn't notice the cold. Above, the stars sparkled clear as distant crystals, and below, the lights of Chicago gleamed peacefully.

It was about three o'clock in the morning. David had taken her up the Wrigley Building again. This time he'd stopped at the top of the building's lower level, seventeen or eighteen stories up, instead of climbing all the way up the clock tower. They'd spent a little while exploring the roof and were sitting now on a flat area only a few feet from the edge of the building.

Though on the surface David seemed the same as always, Veronica felt that her special bond with him was muted, as if he were deliberately blocking his emotions from her.

"Is something wrong, David? You're different tonight. Not while we were making love, but when I first arrived at your house, and now."

"There's nothing wrong," he told her, reaching to take her hand. "We mustn't look at it that way."

"Look at what that way?"

He gazed out at the tops of the buildings for a moment. "Do you still feel muddled about who you are and what you want?"

Veronica began to get apprehensive. He hadn't answered her question, and she could tell he was controlling himself to such an extent that he was mentally separating himself from her. "Only when I'm away from you," she replied. "Is that what's bothering you? Just transform me, and the problem will be solved."

He looked at her, his blue eyes wise and sad. "It's not that simple."

"Sure it is."

"Your confusion comes because you haven't had time to discover who you are yet. You've told me yourself that you've never fully experienced the world. I can't ask you to choose an existence with me when you don't know what you would be giving up."

"But I don't care about what I give up," she insisted. "I want to be with you."

He smiled. "You say that now, after we've made love and I've brought you here to our special place," he said gently. "But what about tomorrow afternoon? Your doubts will return."

"They won't if you transform me," she argued.

David closed his eyes and shook his head. "Once you become like me you may regret your choice." He pointed at his chest. "I thought I was old enough to know what I was doing when I became a vampire. Later I regretted my decision."

"I wouldn't regret it!" she said.

"You don't know that. *I* didn't know what my reaction would be before I was changed. How can you?"

"You weren't in love with the one who transformed you!" she reasoned, her voice betraying how upset she was. "I am. All I want is to be with you forever. How could I ever regret it, if you make my wish come true?"

He studied her in his still way for a long moment, and Veronica thought that her argument had made an impact. She started to smile.

"Veronica, you and I must part for ten years."

She stopped breathing and stared at him. "Wh-what?"

"You need time to discover the world and to live a normal life," David told her. "Ten years will give you the time to find out if you want to give it all up for me."

She felt icy cold and sick, but could do nothing more than look at him in shock. Uncontrolled emotion welled up within her. She began to grow dizzy.

All at once David shook her hard by the shoulders. "Breathe!"

She took in air in a harrowing gasp. She hadn't even realized she'd stopped breathing. For a moment she couldn't exhale, and then she began to breathe in gulps, which soon turned to sobs.

David held her close in his arms. "Shhh. Calm down," he said. She could feel him trying to impose his own composure on her, but she mentally fought him and clung to her hysteria. She would not let him do this!

"How can you even suggest such a thing?" she cried. "You say you love me!"

"It's because I love you so much that I must do this," David explained, emotion finally entering his voice. "If I didn't cherish you, deciding to transform you would be easy."

"Then don't love me so much," she pleaded, the reality of his intentions sinking deeper into her soul. "Anything, just don't leave me."

"I won't ever leave you," he said, stroking her hair. "Not in my mind and heart. You and I are bonded forever, whatever happens. Ten years is not so long when you compare it to eternity. If you honestly believe you'll choose eternity, then look upon this as your time of preparation for immortality, and it won't seem so long."

"Why, David?" she asked, feeling impotent against his resolve. "I never expected this."

"I didn't, either," he said in a grave voice. "When I met you, I saw only you, and put aside the consequences." His eyes grew melancholy. "There's a poem by Wordsworth:

> "She was a phantom of delight
> When first she gleamed upon my sight;
> A lovely apparition, sent
> To be a moment's ornament;
> Her eyes as stars of twilight fair;
> Like twilight's, too, her dusky hair;
> But all things else about her drawn
> From May-time and the cheerful dawn . . ."

His voice broke on the last word and he took a moment to compose himself. "You see, I met you too soon. I must return you for a while to the May-time I plucked you from. Dawn should still be a cheerful thing to you, not an instrument of destruction as it is to me."

"But I can't go on for ten years without you," she said, clenching her hands into fists, her words choked with tears.

David reached to wipe the wetness from her cheeks, but more tears spilled from her eyes. "I don't know how I'll carry on without you," he said. Tears began to fill his own eyes. "Every night I'll be tempted to summon you to me."

"But you won't!" she taunted, growing angry now. "You're too honorable! I don't *want* you to do this for me. Take me now and let me be yours forever! Why should we both suffer?"

"I couldn't bear it if you blamed me afterward because I took you before you had enough experience to choose your destiny."

Veronica broke into sobs again, not knowing how to argue with him. "I'll hate you if you do this!"

"If you hate me, I must accept that and hope that your love for me will eventually overcome your hate. I think one day you'll understand why I'm doing this for you. But now," he said, glancing out toward the dim, flat horizon of the lake, "time is passing quickly, and there are things I must tell you."

Veronica felt listless and hopeless. She let her gaze fall to the cold, stone roof they were sitting on. There seemed to be nothing she could do or say to change his mind. He was bent on torturing them both, as if they deserved punishment for loving each other. It wasn't fair. It didn't make sense to her. He was wrong to do this! How could she make him see that?

Her thoughts scattered as David took her by the shoulders again, this time shaking her gently. "Listen to me!" he said. "I want you to remember all I'm going to tell you now."

She nodded, drawing her lips tightly over her teeth to keep from shouting at him in anger or abjectly pleading with him.

"While we are separated—" he began.

"I don't want to hear it!"

He took her by the upper arms and lifted her slightly, making her look at him face-to-face. "You must hear every word I say!" He stared at her a moment to be sure he had her full attention. "While we're apart, I want you to lead a normal life. You must continue to work and do well at your job. Go after your old goals. I want you to travel, and also to spend time with your friends and relatives. Make an effort to meet new friends. I want you to see other men—this is very important. Have an affair, if you wish. You might even marry someone, if you care for him."

"How can you want me to—"

"Shhh. I want you to experience life fully. Only then will you know what you would be giving up. You must also decide if you want the experience of growing old. And I want you to think a great deal about the consequences of living forever. It's not as wonderful as it sounds, believe me. You must also explore all the unanswered questions about God and humanity. What does God mean to you? Could you risk alienating yourself from Him, perhaps forever? What does being a part of the human world mean to you? You've already had cause to question this. When you begin to mull over all these things, you'll realize that ten years is not much time to come to a decision."

"And what then?" she asked bitterly, not caring about any of this now that she was about to lose David.

"In ten years I'll summon you again. If you still want to be with me, I'll commingle my blood with yours. I'll drink from you, and then you will drink from me. And after you're transformed," he said, his voice growing rueful, "you may choose to leave me, if you wish. You will have all my powers and be my equal."

"I wouldn't leave you," she whispered, looking into his eyes.

"Keep in mind," he continued, as if determined not to be swayed by her feelings, sincere though they might be, "that as a vampiress, you would have to exist only by night, as I do. You'd have to sleep in a coffin by day and live in secrecy and separation from mortals in anything other than superficial contact."

"I know all that," she said. "I know that now. I don't need ten years to understand it."

"Yes, you do," David insisted, "but you're still too young to know what you don't know. Now, here is the last thing I have to tell you: in ten years, if you've thought all this through and you choose to live out your mortal life in a normal way, I will respect your decision and allow you to do so. I will never call you to me again."

"But I won't ever do that, David. This is all so pointless!"

"In ten years I believe you'll understand why I'm doing this."

"Why ten years? Why not five? Or one?"

"In a decade you'll be the age I was when I became a vampire—thirty-four. Even that's too young. I ought to make it more, not less."

"What if I die during the next ten years?" she argued. "If I die in a car accident or something, we'll be lost to each other forever!"

David hesitated and reached out to touch her face. Veronica felt his hand shaking.

"I've thought of that," he said at last. "But it's a risk we must take. If it happens, you may be better off. If there is a heaven, I'm sure you will go there for eternity, and it must be an infinitely more pleasant existence than wandering the earth with me."

Veronica put her hand to her mouth to stifle a sob. "I can't believe that."

"Then God help you." He uttered the words like a prayer, as if she'd said something blasphemous. She realized perhaps she had, and it made her pause. David's tone was softer as he added, "And may He lead you to the right decision."

He turned away from her. His shoulders shook as he wept silently.

Veronica sensed he felt that her choosing him would be the wrong decision. For the first time she began to understand some of his torment. She reached out to touch him. "David—"

He stood and moved away from her. "We have to go now," he said, fiercely controlling his emotion. "Dawn is coming."

Dawn was coming. She realized there was nothing more she could say or do. She could only abide by his wishes and let the future take its course.

They climbed back down the building, Veronica on David's back. By the time they reached his mansion, it was only a few minutes before sunrise. They went directly to the secret room in the basement.

After she lit a candle and set it on the floor, David took her in his arms. Veronica pressed her forehead into his shoulder, shutting her eyes. "What'll I do every evening? My life will be empty without you."

"You must work to give yourself the fullest life possible. If you choose my existence, I want you to feel sure you won't miss the daylight world. And if you choose mortality, then you will appreciate your normal life span that much more, because you will have tested its worth against immortality." He lifted her chin and made her look at him in the candlelight. "Perhaps you're fortunate to have such a choice. Very few humans do. Choose well."

"I'll choose you," she said, tears gathering again in her eyes.

David kissed her before she started to cry. She wound her arms around his neck and stretched up on her toes. The strength and warmth of his embrace comforted her. But ten years until she felt his arms around her again—how could she survive?

She took her lips from his mouth. "David, I'll be so lonely."

"You mustn't let yourself be lonely. Mingle with people. Through them, you'll find out who you are."

"What about our bond?"

"I believe, as time passes by, our bond will grow dormant, just as the marks on your neck will gradually heal. You and I must resolve not to concentrate on each other, because it would only keep the bond fresh and cause us anguish. We must allow our bond to sleep. In ten years I will use it again, to bring you to me."

"Don't forget me," she said, her lips trembling.

"Never could I forget you."

They kissed once more with a fierce passion that seared her bones. She could feel their bond uniting them, body and spirit, in a way she knew she could never experience with anyone else, in a way she would have to wait a decade to experience again.

"Dawn is here," he said, pulling away. "Stay with me until I sleep? I want your face to be the last thing I see."

Veronica nodded, biting her lower lip in order not to cry. When he'd stretched out in his coffin, she picked up the candle and held it so they could see each other. She took his hand in hers. He held it tightly.

"The sun is piercing the horizon," he said, looking at her. "Can you feel it?"

She concentrated and felt the pulsing radiation he was able to sense. In a moment she felt his growing languor.

"Now you must disconnect," he whispered. "Part from me mentally as well as physically. Only think of me once in a while, when you remember all I told you you must do during our separation."

The grip of his hand on hers was growing weak. Soon his fingers could no longer cling to hers. "I love you, my sweet, sweet angel," he murmured, almost too feeble to speak. His eyes took on their strange iridescence of sleep.

She leaned over him. "I love you, David. I love you more than the world. Someday you'll believe me." As his eyes closed, she kissed him a last time.

Veronica drew back then and looked at David in the candle glow. The squareness of his jaw, the breadth of his forehead, the aristocratic line of his nose—all these she tried to memorize. How could she carry on for ten years without even seeing his face? Her vision blurred as tears of helplessness and despair streamed down her cheeks.

And then, as she told herself she had to leave, she remembered the keys he had given her. The keys. He hadn't asked her for them. Had he forgotten?

She sniffed and dried her tears. She still had his keys! She wouldn't have to wait a decade to look upon him again! All at once she was almost jubilant.

All right, then. Because it was what he wanted, she would *try* to abide by his instructions. But ten years! If the agony of loneliness for him became too hard to bear, she could come here and look at him and hold his hand, taking comfort from that. David would never know. If he sensed her presence, he would assume he'd dreamed it. Perhaps it would comfort him, too.

With this thought to give her some emotional stability, Veronica stayed with him a while longer. When at last she thought she had the strength to leave, she squeezed David's hand one last time. Carefully she closed the lid on his coffin. After locking the door to the secret room, she left the basement and went upstairs. She paused in the grand entryway, looking up at the spiral steps she'd climbed so many times. Quickly, before emotion could overcome her again, she went out the large front door, closed it and locked it, too. She held the two keys tightly in her hand all the way home.

*   *   *

The following Monday Veronica sat at her desk, crying. It was after five o'clock, and everyone seemed to have gone home. Her heart ached with acute loneliness. For months she had grown accustomed to going to David directly after work, but now she had nowhere to go but her empty apartment. And how she missed David already! What was he doing at this moment? she wondered.

She tried to concentrate on him, but could barely connect with him mentally. He was blocking her out, she was certain of it. She began to cry that much harder, feeling bereft and shut out from David's world. How could he do this to her and think it was for her good?

"Veronica! What's wrong?"

She looked up to find Rob in her doorway. She tried to stop crying but couldn't. "Nothing," she said. "Please go away."

Rob approached her desk. "I can't leave you like this. What's wrong? Ed didn't fire you, did he?"

"No." She reached for a tissue to wipe her face.

"Did someone in your family die?"

"No."

He walked around her desk and squatted on his heels near her chair. "What, then? Maybe I can help."

"David won't see me anymore. I can't be with the man I love."

Rob searched her face as if puzzled. "He broke up with you?"

"Sort of."

"That's too bad."

She turned and looked at him. "I thought you'd be glad."

"Why?"

"You didn't approve of him."

"Didn't I?"

She studied Rob to see if he was trying to tease her, but he seemed genuinely surprised. "You remember. You told me I should stop seeing David. So did Mr. Malloy."

He rubbed one eye and brought his hand up to furrow roughly through his blond hair. There was a hint of confusion in his eyes. "I said that?"

"How can you not remember?"

"I don't know. There's a whole night recently I don't remember. And other gaps in my memory. I've been wondering if I should see a doctor."

"Really?" she said, growing concerned for him. "Have you been feeling all right?"

"Yes. But every now and then something odd comes up. Like I found some books at my place from the Chicago Public Library, and I don't even remember going there or checking them out."

"You've been working hard lately. You had that tight deadline. Maybe that's why."

"Maybe." He smiled a little. "At least I've taken your mind off your problem. You've stopped crying."

Veronica nodded, but as she thought of David again, new tears filled her eyes.

"Now, now," Rob said, and knelt next to her. He put his arm around her shoulders and tried to pull her close to him. She tried to keep her distance at first. But then she remembered what David had said, that he wanted her to experience a normal relationship with a mortal man. Reluctantly she made her muscles relax and allowed Rob to hold her.

"That's right," he said. "There are other guys in the world. Don't cry over one who was stupid enough to let you go. How about going out for dinner tonight? It might do you good to have some company."

She wet her lips and tried to smile. "All right."

"Great! Why don't we go someplace special, to cheer you up? The top of the Hancock, maybe."

"No. Any place but there."

"Afraid of heights? Well, we'll think of somewhere to go. Put on your coat and we'll figure it out along the way."

She nodded. "Thank you, Rob." Hesitantly she looked into his cheerful eyes. They were green, not translucent blue; amiable, not filled with the wisdom of years. But if this was what David wanted, then it would have to do. For now.

David gazed through the front window of his living room into the darkness. He wanted so much to attune his mind to Veronica's, but he refused to allow himself to give in. Earlier he'd felt her trying to connect with him. He must be firm or she would try to come back to him. For her sake he had to stick to his resolve. But all the lonely nights that stretched ahead of him!

Something caught his eye, and he saw Darienne in her fur coat standing below on the sidewalk. His spirits picked up a bit. She waved at him and he pointed to the door. He buzzed her in and met her at the top of the spiral steps.

"I thought you'd gone abroad again," he said as they walked into his living room.

"No, I've stayed in Chicago." She curled her arm through his. "I had the feeling you would need me one day soon."

David looked down at the Oriental rug. He hated the way Darienne found him so predictable. "How did you know?"

She shrugged. "I knew." She took off her coat and tossed it on a nearby easy chair. "You like?" she asked, twirling like a model so he could see her outfit. She wore formfitting leather pants the color of fuchsia and a silky, almost transparent blouse of the same color with hide-and-seek front pockets.

"Is this for my benefit or for Rush Street?"

"For you, if you like it."

"It's very striking, but I'll take a rain check."

She walked up and put her hands at the sides of his waist. "Where is Veronica?"

"I honestly don't know where she is at this moment," he said, breaking away from Darienne.

"What happened, David?" she asked, her tone sympathetic.

"I told her we must separate for ten years."

"Why on earth did you do that?"

"So she has time to be sure whether or not she should spend eternity with me."

"I imagine she *was* sure."

"She's too young to make such a decision."

"Oh, David," Darienne said with a sigh. Coming up to him again, she draped her hands over his shoulders. "You always stand in the way of your own happiness. You're much too moral. No one I've ever known worries the way you do."

David tried to control his impatience, wondering how Darienne could have lived all these centuries and still be so shallow. "I was brought up to believe high morals and a sense of responsibility were admirable traits."

"And who taught you all that? Father Armand, who sinned with me."

"I have the feeling that may not have been his fault," David muttered.

"Always blame it on the woman. Isn't that just like a man!"

"I know you, Darienne, and you're a manipulator. You're beautiful, feminine, and charming, but you are never, ever an innocent bystander. I don't think you were ever innocent, for that matter."

"Not like your Veronica, no," Darienne admitted.

"No, indeed."

"You silly man. You worship her and she worships you. And yet you banish her and punish yourself with this separation. I find it hard to have sympathy for you."

"Go out and have your fun, then," he said in a cutting tone. "I'm not making you stay here."

The corner of her mouth turned up in a coy half smile. "But you were happy when you saw me on your doorstep."

"I'm lonely and sad, that's all. You can't change that."

"And you're in a sniping mood, too! Use me for target practice if you need to, but I'm here to make you feel better."

"Why?"

Her puckish expression changed and her eyes grew tender. "Because I love you."

Her apparent sincerity touched him. He swallowed and rethought his attitude. "I'm sorry," he said, putting his arm around her. "I just miss Veronica so much."

"Then summon her and forget this nonsense."

"I can't." David shook his head. "I know you don't understand, but it's important to me that I follow my principles to the best of my ability. I might hurt her otherwise. And I would never feel worthy of her if I didn't do what's right. Spending eternity with me must be her choice, and she must make that choice with wisdom. Wisdom requires time. There's no other way."

"You *are* noble, David. I do respect that."

He chuckled with irony. "I'm glad. But I don't know how I'll get through the next decade waiting for her decision, knowing I could lose her in the end to some mortal man."

Darienne tapped his cheek. "How could any mortal compare with you?"

"Even if she chooses to become an immortal, I have no guarantee she would stay with me." He looked into Darienne's beautiful eyes, which reflected her independent spirit. "I might only wind up with another *you.*"

Her eyes widened with mock insult. "I'm offended! You should be pleased—flattered!—to have another like me to dance attention on you. We can take turns stroking your brow when you're depressed, and pleasing you in more intimate ways. Two beautiful vampiresses should keep you more than busy for at least the next several centuries!"

"Why am I not thrilled?" David said with a sardonic smile.

"Because the thing you like best is to complain!" She laughed and kissed him on the cheek. "David, try to look on the bright side. I believe Veronica loves you so much, she'd choose you even if you made her wait fifty years. She won't leave you after you've transformed her, either. For the next decade you can exist on the promise that you will finally have what you've wanted all these past centuries. And what's a mere decade? You should be happy, not despairing!"

David was almost afraid to admit it to himself, but what she said seemed to make sense. Perhaps he shouldn't feel so hopeless. In ten years he might begin unending centuries of happiness with Veronica.

He pulled on a ringlet of Darienne's blond hair. "You've done it. You've made me feel better."

"Only better? I want you to feel wonderful!" Her eyes took on a deeper, sensual light. "If it would help, we could—"

"No," he said, drawing away from her a bit. "I'm not ready for that. I would only think of Veronica and miss her all the more."

If Darienne was disappointed, she hid it quickly. "No, we can't have that. Well, what shall we do?"

"Do?" The question took him by surprise. "I have no idea."

"That's the difference between us. I do things and you brood."

He took a deep breath. "You have any suggestions?"

"Rush Street?"

"No, no."

"A walk?"

"I'm not in the mood."

"Gin rummy?"

"Good grief!"

"We can plan a trip. I've been telling you you should see Paris again. Or we could go to Switzerland. I'll introduce you to Herman, and we can see what he's doing at his lab."

"That ridiculous sunblock cream?" David laughed. "No, thank you! You know I hate to travel anyway."

Darienne shook her head. "It always puzzles me. How have you spent the past four centuries?"

"Studying and writing."

"No wonder you can be so boring!" Then she smiled delightedly. "I know, what about those old movies you like to watch? Do you feel like dancing?"

David leaned his head to one side. "Not especially."

"Well, maybe you will when you hear the music." She took him by the hand, leading him toward the ballroom. "Come on, *chéri*. If you'll be Fred, I'll try to be Ginger!"

David allowed himself to be pulled along. It wasn't really what he wanted, but he'd rarely ever had what he wanted. For now he would let Darienne try to cheer him up and help him pass the time. He would be patient and try to hold on to hope as weeks and months and years passed by.

And then on that distant night, that lovely evening in the future when he called his true love on the wind, his beloved Veronica would come back to him. Perhaps when she returned, dewy brown eyes filled with love, she would bring all her sweet devotion, having saved herself for him alone. And perhaps she would tell him she'd chosen to stay with him forever, until the end of time.

What a beautiful vision. A rapturous dream. David would cling as best he could to that fragile hope.

BIRTHSTONE
New From
Mollie Gregory

Bestselling author of <u>Triplets</u>

*"Dazzling. Mollie Gregory dishes the dirt
with wicked finesse." —Rex Reed*

*"A novel that has it all: Hollywood, opulence and
decadence and primitive passions in high places."
—Maureen Dean, bestselling author of
<u>Washington Wives</u>*

*"A perfect diamond — faceted with a dynamic story,
fascinating characters, and sparkling settings."
—Johanna Kingsley, bestselling author of
<u>Scents and Treasures</u>*

*Nearly destroyed by a shocking crime of passion, the
Wyman family has triumphed over their tragedy: award-
winning director Sara, noted movie critic Vail and their
steel-willed mother Diana are in the spotlight of fame
and success. Then, Sara's daughter Lindy returns, forc-
ing secrets out of the shadows, opening old wounds and
igniting new desires.*

*From Hollywood's glitter to the exotic allure of Sin-
gapore and Budapest, Lindy fights for her dreams — and
then risks losing everything in a tide of passion and
revenge.*

A Jove Paperback
On Sale in December

Author of the #1
New York Times Bestseller

THE BAD PLACE
and
COLD FIRE

Dean R. Koontz

Dean R. Koontz is one of today's most popular writers. His chilling tales catch you by the throat, grip the pit of your stomach, and dare you to turn the page.

____WATCHERS	0-425-10746-9/$5.99
____WHISPERS	0-425-09760-9/$5.95
____NIGHT CHILLS	0-425-09864-8/$4.95
____PHANTOMS	0-425-10145-2/$5.95
____SHATTERED	0-425-09933-4/$5.50
____DARKFALL	0-425-10434-6/$5.99
____THE FACE OF FEAR	0-425-11984-X/$5.50
____THE VISION	0-425-09860-5/$4.95
____TWILIGHT EYES	0-425-10065-0/$5.95
____STRANGERS	0-425-11992-0/$5.95
____THE MASK	0-425-12758-3/$4.95
____LIGHTNING	0-425-11580-1/$5.95
____MIDNIGHT	0-425-11870-3/$5.95
____THE SERVANTS OF TWILIGHT	0-425-12125-9/$5.50
____THE BAD PLACE	0-425-12434-7/$5.95
____THE VOICE OF THE NIGHT	0-425-12816-4/$5.95

For Visa , MasterCard and American Express orders ($10 minimum) call: **1-800-631-8571**

FOR MAIL ORDERS: CHECK BOOK(S). FILL OUT COUPON. SEND TO:

BERKLEY PUBLISHING GROUP
390 Murray Hill Pkwy., Dept. B
East Rutherford, NJ 07073

NAME_____

ADDRESS _____

CITY_____

STATE_____ ZIP_____

PLEASE ALLOW 6 WEEKS FOR DELIVERY.
PRICES ARE SUBJECT TO CHANGE WITHOUT NOTICE.

POSTAGE AND HANDLING:
$1.00 for one book, 25¢ for each additional. Do not exceed $3.50.

BOOK TOTAL $ _____

POSTAGE & HANDLING $ _____

APPLICABLE SALES TAX $ _____
(CA, NJ, NY, PA)

TOTAL AMOUNT DUE $ _____

PAYABLE IN US FUNDS.
(No cash orders accepted.)

227d